She lean
"What just ha...

How was he to answer a question like that? Hell, he was more unnerved by what hadn't happened, and the tightness of his buckskin trousers had relented little. He glanced across the meadow, his mind racing but his heart sure. "What would you want it to be?"

The pink blush across her face hadn't abated. "The beginning of something very beautiful."

He gave a slight chuckle. "If you knew my thoughts, you'd run faster than you did from those Dog Soldiers."

She took his hand again. "I have no fear of you, Dawson McCade."

He stood with a smile, tugging her up beside him. "You should."

Dawson's Haven

by

Kim Turner

The McCades of Cheyenne, Book 3

This is a work of fiction. Names, characters, places, and incidents are either the product of the author's imagination or are used fictitiously, and any resemblance to actual persons living or dead, business establishments, events, or locales, is entirely coincidental.

Dawson's Haven

COPYRIGHT © 2019 by Kimberly Williamon Turner

All rights reserved. No part of this book may be used or reproduced in any manner whatsoever without written permission of the author or The Wild Rose Press, Inc. except in the case of brief quotations embodied in critical articles or reviews.
Contact Information: info@thewildrosepress.com

Cover Art by *Debbie Taylor*

The Wild Rose Press, Inc.
PO Box 708
Adams Basin, NY 14410-0708
Visit us at www.thewildrosepress.com

Publishing History
First Cactus Rose Edition, 2019
Print ISBN 978-1-5092-2849-2
Digital ISBN 978-1-5092-2850-8

The McCades of Cheyenne, Book 3
Published in the United States of America

Acknowledgements

Thanks to the following people for helping make this a better story and me a better writer. Hugs to: Kim Simmons, Marcia Scott, Clare Roden Dennie Garrett, Dianna Shuford and Connie White.

~

And a special thanks to Cynthia Smith for adding to the journey of bringing this story to life!

Dedication

For Marcia…
because those late-night chats keep me going.

~

And for Nicole…
because I never expected to call an editor friend.

~

Lastly, for Pam…
for all the fun and laughter along this writing journey.

Prologue

Wyoming Territory, 1869

The scorch of the sun stung his eyes and burned his skin, sweat trickling beaded lines down his chest and back. The wind did not move as Dawson McCade gulped for air, disturbed by the visions that kept him company day and night. Thirst plagued him, his tongue parched and his belly groaning in complaint of hunger. Left to his dance with the sun, he fought for reality in an effort to prove his worth as a Cheyenne brave.

At the fire, Leaning Bear, the medicine man, chanted and the old chief, Stalking Eagle, smoked his pipe, but it was his father's voice that had spoken to him. *Go well to the job that calls you, son.*

He staggered against the tethered rawhide straps connecting him to the cottonwood trunk, grimacing against the pull of the hard bones that pierced the skin of his upper chest. He swayed, his chest raw and bloody. Soon, the bones would rip through his skin, setting him free and though he wasn't Cheyenne, he would be accepted as part of the tribe.

He drew a ragged breath, the strength in his back all that was holding him upright as he leaned against the painful tethers. He wanted to give up, but '*Heammawihio*' -the wise one above- hadn't answered his prayers for relief any better than the white man's

God of his childhood.

Panic took him, and he wanted to ask for water he'd been denied. He squinted into the distance, the mirage of grasslands hindering his perception as the visions began once more. His animal totem, the Great Spirit Wolf, returned to him with a growl of warning, the animal's large hazel eyes regarding him.

Sweat dripped down Dawson's face and in spite of the heat, he shivered, though not in fear, as the wolf jumped. He grabbed the fur on the predator's neck, rolling in the grass, fighting for his place in the tribe. The wolf didn't want him, recognizing he wasn't Cheyenne and that he'd had no right to the view of the camp of the dead he'd taken in his visions. But his father had not been there, and he pushed the creature back and the canine bared its fangs.

Dawson cried in triumph—the war cry of ancestors that did not carry the same blood. Wisdom had left the Great Spirit Wolf and bolted through him, leaving him to shudder in victory. He lifted his hand to touch the animal's spirit and the wolf bowed its head. She appeared then, the woman with hair of fire the wolf had brought to him more than once over the years.

She moved closer, confusing his vision, his chest heaving in the effort it took to breathe in the bitter heat that scorched him. She brought the wind and her flaming red hair whipped across the wolf and teased his own flesh. She was a haven between them, though the predator bared his teeth once more in warning.

Dawson gave a guttural scream and fell into the high grass, the skin of his chest shredding free of the tethered bones. The pain scoring through him was at last a relief, but it was the woman who called his name in an echo as he fell. *Dawson...*

He reached for her, though she drifted, following the path the wolf had opened toward the mountains. He closed his eyes, his chest dripping blood and the howl of the Great Spirit Wolf left in the wake of his fading vision.

Stalking Eagle lifted Dawson's head and placed a hollowed gourd to his lips, the bitter liquid to ease his pain. He sipped, grimacing as Leaning Bear rubbed salve into the torn flesh of his chest. Weakness clutched him, but he was by all rights a Cheyenne warrior, gaining the Great Spirit Wolf's wisdom for his lifetime.

"It is with you, Proud Wolf." Stalking Eagle offered him more of the bitter drink speaking in his native Cheyenne tongue. "The great wolf has given you his spirit."

Leaning Bear traced a thumb across Dawson's forehead, painting him in the colors of the tribe. "Rest, my brother."

Dawson fought confusion as he was carried into one of the tepees and laid on a buffalo hide. The medicine man offered him water and he drank from the cool leather pouch until he was breathless.

"Sleep, Proud Wolf." A cool rag touched his forehead and a heavy fur covered him. He let his mind drift back to the woman, the echo of her voice a comfort of which he didn't understand. Flaming red hair flowed around him along with the briskness of a cool wind. He reached for her as she faded into the darkness of his confused slumber.

Chapter One

Wyoming Territory, 1881

Dawson McCade slowed his horse, Viho, turning to glance behind him. The setting sun shone brilliant, warming him little against the impending threat of weather. The horse leered from the drop-off of rocks at the edge of the ridge, pulling his attention from his thoughts. He loosened the grip of his gloved hands on the reins, but the mustang's ears perked in further warning.

He scanned the brash cut of cottonwood and pine, miles from home and the waiting warmth of his cabin. Peering ahead, he stopped the horse with a gentle tug of the reins, spotting them. Across the ridge, a band of horse-mounted Indians, four, with a quick count, were scattered across the rise. By the looks of them a hunting party, though by all rights, they shouldn't be in the area with the Cavalry's strict enforcement of no more than two Indians at a time off the reservations.

He urged the anxious horse behind an outcrop of trees, so as not to attract attention. The Indians were searching from what he could tell. The lead brave lifted a hand, halting the others, the reins to a saddled roan in his grasp. Then the fur-clad Indian turned his head and Dawson froze at the sight of his painted face. Cheyenne Dog Soldiers. And this was no hunting party.

He stifled a curse, the dead quiet lifted by a hiss of frigid wind. While he didn't recognize them, the painted faces told the story. And for every effort he'd rendered for peace between the soldiers and Indians, this meant nothing but trouble. He held Viho steady, but a flurry of brown skirts scurrying down the far side of the slope caught his attention. A white woman and now things were very clear.

He dismounted, tying the horse and followed the direction the woman had moved. It was apparent the Indians had taken her horse, and she was the reason for their search. He ducked behind a patch of tall grass at the bottom of the ridge, spotting her again. She moved with swift but cautious ease and if nothing else, he needed to get to her before they did.

He continued on foot, closing the gap, but a twig snapped in the distance and one of the Indians turned his horse.

Dawson raced to circle behind the woman. His moccasins made no sound as he moved within a hundred yards of where she huddled behind an old tree, the trunk large enough to hide them both if he could get to her.

The Indian rode with slow deliberation, ever closer. Dawson took a step, then another, his buckskins worthy of camouflage in the sleeping trees of winter. Just a bit more and—he grabbed the unsuspecting woman, placing his gloved hand across her mouth and nose to stifle her scream, fighting to hold her still.

"Shhh." He whispered, and she stopped the struggle, the full length of her body against him. He pressed her to the tree, shielding her as the Indian, yards away, stopped his horse at their brief scuffle.

The woman grasped his hand with both of hers, trying to tug them away from her face in an effort to breathe.

"Quiet." His voice was less than a whisper as he lowered his hand, uncertain it was wise to do so. But she remained still, all except for the rise and fall of her panting chest. If she let any sound escape, they'd both die, and it was apparent she'd figured that for herself.

Fallen leaves crunched under the horse's hooves as the Dog Soldier moved closer, black paint across his eyes as if he wore a mask. Dawson eased a gloved hand to his tomahawk, lifting it from his belt, the smell of lilac invading his senses and confusing his focus. The woman was a real beauty. Strong too, as it had taken some strength to subdue her, but it hadn't gone past him that she clutched her side in injury he hadn't inflicted.

"Shhh." The slight whisper escaped his lips and while she didn't move, her body shivered hard. A mix of fear and cold would do her no good, but the real concern was what any woman might be doing out this far alone.

If the Indian continued to advance, they'd be discovered, and with Viho at the top of the ridge, there was no other escape. But for all the ways he'd one day die, this wasn't one of them. He held her steady, though she tugged his hand away from her side, replacing it with her own. She *was* injured, and he eased the press of his body, though it had been a long damn time since he'd held a woman against him.

Gripping the tomahawk tighter, he was all too sure the smell of lilac would alert the Indian how close they were. Another few feet and he'd have a decision to make. Killing wasn't to his liking, but neither was dying. The crunch of twigs under the horse's hooves drew closer as he kept them out of view. Seconds passed and a call from beyond the rise turned the Indian back toward the others, scattering a flock of birds from the trees overhead.

Dawson waited until the Indian was over the hillside and grabbed the woman's hand, it being imperative to get to Viho. She turned and wide hazel eyes met him. He froze. She was tall with a disarray of long orange hair falling free from under her floppy brown hat. He gave her a nod of reassurance.

She whispered, digging in her heels. "They have my horse."

He placed a finger to his lips and urged her to follow. They were lucky to be alive, never mind the damn horse. He assisted her up the incline where Viho waited, but she slipped, holding her side. He put her back on her feet, noting her newfound tears.

Of all the things he hadn't expected on an afternoon hunt for dinner. He wanted to curse but continued on, assisting her up the final ledge. He grabbed the reins and climbed into the saddle, offering her his hand.

She shook her head, those large hazel eyes scanning the length of him. "They have Josie, my horse. We can't leave her."

He let his hand drop to his thigh, speaking in a stifled whisper. "Can't worry about the horse right now."

"But..." She glanced behind them as a high-pitched scream echoed across the ridge.

They'd been discovered, and this time she didn't hesitate to take his hand and climb up behind him, though she yelped in pain. He turned Viho, the light creamy flesh of her exposed knee not escaping his glance as she settled behind him, her arms around his middle. He snapped the reins and took the horse to a full gallop toward the river.

"They're coming." She scooted so close, the heat of her body warmed his back, even through her heavy brown coat and his thick deerskin tunic.

It was miles to his cabin, further to Cheyenne, and out of the question to turn back for Fort Laramie. But if they could make it to the river, there was the slightest chance of escape, providing the Dog Soldiers' didn't know what he did.

He hunkered down across the animal, chanting in Cheyenne. The mustang mix, bred for speed, widened the gap. The wind whipped across them as the woman rested against his back, her arms so tight around him, his breath stifled along with his thoughts about who she might be.

Moments later, the river came into view, and he urged Viho toward the falls, behind an outcropping of boulders. He slowed the horse to maneuver the rocks, coaxing the animal down the steep bank and into the frigid water.

The woman bent her knees as the water touched the hem of her skirts but didn't protest as he thought she might. He coaxed the mustang to the falls, under an overhang of earth where roots and moss draped from deep inside. The smell of molten earth became stronger than the woman's lilac perfume, the darkness of the deep overhang swallowing them and the horse.

Out of view of anyone passing the banks of the river, they'd remain hidden, the falls loud enough to cover the sounds coming from the winded horse. With any luck the Dog Soldiers would ride on by, thinking they had taken the trail ahead with the darkening sky.

Dawson fought to catch his breath. Glancing to his middle, the woman's fingers still gripped his leather tunic, her knuckles white and her body shivering hard. There was an open scratch on the back of her hand, matching the bruise she wore across her cheek. By the looks of her, she'd taken a fall or jumped from the horse, either way saving her from certain capture.

There were several homesteads in the area, and while something of her was familiar, he wouldn't soon have forgotten a woman of her beauty. He shook thoughts he had no right to own as the heat of her body curled around him.

"They won't hear us with the falls." He glanced at her tearstained face and she nodded. He wasn't sure what possessed him, but he removed his gloves one at a time, noting she wore no ring as he placed them onto her ice-cold hands. Some married women wore nothing to prove themselves as such, and what the hell was he thinking anyway?

He was sure the Indians knew nothing of this semblance of a cave where they were hiding, otherwise—he scanned the far bank of the river. They might chance the frigid water and make it to the other side but fighting the rapids and cold wouldn't help their plight.

Viho's ears perked and the woman gripped Dawson's tunic tighter. Her body trembled as hooves shook the earth above, and wet dirt fell across them and the anxious animal. She hid her face in his back as they waited within the damp earth. His heart raced and he wasn't sure if it was the idea of being discovered or the warmth of her against him. He lifted his head as the pounding hooves lessened into the distance.

When she did the same, he held his hand up to halt her from speech. The falls drowned out the thumping in his chest, but while things were quiet above them, it didn't mean the Indians were gone. The rush of the river was deafening and when she tightened her grasp again, it was he who shivered. His leather fringed tunic was lined but was not as much protection, given the mist covering them. He'd been out for a few hours of hunting, since the sky called for snow, but he hadn't expected this delay. He glanced down where two skinned and gutted rabbits were still tied to the saddle, their pelts folded inside his saddle bags.

Viho rocked his head, anxious to be free of the confinement. He spoke to the horse in Cheyenne, calming the animal with his words.

"You're an Indian?" Her whisper held no alarm, though she peered around at him.

It wasn't the first time he'd been thought of as an Indian, given his buckskins and the fact his hair hung past his collar, a braid and feathers attached. "I speak the language." His reply was short, with there being no time at present for a full explanation as to why he appeared the way he did.

He wasn't expecting the horse to cooperate for much longer and didn't give her another chance to respond. It would take a moment to free them of the earthen hole, and a bit longer to get them across the river, further south. "Hang on."

She squeezed, ducking against him. He clucked his tongue and Viho drove from the ground, the cold water splashing them as he took the incline. Once on solid ground, the animal never slowed, the cold wind almost unbearable as the woman hid her face against his back.

Dawson glanced over his shoulder, the Dog Soldiers nowhere in sight. After a time, he slowed Viho to a canter, the sun disappearing altogether by the time they crossed the shallow part of the river miles south of where he'd found her.

"Will they follow?" She clung to him but bent to protect her side.

"Not likely." He glanced at her. The Indians would've moved on, though the wolf inside him had settled little. He'd heard of random bands of Dog Soldiers that still roamed the Northwest, long after most of the tribes had been banished to reservations, and this was more than concerning.

"Where're you taking me?" she asked. The awareness of her warmth continued to be overwhelming.

"My cabin's not far." Taking her there was best, it being too far to his family's ranch given her injuries and the impending weather. Snow flurries had begun, and the ground would be a solid sheet of ice by morning.

"But I must get home, to my brothers." A length of auburn hair fell from beneath the floppy brown hat, snagging his full attention.

"I'll get ya home once it's safe. Weather's turning. That and you're injured." He turned back to the trail as Viho broke through the dense forest near the cabin.

"You've a family? A husband?" He cursed himself for asking, but he'd have words with the man who'd let her ride far enough for the kind of trouble she'd found.

"Only me and my brothers. We live on the old Harper homestead. My father passed away last year." She bent her elbow in protection of her side as Viho took a dip. "I'm Haven Oakley."

He urged Viho ahead, the new moon offering little light for the darkened trail as snow fell around them. Taking her back the way they had come wouldn't be wise for several days, but he didn't want to leave youngsters alone. "Your brothers are young?"

She panted to breathe. "Levi's fourteen and James five, but I must get home."

"I'll get you back when the weather clears. I'm sure they'll be fine for a couple of days. Weather permitting, I might check on 'em." That appeased her for the moment, though it would be tough to backtrack in the weather he was anticipating.

She grabbed her side and leaned against him as Viho maneuvered the uneven trail. "I left Sosha with them and I suppose Thorn might drop by as he does a few times a week."

"Thorn?" Dawson chuckled. The old man had lived in the mountains for all the years he could remember, panning gold and often lucrative at it. Some thought him *touched*, and most steered clear of him, even the Indians. "I'm surprised he's still gettin' around."

"You know Thorn, then?" She peered around at him with a lift of her auburn brows.

"Been in these parts as many years as I can remember." He glanced back at her then and ahead to the trail. He didn't mention the fact that he and his brothers had grown up thinking Thorn something like the boogeyman.

"He's been very kind to us since my father died."

Her voice held a hint of sadness.

"And Sosha?" He no longer had to guide the horse toward home and lessened his grip on the reins.

"Our dog. They'll be safe for a time, but I mustn't leave them for long." The urgency of her voice lessened.

Dawson glanced down again, where her gloved hands held tight to his tunic.

"I hesitate to think what might've happened had you not come along. Thank you." She settled to the idea she couldn't be taken home, he supposed.

"It'd be wise if you didn't stray that far away from home anymore." He added in warning, though he offered another question. "May I ask of your mother?"

She remained quiet for a moment but then spoke. "She died several weeks after giving birth to James."

Managing even a small homestead wasn't easy for a man, much less a young woman. "It must be difficult to run a homestead and care for your brothers alone."

"Sometimes life doesn't give us choices. But we do fine. I collect herbs to trade at the fort. When I saw the Indians, I raced Josie away from the homestead, but they kept gaining. I jumped…knowing I would lose her…" Her voice dropped an octave. "I raised her from a foal in Georgia."

He'd placed her accent as southern, a soft tender drawl. "I'm sorry the Dog Soldiers took her, but leastwise we're alive."

"Dog Soldiers?" Concern edged her voice.

He took a deep breath and let it out, the vapor from his lungs white against the darkness of the sky. "Cheyenne. Not the friendly sort."

Her teeth chattered. "They'd have killed me then?"

"There are worse things than death." He should've held his tongue, that not being the smartest of things to say to a frightened woman. The Indians might have killed her after they'd had their fill of her or if they hadn't traded her off to a far worse fate. He offered her a hand as Viho stopped before the small barn near his cabin.

She worked her way down until she had her feet on the ground, bending at the waist and wincing before standing erect. Large flakes of snow fell across her, landing in the strands of copper hair that splayed across her shoulders from under her hat. "You were right about the weather."

He dismounted, keeping Viho's reins in his grip, the sky heavy and dark. "Be a foot or more by mornin'. Go sit by the fire. I'll get him brushed down."

She glanced at the cabin, hesitating.

"You'll come to no harm here." He turned for the barn, tugging the horse along, and glancing behind him until she entered the cabin. She was tall and slender, and he could still feel the grip of her hands across his middle, stirring warmth inside him that he hadn't known in years.

He removed Viho's saddle, lugging it in one hand and leading the horse inside the barn. Letting go of the reins, he lifted the saddle to the mount to dry. Sliding the wet saddle blanket from the animal, he laid it over another. He allowed Viho into the stall, brushing the horse with effort, ice crystals flying free. The mustang gave him a nudge.

"You did well, my friend." He thanked the animal in Cheyenne, as Viho pranced toward the fencing in the next stall, hanging his large head over with a heavy snort.

"She'll be back soon enough." He closed the gate. He'd taken Neha, his expectant mare, to his family's ranch outside of Cheyenne several weeks before. The mustang would foal within the month and he'd left her to Evan's charge, his youngest brother having a knack with horses.

He lifted a bucket of oats and filled the trough, the horse ambling across to eat. Setting the bucket aside, he untied the skinned rabbits from the saddle and headed to the cabin. Snow fell in heavy droves and wind whipped in gusts around him. He'd never have made it in this weather to get Miss Oakley home, but now he wondered what he'd gotten himself into. Leastwise, he needed to see to her injuries and let her have a couple of days to rest before he took her back. He grabbed the door latch and stepped inside the cabin and damn near forgot his body required breath.

Chapter Two

Miss Oakley stood at the hearth, her long auburn hair hanging across her shoulders. He gulped for the breath he'd missed and glanced down to remove his moccasins. The warmth of the cabin made him shiver, his hands near frozen, but she was a sight to behold, quite beautiful, if it was any of his business.

"It's a nice cabin." She glanced around, holding the coat tight about her. "Our barn roof is in need of repair. Levi promises to get to it, but winter's here once again."

He walked closer to the fire and warmed his hands, struck in awe at her hazel eyes and the sprinkle of freckles across her nose. "A roof's a big job for a boy."

"He works so hard sometimes." She eased a hand to her side, frowning.

"Best we get out of our wet clothing." He tugged his damp buckskin tunic over his head as he stepped into the next room and grabbed a dry shirt from the chest. He pulled it on as he returned, noticing she'd dropped her gaze. It hadn't occurred to him to be modest in her presence.

"Uh, there's a shirt and trousers in the top drawer of the chest, probably a might too big for you, but they'll have to do. The door closes." He'd never pushed out more difficult words.

She opened her coat, glancing down at her blouse,

which was covered in bloodstains below her left breast. All the color left her face and she swayed, the coat falling to the floor.

Dawson darted to scoop her into his arms, carrying her through the doorway to his bed. He laid her along the length and patted her face. "Hey..."

She was pale and unmoving. There was no way he'd make it to the ranch for the doctor. He adjusted the pillow behind her head and as he drew the blanket up, she moaned.

"Easy." He brushed a palm across her cheek.

She startled to full alertness, scooting from him. "I must've...passed out."

He bent, concerned at her worsening symptoms. "Better let me take a look."

She leaned away with a hiss, her face distorting with the pain. "I'm fine, just need rest is all."

He lifted his brows and waited on her reluctant nod. He could understand her concern given the situation. "Look, have I harmed you so far?"

She frowned. "No, but you're a...man."

"Miss Oakley..." He sat on the bed beside her.

Her mouth dropped open as she held her side. "Call me Haven."

He was well aware of the dangers in using her given name—using a woman's name insinuated a closeness the two didn't carry, but he spoke it anyway. "Haven, we're in the middle of a snowstorm. It's long after dark and the nearest doctor's just outside of Cheyenne. Seems I'm all you've got." He was tired and hungry, and this was not how he'd expected his evening to progress, even if she did add more decoration than had ever been inside his cabin.

She began with the buttons of her blouse and opened her shirt. She worked at the ties of the corset, struggling to free the ripped garment. "It's quite painful."

He added his fumbling fingers to the mix and gulped another breath when the stays fell away, and she lifted her chemise to expose her side. Folding the linen of the garment underneath the swell of her rounded breast, she hissed.

Hell, it had been a long time since he'd undressed a woman and he lifted a brow as he touched her bruised skin.

"My coat must have slid up when I fell." She leaned to see her side, her face wrinkling in pain.

"You hit hard, from the looks of it." He traced a hand across two protrusions along her lowest ribs.

She sucked a stifled breath, tears rimming her eyes. "Please…I can't bare it."

As he'd suspected. Broken. Her side was covered in scrapes, the two protrusions red and angry. How had she even held on for the ride they'd taken? Broken ribs were enough to bring a grown man to his knees, but she was a woman—a fact he was all too aware of at this moment. "Looks like broken ribs. I'll get ya wrapped so you can rest."

She gave a reluctant nod, straining to pull the quilt to cover herself.

He escaped the room and opened the cabinet above the sink, lifting a crate of bandages down. Grabbing a cloth, he dunked it into the steaming bucket of water he kept on the fire. Wringing the hot rag, he tossed it hand to hand until he let it rest over the edge of the crate.

Returning, he found Haven, brushing away tears.

He supposed this entire ordeal was more than a shock and given her pain, the loss of the horse and worry of her brothers, he expected no less than tears from any woman. He sat beside her once more.

Haven sniffled. "I'm sorry."

"I think you're entitled to a few tears." He lifted the hot rag and used both hands to open and fan it, then folded it into his right hand and eased it against her side.

She bit her bottom lip, tossing her head back to the pillows in a full shudder of her body. When she caught her breath, he used the rag to clean around the open scrapes across her side. Her ivory skin held the tiniest freckles and her short panting breaths drew his attention to her breasts, where pert nipples pressed dark against the light fabric of her chemise.

He went back to her injuries, opting for conversation. "My brother Wyatt's married to Doc Tess, who says to wrap broken ribs tight." He pulled her to sit up and she opened those big hazel eyes watching him. She shivered as he medicated her scrapes with ointment and began wrapping the rolled dressing about her. She looked a mess with her dirty face and rumpled hair, but the smell of lilac held him hostage each time he passed the dressing around her.

She held her side, fighting against the bindings when he tucked the tail of the cloth under itself. "I think it's…too tight."

"Gotta be a little tight to help." He lifted her chin and used the edge of the wet cloth to clean her cheek, dabbing a bit of salve to the cut, landing his sights on her plump pink lips. She couldn't be more than seventeen. He cleaned the blood from both hands, adding the balm to the open scrape to the back of one. Her nails were short, and her hands as callused as his own. She was no stranger to hard work.

"You've family nearby?" she asked through panting breaths.

That fact would be an understatement, but he answered. "My oldest brother, Sawyer, is sheriff. Wyatt deputies and my youngest brother, Evan, manages the ranch outside Cheyenne. My mother, Dodge, runs the mercantile in town."

She angled her head, studying him. "Mrs. McCade allowed me to continue my father's line of credit at the mercantile. She's a very kind woman."

He nodded at her recognition, though the fact she seemed familiar with town threw him again. A woman like her would not have slipped his mind had he ever laid eyes on her. He went to the chest for the shirt and trousers. He didn't have anything by the way of clothing for a woman and his clothes would shroud her. Turning back to her he laid them on the bed and stepped to the door. "You need to change your wet clothing. I'll get you something for pain."

"I'll manage." She surveyed the bedroom. "Mr. McCade, your given name?"

"Dawson."

Haven repeated his name in a whisper. "Dawson, thank you."

He closed the door, sucking in a much-needed deep breath since the glimpse of her pert breasts beneath the chemise. After putting the willow bark tea on to steep, he made quick work of creating a rabbit stew, placing the small black pot into the ash of the fire to simmer.

He filled a tin mug with the tea, stirring the dark

liquid. He had nothing more for her pain, but this would let her rest. He stepped back to his bedroom. "I've tea…"

He stopped. She was covered by the quilt, propped on several pillows, her hair splayed across them, asleep. He touched her arm. "Hey…"

Haven startled awake.

"I've tea for the pain." He lifted her upper body, placing the tin cup to her lips, lilac surrounding him again.

She sipped and pushed the cup away with a groan.

"Come on, finish. It'll help you sleep." He encouraged her, tilting the cup to her again.

In seconds, Haven took the rest of the liquid and he laid her back to the bed, assuming she slept before he'd placed her head to the pillows. He drew the quilt back over her.

He studied her for some time, lying there with her flaming hair…and it dawned on him in an instant. He scooted to the edge of the chair, the wolf inside him stirring the memory to full. She was the living replica of the woman his totem had brought to him in his dreams. He uttered a whispered Cheyenne curse.

Chapter Three

"Josie!" Haven sat up and grabbed her side, cringing in pain. Moving had been a mistake and she collapsed back against the pillows. She was in bed, but not her own, and she blinked hard as it all came back.

Jumping from Josie had allowed her to escape the Indians who'd found her miles south of the homestead. And she'd run, trying to hide, until she'd been rescued by Dawson McCade. Now she rested in his bed inside his cabin, all of it a very bad dream it seemed, as she thought of her brothers.

She'd never left them more than the few hours it took her to search for plants and herbs or to ride to the fort and back. Levi liked to think he was the man of the house with their father gone, but he was still young. And James, would have fretted without her there to tuck him in. She needed to get home and hadn't a clue how long she'd slept.

The light from the small window let her know it was day. No matter the pain, she had to try, and she sat up with some effort.

"How're you feeling?"

Startled, she lifted her gaze to Dawson's deep voice. His large frame filled the doorway and he held a hot bowl and wooden spoon as he sat in the chair beside the bed. How was she to respond to his question? Her head pounded, and it hurt to breathe to the point she could have brought forth tears. She forced a whisper. "I suppose I've been trampled by a herd of buffalo."

"That good, huh?" His smile was genuine, his eyes a deep sapphire blue. The intensity of them had been the first thing she'd noticed about him, that and the thick white scar above his one brow.

She adjusted to a comfortable position, self-conscious at his continued stare. "How long has it been?"

"Two days. Hungry? I've hot broth. It'll help get your strength back." He lifted the bowl and spoon toward her.

"I must get home." She tried to move to the side of the bed and yelped in pain, tears no longer held at bay.

When she looked up again, he was shaking his head. "They're fine. Wyatt came through. Said he'd check on 'em every few days 'til we can get you home."

A few more days was too long, though she was sure Thorn would have come by if nothing more. "I've never left them so long."

"Can't ride far in the kind of pain you're in." He handed her the bowl with the spoon resting inside. The hearty smell of the broth was enticing as she brought the spoon to her lips. To her surprise, it was good, or she was so hungry it mattered little.

She studied him for a moment. Dark brown hair fell past his shoulders. A single braid hung behind his left ear; a feather attached with beads. He wore buckskins, and a small leather pouch adorned with beads hung around his neck and the beginnings of a beard rode his face. He'd denied being an Indian, though he could all but pass for one, save those blue eyes.

"I'm obliged to your brother." She licked her lips, wishing she had a proper napkin. "I was so afraid…when you grabbed me. I hadn't known you were there, of course."

"Thought you might scream and give us away." His deep voice was as low as she'd ever heard.

He'd been very kind to her so far when he'd cared for her injuries. Heat rose to her cheeks in remembering, but there was no point in dwelling on the issue of her modesty when there was naught she could do.

"As I recall, I did try to scream, but…you kept me from it." She gave a hesitant smile.

"Thought you might bite, then *I* would've screamed," he teased with a tilt of his head and a grin.

She giggled, but then stopped abruptly, wincing and holding her ribs.

He stood, the fringe from his buckskin tunic hanging more than a few inches up the entire sleeve to his shoulder. "Rest a couple more days. Snow's not melting any time soon, but I'll get you home as soon as you can manage the ride."

She nodded, the ache in her chest visceral, and he was right, given the pain she was suffering.

"I've more tea." He stepped from the room and returned with a steaming mug, placing it into her grip.

She inhaled the pungent smell and wrinkled her nose. " Willow bark tea again."

"It'll dull the pain, let you rest." He folded his arms.

"It's one of the herbs I sell at the fort." She sipped the dark chalky liquid, shivering at the bitterness.

He leaned against the door frame, watching her. He was tall and thick with muscles, his size overwhelming, but she'd known that from riding behind him on his horse.

She lifted the tea once more, his piercing gaze too intense. "I've always dreamt of opening my own apothecary, but for now selling the herbs keeps up the payments on the homestead."

"Sounds like a lot of work for a woman alone." The braid fell across his shoulder, the small beads clicking.

Had she not been in pain, she might have told him more of her dreams, but right now she was at his mercy. "My father always said working hard for things makes them worth it."

He shrugged, giving it some thought. "It's a right fine dream."

She wasn't certain his remark was sincere and drank more of the tea, hoping indeed it would help the pain. How had she slept for two days like this? She fought a bout of coughing, the bindings searing her painful ribs.

"Rest. I've got a few chores but won't be far." With that he turned but glanced back. "Uh, if you need to..."

She caught the idea of his meaning and heat rose to her cheeks. She did need to go, but she'd manage that for herself no matter.

"Outhouse's just through the back door." He turned, and a whip of bitter wind stirred through the cabin as he went outside.

After a struggle to work her coat on, she managed the jaunt to the outhouse. Back inside, she continued to shiver, crouching in pain. She had to rest and let the tea work, so she could go home. Taking a look around the cabin, it held no touches of a woman. Piles of papers and maps lined the table and a disorganized stack of wood lay in a heap on the floor. The dishes on the counter were stacked in disarray as were the various pans near the fire on the rock hearth. Along the mantel, books lay in uneven piles and the floors were in need of a good sweeping.

Fatigue gripped her, and she managed to slip underneath the covers, grateful for the warmth of the bed. She curled to her side, rubbing the wraps pulled tight around her ribs. She inhaled the scent of leather, a hint of Dawson on the bedding. He was a might older than her, maybe even thirty, but some part of her thought him handsome and she could still feel the tenderness of his touch.

Her thoughts roamed to Josie, tears welling in her eyes. She missed the horse and always would, though her arms ached to hug her brothers. And she missed Sosha, the furry wolf mix her father had raised from a pup. The dog and Josie had somehow become her best friends over the years.

The tears slid down her cheeks, though she hadn't the energy to sob. Closing her eyes, she uttered a silent prayer that her brothers were safe and that somehow Josie would be returned to her, though she relinquished the latter prayer would go unanswered for her lifetime.

****

Dawson entered the cabin, hanging his buffalo robe on the hook on the wall. It had turned colder; the bitter winds hindering his work. He shook off the chill and narrowed his sights on Haven, who sat at the table, a full meal before them both.

"I thought you would be hungry." She wore one of his long-sleeved undershirts tucked into her brown skirt, offering a glimpse of her full rounded breasts; his mouth went dry.

He stepped from his moccasins, glancing around the cabin. The floor had been swept, the messy items of this or that were in neat piles, and the hearth was clear of the clutter. Even the various stacks of books that lay around the cabin were all tidy and in alphabetical order across the mantel. He wasn't sure what to make of it.

She tucked stray strands of hair behind one ear. "I figured to earn my keep."

"You should rest." It wasn't that he minded her care of his home, but she owed him nothing. He turned to warm his hands, not allowing himself a second scan of her breasts.

She nodded in agreement. "I'm little good at sitting still. I fried the rabbit up with a few of the vegetables in your cupboard. Please, eat while it's hot."

He took his seat at the table, the aroma of the meat enticing. "Thank you. Who gave you the name Haven?"

Her smile warmed his chest and he wasn't sure what to think of that either. "My mother was from New Haven, Connecticut and never did get used to living in the south. He sent her back there to have me and she didn't return until the war was over."

"It's a nice name." He lifted the cloth napkin and placed it across his knee. Hell, he didn't even know he had napkins. He studied her for a moment. Her face held a bit of color, and with her up and around, he might be able to see her home tomorrow. Why did that thought send a course of regret through him? The fire crackled as he picked up his fork and began eating.

She added a biscuit to his plate, holding her side all the while. "Biscuits, too."

He eyed her with suspicion. "I have a feeling you rested little."

A hint of rosy pink splashed across her cheeks. "I'm feeling better. It's still so cold outside. Do you think there'll be more snow?"

He broke the biscuit, a piece in each hand. "Temperature's holding, but the sky's clear."

"I would ask a favor, once you're done eating. I've warmed the water and would…like to bathe. If you could carry the bucket into the bedroom, please. It was easy to get the snow bit by bit, but now the water's too heavy." She spat all the words in a flurry, glancing at the bucket of water by the hearth.

He nodded, though the idea of her bathing was about as darn interesting as her appearance in his shirt. And no, he didn't mind, though if she were aware of his thoughts she'd run like hell. He went back to his food.

"I sewed my blouse and cleaned what dirt I could from my skirt." She brushed the garment with her hand. "I also cleaned your shirt and trousers and hung them in the out room to dry."

He took a bite of the meat, savoring the flavor as he chewed, and hoped to calm his racing pulse. She'd accomplished quite a bit for a woman who'd taken a terrible fall from her horse days ago. "Now I know you didn't rest enough."

"I should make myself useful." She watched as he continued to eat. "Otherwise I will simply worry about my brothers and fret over Josie."

"I'm sure they'll be happy to have ya home."

Returning her home was what he had to do, but he couldn't shake the feeling that he'd miss her presence. He'd been out working in the frigid weather, but she'd left his mind little. He couldn't pass a moment without picturing her as she had looked when she slept in his bed, her hair splayed across the pillow.

"Levi's a really hard worker, even before my father..." She hesitated, but then continued. "He's good with the animals and figures. And James is very smart, already reading."

"He must have a good teacher." He answered, catching himself taking in the sight of her. She was beautiful, wasn't she? Her wide hazel eyes were bright and her lips rosy and plump. The bruise to her cheek was fading, and when she smiled, he caught himself trying to memorize all the things about her. Yep, best he got her home as soon as possible.

"You said you work with the Cheyenne, like an agent?" She sipped the coffee in the tin mug before her.

"I'm not an agent. I translate for the tribes at Treaty Council, paid by the Bureau of Indian Affairs." It was the best answer that he had for the moment. "I translate so the Indians know the treaties are written accordingly. I help on the reservations, fight for the Cheyenne to trade their goods for fair prices."

"I sell my plants at the fort every month or so, but visits there..." She tucked another strand of hair behind an ear.

Damn, he'd like to do that, but why did she stop? "Not to your liking?"

"The soldiers can be very rude, but it's worse in town paying Mr. Scott on the homestead." She dropped her gaze to the steaming mug.

"The fort's not a good place for any woman, and Dodge isn't too fond of the man at the bank in Cheyenne either." He sucked down a long sip of the hot coffee. The soldiers under Captain Simmons' command were a rowdy bunch, most often drunk, and he'd heard Dodge speak of the crooked antics of Mr. Whitney Scott who ran the bank in Cheyenne.

Her tone sharpened. "Mr. Scott holds me to those payments, threatening to take our homestead should we fall behind. I suppose he sees me as an incapable woman. Perhaps you see me the same?"

He set his mug of coffee aside. Her question was rather lethal come to think of it. She squirmed in her chair but held his gaze. How *did* he see her? She was determined, he'd give her that, and strong spirited, but… "No. I don't see that at all. I see a beautiful. strong woman trying to make her way. Nothing wrong with that."

Her blush was expected but not her words. "You're a very kind man, Dawson, much like my father."

He hadn't asked of her father. "How was it he died?"

"He was drowned at the falls near our homestead. An accident we were told…" She took a shallow breath and went on, "I pour myself into work to avoid thinking too hard about things, just as I worked today to keep my mind from worry over Levi and James. We lost our mother, and now our father, and my brothers deserve the best life I can give them. Oh, listen at me ramble…"

He sipped the last of his coffee and stood, walking to the hearth and lifting the bucket. "I'll get your water."

She followed him.

He shrugged entering his bedroom, aware how close she stood, with his fragile thoughts of her bathing. "No trouble."

She touched his arm as he set the bucket of water beside the bed.

"No, I thank you that I may return to my brothers. I shudder at what might have happened to me, and to them if I wasn't able to return home."

"Thanks aren't necessary." Some part of him melted at the physical contact she'd made with ease. The tenderness of a woman was almost foreign to him anymore.

"After you take me home, you'll go to the fort again." She adjusted the bucket nearer to the bed with her foot. "Perhaps I'll see you there."

He'd shared some of his plans with her and she'd seemed interested in his travels, but the tenderness in her voice caught him off guard. "Perhaps. But I may be able to get you home tomorrow afternoon, if the ride wouldn't be too much."

Her hazel eyes lit up. "Do you really think so? I can ride. I'm sure of it."

He shrugged, not understanding the uncertainty he was feeling. "We'll try."

She was quick to wrap her arms around him in her excitement. "Thank you, Dawson."

He inhaled the sweetness of her but stepped back with reluctance as she let go.

"There's lye soap in the dish and some wash and drying cloths in the second drawer there in the chest. I'll...take care of the dishes." He made his quick escape, his heart pounding and a deep ache of wanting emerging inside him.

He glanced around the cabin again. It had never looked better. Everything was tidy and even the pallet he'd made for himself by the fire had been made up to look like a bed. He shook his head and went to the table, picking up their plates at the same time he heard a splash of dripping water—

He growled low to himself and washed and dried each dish, setting it aside, forcing the idea of Haven's naked body from his thoughts. Hell, the sooner he got her home the better. He had to get back to Fort Laramie for passes for the reservation, and while she was a pleasant distraction, it was time to get back to work.

He walked across the room, tossing a few more logs on the fire, and propped his socked foot up on the hearth, using a poker to stoke the flames, still unable to shake the feeling of her arms embracing him. He'd wanted to touch her, pull her hair close and smell the lilac, and feel its touch to his face as he…

"Thank you, again." She stood in the doorway of the bedroom, toweling her long hair, and his groin tightened. She still wore his shirt, but her damp hair was breathtaking, a deep burnt orange across her shoulders, and all he could manage was a slight nod.

"Do you really think we can make it tomorrow?" Her eyes glowed in anticipation and the edge of a smile on her still-bruised face captivated him.

He leaned an elbow on his knee, not taking a chance on dropping his gaze from the view of her. "It's not an easy trail and it's right cold."

"I'll be fine, though I don't remember so much about the ride once we left the river. It hid us well." She draped the drying cloth across her shoulders, swinging her long copper hair behind her. He froze, mesmerized at her pert nipples tenting underneath his dampened shirt. Yep, the sooner he got her home the better off he'd be.

He turned back to the fire out of necessity. "We got lucky."

"Well, I won't think of the alternative." She folded her arms across her breasts, cutting off the peripheral view he'd allowed himself. "I'll bid you good night."

"'Night." He took two full breaths before he could clear his thoughts of her body under his shirt. He had no rights to those thoughts, but after spending the last few days with her... Nope, he needed no woman or tidy cabin. It was best he took her back where she belonged and never looked back.

Chapter Four

Dawson hammered another nail into the thick wood of the fencing. Widening the corral was something he'd put off with the weather, but given the present company in his cabin, hard work was a good thing.

He'd spent the night before standing in the doorway to his bedroom, watching Haven as she slumbered, once again memorizing her. He'd been on his own for so long the thoughts he carried of her had become confusing, stirring the wolf inside him. He couldn't keep her off his mind even for a second, but what to do about it? He'd never thought much about marriage given what he did for a living, but when it came to Haven…pictures of the possibilities were emerging.

He glanced at the cabin. When he'd been fourteen, his father had helped him lay the foundation, even though he'd been young for the endeavor. Somehow, the cabin made him feel close to the father he'd lost long ago, killed in cold blood. And it had been Sawyer and Wyatt who had seen justice done. Their father now dwelled in peace—wherever that might be.

A cloud of thin black smoke left the rock chimney, bringing his thoughts back to Haven. She'd warmed biscuits and dried beef, insisting he eat before the morning's work. He'd enjoyed the meals she had prepared, but more than that, he'd relished her presence and conversations. Her eyes lit up as she listened to him talk about his work and when she spoke of her brothers.

She'd dressed in her own clothing, leaving his shirt and buckskins folded on the bed. He'd miss the view of her in his oversized clothing, cinched up with one of his leather belts. She was ready to return home, though he ventured the ride would be harder than she was anticipating, and taking her back was going to leave him empty whether he wanted to admit it or not.

He slammed another nail into the cross board and cursed in Cheyenne when he hit his thumb. It was like that with her around. He couldn't focus on one damn thing. He batted the nail back into place with a growl. It *had* been a long time since he'd enjoyed the company of a woman for conversation and damn longer since he'd—

"Ahhhhh..." he stopped the hammering. Why did she ride his thoughts so much? But then he knew. She'd been the woman in his visions and his totem was a strong one. He hadn't bothered to tell her about the wolf, but she'd been intrigued to learn a bit of the Cheyenne language and he'd enjoyed teaching her.

A shrill scream from the cabin turned him. He dropped the hammer and took off on a full run. The door was ajar as he tore through and stopped in mid-step, yielding his tomahawk from his belt.

Across the room, Haven held a large frying pan with both hands, and on the floor at her feet, rubbing his head, was Leaning Bear, the Cheyenne medicine man he'd called friend since his youth.

"An Indian!" Haven raised the pan higher, poised for action.

Dawson scrambled to the medicine man, lifting him to his feet. "Wait, he's a friend."

"What?" She lowered the skillet, her hazel eyes wide with fear. "But..."

"He's a medicine man, the friendly sort." Dawson gave her a wink and slid a chair under the Indian, who grumbled in native curses.

Haven took a tentative step, still holding the iron skillet. "I'm sorry, but...God in heaven, is he all right?"

"Ah, he's hardheaded." Dawson spoke to Leaning Bear in Cheyenne.

The Indian opened his eyes, blinking in confusion and sizing up Haven. "Not expect woman in cabin but pleasure mine."

"This is Miss Oakley, from a nearby homestead. She was injured when Dog Soldiers took her horse." Dawson nodded her direction, wishing better than to have to explain this one to his friend. "I'll be taking her home this afternoon."

The Indian scooted the chair further away from her. "White soldiers shoot rifles at all Cheyenne braves with Dog Soldiers spotted near fort."

Dawson wanted to curse. "Captain Simmons behind that?"

Leaning Bear held a hand to the back of his head. "It is as you say."

"Captain Simmons?" Haven dropped the skillet, startling both men to turn.

"You know him?" Dawson angled a sidelong glance at her.

She bent to lift the skillet and placed it on the counter, answering without turning around. "From visits to the fort, as I told you."

Dawson folded his arms, concerned she'd turned from the conversation. She'd mentioned selling herbs at the fort and that the soldiers could be rude, but why had she been startled by the mention of the captain?

"Captain ask speak with you." The Indian held his gaze steady on Haven as she turned back around.

Dawson's pulse raced. He'd been held for questioning by Simmons more than once, related to his leniency with the Cheyenne on the reservations. Lectured on his duties according to the captain, he'd most often been released with verbal warnings and threats he never heeded. His Indian counterpart had not been as lucky, often beaten or mocked in other fashion by the soldiers under Simmons' command.

The one help he had besides Leaning Bear was First Lieutenant Carl Bartley, who had been sent from back East to work alongside him at the reservations. The young man was hard-working and honest, wanting to do his best for the tribes, in spite of the captain's interrogations.

Dawson glanced at Haven as she approached with apprehension, taking the chair he pulled back from the table. She studied the medicine man, her curiosity apparent, and for a moment, he remained focused on her.

Leaning Bear continued. "Dog Soldiers bring trouble. Spirits restless."

Dawson ran a hand through his hair. The elders of the tribe had long thought war with white men far from over, even though it had been a couple of decades since they'd been mandated to reservations. But the presence of a random band of Dog Soldiers was proof enough things were at unrest, just as the pacing wolf inside him had known.

Leaning Bear continued. "Dog Soldiers bring no peace to tribes or white men."

The Indian was right. There'd been few sightings of them back during the Indian wars. Something wasn't right, and the hair on the back of his neck stood.

Haven broke the silence, her voice tender with regret. "I'm terribly sorry I hit you, but you frightened me. Please accept my apologies."

Leaning Bear's brows narrowed on her and he stood. "Apology accepted. Not enter cabin without knock first. Pan for cooking."

"Of course," she said, as he yielded a wide berth for the door.

Dawson followed with a quick glance her way. It surprised him she hadn't been more fearful, and he'd been intrigued that she had sat alongside his friend at the table.

Leaning Bear stepped off the porch, lifting his dark brows. "Take woman with frying pan for wife, good choice."

Dawson shook his head. "Not looking for a wife. Taking her back home this afternoon."

The medicine man glanced at him for a long speculative moment, folding his arms. "You good liar."

Dawson scowled. "Get the hell out of here. Maybe she knocked some sense into that thick skull of yours."

The Indian gave a hearty belt of laughter as he sauntered off toward the woods where his horse waited. "Meet fort."

"Yep." Dawson turned to enter the cabin again, meeting Haven's gaze. "I'm sorry he frightened you. He uses the cabin from time to time. Helps himself inside."

She folded her arms with the chill. "I feel awful. Perhaps he should see a doctor."

"He'll be fine, though I think he'll wear a headache for a few days." Alone with her, he memorized her yet again. The deep hazel eyes, freckled skin, and high cheekbones, with plump pink lips made for kissing. What was the hold she had on him, where he wasn't sure at all he wanted to take her home?

"I've gathered my things, my coat and hat." She held his gaze, waiting but not saying it was time to go.

"When I get you home, keep yourself closer to the homestead from now on. I'm not sure of the Dog Soldiers showing themselves again. Something isn't right that they haven't moved on." He was hopeful she would heed his warning, but he'd a mind to check on her anyway.

"You thought they had gone." The morning sunlight danced across her hair, kissing it a deep ginger.

He hadn't realized how much he'd like to run his hands through it until now. He lost seconds, his thoughts in disarray any time he focused on her too long. "They've most likely moved on, but it would be best you stay home."

"The Indians on the reservations are harassed by the Cavalry as well?" She asked in the southern accent he'd grown fond of hearing. "I thought the reservations were a safe place for the Indians."

He'd never have all the answers where the plight of the Cheyenne was concerned, but her question was innocent enough. "It's hard to predict what the Dog Soldiers bring by being here. Those on the reservations are harassed by the soldiers more times than not, most often when they visit the fort to trade their goods."

She held his gaze, folding her arms. "I must sell my herbs regardless but will search closer to home."

Dawson angled his head, still caught up in admiring her features. "Then take your dog along and make the visits quick."

She took a moment to respond. "I seldom linger, but now without Josie...I've been meaning to get Levi a horse, seems it's time now."

Dawson inhaled a deep breath and let it out. "You might sell the herbs in Cheyenne, at the mercantile."

"Perhaps." Her voice trailed off.

"I'll saddle Viho if you're ready." He lifted his buffalo robe from the hook by the door. He wouldn't need it for the ride to the homestead, but it would be a mite cold on his return.

A pleasant glow crossed her cheeks. "Oh, my goodness, yes."

"Viho should make the trail with no trouble." He turned toward the door, the intensity of her gaze too much.

"Dawson?" She was still standing at her chair. "I thank you again."

This was goodbye of sorts, and somehow the time with her wasn't enough, and before he could rationalize his thoughts, he spoke them. "I'd do it all over again if needed."

Her tender smile sent him out the door. He'd never fallen for a woman so fast. He'd never been like his brothers when they were younger, sneaking off to the brothels. He'd stayed away from women like that on purpose, seeking something with meaning.

He'd found it once—with Winona. He'd been

young then and she'd been older, teaching him the ways of a woman even if in the end her heart had belonged to another. He'd never thought much about marriage even then, but last night he'd spent time wondering how that might go with Haven. Ah, hell, he had no business at all thinking thoughts about a future with her. He had his work and she had her brothers to care for.

He ambled into the barn, finding Viho anxious to be free of his stall. He held his hand up giving the signal to the animal it was time to ride. The horse gave him a snort, Dawson walking to him and grabbing the halter and bit.

"What would you know about any of it?" He spoke to the animal in Cheyenne and led the horse outside to saddle him for the trip. "Make sure you do your part in getting her home and watch your manners. She's a lady."

He examined his own words, reluctance scoring through him. Haven was a beautiful woman, and it was long past time for him to get back to whatever he'd been doing before he'd found her running in the woods, before he'd watched her undress so he could care for her injuries and before she'd slept in his bed for enough nights to keep him thinking of what it would be like to have her as his own.

Chapter Five

The wind whipped, and Haven pulled Dawson's heavy buffalo robe tighter, though she worried he wore a tunic and undershirt alone. The snow had melted little and temperatures, even in the full sunlight, were more frigid than she'd imagined.

She held him around the middle, not wanting to admit she enjoyed the rumble of his deep voice through her when he spoke. She'd gotten up to begin breakfast and found him outside in the bitter dawn, bent in the snow chanting Cheyenne words she didn't understand, something he did each morning. He'd worn no shirt and the picture of his naked tanned skin against the white brilliance of snow had somehow been beautiful. She'd been in his care for a week and some part of her would miss him when she got home.

He'd worked most of the morning, saying the trip would be warmer in the afternoon, but she wasn't so sure now. She held tighter to him, sitting behind him on the horse he called Viho, the animal that had taken part in her rescue. She'd be home within the next few miles and was anxious to see her brothers, though they would be saddened by the loss of Josie. She'd never been away from Levi or James for this long and the pain was as real as her injuries, though she hadn't forgotten that things could have happened much worse.

"Not long now." Dawson urged the horse across a

small stream that held ice around the boulders. He coaxed the animal with whispered Cheyenne words, which vibrated through her.

"Yes." Haven had started recognizing the terrain miles back, the same places she'd often ridden Josie when she was out searching for herbs. Poor Josie. The hole in her heart would remain there for the rest of her days, she supposed. She hid her face from the wind, by turning into Dawson's back. He'd made small talk along the way, but she kept repeating what he'd said to her inside her mind. *'I'd do it all over again if needed.'*

Dawson had risked his life to protect her and she hadn't taken that for granted. Though words as such wouldn't be casual for a man like him, would they? And as anxious as she was to be with her brothers, there was a hint of sadness over the fact perhaps she'd never see Dawson McCade again.

"I do hope Leaning Bear will be all right." She apologized once more, wanting conversation with him before they arrived home.

"He'll be fine." His chuckle filled her ears. She would miss him. She leaned in closer as the wind crossed them, conscious of her hands that touched the hard ripples of his belly. He was such a handsome man, tall and thick with muscles. He towered over her, which drew warmth to her center at the thought of falling in love with such a man. Heat stroked her cheeks as she'd even gone so far as to wonder what it would be like to lie in his arms as he made her a woman.

"Dawson?" She leaned around to catch his gaze, knowing thoughts like that weren't proper so she changed the subject. "What did Leaning Bear mean about Captain Simmons' aggressions toward you?" It wasn't her business, but she'd seen the anger that had crossed his face at the mention of the captain.

"I'm hired as interpreter, but I'm not an agent. I think in that respect I fall short of what the captain desires from my work. I've no interest in changing the Cheyenne's way of life. I don't see the point in forcing them to acclimate to the white man's world, so I fight harder for their freedom to hunt off the reservations and trade in the towns for fair prices." His body tensed where she held him around his middle. "But as for the captain, I'd like to know why mention of him startled you."

His observation surprised her. "He's been very forward, but I have quickly put him in his place."

He laughed as the horse took an incline. "I suppose I can see that."

"I'm used to putting off soldiers' advances at the fort." She was often a spectacle when she showed up there, but she let go of her thoughts as they arrived home. "We're here."

As expected, Sosha ran from the barn, the large dog barking in warning as they approached the house. "Stay here but help me down." She took his hand, finding her footing as he lifted her down. "Sosha, come."

The dog ran to her and she thought for a moment she'd weep with joy. "Oh, Sosha, I hope you took care of the boys. Come on, I'll introduce you."

Dawson dismounted and tied Viho as Sosha began a low rumble of a growl, the horse anxious enough to sidestep.

"Sosha, no." Haven touched the dog, who stilled, though he stayed at her side.

He bent to his knees, lowering his gaze, the dog sniffing his outstretched hand and sticking out a tongue to lick it when he spoke in Cheyenne.

"How did you do that?" Haven was in awe, as Sosha had never taken to anyone. Her father had made sure of that, training Sosha from a pup. He'd wanted Haven and her brothers to have a protector while he was away to his work each day.

"He needs to know I mean you no harm." Dawson stood and stepped back from her.

"Haven!" James bolted from the porch, followed by Levi, both her brothers on a run toward her, it occurring to her the impact of their embrace would hurt. She engulfed both of them as they hit her, ignoring the pain and fighting to hold back tears of joy.

"James." She kissed her youngest brother's cheeks and hugged Levi, who allowed it but stepped back eyeing Dawson.

"Did you really get chased by the Indians? Are ya hurt? Why did they take Josie? Who's that?" James spit out a flurry of questions and hid behind her skirts.

"James, one question at a time. This is Mr. McCade, the man who helped me when I was injured. I escaped the Indians and I'm a bit sore." She turned to Dawson, touching his arm and nodding at her brothers.

"Thank you for what you did for Haven, Sir. Mr. Wyatt's been by twice to check on us and Thorn's been by, too." Levi extended a hand, seeming a grown man.

Dawson took his grip. "I'm glad he made it here."

"James, your manners." Haven scolded as her youngest brother peered around her.

He offered a small hand to Dawson. "It's a pleasure, Sir."

"The pleasure's all mine." Dawson bent to his level with a smile, taking his hand.

Levi ambled closer to Viho. "This is some horse. What kind is he?"

Dawson stepped to the animal. "Part mustang; runs with the wind."

Levi whistled with interest and Viho's ears perked as the boy ran a palm along his flanks. "I'm gonna get a horse like this one day."

James peeked around Haven's skirt again. "Mr. Wyatt's real nice, brought us candy, biscuits and a pie. He's really your brother?"

Dawson chuckled. "Yep, he's my big brother."

"He's a bounty hunter." James' eyes widened with explanation. "He catches outlaws all the time."

Dawson shook his head, a grin crossing his cheeks. "My guess is my brother made that sound a bit more fun than it really is."

"Will you come inside, sup with us at least?" Haven asked, hoping goodbye wouldn't come.

"It'll be dusk soon. Best I head back, with the temperatures." He held her gaze. Lingering past dark would make the journey home for him more dangerous, and she gave him a reluctant nod.

"Come inside, Haven, I'm freezing out here." James tugged her hand, shivering though he was bundled.

"Levi, take him back inside and I'll be there shortly." She waited as Levi followed James into the house and turned back to Dawson.

"They're both right handsome boys," he offered.

She stepped closer to him again, returning his buffalo robe, Sosha sitting beside her as if in protection.

"I'm relieved they're well. You must thank your brother. Bringing candy will mean he's made a friend of James for a lifetime."

"Wyatt and Sawyer both have children. I suppose he knows how that works." He put the robe on, wrapping it tight.

"I thank you again for all you have done for me." Her throat tightened with the impending goodbye, the moment harder than she'd thought it might be. It was strange but the possibility of not seeing him again caused dread to roll through her.

"I'm glad you're home." His voice was a whisper and his deep blue eyes gazed across her face. "Stay close to home, will ya?"

"I promise." She clasped her hands together, self-conscious at his continued stare, but in spite of her nerves, rose up on her toes to kiss his cheek. "Thank you, Dawson, for bringing me home to my brothers."

She'd shocked him, given the surprised look on his face. He grabbed Viho by the reins, saying no more. Somehow, she wanted to follow, uncertain when, if ever, she would see him again, but knowing it couldn't be the last, could it?

She called to him as he turned the horse. "Dawson?"

He glanced up, his blue eyes clear and his brown hair blowing across his shoulders with the brisk chill of winds.

"Did you mean what you said when you told me you would never hesitate to do it all again?" There, she'd gotten it out, hopeful for his positive reply.

He held the reins and her gaze, the horse prancing in anticipation. "A thousand times over. I'll see you again soon, Haven Oakley."

With that he raced off in the direction they'd come, and she stepped closer to the stairs, watching until he disappeared from sight. So this would not be their last meeting? Her heart raced at the prospect this wasn't the goodbye she'd thought it might be. She smiled and hugged her arms about herself shivering, though not from the cold but from the idea their parting was not final, and she would indeed see Dawson McCade soon.

Chapter Six

The afternoon sun warmed Haven's back as she bent to dig a sprig of horsemint from the edge of a cottonwood. She pulled the small plant free, smelling the sweet fragrance along with earth. The dried leaves would produce a bitter drink that would help with chest congestion. Sliding the herb into the bag across her shoulder, she glanced at James who panned for gold alongside Levi at the small stream a mile from the homestead.

"Haven, we need to work the cave." Levi stretched his shoulders and bent again. "Not even a small nugget today."

Haven walked closer, glancing around them. "We'll come back one night soon. We can't risk anyone finding out." The cave had been more than lucrative, but if anyone discovered it, they would lose all their father had died to protect.

He shook his brown curly locks panning, sending her a sidelong glance. "Seems a waste to spend all day out here."

"Aw, I hate the cave, ghosts live there." James added his two cents.

"Ain't no such thing as ghosts," Levi retorted, not looking up. "You're just a 'fraidy cat."

"Thorn says ghosts are real and he's seen 'em. I ain't no 'fraidy cat," James belted.

"Are too." Levi gave his younger brother a smirk and dipped his pan again.

"All right, both of you." Haven grabbed a pan and placed her brown boots in the edge of the frigid water. The cold stung enough to take her breath even though the oiled boots remained dry. She understood Levi's frustration but keeping the cave a secret was best. The nuggets and dust they continued to find inside had kept the homestead paid, and with what they had hidden, each of their futures would be secure. And that was as her father had planned as well, never a man who paid with or accepted paper money.

"There're no ghosts in the cave, James. The sounds come from the earth shifting and most often the wind. Mr. Thorn's stories are meant to be frightening for fun, but they aren't real stories." She bent, scooping the wet dirt and rocks into the pan and swirling it to reveal nothing.

Well, at least there was no ghost in the cave unless something of her father remained. Nope, her father was hardly a ghost, but something told her until she proved his death had been no accident, it was her own spirit that would remain as restless as Levi's.

She glanced at Sosha, who sunned himself in a small patch of grass as happy for the break of warmth as any of them, though the full winter was on the way.

"Ain't no one gonna know." Levi panned closer to her, keeping his voice to a whisper.

"Isn't. We can't be too careful, Levi. All we have is this claim to keep the homestead without Papa." Haven rinsed and scooped again, glancing behind her as James tumbled into the tall grass near the dog, giving up his efforts.

She giggled as her youngest brother didn't last long with working the claim. She glanced in the distance, where the cave remained hidden beneath the earth. Her father had discovered gold in this very stream several years before and sworn his children to the secrecy that had taken his life.

"Not so cold this morning, but I think the weather's coming full again." Levi made small talk as he continued to work.

She went back to panning. "You and James might need to add to the wood pile, and Levi, the barn roof may not hold with a big snow, if you could work on it again."

Her brother nodded. "I keep patching but guess I'm not good as Pa in keeping it leak proof."

He was just fourteen and maybe she expected too much of him. Maybe it would be best if she tried to help him, though she had less know-how than he. She sighed. "I'll help you all I can."

Sosha bolted to the edge of the stream, growling in ferocious warning.

Haven glanced up in alarm as did her brothers. Across the water, several men on horseback approached, her pulse racing to her throat. Mr. Scott from the bank, along with the two men who always rode with him.

Levi dropped his pan in the sand and lifted the shotgun, walking closer to her and grabbing Sosha to keep the dog at his side.

Haven whispered, "Lower the gun but hold tight to Sosha."

James ran to her, hugging her hips as the men edged closer.

She met gazes with Mr. Scott as he pranced his horse across the stream, lifting the hat. "Good afternoon, Miss Oakley."

Sosha's heavy growls turned into ferocious barks as he tried to free himself from Levi. She and Levi had long suspected the dog of witnessing their father's death but there was no way of proving such.

Haven reined in her racing pulse. "Good afternoon, Mr. Scott." His presence here wasn't expected, though it was no surprise.

"Boys." He rode closer, his horse shying with Sosha's continued display. "Wanted to remind you of the payment due the first of the month on your homestead."

Haven's brows narrowed. She had paid every month on the deed and timely since her father had died. "Mr. Scott, I make payments every month without fail."

He nodded as the men with him rode across the stream to join him. James hid behind her, peeking around as Levi fought to hold Sosha.

Mr. Scott studied her for a time. "Gold's bound to dry up sometime. Seems them pans there are empty, makes me wonder just how it is you do make your payments in gold most of the time."

Haven forced her manners. "We've made our payments timely, Sir, and will continue to do so. Don't let us keep you."

The man to his right chuckled, urging his horse past them, following the stream up river as the second followed, both inspecting the landscape as they rode.

"Seems you're the only one paying these days in real gold. But it ain't this stream yielding your find." Mr. Scott tilted his hat back. "Prime estate runs dry sooner or later and you need to plan accordingly, or the homestead will be owned by the bank."

Haven said nothing. This man was behind her father's death and she had no doubts about that. And her father had died keeping the cave secret in an effort to protect her and the boys. Mr. Scott had no interest in owning the homestead. He wanted the gold that he knew existed.

Mr. Scott moved his horse closer. "First of the month, Ma'am."

"We'll bid you a good day, then." Haven's tone was cold as he eyed her up and down.

Thorn's loud cackle came from the rise, turning them all. "Ya know they say, in these parts, the gold can be found in a cheat's back pocket just as the ghosts will haunt those that take it." The old trapper's Scottish accent echoed around them.

Scott's men rounded on their horses as Mr. Scott responded. "Best you get out of here, crazy old man. No one cares what you have to say."

Thorn's laughter filled the ridge. "Never know who's watching when you dig up your ghosts, Mr. Scott, ghosts or goblin, thief, friend or foe. The mysteries of the afterlife find their way back to the evils that took 'em."

Mr. Scott narrowed his gaze but turned back to her. "First of the month, Miss Oakley."

Haven looked on as the three men disappeared up river out of sight. She turned back to the ridge. "Thank you, Thorn. Would you care to sup with us tonight?"

"Much obliged, Miss Haven, but you'll save me a plate for a later time, I thank you. Out checking my traps." The old man raised a hand. "'Tis a fair day before true winter that my belly will hunger for your wonderful stew." And with that he was gone as fast as he had appeared.

"Is Mr. Scott gonna take our homestead, Haven?" James frowned, near tears.

Haven bent to her knees hugging him. "Of course not. We already have more than enough money to pay for the deed in full, but it's best we keep paying monthly. You understand not to tell anyone at all about the cave or the gold?"

"I know." He yawned. "But Thorn did say there was ghosts. You heard him, Levi!"

Levi lifted the rifle over his shoulder, ignoring his younger brother.

Haven stood as James scampered away, catching up with Sosha who sniffed along the trail, the dog still growling.

Levi moved closer to her, glancing back to make sure that James was out of hearing reach. "Haven, we gotta tell somebody or Papa just died in vain. Even if Thorn doesn't say, he must know what they did to Papa, just like Sosha does. Every time I see that Mr. Scott..."

She shook her head. "As long as he doesn't find out about the cave, we're safe. By not telling anyone we stay alive, Levi. If we say too much, every claim jumper in the area will top this mountain."

The last year had changed her brother, forcing him to grow up quick. The scattering of freckles across his face still reminded her of the innocent happy boy she'd once known and now missed.

"He was murdered, and Papa can't rest until we go to the sheriff. People say Sawyer McCade is a fair man, decent for a lawman," Levi tried.

Haven's mind jumped to Dawson with the mention of his brothers. "We can't accuse Mr. Scott with no proof. Best we work this claim as we have been." She glanced behind her, still making sure James was occupied, as he'd been too young to understand anything about their father's death.

"The longer we wait the harder it is to prove anything, and Mr. Scott keeps asking for more," Levi mumbled under his breath.

Her brother was right, but she couldn't prove what she knew to be true about her father's death. She could still picture the day Mr. Scott and his men had ridden up with her father lying across the back of an old mule. She had wanted to fall apart screaming, but she'd glared hard at the man whose knowing gaze had been a warning.

"For now, this is best." She tried as James ambled closer, carrying his bucket filled full of river rocks, Sosha alongside him. Levi began gathering their supplies.

"What do you have there?" She changed the subject, turning to James.

"Pretty rocks to line the garden in spring by Papa and Mama's graves." He dropped one of the rocks and bent to pick it up. Sadness wove its way through Haven's heart that either of her brothers had to understand death so young.

"Put some in here." She offered him the small pail she carried for adding mushrooms she hadn't found on this trip.

He took the pail and bent to put one rock at a time inside. "I'm hungry."

"We'll head home in a minute." She gathered the

pans, thinking it would have been much easier with Josie. Sometimes she missed the horse enough to cry, most often at night when the house was quiet.

That was also when her mind drifted to Dawson McCade and lingered over where and what he might be doing. Any time her thoughts went to him, her heart raced, and her body flushed, leaving her to think she loved him.

She called to Levi. "It's about time we got back home, near supper time."

"Yeah." He glanced at her with his dark brown eyes much like their mother's. "Only a couple of small grains today."

"Grab your things and we'll head back. Come, Sosha." She followed James, who took the lead, Sosha running to catch him as she waited on Levi.

The warmth of the sun struck her, and she lifted her face toward the sky. There was still a bit of chill in the air and she'd bundled James and worn her coat, but the temperature was warm enough that she now carried it as they made their way back to the homestead.

With her recent injuries they hadn't worked the inside of the cave much at all, which was best, given Mr. Scott had a mind to check up on them. She touched her side, where her ribs were still tender, and let her thoughts drift back to Dawson.

He'd said he would see her soon, but it seemed weeks had passed with no word. She'd often found herself scanning the horizon for his return.

"You're thinking about him again, aren't you?" Levi aimed a glance her direction.

"I was thinking what I might pull together for supper tonight." She lied.

"He's too old for you anyway." Levi shrugged, and a hint of a smile crossed his lips. "Leastwise Papa would have thought so."

"He is not too old, but it isn't likely we will see him any time soon. He's busy with his work." She made idle talk, but she wasn't fooling her brother any more than she was fooling herself. "And Papa wouldn't have cared greatly for any man who might have shown interest in me."

"Papa said you'd marry one day and leave us, but…" Levi looked away.

"Levi, I would never leave you or James, and my recent almost abduction should be proof enough I would do all I could to get back to you." She waited until her brother gave her a reluctant nod.

"Come on. I'm hungry." James ran back to them in complaint once they were near the cabin.

"Oh, by the time you put your rocks away, I'll have us a stew and biscuits." Haven teased, taking the bucket he was having a hard time carrying. "I'll dry out my herbs by the fire, so Levi, bring in a bit more kindling when you come in."

"All right." Levi turned for the barn. "And I'll milk the cow and clean the barn and put fresh hay and chop the wood. Call me when it's time for supper."

Her brother's complaints were sound, but she called to him anyway. "Thank you, Levi."

"Yeah." Her brother made his way into the barn with a shrug. Inside the house she lifted her bag from her shoulder and placed the horsemint and several herb species on a spread cloth at the counter. She grabbed her tablet from the shelf above the counter. It was a brand-new book she had yet to write in, since the

Indians had taken her old tablet, full of years of information.

Once she'd tossed together a semblance of stew and had it simmering on the old stove, she uncovered the morning's leftover biscuits and laid them on a cloth on top of the stove to warm. She sat and opened the first page of the tablet and began sketching the horsemint leaves.

In no time, Levi entered the cabin, carrying a bucket of milk from the cow and calling for James to follow. "Come on, slow poke."

"I'm coming." James bobbled with the kindling but made it to the hearth, tossing it all in the wood box, dusting his hands.

Levi put the milk on the counter and poured three tin cups full, bringing them to the table. "Haven, I've been thinking. Maybe we should take the gold and put it in the bank for safe measure."

"Shhh," She cut him off glancing toward where James had gone to play in the corner where he kept his toys. "It's too much risk. As long as we make the payments, Mr. Scott will just make his threats and leave us alone." She glanced at her brother with a lift of her brows to change the subject. "I was thinking, without Josie it's time to get you a horse and James needs new boots. We can make the trip to Cheyenne together."

"Sure, like to have a horse like Mr. Dawson's." Her brother began washing his hands at the sink pump.

The mention of Dawson once more caused her heart to race. "I'm sure such a horse is very costly, but we can go to the livery in Cheyenne and you can choose the best animal there. And in a year's time the homestead will be paid in full, and then…"

Her brother interrupted. "I know. Then you can build your apothecary and sell your herbs..." Levi sipped his milk, the sarcasm in his voice apparent as he sat at the table.

She turned back to the stew. Her brother couldn't understand her dream now, but maybe one day she would own such a business.

"I want a horse too, a pony." James plopped in his chair.

"Not right now, but maybe we can manage that by next spring." She tried, as they had to make larger purchases few and far between.

She added a bit of stew to each of their bowls, uttering a quick prayer after she sat. "Eat up, the biscuits are left over, but I'll make fresh ones in the morning. And the chickens are laying better, since you moved them inside, Levi, so we'll have eggs too."

"The livery in Cheyenne had some younger horses last time we were there. Strong ones we can use with a plow for the garden come spring." Levi dug into his stew.

She smiled. "Spring seems so far away."

"We have the barn full of wood, you've canned vegetables and stews, and we've got meat drying. I'll get a start on the roof of the barn soon." Levi sounded a lot like their father with his plans.

"James and I will help all we can," she added, taking a bite of the stew.

Levi glanced at James and chuckled. "Someone's fallen asleep. I'll get him."

Haven nodded as Levi lifted a protesting James from the chair and headed to put him in her bed. Snuggling with him since her return had reminded her of how sweet life was in spite of all their hardships. She stood and cleared the dishes, laying them in the sink and walking to open the front door for Sosha, who scampered away. Night was closing in as she glanced across the homestead and toward the meadow.

"See, you are pining for him." Levi startled her with his return but more so with his continued inquisitions.

She closed the door, pulling the bar down. There was little point in denying her thoughts, and it was clear her brother had figured her anyway.

"He was very kind to me, that's all." She returned to the sink to begin washing the dishes.

"Well, I like him and so does James, but he's still too old for you." Levi turned to let Sosha back inside.

Haven's mouth dropped open. "You have had this conversation with James?" Good Lord, was anything sacred?

"Well, he liked Mr. Wyatt better because of the candy, but I doubt James understands the pining part." Levi chuckled and darted away.

"The pining part, oh you!" She ran after her brother, swatting the rag at him.

"Good night, wake me early." Levi slammed the door to his room.

"Sleep well." Oh, who was she fooling? Her mind *had* been preoccupied with thoughts of Dawson McCade. He paid attention to her and treated her as an adult, something she struggled to feel about herself at times.

She went back to the dishes, drying and laying them on the shelf in the cupboard. There was little time to think of more than the care of the homestead and her brothers. There was a lot at stake in working the claim to make sure they kept the homestead, and she wasn't at liberty to dream of anything more for her own life. Besides, a man like Dawson had work that took him from home a lot of the time. So why couldn't she keep him from staying on the edge of her thoughts most all the time?

Chapter Seven

Riding Viho into Fort Laramie, Dawson scanned the bordered town for Leaning Bear, ignoring the glares of the soldiers posted at the gates. He tugged the reins and urged Viho to a stop, glancing around as he dismounted. The fort had seen its better days but was alive with activity as usual. Soldiers ambled along the streets and like any small town within itself, there was a livery, saloons and even a barber, not that he'd seen one of those in a very long time.

He tugged Viho along, never certain within the fort of his own safety or that of his horse. The soldiers could be trusted little and the few drunken Indians made a mockery of the ones who visited to trade their goods.

"McCade." Behind him the liveryman, Avery Roberts, trotted his direction, the old man limping with his bad back.

He turned, still holding Viho by the reins.

"They got that medicine man in the ring, trying to make him fight." Roberts groaned in pain when he stopped.

Dawson handed off the reins. "Take him."

Roberts gave him a nod and took Viho. "Watch yourself, can't a one of them soldiers be trusted."

Dawson didn't acknowledge. He had no fear of any soldier. He turned the corner to the back street and walked right up to the ring. Shoving his way through soldiers, some of whom cursed, he found Leaning Bear. The medicine man was wearing his buckskins and one of the soldier's hats in mockery. An oversized soldier shouted slurs, trying to entice the Indian to fight.

Dawson spotted Captain Simmons across the ring, chomping on a cigar and laughing with his men. The medicine man well knew how things worked. If he raised a hand, he'd give the soldier reason enough to beat him worse than the bruised cheeks and the bleeding lip he already carried.

"Son of a bitch!" Dawson shoved two soldiers aside and climbed under the roping to enter the makeshift ring. "That's enough."

A hush fell over the crowd, a few soldiers cursing him for stopping the fight.

"Fight's over." Dawson glanced at the captain, who tossed down his cigar with a sadistic smile crossing his lips.

"Aw, we're having a full unprofessional fight and the Indian is allowed to hit if he likes." Simmons smirked, urging his cheering men along. "But the coward won't lift a fist."

"Yeah, let him fight." A young soldier yelled, giving his partner a nudge.

Dawson grabbed Leaning Bear by the sleeve, tossing the hat from the Indian's head. "Let's go."

The crowd of soldiers complained in a ruckus so loud Dawson couldn't make out the individual voices as he led the way. His friend was no coward. The Cheyenne was brave enough with a strength that couldn't be matched when it came down to it, but the soldiers were too stupid to respect that.

Captain Simmons grabbed Dawson's shoulder,

turning him. "I'll have words with you in my office, McCade. Ten minutes."

Dawson held the man's gaze and glanced at his shoulder, the captain dropping his hand. It was a common game with the soldiers, who taunted the drunkard Indians for such display. And while he found it distasteful, Leaning Bear was not one of the usual candidates and they all knew that, the captain included.

He caught up to Leaning Bear at the livery. "You all right?"

The medicine man nodded. "It is as you say."

"Leastwise, you didn't put up a fight." Dawson handed him the canteen and the Indian drank, returning it and wiping his bloody mouth with the back of his hand.

"Must not anger soldiers. Cheyenne need passes to hunt." Leaning Bear sat on a bale of hay, catching his breath. The medicine man was eight years his senior and wise to his actions impacting the tribe, though Dawson wasn't sure how he held back.

"That Capt'n Simmons is just riling you, McCade." Roberts leaned a boot up on the bale of hay as Leaning Bear stood again.

Dawson's mind whirled around the injustice that the jackass captain continued to pull with detaining him and Leaning Bear several times over the last few months. Enough was enough and he'd meet the captain, but he wouldn't wait the full ten minutes.

He turned, though Leaning Bear caught him by the arm.

"Captain will detain you." The medicine man warned with a hard glare of his dark eyes.

"Then he has it to do." Dawson jerked away but

froze in his tracks. Across the opposite corral of Viho was the gray roan that belonged to Haven. "I'll be damned."

Roberts settled his arms across the fencing. "Got her off a couple of Indians a few days ago. A real beauty. You lookin' for another mare?"

Dawson shook his head with no doubts this animal belonged to Haven. "This one's stolen and I know who she belongs to."

Roberts chuckled. "Probably, but I paid right near twenty dollars for her…"

Dawson nodded. "You didn't know those Indians? Cheyenne?"

"Most likely. Never seen 'em before. Said they found her wandering the hillside past the reservation." He spat tobacco to the ground and rubbed his low back. "Probably as good a lie as any. This came with her, though, no saddle." Roberts handed him a small white shoulder sack.

Dawson took the bag, glancing inside. Haven's gloves and a tablet of notes and pressed herbs. Somehow her script drew him to lift the tablet and inhale. Lilac. Damn. "Don't sell her. I'll be back."

Roberts nodded.

Dawson hung the bag on the fencing and made off for the captain's office. The storm inside him raged, but now the picture of Haven lingered in his mind, disrupting any rational thoughts he might have held. He would never have believed the horse to be found. Regardless, he now had a big surprise for the woman who'd left his mind little over the last few weeks.

He made his way across the street, many of the soldiers from the fight now dispersing back to their duties. A few made snide remarks he ignored. At the captain's office he walked right past the soldier at the door. The man jumped to his feet and raced ahead of him inside. "He's here, Captain."

Captain Simmons sat behind his desk, his feet propped on the scratched-up table before him, a lit cigar hanging from his mouth. He dismissed the soldier with the wave of his hand and blew out smoke. "You know, McCade, we were just funnin' the Indian."

Dawson focused to keep his voice steady. "By what, degrading him in public, making a spectacle of him?"

"Come on, McCade, he's an Indian. No one cares." The captain chuckled, sucking on his smoke once more.

"I care." Dawson fisted his hands. "The Indians on both reservations are peaceful, following your damn rules, but you harass them at every chance. It stops now."

The captain slammed his feet to the wooden planked floor, standing. "Look here, this is my fort and I'll run it how I see fit."

Dawson gritted his teeth. "Then do your job!"

Simmons narrowed his gaze. "Careful, McCade. I know you're giving more passes than permitted. The Indians are traveling farther than allowed in larger numbers and not a one of them is working to build the needed housing on those reservations."

Dawson narrowed his gaze, his pulse racing. "They don't live in houses, and I allow them passes to trade in the cities and hunt the game further north. Your restrictions keep them from feeding their families."

Captain Simmons laughed with his jeer. "What keeps you at it, McCade? Is that how you live too, with some squaw in a tepee that will let any member of the tribe rut with her? Hell, I might give that a try myself for one of those pretty young ones…"

Dawson slammed the captain's table over, sending the hulk of a man staggering back to catch his stance, papers flying to the floor.

"You son of a bitch!" The captain swore, dusting his uniform of cigar soot and stepping around the upturned table in a roar.

Dawson held his stance as Lieutenant Carl Bartley ran inside, placing himself between them. "Captain, Sir, I'm sure we can settle this without a fight."

Simmons spit a flurry of words. "Half rations for the reservation, no passes next month, I suggest you use these sparingly." The man lifted the stack of paper passes from the floor and tossed them to Dawson, who caught the bound stack in one hand. "And while we are here, I'm warning you about the upcoming negotiations to keep yourself and that medicine man in check. Do I make myself clear?"

Dawson glared. "Call back your order for half rations and I'll limit the passes. Go through with it and I'll wire Washington about the situation at this fort."

The captain scowled. "That would be unwise. One more outburst from you, and I'll find reason to have you detained by the Federal Marshals. Word has it both you and that Indian know the Dog Soldiers who have been traipsing through this part of the country. Wouldn't that be a story to put together with your past?"

Dawson didn't move. It had been a damn long time but there it was again.

"That's right, McCade, we all know about that, a

soldier losing his life to the hands of a white man dressed like an Indian." He chuckled sadistically.

Dawson said nothing. This wasn't the first time that story had surfaced, and it wouldn't be the last. It had been years, but the knife scar to his belly still burned, even though he'd been relinquished of the charges when he'd defended himself against a drunken soldier set on vengeance.

Simmons spoke to Bartley. "Get him out of here and get back to your post."

Dawson held the man's gaze a moment more and stepped from the tent. He had no connections with the Dog Soldiers, but it was concerning that the captain pulled up his past.

Lieutenant Bartley followed him outside. "He's been asking lots of questions about you."

Dawson continued toward the livery. "Best you not break in like that in the future. You've a family to think about."

The lieutenant trotted to keep up. "Gotta keep you out of trouble, but what the captain said about that soldier…it's true then."

"Some things are best left in the past." He owed no one an explanation, including Carl.

The soldier continued with a nod of respect. "I'm sure the rations will be sent, but the month without passes might be tough. You gotta back off on riling him. He's got ammunition with that, knowing what you did."

Dawson spoke in a stern whisper. "I make no excuses for what happened. That soldier attacked me, and I defended myself, nothing more. I was acquitted of charges."

Bartley nodded, his face red. "Captain says if it wasn't for your brother being sheriff, he'd have already hanged you."

It was no surprise that while his brother, Sawyer, was sheriff in Cheyenne and had no jurisdiction anywhere near the fort, the captain like many others understood McCade law well enough. But what bothered him more was that Bartley, like most of the soldiers under the captain's reign, stayed loyal out of fear alone.

He turned on a dime, handing the passes to Bartley. "You go to the reservation and go home to your family after sundown each day." The least he could do was make sure the hardworking soldier wasn't on the reservation should Dog Soldiers arrive.

"But..." Bartley shook his head.

"Just do your work during the day, allow the elderly men the passes, and go home at night. Then you won't be held responsible for the misuse of the passes." Dawson glanced to the livery and back.

"He'll have reason to arrest you then," Bartley whispered.

"He won't arrest me. He'll need me at the negotiations." Dawson turned for the livery.

"Hey?" Bartley called to him. "You and Leaning Bear gonna enlighten me about these Dog Soldiers? I'm gonna be at the camp, and what do I do if they show up."

Dawson studied him. "You get any word of their presence, you take off on your horse and don't look back."

Lieutenant Bartley held his gaze for a long moment, fear holding his expression.

Dawson finished the conversation. "I'll be by the reservation soon."

Trotting back to the livery, Dawson met Leaning Bear outside. "Only two at a time for the month or we're down to half rations."

"Two not much good for hunt. Snow come soon." The Indian's face never changed no matter his concern. "Spoiled rations still waiting in storage."

Dawson nodded. The latest rations arriving by train had been held by the captain and the spoils never delivered to the reservations. "Keep passes for yourself and stay away from the fort until after the negotiations."

The medicine man nodded. "You stay out of trouble when return horse to woman with frying pan."

Dawson narrowed his gaze. "Be on your way."

The Indian cackled and took off on foot. His horse would be a mile away and he'd disappear again out into the wilderness as always.

Dawson turned to go inside the livery for Viho and the roan. Maybe the Indian's advice was something he should heed, given he now had reason enough to return to Haven. He glanced at her horse, the idea of seeing Haven again calming the pacing wolf inside him.

Chapter Eight

Dawson arrived outside the old Harper homestead, the reins to Haven's roan in his hands and the afternoon sun warming his back. The warm spell gave a bit of relief from the cold and he could still see Haven's face and her copper hair. It had been weeks since he'd returned her home, but she'd stayed on his mind often. He'd not soon forgotten the feel of her hands around his middle as she'd ridden behind him on Viho. And he hadn't forgotten his freely answering her question.

"Ahh..." Frustrated with himself, he urged Viho ahead as the homestead came into view. He should've known better than to be so bold with his response of interest. But as much as he needed no woman in his life, the anticipation of surprising her with the horse made his pulse race, in spite of his confusion of thoughts about her.

He stopped Viho and dismounted, tying the mustang to the corral fencing and grabbing the bag with Haven's book and gloves.

Levi exited the barn, lowering a shotgun, as he tugged the roan behind him. "You found Josie?" The boy gave the animal a good rubbing as Sosha yapped. "Haven isn't going to believe it."

"Found her at the fort. Is Haven inside?" Dawson glanced around the homestead, patting the dog.

"She's out looking for plants. James is sleeping.

Been fightin' a fever." Levi nodded toward the meadow but walked to Viho. "Haven gave him some tea and thinks he's getting better."

Dawson looked on as he admired the horse. "Little ones run a fast fever."

"Haven says we've enough money saved to get a good horse next time in Cheyenne, but I'd sure like to have one like this." Levi ran a hand the length of Viho all the way to his flanks.

"Can you give him a rest, water him?" Good horses were expensive, and he couldn't imagine with the payments on the homestead Haven would have extra for another animal. Selling herbs couldn't be that lucrative.

"Yes, Sir. I'll take 'em." Levi grabbed the reins and was off, followed by Sosha who scampered ahead.

It didn't take Dawson long to find Haven, his chest pounding at the sight of her. She stood at the edge of the large field, searching along the ground. She bent and lifted a small rock, tossing it in her bag. The sun was warm enough she wore no hat and her hair was splayed across her shoulders as she moved along in her search.

At first, all she did was look at him and the horse from the distance in obvious disbelief. But then she placed a hand across her mouth, lost to tears. and she ambled his way. The horse needed no guidance to her, and he let go of the reins. Haven welcomed the animal with a hug, stroking her mane.

"Josie, I thought I'd never see you again…" Tears streaked her face as she spoke to the animal in soft whispers. He hadn't meant to make her cry, though he supposed tears of joy were the best kind.

She was breathtaking, and he hadn't realized how

much he'd missed her until now. After a time, she glanced up and without another word bolted his way, leaving Josie behind. The impact of her embrace caught him off guard as lilac enveloped him. He sucked in a deep breath and held her for a moment, thinking her touch came so easy, so giving, so damn perfect.

"How on earth, Dawson?" She hugged him again, wiping her eyes.

"She was at the fort in the livery. She might've been traded a time or two." He patted the animal's side. "I don't think she's been harmed. The saddle was gone, but there was this." He held out the bag with her things.

She glanced inside, speaking in a whisper. "My tablet. Thank you." She walked around the animal, the horse turning to stay forward of her.

"Looks like she missed you." He was intrigued with Josie's interest in her.

Haven's hazel eyes held a twinkle. "Once again you've come to my rescue."

"That means I've about nine hundred and ninety-eight left." She was beautiful in the sunlight and against the gray of the roan with her flaming hair, and he damn well knew better than the words he was tossing with ease.

She took Josie by the reins. "I should take her to the barn for oats and to check her hooves. And I am sure I owe you for her return."

"Her hooves look good and she's been fed some of Viho's oats. You owe me nothing." He wouldn't let her pay him one dime for this moment.

"I keep looking at her. I can't believe it." She glanced at the horse ambling behind her. "How did you find me?"

"Your brother pointed the way." He shoved his hands in the pocket of his buckskin trousers as he walked. The bruises to Haven's face had faded and her hand held the slightest pink skin where her wound had healed. And she moved with ease, her ribs better with the passing of a few weeks he supposed.

She stopped as the horse bent to nibble the tall grass.

"She's been fed well it seems." He then asked out of curiosity. "And James? Levi mentioned he was ill."

She watched as Josie moseyed along eating and dropped the reins. "James had a mild congestion but has been better the last few days. Come, let's sit for a while and let her eat." She grabbed his hand and led him to an area of lower grass where she sat. "The sun's so nice. It won't be long until winter keeps us inside." She patted the ground and he bent to one knee and settled beside her, drawing a blade of grass from the earth and peeling its layers away. Sitting with Haven for a spell seemed odd, but then she scooted next to him close enough for the warmth of her to touch him.

"You must tell me how you found Josie and of your travels." A slight blush crossed her cheeks, leaving him to think her feelings much like his own. Something had grown between them while he'd cared for her and something even more as he'd taken her on the long ride home.

He shrugged. "I'd work at the fort and I usually leave Viho at the livery. She was in the corral there."

"I've prayed for her safekeeping but never thought she would be returned to me." She glanced at Josie who munched behind them.

She turned back to him lifting the medicine bag he

wore around his neck, weighing it in her palm. "I never asked you about this."

"My medicine bag." He studied her eyes in the sunlight, noting the speckles of brown and slight hints of green that blended.

She asked further. "What do you keep inside?"

He smiled, touching her hand that held it. "It's sacred."

"Sacred to who, the Cheyenne and you?" Her curiosity intrigued him.

"The Cheyenne wear it as a rite of passage to becoming a man. It's sealed when a boy takes his Vision Quest to find his spirit guide," he explained, studying his hand around hers and the fact she didn't draw away from his touch.

"And you did this rite of passage as a Cheyenne, that's why you chant each morning?" She turned the bag back and forth, touching the tiny colorful beads sewn along the outside.

He nodded, letting go with a hint of reluctance. "I was a bit older when I decided to follow the Cheyenne ways, not a boy as most."

She leaned closer to look at the top where the pouch was drawn tight with the leather straps laced through. She glanced up at him and began to open the bag. "May I?"

He placed his hand on hers again, her sweet voice drawing his gaze to her plump rosy lips. "It's for protection and strength."

She glanced up at him, touching the braid hanging across his shoulder. "I thought perhaps your strength might be in your hair. Like Samson."

He laughed, running a hand through his long brown

hair. "I've told Dodge the same when she challenges that I cut it."

"Well, you would be rather convincing as Samson, but what animal became your spirit?" She asked. "My knowledge of the Cheyenne ways is limited except for the words you taught me."

"I'm called Proud Wolf by the Cheyenne." He leaned as if some magnetism was drawing them closer. He held her gaze as she took in the proximity of him at the same time.

"And the bag is sacred enough you can't share its contents?" She still held it closer for viewing, her hair blowing to mingle with his own.

The medicine bag was sacred. He'd never shared what it held with his family as, most often, they didn't approve of his adopted Cheyenne beliefs. "It's for the one who wears it to decide, but most often it isn't shared."

She hesitated. "I've heard there are herbs and seeds inside. I'm curious what the Cheyenne find sacred where it comes to plants."

He took the bag and drew the straps apart and tilted it. A small blue polished stone rolled into his hand and he held it out to her. She lifted it as he leaned ever closer, having never shared anything from the small leather bag with anyone before.

"Turquoise. Polished it myself. For wisdom and protection. It's…" Her cheek brushed against him and he stopped without finishing, wanting the kiss he hadn't taken.

Her breath was on his skin but as he leaned closer, she pulled away, bounding to her feet and taking off on a run, turning back with a giggle, enticing him to follow. "Catch me and I will return your precious stone."

He chuckled. What was it with this woman, so carefree? He scrambled to his feet, giving chase, catching up in a few strides. He caught her around the middle and they fell into the high grass, his body across hers. Her laughter echoed through him as he studied her face and lips and settled his gaze on her wide hazel eyes.

"Kiss me, Dawson McCade." She whispered as she caught her breath.

He wanted the kiss and he'd have it too. He placed his hand on her cheek, brushing the bruise that had faded. He pressed his thumb across her lips and her gaze never left him as he touched her, though she wore a pleasant shade of pink. Her lips were plump and moist and—

The impact of his mouth against hers made his heart race and his groin tighten. She was tender and parted her lips with little coaxing, her hands playing through his hair. Touching his tongue to hers, he wanted to consume all of her. She tasted of mint and her sigh of passion or surprise made him moan with the hard want of her. He rested his hand across her belly and slid it to rest underneath her breast.

She pulled from the kiss breathless, her breasts pushing against his chest and he continued his fervent kisses along her cheeks and to her neck. He raised his head, finding her gaze once more. It surprised him when she lifted her hand and tucked his hair behind his ear, making him shiver. The sensation of her touch went clean through to his heart, warming his chest. He'd never wanted a woman as much, but more than that he wanted to know her mind and her thoughts. All of her...

"My heart's beating so fast." She placed a hand to his chest. "I've thought of you so often."

He had no words but touched her cheek again as Josie came close enough to drag her reins across them.

Haven giggled. "Oh, Josie."

"When you were at my cabin, I wanted this, to touch you, kiss you..." And he was falling ever deeper in admitting anything within his heart.

"Then kiss me again." She ran her hands into his hair, drawing him back to her lips.

In spite of his thoughts, he lowered his mouth to hers, this time kissing her without mercy and letting his hands roam her body. Hell, he'd like to undress her here and now, taste the pert peaks of her breasts and take her as a man, not yielding until she cried her first passions to him. And then he wanted to hold her and lie with her for the rest of his life in a peaceful state of bliss and warmth he hadn't known for a long time.

He sat up, leaving her in the grass. Hell, he had to stop now, or he'd do just what he was thinking.

She sat up and opened her palm, breathless. "Your stone."

He struggled to inhale enough air to recover and glanced at her. He placed his hand under hers and closed her fist around the stone. "It's yours now."

"Oh, no, I couldn't. I mean, it's sacred." She shook her head.

"It's yours." Some part of him wanted her to have it, to keep something of him safe in her grasp.

She leaned against his shoulder studying the stone. "What just happened between us?"

How was he to answer a question like that? Hell, he was more unnerved by what hadn't happened, and the tightness of his buckskin trousers had relented little. He glanced across the meadow, his mind racing but his heart sure. "What would you want it to be?"

The pink blush across her face hadn't abated. "The beginning of something very beautiful."

He gave a slight chuckle. "If you knew my thoughts, you'd run faster than you did from those Dog Soldiers."

She took his hand again. "I have no fear of you, Dawson McCade."

He stood with a smile, tugging her up beside him. "You should."

She grabbed Josie's reins but didn't let go of his hand. "Then perhaps you should come by more often to give me reason enough to fear you."

He shook his head as they headed back toward the homestead. Somehow, she had gotten through to the heart he'd hidden away long ago, but it was going to take him some time to figure things out.

She didn't stop, and she didn't let go of his hand. "You are quiet because you're uncertain?"

He squeezed her hand tighter. "Partly, because of my work, there are many things we have to think about. I'm not the kind of man to make excuses for who I am and what I do, and I wouldn't want that to bring you any harm." No matter his feelings, there were things to consider and he wouldn't make her promises that would leave her pining at the door in wait of him. "There's much to be done for the Cheyenne, for all the tribes. I care for you, Haven, but you have your brothers to raise and I don't want to make promises in haste that I can't keep."

She squeezed his hand again. "I would ask you..."

He gave a slight nod as they continued toward her home.

"Is there someone? I...mean a woman?" Her question was sincere, and she kept moving along not pressing for his response.

"Not since I was a very young man." He continued after giving it quick thought. "She was half Cheyenne. Her mother had been a white woman. In the end, she loved another, as was best."

It surprised him that she would ask. "She went to the northern Cheyenne with him. She later died of pneumonia from some kind of influenza or winter sickness."

"You loved her then?" She asked without any hesitation.

It had been like that, some of the time, but Winona had been older and often times frustrated with him and the fact she wouldn't be accepted in his world any more than he would be in hers. "I believe you love someone you choose to spend time with. I...loved the idea of living the life of the Cheyenne, but she was right. I was too busy trying to prove that point instead of just being who I was supposed to be. In the end, it was best."

She leaned into his upper arm as they strolled along. He had to wonder her thoughts, though his own were in shambles. He'd never made promises to any woman including Winona, but all he could think now was that he wouldn't be able to get two feet from Haven without losing something of himself.

Arriving at the homestead, he lifted her hand and kissed the back of it. "I do...care for you, Haven...best we get to know each other little by little first."

"Yes." She whispered.

He placed his lips to hers, touching her cheek. With a smile he trotted toward Viho. Leaving her was harder than he'd expected, but he mounted up and didn't look back, knowing if he did, he'd have to battle with his inner wolf about ever leaving her again. As Viho took to a gallop, he settled in his mind it was the right thing for now, and no matter, the wolf would bring him back. And he knew this, as did every Cheyenne brave when they'd found their—Heartsong.

Chapter Nine

Dawson slowed Viho as the ranch came into view and he and Zane rode toward the barn. His nephew had ridden up to his cabin earlier that morning to let him know Neha would foal soon.

Cattle sprinkled the hillsides as far as could be seen, wranglers on horseback, idle in watch. The main house always brought a sense of home, even though he hadn't lived there for years. All his childhood memories and those of his father lingered here.

"Bet Neha's close now." Zane dismounted outside the barn, Sirius yapping their arrival. "Go ahead, she's inside. I'll separate these two in the corrals."

Dawson relinquished Viho's reins to his nephew and made his way inside the main barn on a trot.

"Speak of the devil, the nervous father arrives." Wyatt slapped him on the back and urged him closer to the corral where Neha labored.

"How's she doing?" He glanced at Evan, who was leaning against the inside of the corral, arms folded across his broad chest.

Evan nodded at Neha. "She's struggled through the last few contractions. Thought she might have delivered by now, but it's her first foal. I'll check her in a bit, might have the legs under."

"Give her time." Sawyer braced across the fencing alongside Brett and the old man tipped his hat in greeting.

Dawson entered the stall, laying a hand on the horse's belly, waiting for it to tighten. Neha neighed, rocking her head. He spoke to her in Cheyenne and the animal calmed for the moment.

"Ah, she don't know Cheyenne, she knows your voice is all." Evan leaned closer. "Easy, girl."

"She understands." Dawson darted a glance at his younger brother, who had little in respect in how the Cheyenne trained their animals.

"She understands little with the pain of foaling, like any woman giving birth." Brett walked outside the barn and spit tobacco juice across the ground and returned.

Dawson nodded in agreement. "How ya feeling, Brett?"

"I'm doing right fine. Doc won't hear of me doing a full day's work, though." He scoffed toward Wyatt.

"You're still out to pasture." Wyatt chuckled, brushing the sleeves of his fancy shirt.

Dawson glanced again at Brett. He was pale and thin, but better than he'd initially been. He'd almost died from a gunshot injury, but the old man was as tough as nails when it came down to it. Dodge had nursed him back to health every step of the way, insisting he stay at the ranch for most of it.

Neha stamped her feet and snorted, uneasy once more.

"Who braided her tail?" Zane jumped up on the fencing beside Sawyer.

Sawyer answered, with a roll of his gray eyes. "Rose. Said every woman wants to look her best at delivery."

Dawson chuckled. It wasn't the first time the ladies

on the ranch had put their hands into helping at delivery time. He glanced at Wyatt. "How's Zachariah doing? Getting any sleep?"

Wyatt beamed, folding his arms. "No rest for the weary but thought you might like to know that pretty little redhead rode in here early yesterday morning. James is ill, got Tess looking after him."

Dawson froze at the mention of Haven and at the fact James was ill enough for her to seek help.

"You can, uh, close your mouth now." Sawyer lifted a dark brow and laughed with the others.

Well, he expected no less from his passel of brothers and even his nephew, but James being ill was a concern. "He's bad off, James?"

Wyatt shook his head and folded his arms. "Heavy fever, though Tess has it down. Says he'll be fine."

Dawson turned back to Neha, who rocked her large head, trying to lie down though Evan grabbed her harness.

"No, girl, gotta keep you upright. This is taking too long." Evan rubbed Neha's belly, leaning against the horse. "Zane, you and Dawson hold her steady."

Zane jumped the fencing as Evan removed his shirt and soaped his arm to the shoulder in a bucket of suds. He returned to the animal, lifting her braided tail and inserting his arm to his elbow and then shoulder. Dawson held Neha steady, waiting.

"Yep, got the feet beneath." He groaned as he pulled and tugged inside the anxious animal.

"Can't figure it, the man passes out at the sight of blood, but he can deliver a horse like it's nothing." Wyatt stepped back, glancing at the front of his shirt.

"Well, this one's about out." Evan tugged with his

full might and pulled a pair of tiny matching hooves from the struggling mare. He continued to pull with each contraction until the blob of a foal plundered free into a heap in the straw below.

Dawson calmed Neha with more Cheyenne words as the animal bent to smell the damp wiggling foal.

Zane grabbed a blanket and rubbed the foal's body, drying the animal's face as it struggled already trying to stand. "Hey, a colt."

Dawson bent to touch the animal. The painted colt had beautiful markings of brown and white, speckled much like Neha. He'd have to send a wire to Samuel Hagen first of the week and let him know Viho had sired a male. The horse rancher liked to keep up with the lineage of the horses that came from the ranch outside of Rapid City.

Evan went to the bucket to wash his arms and chest. "Let him be. He'll stand when he's ready."

Dawson and Zane stepped back, and Neha took over, nudging and licking the colt that leaned upright and then after several attempts rocked up onto his unsteady legs.

"There he goes." Evan turned, using a towel to dry himself.

"He's a beauty." Sawyer admired the colt.

Wyatt eased closer to take a look at the foal, then crinkling his nose with purpose at Evan. "You will, uh, wash up before dinner?"

"Shut the hell up!" Evan kicked straw his way. "Might not hurt you to get dirty now and then."

Wyatt darted from the barn, following Sawyer and Brett, who were already heading back to the house.

"Wyatt doesn't like anything about getting his shirt

stained, does he." Zane's statement wasn't a question as he traced the drying cloth back down the colt. "What you gonna do with the colt, keep him?"

Dawson nodded, taking a long look at the toddling animal. "For a time, let him stay with his mama here on the ranch. Safer that way with winter coming. I finally have the corral finished, so by spring, he'll have a better run." He'd worked hard on the corral, trying to keep his mind off Haven. His brothers might make light of him, but that she was near, his pulse raced, and he couldn't help but glance outside the barn toward the house.

Evan put his shirt back on. "Haven said you found the horse she'd lost."

"At the fort, likely sold through several hands." Dawson glanced at the colt once more, not interested in the interrogation.

"She's a right pretty thing." Evan's comment turned him from the colt, his brother's light brows lifting high as he buttoned his shirt. "Seems smitten with likes of you."

Dawson glanced at Zane, who shrugged and left the barn on a trot, carrying a smile.

"Seems Wyatt had a rather big mouth, come to think of it." He glared at his younger brother and made his way toward the big house without a second glance at his brother.

Inside, Ella, Wyatt's daughter, toddled past him carrying a rag doll larger than she was. He tousled her dark hair as she scampered away jabbering baby talk. Dodge passed him close on her heels, carrying Ella's newborn brother, Zachariah, over her shoulder.

"I hear Neha did well." His mother adjusted her grandson to the other shoulder.

He kissed her outstretched cheek and touched the baby's tiny head. "A colt. Haven and her brother?"

Dodge trotted after Ella. "Your old room. She was asking of you."

He held her gaze, too aware of the meaning behind her knowing blue eyes as she disappeared into the living area, leaving him grateful for his rambunctious niece. He turned toward his old room, stopping outside the door. Inside, Tess hovered over James, who was covered in blankets. Haven sat on the side of the bed, running a cool cloth across his brow. Dawson's breath hitched at the sight of her.

"Oh, Dawson." Tess glanced at him and turned to her medical bag, speaking to Haven. "His fever's much better with the Quinine. You can take him home in a few days."

"Thank you, Doctor." Haven's voice was but a whisper as Tess left them alone with James.

Dawson touched James' brow, which was cool. Haven's worried gaze found his as she spoke. "His fever was so high. I was frightened, and the willow bark tea helped little. I rode all night to get him here."

"She's a good doctor." He looked on as she sponged her brother's forehead. His sister-in-law, Tess, had trained in Boston and was the best physician in the territory.

"If you hadn't returned Josie, we never would've made it." She was on the edge of tears and turned back to James to avoid looking at him.

In spite of thinking better of it, he drew her up and wrapped his arms around her. Not because she'd asked him, but because he wanted to be the one to comfort her in times like this. And he held her in the quiet for a long moment closing his eyes and inhaling the sweet scent of lilac that always rode her long copper hair. "Shhh, Doc Tess said he'll be all right."

She wiped her eyes with her sleeve. "I was so worried. Your family has been very kind."

"When did you last eat?" He let her go and pushed her to sit by James again. She was weary, and her hazel eyes showed it, exhaustion across her expression.

"I left Levi with Sosha." She shook her head, touching James' cheek. "It's all a blur. James' fever wouldn't break, and Josie could only carry me and James. I don't know…yes, I had some bread, a muffin, a bit earlier or…last night."

"How about I get you a little something to eat?" He didn't figure her to leave James even for food.

She tried for a smile that faded. "Your mare foaled, then?"

"A colt. Neha did well. You can see him tomorrow." He offered, wanting to hold her again and take away the struggle.

"I'd like that." She wiped James' cheeks. "Never seen James so sick. When he was born…" She started but then seemed to be trying to gain her emotions. "My Mama had a hard time of the birth and died with fever a few days later. I'm the only mother James has known."

"He's lucky to have you." He squeezed her shoulder. "You'll feel better if ya eat."

She gave him the hint of a thankful smile, something inside him all but melting. With one more glance of her caring for her brother, he walked back down the hallway and pushed through the swinging door of the kitchen.

Inside, Mei Ling was at the stove and Tess at the

sink. "Mei Ling, you got something she can eat?"

"She eat little. Too thin, but hair like setting sun and much tall for woman." Mei Ling handed the bowl of chicken and dumplings to him, lifting her knowing almond eyes to hold his gaze. "Young and smart. Make good wife for you, Dawson."

Dawson fought the urge to react. Mei Ling had never been one to hold her tongue and as his mother's best friend, had been like an all-knowing aunt as he and his brothers had grown up. Well, he knew better than to respond to that and glanced at Tess who held the same hopeful smile.

"She really is a sweet woman..." Tess added her two cents, a comment that justified his thoughts. Haven was a woman. A beautiful one, but it plagued him his entire family being in on all the details. Regardless, the air was getting thin and he turned to escape the kitchen, running right into Sawyer's wife, Rose. She held their youngest son, Uriah, who chewed his fingers, grinning.

"Dawson, the colt is beautiful." She gave him a quick hug as he juggled the bowl of dumplings.

He gave Uriah a tender poke to the belly, getting a slobbery giggle in return. "He's growing fast."

Rose smiled and angled her head to study him with an inquisitive gaze. "Yes, faster than I can fathom. I've enjoyed talking to Haven."

Well, there it was again, the lift of another sister-in-law's brows of question. Was there going to be no mercy in this house? "I've gotta get her to eat." He made a quick escape, returning down the hall to his old room.

Turning inside, he found Haven still sitting on the bed beside James. She accepted the bowl, using the spoon to take a small bite. "Thank you."

"Mei Ling does some fine cooking, Asian spices with the chicken and dumplings changes it up a bit." He took the chair beside the bed.

She narrowed her gaze on the contents of the bowl. "I could smell this simmering, but the spices are not ones I recognized."

"Mei Ling purchases spices from San Francisco." He explained, the full picture of her with her hair pulled up onto her head and her neck exposed drawing his attention. She was downright captivating.

She took another few bites, closing her eyes. He thought at first she was enjoying the food until she swayed and set the bowl aside. "I'm…so tired."

He tugged her up. She needed rest, and he could sit with James.

"I mustn't leave him…" She protested and without a thought he scooped her into his arms.

"Shhh, I'll stay with him." Dawson whispered as he walked from the room carrying her. Her eyes closed, and she leaned into his chest, wrapping her arms around his neck. He kissed the top of her head, inhaling the sweet scent of lilac as he laid her on the bed in the room across the hall. He covered her with the quilt from the foot of the bed and slipped her boots from her feet, dropping them to the floor and lingering. In spite of it all, he placed his lips to hers.

Haven looked at him, smiled and closed her eyes once more.

Dawson waited for a long moment, until he was sure she slept, and then he eased the door almost closed.

"Tess seems to think James will be fine." Dodge met him in the hallway and peeked through the crack in the door at Haven. "Wyatt took Tess home for the night."

Dawson leaned against the door frame, thinking about a quick escape if he knew what was good for him. His mother knew him well, and her waiting gaze was the same he'd suffered from Tess, Rose and Mei Ling. "Haven was exhausted. Didn't give her much choice but rest as well."

Dodge followed him back into his old room, touching James' brow. "She's very lovely. She's been in the mercantile a number of times. Evidently, exchanges gold for being able to pay in cash. Never keeps much of a tab. Says she's nineteen and carrying the weight of the world on her if I know anything."

He hadn't asked Haven her age. Nineteen. A good bit younger than his thirty years as he'd suspected, but well old enough for the kisses he'd stolen. "She sells herbs at the fort, must do well with it."

Dodge eyed him with speculation. "Herbs pay little, though I suspect her father had some money put away. He paid his tab in full every month as well. She's usually with the older boy when she comes to town."

"Levi." He ran a hand through his hair, banding it with a leather strap from his wrist.

Dodge tugged the quilt higher across James. "She praises your care in rescuing her and returning her horse."

"I did what needed doing. We're both lucky those Dog Soldiers moved along." He held her gaze as he leaned against the chest of drawers.

"I assume you're planning to visit with her now and then?" Her light brows lifted. "She is quite smitten with you. Said you were one of the kindest men she had ever met, and I happen to know she's right."

He shook his head, avoiding the curse he wanted to toss. "There you have it, the entire story."

She smiled, ignoring his tone. "It's been some time since a woman has caught your fancy. You've protected that heart of yours for a long time now."

He narrowed his gaze. Dodge might be interested in his concern over Haven, but this was *not* where the conversation was heading. "We both know this isn't about my intentions toward her. This is about keeping me busy with the upcoming negotiations." He inhaled a deep breath.

"It would do me little good to insist you don't go, I suppose." Dodge didn't raise her voice but held his gaze, hands on her hips.

"It's not that easy, Dodge." He shook his head. "I'm obligated to translate, or a lot gets omitted."

She walked closer to him. "And what of her? She is more than smitten, Dawson, leaving me to guess, based on your tenderly tucking her in, that she has reason for such thought."

He hadn't known he was being watched, but little slipped past his mother. "Not sure I've promises enough a woman would want to hear, and I've given my word on the negotiations."

Dodge took a long deep breath and squeezed his hand. "That you are smitten enough to speak of the promises for the future, no one can decide that save you. But worse would be regrets over letting her slip from your grasp."

With that she let go of his hand and left him. As much as he hadn't wanted to think it, Dodge was right. He'd somehow fallen hard for Haven. He'd already expressed words to her that would be considered a promise to any woman and damn if kissing her hadn't stirred the song in his heart. He didn't know whether to chuckle or curse the situation but turned back down the hallway to his doom. Dinner with his brothers.

Chapter Ten

The sound of a barking dog pulled Haven from a deep slumber, though she sat upright knowing right away the dog wasn't Sosha. She glanced around, tugging the heavy quilt away, remembering James and the fact she was in the McCade home. She jumped up, smoothing her hair and rumpled skirts. It had been Dawson who had placed her here in the bed, carrying her and easing her worries. And he'd kissed her, she was sure of it.

She crossed the hall, Dawson's voice rumbling soft as she stopped at the door. He was sitting on the bed beside James, reading from a book with her little brother curled against him. He'd stayed as promised.

Dawson lifted his gaze. "Afternoon."

"Haven!" James scrambled across the covers and into her arms. She hugged him to her, his warmth nothing of the fever he'd held before.

"His fever's gone." She glanced at Dawson, placing James back on the bed.

"Mr. Dawson's readin' me a story 'bout a giant whale." James crawled back to his spot, though he gave a long yawn.

Dawson lifted the book. "Moby Dick."

She smiled at the story she'd borrowed a few years before but had returned to one of the neighbors. "Yes, I've read that one myself, but it's got some very frightening parts."

"I ain't a 'fraidy cat of no whale. Can we go home?" James asked, though he was pale, and his voice was hoarse.

"Doc Tess said a day or two." She sat on the edge of the bed, James between them. "I didn't mean to sleep so long."

"I'm thinking maybe you needed it." Dawson set the book aside. "Tess came by earlier, said we can take him home tomorrow."

"We...I can't ask you to..." She shook her head.

"No isn't an option." He scanned the features of her face, reminding her of his kiss and sending a rush of heat back through her body.

The moment held between them as James flipped through the book oblivious to them both and she gave in to a nod, which wasn't difficult. It had been a frightening ride to the ranch with James so ill, and the help in getting him home would be appreciated. "Thank you."

James yawned as the book settled to his chest and he closed his eyes.

"He's been fighting sleep for about an hour." Dawson eased from beside her brother, standing and stretching his arms above his head, able to touch the ceiling with his extended fingertips.

Haven brushed her fingers through James' dark hair again. "His hair is the color of our mother's. He's always had her gentle spirit."

"I think he's a lot like you." Dawson stepped closer, his blue eyes gazing at her to the point she was sure he wanted to kiss her again. And she'd let him, maybe she even wanted him to.

"I've always thought I was most like my father, though as Levi gets older, he is Papa all over again." She dropped her gaze to James, turning away from Dawson's continued stare. "Levi's got a start on the roof."

And then Dawson was there, taking her in his embrace. She shivered at his touch and met his gaze, her heart pounding against her chest.

"It's gonna be all right, you'll see." He held her to him a moment, the smell of earth and man intoxicating. "I've missed you."

She leaned closer, the feelings of desire flowing through her so foreign. Her mother had told her one day she would fall in love, but she'd never thought it would be so consuming. "I've thought of you every moment."

"The noon meal is ready." Dodge popped into the room unannounced, causing Dawson to let Haven go. Heat flew to her cheeks and she turned to James, but not before she caught his mother's knowing smile.

"We'll join in a minute." Dawson stepped into his moccasins, bending to lace them over his buckskins.

"It'll keep if you need a bit of time." Dodge took her leave.

Dawson took Haven's hand in his. "How about we eat, and I show you the colt while James rests?"

She nodded, anxious to check on Josie and see the foal. "I think leaving him for a short time would be fine." She tugged the blankets higher on her brother and followed Dawson down the hallway to the dining room.

He pushed the door open where Dodge and Mei Ling already sat. "After you."

"Thank you." The smell of the midday meal coursed through the house.

Haven sat by Dawson as Rose wandered in carrying her youngest son, Uriah, with Nicholas scampering in behind her.

"I'm hungry." The toddler bounced into the chair across from Haven and eyed her with suspicion. "Where's your boy? He's still sick?"

Haven smiled. "He's my little brother and he's napping, but much better. Thank you."

"Nicholas, manners." Rose spoke to him as she held Uriah in her lap, the baby chewing the spoon his mother offered him.

"Yes, Mama." The boy's curly blond locks, much like his mother's, dropped across his brow as he placed his napkin in his lap.

Haven had spoken with Rose a few times and was surprised she wrote for the local paper even with caring for her children.

"Snow will come." Mei Ling lifted her dark brows and dipped her head to sip the tea before her.

"Winter's on the way." Dodge forked a piece of roast beef and pushed the plate to Dawson.

"Leaning Bear says the same." He added meat to his plate and then to Havens.

"Well, the medicine man seems to know these things much better than do we." Dodge answered, though her tone tightened as she held Dawson's gaze.

Haven spoke. "I thank you all for the care of my brother and the meals. I'm not sure what I would have done without your help."

"It's our pleasure. Tess will check on James again before nightfall." Dodge said adding a biscuit to her plate. "She's home resting. Newly delivered, she hasn't taken much time to care for herself."

"The doctor has been very kind to teach me about herbs," Haven added, "since I've never had the chance to learn from a physician before."

"Tess trained in Boston with some of the finest physicians." Rose fed her youngest son small bites of meat.

Haven wiped her mouth with a linen napkin, setting her sights on Dodge. "I wanted to ask of you, Mrs. McCade, if it isn't an imposition, that you would consider the purchase of my herbs for resale in the mercantile." Dodge nodded, her expression much like Dawson's. "Bert Lester and I have a partnership, but I can see no reason why he wouldn't want to purchase a few items to sell."

"Partnership." Mei Ling cackled, drawing all their attention. "He say you swindle of him."

"I'm a partner simply because I bailed him out of making bad choices on what he sells and when. He arrived in Cheyenne all those years ago with no inkling of how to run a mercantile and I am a woman of business," Dodge defended.

Mei Ling set her brows high. "As I say. Swindler."

It was Dawson who chuckled, amused with the banter of the women as he began eating.

Mei Ling explained further. "She swindles a little of all in town except bank."

Dodge sipped her coffee. "I am making investments in the future of Cheyenne and if my endeavors are profitable, then it serves this family well."

"Good swindle, then." Mei Ling gave a giggling grunt.

"You're to be admired, as I've aspirations to

operate my own apothecary someday." Haven smiled, gripping the edge of the table. She was bound and determined to find a way, part of the reason for keeping quiet about the claim, so there would be money enough.

Dodge rested a gaze on her after a quick smirk to Mei Ling. "Every woman should have the right to see her dreams come to fruition."

Mei Ling stood and took Uriah from Rose and carried him to the counter and handed him half a biscuit.

Rose rubbed her temples. "Maybe the snow is coming. Sawyer says he can feel the cold in his shoulder."

"Snow several weeks, much snow." Mei Ling added, taking her seat and placing Uriah on her lap.

"The sheriff was injured?" Haven asked, not understanding.

Rose nodded, but it was Dodge who answered. "Sawyer was shot a few years ago, nearly died if it had not been for Doc Tess. The shoulder still pains him most of the time."

Rose took a small bite of the biscuit before her, but it was clear she wasn't feeling well.

Haven wasn't sure how to respond, though she was certain there were so many dangers for men of the law. "It must have been very frightening."

Rose nodded in agreement, closing her eyes.

"Rose, why don't you rest, and we'll look after the boys for a while." Dodge sipped her coffee, holding the hot brew away from Nicholas, who had crawled into her lap.

Rose gave a simple nod. "The nausea will pass in a bit."

"You're expecting?" Haven hadn't realized.

Rose smiled. "Yes, but so much nausea this time, I'm afraid."

Mei Ling set her tea cup back on the saucer further than the baby's reach. "You have girl this time."

"A girl would be nice, even Sawyer thinks so." Rose stood, gaining her balance, smiling in spite of her discomfort.

"Should I have Tess check on you?" Dodge asked, narrowing her brows.

Rose shook her head. "No, of course not. I'll be fine."

"I bring herb tea to your bed." Mei Ling went to the cupboards with the baby on her hip, picking up a small porcelain tea cup, and went to the kitchen.

Rose spoke to Nicholas. "Be a good boy, Nicholas, and Papa will let you ride your pony when he comes home."

"Yes'm." Nicholas shoved a heaping spoon of mashed potatoes into his mouth. Dodge landed a gaze on her. "Tell me about you, Haven, how you manage the homestead with your brothers. I was very sorry last year to hear of your father's death. He was a very kind man, often generous to others in need."

Haven set her fork down. "Thank you. We do fine with the money my father had put away and what I make off selling herbs. Levi's fourteen and helps a great deal."

Dodge's gray brows lifted in question. "It must be difficult."

"I suppose an easy path isn't found by all." She was a bit perplexed by Dawson's mother's inquisition.

Dawson took them both away from the

conversation, much to her relief. "We're gonna go check on her horse, if you can listen for James."

Dodge held both their gazes a moment longer and smiled with a brush of her hand. "Be on your way. I'll check on James."

"Thank you for the fine meal." Haven followed Dawson outside the house.

"Once again you, or at least your family, have come to my rescue." She made small talk on the way to the barn.

Dawson glanced at her with a smile. "No one's counting."

"I thought you might say nine hundred and ninety-seven or even lower at the rate we are going." She couldn't help but grin as he chuckled leading them inside the barn.

Dawson leaned on the stall that held Neha and her colt.

Haven glanced over. "Oh, they're both so beautiful. He has similar markings to her."

He admired the animals but turned to face her. "I've been thinking. Maybe in getting you and James back home, I can stay and help Levi get that roof on the barn before the cold snap hits."

Haven wasn't sure what to say. "But…your work."

He shrugged, "got a little while before the negotiations, if you think Levi won't mind my help."

The idea was a good one, but how would they work the claim? No matter, the barn did need completing and Levi was struggling. "I think Levi would appreciate the help."

He admired the horses again. "It won't take us long working together. Get the homestead ready for winter."

Haven's heart pounded to the surface of her chest. "I can't promise you more than a good meal each day."

Josie whinnied at the edge of the corral, turning them both.

"She knows you well." He spoke as he followed her to the corral.

"I still can't believe I have her back." She rubbed the mane hanging across Josie's large eyes, tucking the strands back. "I just knew I'd never see her again, but she must love it here."

"Ah, she knows home like she knows you. We'll get an early start in the morning. Get James home to rest." His deep voice enfolded her and somehow gave her a comfort she'd missed since the loss of her father.

"It will be a relief not to ride home alone," she added.

"You know what I think?" He studied her with the haze of those deep blue eyes. "I think maybe it's been a long time since you've let anyone care for you."

She wasn't sure what to say. "Maybe, but your mother worries of the coming negotiations."

Loose strands of his banded hair blew in the slight breeze. He was so handsome she had to remind herself to take a breath. "They all worry, I suppose."

"They must have just reason."

He took in a breath, letting it out with controlled effort. "Don't you go worrying the same."

"I understand little about such things, the treaties and peace negotiations." She ran her palm down Josie's neck. "Will you be gone for long?"

He hesitated in answering, glancing away to the other horses in the corral. "It's still a ways off. Be gone about a month."

"That's a long time." She said. The last few weeks of not seeing him had left her longing for his return.

"I've given my word, and without me there to make sure it's done right, the tribes gain little." He took her hand, leading her away from the corral and out into the pastures toward the trees. "Come on, I want to show you something."

The brisk wind caused her to shiver, or was it his touch that gave her a chill? His fingers tangled with hers and heat warmed her with the ease with which he'd taken her hand.

"Where are we going?" She glanced ahead, the vast pastures full of brown winter grasses as far as she could see.

He shrugged, giving her hand a squeeze. "For a walk, so we can talk."

"About?" She trotted to keep up and he slowed his pace.

"Maybe I just wanted to be with you alone. Got a lot of family back there." He took in the landscape before them and grinned. "My intentions are honest enough."

"You once told me I should run from the likes of you." She lifted her brows.

"As I recall, you said you have no fear of me."

"Still don't. Perhaps you should try to catch me again, because I kept your precious stone." She tried to tug away, but he didn't let go of her hand, turning her and capturing her lips with his. And somehow, she found herself resting against one of the large cottonwood trees they'd reached. Dawson teased her lips apart. Haven allowing his access as she had at the meadow.

He was tender and tasted of coffee, his hands roaming her body. She pulled free gasping for air, the intensity of him leaving her breathless once more.

He kept his face near as he whispered, "So, you kept my stone, after all?"

Her heart raced at his continued touch, his hands along her hips. "It's safe at home in my box of special items."

"Special items?" He tilted his gaze, still so close his breath mingled with hers.

"A woman has to have some secrets." She whispered, his intense blue-eyed gaze holding her captive. "The last time I was against a tree like this…"

He finished for her. "I was holding you quiet from those Dog Soldiers. Don't want you in that kind of danger again." He drew back from her, taking her hand once more. "There's a stream just ahead."

She followed, and as the small moving water came into view, he tugged her to sit beside him on one of the huge boulders. "It's quiet here."

He leaned back on the rock, lying flat, letting the sun streak his face through the shade of the trees. "Used to come sit here to read and study. Dodge would have to come and hunt me after dark."

He sat up, reaching for her hand. "Haven, I…"

"Dawson, I…"

"You first." She glanced down where he stroked her fingers.

He glanced across the stream. "When I took you to my cabin…you slept for a few days, but…"

He seemed to struggle with his choice of words, though he continued. "When a Cheyenne takes a totem, it's as if the animal and he are one. When I did my dance with the sun, the wolf brought to my visions...a woman with flaming hair like yours." He touched her hair and tugged her closer, wrapping his arm around her shoulders.

She held his gaze, trying to understand, so close the deep blue of his eyes captivated her.

"I never understood why or who she was...until now." He went on. "She was you, Haven."

She understood little of the beliefs of the Cheyenne or of the chanting he did early mornings. "Me?"

"When you were lying there injured, I kept looking at you. I knew I hadn't seen you before, but then, the wolf reminded me why I thought you familiar." He touched her chin. "The woman looked like you, with your fire-colored hair and the same eyes as yours."

She wasn't certain how to respond. "Why does a totem bring a person to you?"

"The Cheyenne believe they bring those who are to be a part of your life, sometimes those who have gone before, or someone from the future..."

"I'm not sure I understand, but I believe in your vision, like in dreams..." She hoped to say the right thing. "I've seen my mother at times in my dreams. She never says anything, just smiles...and I know things will be all right."

"Visions are like dreams, I suppose. But Haven, I want to do right by you." He took a deep breath and pushed it out. "Promises...sometimes those are broken even with the best of intentions, but...I would like to come by when I can to see you."

Was he asking her to court her? "Courting?"

He shook his head. "Courting is full of promises a man makes. I won't ever lie to you, Haven, but to set a promise I may not have the ability to keep with my work wouldn't be right...but I do want to spend more time with you."

Haven glanced down at their hands. There were so many things...her brothers, their different homes, his large family and her dreams of an apothecary. "I would like that too."

He kissed the back of her hand. "My work takes me away a lot, but it would be nice to know I can come home, see your pretty face, spend time with you, taking walks, talking, kissing..."

"Kissing. Well, I'm afraid I know little about that, it seems." She whispered, wondering often if she had done so the right way.

He gave her a nudge. "You've never been kissed before me?"

Now she was sure she was glowing a deep burnt red. "No, but you're making light of me."

"No, not laughing." He leaned closer, so close she could scarce focus her eyes on him. "But you know what might help?"

She shook her head.

"Practice." He took her lips slow and sure, tangling his hands in her hair and taking what breath remained in her lungs. "But I know the boundaries."

She relished the closeness but spoke her mind. "And I know very little of what is past those boundaries anyway."

Now he did laugh at her while at the same time pulling her to him and laying her across the warm rocks, his body covering hers. "No need to worry on that right now, but kissing...best you worry, Haven Oakley."

He placed his mouth on hers again, their tongues mingling, the heat flowing through her body she didn't understand. Strange, she'd never thought of courting or marriage because of caring for her brothers, but Dawson didn't seem concerned that she had to look after them. In fact, he was coming to help with the roof. Somehow, her heart was as full as she had ever allowed it, all except for what on earth she and Levi were going to do about the claim.

Dawson lifted from her, his body having been hard against her side, making her aware of the heat of him. His breath was as short as her own, and he studied her again as he often did, as if memorizing her.

She sat up and touched a length of his hair that was free of the band. "I've not had much liberty with taking care of the boys to think of anything more than the day to day, week to week."

"I'm not making promises, Haven, but I am giving you of myself what I can. This land here..." He glanced around them. "My father purchased this land years ago, grew this ranch. Smart when it came to business. Was behind a lot of getting the railroads here in the West and growing the cities. But..."

"But?" She asked, his tender words and his emotions surprising.

"Father was rarely here, never home. We all traveled with him at times, Sawyer, Wyatt and me, but he was never here when we needed him." He took a slow breath. "Business took him away, and I don't want that for you."

He let a moment pass and continued. "I've been alone for a long time, Haven, but...when I get ready to make promises, I want to make them to you. And I want to be here for all that will mean."

"Dawson, I…" What was he telling her?

He placed a thumb to her lips to stop her. "But for now…I do have business and I don't want you worrying. I have little to fear from the Cheyenne. Besides, Leaning Bear looks out for me."

How could she not worry with him off to work alongside the Cavalry, helping the Indians it seemed few trusted. "And how is he? I still feel terrible about hitting him."

He laughed. "Ah, he's fine, though he had a recent run in with the soldiers at the fort. He never lets them rile him…just takes it…"

"He's very important to you?" she asked, having thought now and then about the relationship he carried with the medicine man. "How was it you became friends?"

He smiled, staring at the water. "When I was maybe twelve, I was with my father on one of his expeditions. We were camped along a river in Nebraska. I woke one morning and went to the river to wash, and when I glanced up there was an Indian, a young man like myself on the opposite bank. I froze, as did he."

Haven listened with interest, the sound of his deep voice calming.

"We studied each other for a long moment, me thinking I needed my knife on the bank, but not moving to reach for it. When all we did was look at each other, I bent and filled my canteen and he went about filling his water bag, a truce of sorts." His grin was contagious.

"My father had always offered Indians he

encountered some sort of trade, and all I had at the time was my knife. So I carefully took it up, blade in hand, and held out the handle to him, even though there were small rapids between us."

"You were afraid?" she asked, though it was hard to imagine him a vulnerable boy.

"Shaking out of my skin." He chuckled in remembering, lifting a necklace from beneath his tunic. "But he waded into the water and removed his necklace of beads and a bear claw and we swapped."

"Instant friends then?" She asked as she admired the large claw.

"I didn't see him again until a few years later, at the fort where he was trading his pelts. We've swapped time and again over the years. Finally, I spent time with him, with his tribe. We hunted together, teaching each other our languages. Later, he was the reason I took the spirit journey."

"And your family allowed the closeness with the Cheyenne?" She questioned, having wondered if that had been difficult.

He shrugged. "Dodge never cared for my beliefs, afraid I'm not worshiping the God who counts. Sawyer respects the Indians much like my father did, but Wyatt tends to bicker with Leaning Bear and Evan has no fondness for any of the tribes."

"Well, it's a beautiful story, your friendship," she whispered, leaning against his shoulder and relishing the closeness. "Maybe you could keep teaching me some of the Cheyenne language."

"You'd really want to learn?" He seemed surprised.

She smiled, "Learning would give me more time

with you and might come in handy."

He kissed the back of her hand. She closed her eyes and inhaled the scent of him, content for the moment that he'd made his interest known. No promises, but words full of hope and a future she'd never been certain to claim for herself. She closed her eyes and let the moments go by them without moving from his embrace.

Chapter Eleven

Haven drifted along the edge of a dream she couldn't hold, the pounding outside drawing her from a deep slumber. Lifting her head, she glanced around her bedroom and settled her gaze on James, who slept beside her. He'd been better since Dawson had escorted them home the night before, but Doc Tess had warned he needed rest and water for several more weeks.

The pounding continued outside, leaving her to wonder how early Levi and Dawson were beginning on the barn roof. She glanced at the curtain where it wasn't light yet, wrapping her arms around herself. Drawing up the heavy quilt, she tucked it around her sleeping little brother.

She tiptoed to the front room and tossed more wood onto the fire and shivered. Taking a peek outside the front window, Josie grazed in the corral along with the cow, Buttercup, and Viho was hobbled further out near the trees, munching on a bucket of oats. The hammering continued as she glanced in the direction of the barn. His back to her, Levi banged the hammer hard, with Dawson pointing and handing her brother another shingle.

Levi had been happy to have help but like her, he'd been worried of the claim. She had settled him to hold off on panning inside the cave until Dawson left for the negotiations.

She wrapped her robe tighter, stepping to the porch. She shouldn't have slept if they were working so hard, but the travel back from the McCade ranch had been tiring with James, who had fretted. And while she'd gone to her warm bed to keep an eye on her brother, Dawson had made a place to sleep by the hearth. The least she could do was make them breakfast.

"Mornin'," Dawson called from the roof of the barn, standing with a hammer in his hand.

"It's barely morning, but I'll have breakfast in just a little." It dawned on her that he was eyeing her in her night robe, and her body flushed warm in spite of the chill.

Sosha ran to greet her, licking her hand and sitting beside her.

"Breakfast sounds good." Levi glanced at her and hammered another shingle in place.

"How do biscuits and gravy with sausage sound?" she asked walking a bit closer to the edge of the porch, folding her arms.

"Best you stay in with James, cold's bitter this mornin', but I think we'd both enjoy the meal." Dawson spoke as he lifted a pile of shingles from near the roof's edge.

She thought maybe he was right, as she hadn't expected the snap of cold to be so harsh. James would sleep for a while, and even when he did wake, she needed to keep him still. She turned back to enter the house, letting Sosha inside. The dog shook his heavy gray coat and curled up on the rug by the hearth as she made her way to dress for the day.

Back in the kitchen, she stoked the fire back to life

inside the old stove and placed the coffee pot to simmer and the large iron skillet to heat. In a short time, she had biscuits in the stove and scrambled sausage simmering in a white gravy.

She glanced over her shoulder as Levi and Dawson bolted through the door, shaking off the cold and tossing their coats and gloves aside.

"You boys look frozen." She served up a plate with two biscuits and heaped a large portion of the sausage gravy over them, setting the first to the table for Dawson and doing the same for Levi.

"We got a good start, Haven, it's looking better. I milked Buttercup. The bucket's on the porch." Levi went to the hearth and kicked from his boots.

"James is still sleeping." She fussed over filling Dawson's tin cup with coffee and smiled when he nodded his thanks.

"I'll have coffee too." Levi made his way to the table and sat in their father's chair, something he'd never done.

Haven eyed her brother, surprised, but she supposed he'd worked as hard as any man and if he also wanted coffee then it might warm him up. "All right."

She poured a tin cup of the black liquid and set it before Levi, reaching for her own plate of the biscuits and gravy. "Well, I thank you men for the hard work."

James sauntered in, dragging his blanket along. Sosha ran to greet the boy, who climbed up into her lap and curled against her. Haven felt his forehead and smiled. "No fever."

"I wanna help with the roof," James fussed, though he closed his sleepy eyes.

"You're too little." Levi was quick to answer as he

shoved a bite of the coated biscuit into his mouth.

"Am not. I wanna hammer." James sat up and eyed Dawson. "You said I could learn to hammer shingles, too."

Dawson nodded, holding his mug of coffee. "Only once you're well. You've gotta get your strength back."

"Here, biscuits and gravy that you love." Haven shoved her plate his way and scooted him into the chair beside her. She went to the stove to make herself another plate, sitting to begin eating.

Dawson lifted his brows. "Haven't had this in a while, it's really good."

"There's more." She started to stand but he shook his head, holding up a hand to halt her.

"This is plenty." He took the last bite. "Best we keep working, with this cold."

"It's something frigid," Levi added as he sipped the coffee before him.

"Well, James and I will take care of some of the house chores and let him rest." She tousled James' dark hair, relieved he was better.

"Aw, I'd rather hammer." James stuffed his mouth with a thick bite of gravy.

"And Levi, you'll have your studies tonight after supper to catch up on," she added, not wanting to let her brother have too much time away from his learning.

"You worry too much about books. I've got man's work to do." Levi stepped into his boots and tugged on his coat and went back outside with Sosha following.

Dawson held her gaze. "He's doing a very good job of it. What he completed on his own is solid. Let him grow up for today. I'll talk to him about his studies."

"He used to work alongside Papa. I think he is enjoying the time with you, though I'm not sure how he grew up overnight, coffee and thinking he's a man." The sudden memory of Levi as young as James still seemed recent.

"He's done a good job, just needed to layer the shingles tighter." Dawson sipped his coffee and rose. "Best get back to it."

"James, get your slate and maybe later after a rest you can help me make cookies," she suggested as James headed to the window to peer outside.

"Aw, I don't need to rest anymore." He fussed but made his way to get the slate.

Haven followed Dawson as he lifted his gloves from the table and walked to the door for his buffalo robe.

He glanced behind her and back. "There is this one more thing…before I go."

"Oh, there is…" Haven's knees went weak as he leaned closer, wrapping one arm around her, tugging her close to his body.

"Yep, and I've waited all morning…" He took her tender lips, a sweet kiss that robbed her of all sanity. "You always smell like spring, even in the cold."

"You make me blush." She stepped back as James returned and she gave him a gentle nudge when he didn't move right away. "Back to work with you."

"Haven." James held up his slate as he sat at the table. "I'm ready."

She sat beside him, pulling out the schoolbook that sat on the counter behind her. She opened the pages to where James had left off. "You write all these words several times and we'll work on seeing if you can spell them without looking in a bit. I need to dig the last of the potatoes out of the garden. Do you think you can stay inside for a bit by yourself? I'll let you use my pencils and the new tablet I have."

"Yes'm. I can use your special pencils and the paper?" James shrugged using the chalk with the slate to begin writing.

She had to giggle at his excitement. "Of course, but in your bed so you can rest while you draw."

With her brother content, it took no time to clean up breakfast and settle him in his bed in his room with her pencils and tablet.

"Now you stay right here, and I'll be back shortly. Don't go near the fire and call for me from the door if you need me." Haven waited for the short nod that came from her brother.

"I'll be careful with your pencils." He opened the tablet.

Haven smiled, not at his excitement in using her drawing pencils, but that he was doing much better. The night she'd raced him to the McCade ranch, she thought he might…well, she wouldn't think of that as he was doing fine now.

Outside, it was Sosha who greeted her and followed her to the edge of the garden, where she grabbed the hoe to dig the last of the sweet potatoes. She should scold herself for not having gotten to them before the ground had frozen. Above her Dawson and Levi were hard at work, Dawson making his way down several times for loads of shingles. It seemed hard work, but he climbed that ladder with ease, and she caught herself just watching him and the sheer strength in all he did.

She carried on with the potatoes thinking, with any luck, she'd finish today and could get to the canning she'd put off over a week ago. Though she had enough of the late blackberries, it might be that she could make a pie later along with the cookies she'd promised for James.

She glanced at Dawson again, her lips still tingling with his kiss. She should find him too improper, but she'd caught herself wondering what it might be like to lie in his arms. Even that thought brought heat to her center. Was it wrong of her to dream of that? He'd said he knew the boundaries, but her body somehow betrayed her when he touched her, and she'd understood it little.

She focused on digging, sweat forming across her brow. In no time she was at the end of the row and done until planting next spring. She leaned on the hoe, catching her breath, and a high-pitched scream turned her. "James?"

She stifled her panic for fear of startling her little brother, who was hanging onto the ladder and part of the roof, his legs off the ladder, which leaned. She should have been watching him, but she hadn't even noticed he'd come outside. She ran toward the barn.

Dawson held up a hand to stop her as he lay down on his belly on the slanted roof, looking down at James and scooting as close as he could, Levi holding his legs.

Her heart in her throat, she forced herself closer little by little, trying to get below the ladder in time.

"Hang on, James. Look up." Dawson spoke in a calm loud voice. "That's good, squeeze your hands tight."

Haven grabbed the bottom of the ladder, not daring

to distract James. He'd fall if Dawson couldn't grab him, and she wasn't sure she could catch him at that angle.

"Good boy, grab hold..." Dawson kept speaking as he scooted closer to the edge, trying to reach for James.

James struggled, crying. "Gonna fall."

Dawson eased further, so close to the edge Haven held her breath as he worked his way to her brother.

"It's all right, James. Hang on." Haven tried to keep her voice calm, but then James slipped more, struggling for a grip.

"Uh-oh," he whimpered.

"Get him," Levi yelled at the same time Dawson let go of his own grip and grabbed James by both his wrists, her brother dangling in his grip.

Dawson struggled to pull James up with Levi lying across his legs on the steep pitch of the barn roof.

Haven pushed the ladder closer to where James was hanging and held it as Dawson shuffled James to get his footing. "Kick your feet over, James, put your feet on the ladder. I got you." Dawson spoke, and James obeyed, catching hold of the ladder and starting the climb down with Dawson following.

Haven leaned on the ladder fighting tears. She was shaking so hard, it was all she could do to speak when Dawson lifted James to her.

"He's all right." Dawson touched the boy's back as he clung to her.

Haven set James to his feet. "That ladder is much too high, James. You know better than to go on the ladder without help, and I told you to stay inside."

"I just wanted to help hammer." He leaned back to look at her face, his chin quivering.

"But you disobeyed." She scolded and pointed. "You go and sit on the porch steps until I tell you to get up."

James burst into tears but marched over to the porch and sat crying, bundled in his coat and hat. Well, at least he had done that much.

She turned away, brushing back tears. "I'm sorry, but...I should've known he might try."

"I never saw him come out." Dawson placed a hand on her arm. "You all right?"

"Yes. No. But I am teaching him to obey me." She glanced back where James was still wailing. "The porch is our new thing when he is in trouble, or the hearth inside."

"Haven, can I get up now?" James yelled as he stood from the steps.

Haven turned. "A minute longer because you are not to climb the ladder."

The boy sat back down and sniffled. "I said I was sorry."

She wiped her eyes and turned back to Dawson and stifled a grin. "It is very difficult to scold him."

"Haven, I'll be good." James tried again.

Dawson chuckled this time. "Are you all right?"

She fell into the open embrace he offered, wiping the hint of tears that threatened. "If anything ever happened to him..."

He hugged her tight for a second. "Go on, take him back inside. it's too cold for him out here."

"Well, at least I've finished the potatoes, and the wash is next, but I'll do it inside by the fire where I can keep an eye on him." She turned back toward the steps where James still sat, his little wet face red and puffy.

"I'll be good, Haven," he said, his sweet voice enough to bring her tears again.

"You're not a bad boy, James, but you could get hurt on the ladder and I told you to stay inside. Leastwise you put on your coat and cap." She leaned to get his attention again. "You were afraid on the top of the ladder, weren't you?"

"Yes, but Levi gets to hammer," he added, glancing around her.

"Yes, but Levi is older. James, I have to know you will obey me or I cannot leave you alone anymore. Do you understand?" Haven lifted him into a hug. "Come on, you and I will go inside to fix up some soup for lunch and make those cookies."

James relinquished the argument and followed her inside. She hated scolding him, or even Levi for that matter, but like it or not, she was their one parent.

"Haven, are we going to the cave tonight?" James asked once they were inside.

She bent to him. "No, James. But I must ask you not to mention the cave or the claim to anyone, not even Mr. McCade, all right?"

Her brother studied her for a moment. "Why? Don't you like Mr. Dawson? Sosha likes him a lot and he don't like no strangers."

She nodded. "Of course, I like Mr. McCade, but the cave and the claim are a secret for just me and you and Levi. No one but us gets to know about it, all right?"

James nodded. "I'm good at keeping secrets."

"You are very good at that. It's like in the story I read you about the pirate's gold. We have to keep it quiet." She smiled at her brother, though he was too young to understand all the reasons why. And while she trusted Dawson, the cave was something she couldn't share even with him—at least for now.

"Levi says you're smitten with Mr. Dawson." James searched her face which she was well aware had flushed pink.

"Well, he's a very nice man, but I think you can wash the potatoes while I cut them for frying up." She tried for distraction, handing him the first potato.

"I wanna go draw again." He scampered away after eyeing the potato, leaving her to giggle. She wandered to the window, glancing out to watch Dawson on the roof of the barn. It hadn't been her fault that she'd run into those dangerous Dog Soldiers, but had she not, she would never have met Dawson McCade. She touched her lips again as he bent to hammer more shingles into place. Well, as frightening as it had been, she'd never be sorry.

Chapter Twelve

Dawson bent in the heavy shrubs near the river, huddling in the cold. He'd much rather have stayed on the warm pallet by the fire with Haven near, instead of traipsing along the trail to the river, following Levi. He and the boy had been working on the barn roof and would finish in a few more days, but Levi's efforts were slowing with fatigue by early afternoon. And he hadn't returned with any meat for the hours he spent claiming to hunt. Something wasn't adding up and Haven had been a bit nervous at his questions, telling him her brother hunted well when there was game.

He waited as Levi crossed the stream before he did the same a bit further down, glad the boy hadn't brought along Sosha. Levi turned and glanced around and stepped up, near the wall of trees at the edge of the far side of the stream and disappeared.

Dawson moved closer. Best he waited Levi out, which by his judgment was lasting about an hour, this being the second time he'd followed. Hell, he should have come right out and asked, but he wanted to be sure. With Dodge mentioning that Haven often paid in gold, it wasn't just herbs she was selling. He had every reason to believe they were still working their father's claim, though he hadn't known the location until now.

He'd never seen nor met their father but talk in town had let him know that Mr. Oakley had proved lucrative on his claim. Jacob Sanders had mentioned the man had lost his life for it, in not so many words but talk at Jacob's saloon was cheap.

He settled on his knees, wondering at the fact Haven hadn't shared anything about this with him. She'd made excuses for what Levi was up to, saying the chores and roof work had fatigued him. He supposed she had reason enough to keep the claim hidden, but what they were doing put them at risk.

By the time a hint of the sun was dawning, Levi emerged, crawling up from what Dawson could tell. Levi glanced around and scampered back off toward the homestead. Dawson gave the boy a bit of time before he made his way there.

The wall of trees rose with a steep incline above, to the point climbing would not have been an option. He bent and traced the earth that Levi had been careful to cover, and his hand caught the edge where the rock gave way. He scooted to lie on the ground and pushed through an opening, his frame almost too large to let him maneuver inside as he edged his way through.

He stood in a semblance of a small cave and ducked to avoid hitting his head, waiting for his eyes to adjust to the darkness. The little light from the opening he'd crawled through allowed him a glance at the tools stacked in a corner along with a pile of blankets. He walked to the tools and found a lantern, lighting it with the flint from his pocket. The cave came aglow, and he turned a full circle. The walls of the cave were intact, but on the far side, where the stream flowed, pans and shovels had unearthed the dirt and rock. They were panning inside the cave, as he'd suspected.

He wasn't interested in their gold, but he would be

doing some talking to Haven. It was dangerous for Levi to be out on his own, but it would be far worse that the claim be discovered.

He snuffed the flame in the lantern, returning it, and escaped the tomblike cave with some effort. He replaced the stone covering and turned back for the homestead perplexed at how to handle the conversation he'd have with Haven. He didn't want to make her angry, but he couldn't protect her if she didn't trust him, and with the Dog Soldiers still around, it wasn't safe for her or her brother to be out working the claim alone.

He ran through the woods, intending to beat Levi back to the barn roof as if he'd never left the homestead. The cold wind filled his nostrils and he became the wolf again, tracking through the forest with ease.

Outside the homestead, he bent to his knees at the edge of the trees, shucking his tunic and shivering hard in the cold. Closing his eyes he began with his morning prayer, his arms splayed high. He offered peace for the tribes, well-being and equality which had become routine, but the newness of his prayers included Haven. The wolf had selected her, and maybe when these negotiations were over, he'd see just what he might do about that once and for all.

****

Dawson jumped down from the ladder. The impending weather was coming, and he'd continued to work the rooftop long after supper. His hands were so frozen, he could scarce make a fist. He climbed the steps to the porch and removed his leather gloves and the heavy buffalo robe, which had served its purpose.

Haven opened the door and he hung the coat and dusted his buckskins, kicking from his moccasins.

"I saved your supper." She tugged him toward the hearth to the warmth of the fire. "You must be freezing. I was beginning to worry." She laid the gloves on the counter, turning back to him.

He caught his breath for a moment and walked closer to the fire, stretching out his fingers to the warmth, making small talk. "Not sure what this cold snap will bring, best I work as long as I can."

"I'm afraid it's not much." She fussed over the plate and poured steaming coffee into the mug before him.

"Anything's fine at this point." He studied her for a long moment.

She moved into the chair beside him as he began eating, offering him the smile that had become his reward each day.

"I worry with you and Levi working so hard. He fell asleep soon after he ate, though it took a bit to tire James." She watched as he consumed the stew.

He held her gaze, figuring with both her brothers in bed, now was as good a time as any since she'd brought it up. "I think maybe Levi's exhaustion comes from lack of sleep with his early morning jaunts to hunt."

She dropped her gaze, playing with her napkin. "Well, you both work so hard and…"

There was no point in delaying what he needed to say. "Haven, I know about the claim he's working each morning."

It took her a moment to answer but she didn't deny it as he thought she might have. "Levi told you, then?"

"I followed him, wondering why he never returns

from hunting with any meat. Why he's so tired before dark and where you disappear off to while you're hunting herbs which are rather scant at times too." He waited, a brow lifted to her.

"The claim is best kept a secret." It was the first time she had raised her tone with him, catching him a bit off guard.

"I'm not interested in the claim or what it yields, Haven." He leaned up. "Having a claim is dangerous, and so's Levi working that area alone each morning. And it's not safe for you either."

She rose from the table turning her back to him and folding her arms. So she was angry, as he'd suspected she might be given that sun-kissed hair of hers. But she glanced at the ceiling her voice cracking as she spoke. "I suppose I thought I could keep everything hidden to keep my brothers safe…keep this homestead, but you mustn't tell anyone, Dawson, please."

Now things were coming together. If she was living under threats, that had come from one person. "Mr. Scott threatens about your payments?"

She didn't answer for a long time, tears rimming her eyes. "I believe he…killed my father. Levi and I both think so. And Sosha knows it was Mr. Scott, though we can hardly prove that. But my father died never telling where it is hidden, and you mustn't either."

"Haven, I have no interest other than your safety, but if you know this…" He stopped as tears spilled down her cheeks. He hadn't meant to make her cry.

"Mr. Scott thought with my father out of the way we couldn't keep making the payments on the homestead, which includes the claim, but…" Her voice faded to a whisper making him want to hold her against him.

"Mr. Scott knows we suspect him, so he threatens, wants more gold than is due. That we pay is most likely how he knew there was more. And I've paid it to keep my brothers safe." She turned back to him. "I'm sorry I didn't tell you…"

He finished for her. "My being here has halted your progress."

She sniffled with a nod. "The mortgage will be paid next year in full, but the fees to Mr. Scott…maybe they will never end."

Dawson got up and placed his hands on her shoulders, though she tensed at his touch. "I'm sorry about your father, but how do you know it was Scott?"

She shook her head, though she didn't meet his gaze. "Mr. Scott and his men brought Papa back to us across a pack mule. They said they found him drowned down river, but Levi checked, and the tracks came from the claim. Papa was a fine swimmer, taught us all, even James has been able to swim since he was three. They drowned him because he wouldn't tell them where the claim was located, and neither have we…which keeps us alive."

More tears spilled as she walked a full circle, explaining further. "It's why Levi works so hard. He's just a boy who should be fishing and complaining about his chores, but he does all I ask of him." She brushed her face of tears and looked at him with her sad hazel eyes. "You must hate me now with not trusting you with this, but…"

Is that how she saw it? "Haven, I could never hate you for trying to protect yourself and your brothers."

He drew her against him as she cried hard into his chest, ripping his heart out altogether. "Shhh, I'd never find reason on this earth for hating you, Haven, but you must trust me."

"I do trust you, but we have kept it a secret for so long." She lifted her head to hold his gaze.

"How much gold have you discovered?" He'd come to the conclusion she wasn't talking about small amounts.

She hesitated a long moment and whispered, "My father left enough for all of our futures, but we live off what we find to leave that hidden, nuggets and a lot of dust bits."

"No one else knows, then?" He narrowed his gaze on her.

"Thorn knows. He taught my father what he knew, but Thorn has his own claims and is no danger to us. He's even let me know where his hiding place is, in the event something happens to him," she added with a shrug.

He brushed back a tendril of her auburn hair. "You don't hide it here at the homestead, then?"

"No, just what we currently have, the rest is safe for now." She shook her head. "But I would trade it all to keep the boys from harm."

He nodded, thinking the best way he might help. "It would be best you pay only the required amount, Haven, and no more." If Scott continued to harass her, he'd put a stop to it the next time he was in town.

She wiped more tears he now suspected of relief. "I did want to tell you, but Mr. Scott already killed my father. I try so hard to do right by the boys, make them learn their lessons, taking care of them when they fall ill. They deserve a good life after all they have been through, and I am doing the best I can. My intentions were sincere, but now I wouldn't blame you if you leave for good."

He grabbed her then, steadying her to face him. "No. I'm not leaving, Haven. I'm not going anywhere. I will be here come morning and every day after that and after that and after that, except when my work calls me, and then I am still coming back to you...I love you, Haven, always."

And with that she clung to him and let go of her tears. He sat and pulled her into his lap, cradling her against him and whispering in Cheyenne, "You are my Heartsong and nothing will ever come between us now or ever."

Chapter Thirteen

Haven pulled the scarf around her hat, the wind howling across the prairie. The weather had remained too cold for making the trip to Cheyenne with James, and it had taken some convincing to keep Levi home with him. The mortgage was due and paying it early was best, and he knew that too. She'd promised her brother a horse the next time they were in town, but with James ill and the bitter cold, it was one more thing that would have to wait.

It had been near a week since Dawson had taken off to meet his friend Leaning Bear at the reservation, with the promise of seeing her in town today. He hadn't said much about the work other than he had to go by the fort for business. He'd seemed annoyed in leaving her, uncertain at her promise to keep herself and her brothers away from the claim for now. She supposed she should have told him about the claim and about her father, but it had been best to tell no one. Though now he knew, it had been a relief in some ways that he was only trying to protect her and her family.

Josie whinnied as they approached Cheyenne. Haven patted her chest. The gold tucked in her coat pocket weighed heavy. Her heart pounded hard as she arrived in town, and she wasn't certain if that was at the prospect of seeing Dawson or because she needed to make her payment to Mr. Scott.

The usual bustle of people roamed the streets in spite of the chill. Teams of oxen stalled outside the mercantile and ladies with small children tagging along shopped along the outdoor markets, everyone bundled against the cold. Men on horseback moved with ease through town, and as usual, a group of men hung outside the saloon, some of them eyeing her.

She studied the bank in the distance and urged Josie ahead. Dawson had insisted he would make her payments for her, but she'd argued that she needed to do it herself. Arriving at Cheyenne was one thing, but paying Mr. Scott was another. She stopped Josie at the bank and dismounted, the whip of wind making her shiver. Tying off the horse, she made her way toward the bank steps, tugging free the pouch of weighted gold from her coat.

"I'll take that right here, Miss Oakley." The deep guttural voice stopped Haven at the top of the stairs.

Mr. Scott was leaning against the bank wall in the shadows and stepped out, tipping his hat and gazing the full length of her body.

"I'd prefer inside the bank to make things official, all except for the bit extra you require, but you will see it's all there in full." She kept her voice steady, making an effort to not even blink.

He placed his hand over hers, rubbing along her fingers, the pouch in her hand. "It's official enough here. I'll be sure to mark it to the ledger."

Haven tried to pull her hand away, but he held her tighter, pain gripping her fist as he squeezed, narrowing his evil gaze.

He smiled sadistically. "If that brother of yours is having trouble making a yield, you and I might be able to work out a little something more for the extra payments from now on." He bent closer, intending to kiss her, the alcohol on his breath taking hers.

Haven tried to free herself from his grip as his lips found the side of her neck. She pushed away with a gasp as he let go with a huge bout of laughter.

Haven backed away, leaving the pouch in his hand. "I will not be providing you any such favors. You will get your payments, Mr. Scott, as you always have, but nothing extra ever again."

He grabbed her by the wrist and twisted. "Careful, Missy, or I may have a mind to visit you one night at your homestead, take care of a little business each time your payments are short."

Haven jerked free and fled down the steps to Josie, her eyes filling with tears, aware he still watched her. She struggled to inhale enough air to breathe as she led the horse toward the mercantile, her wrist burning. Once out of Scott's view, she couldn't hold back the silent tears that streaked her face. She wasn't hurt, only fearful and angry. She didn't know she'd even gotten to the mercantile, but she had. And there was Dawson, waiting, a smile easing across his face. And every fear inside her vanished as she fell into his arms, unable to stop her sobs.

"Haven?" His voice vibrated through her chest.

She couldn't answer, but with purpose stopped her crying, her body inhaling several broken breaths. He wouldn't let Scott get away with this and she couldn't let him start any fights with the forward banker.

Dawson pulled her back, holding her upper arms. "Haven. What happened?"

His words seemed a blur as if she couldn't hear

what he was saying, her mind unable to focus. "It's...it's all right. I just let him...upset me. That's all."

Dawson's blue eyes narrowed, understanding crossing his face. "Mr. Scott?"

She held her paining wrist, but Dawson took her hand away and inspected the redness on her skin. "He hurt you?"

Haven shook her head. "I'm all right, just...more threats."

Dawson rubbed her wrist with a tenderness that didn't match his tone. "Scott put his hands on you?"

She shouldn't have shown Dawson her tears or her minimal injury. His blue eyes went dark and he glanced toward the bank and let go of her.

She tried. "Really, I'm all right."

He grabbed Josie by the reins, putting them in her hands. "Tie her and go on in for your shopping."

Haven followed as he headed toward the bank. "No, please, Dawson, you can't...it'll make things much worse."

He turned and held her gaze for a breath of seconds. "Haven, I can't let him put his hands on you...touch you...ever."

"No, please, Dawson." She grabbed him by the sleeve of his tunic, but he brushed her hand away.

"Go inside, Haven."

****

Dawson took the steps to the bank two at a time. He'd had little dealings with Mr. Scott, but it was no secret the banker had been more than ruthless to the citizens around Cheyenne. Since his takeover of the bank, Dodge had removed most of the McCade monies to banks in Denver. She trusted the man little and had tangled with him more times than not. But now Scott had made a mistake, a rather big one.

At the top step of the bank, Dawson was met by one of the armed men Scott kept there.

"You've business here, McCade?" The man, tall and wearing a dark hat, blocked his way by placing his rifle sideways across Dawson's chest.

He held the man's gaze, the weight of his revolver and tomahawk on his belt within reach.

The man turned the weapon on him in a quick jerk of his hands. "We don't serve Cheyenne or the like here."

Without warning, Dawson grabbed the barrel of the rifle, with both hands jerking the man to his knees and shoving him to the porch floor, a moccasin across his neck.

The man sputtered, trying to free himself. "Can't breathe…"

Dawson applied more pressure as the man's face turned red and he gagged audibly. With that, he flung the rifle off the bank porch and unarmed the man further by pulling the revolver from its holster at his hip and tossing it the same. "I have business in the bank, and if you point that gun at me again, best you be ready to use it."

He walked into the bank, moving with purpose to Scott's office and flinging open the door.

The gentleman he'd left on the porch scurried up behind him, his revolver in hand. "Sorry, boss, he wrestled my guns away and…"

Whitney Scott stayed in his chair and tilted his hat back, unalarmed, waving off the assistance. "It's all right, Pete, I'm sure Mr. McCade can conduct himself as a gentleman."

The man drew away from the door, leaving Dawson holding Scott's narrowed glare.

"Now, what might I help you with, Mr. McCade? Seems you've not had business here at the bank since my ownership." He stood and offered a hand.

Scott's first mistake was touching Haven and his second was coming around his desk.

Dawson grabbed his hand and with all the might he could muster shoved the man, near his same size, against the wall, pressing the tomahawk from his belt to Scott's throat. He'd never been one for idle words and most often walked away from a fight, but this one had become personal. "I'm gonna say this once. Miss Oakley will pay on her deed in full each month with no extra. If you ever place your hands on her again, you will breathe your last."

Scott struggled to free himself, his hand reaching toward his belt. Well, this was a hell of a predicament, though he'd expected no less.

"Boss?" Pete questioned, another man with him.

Dawson pressured the tomahawk, contemplating a jump through the glass window, a step away. Nah, these men didn't want the fight they thought they did, if it came down to it.

"Seems you're a bit outnumbered." Scott strained to talk through his teeth.

With that, and in one fell swoop, Dawson flipped Scott in front of him, the tomahawk still at the man's neck. "Walk."

He never looked at the men who waited, aiming weapons at him, but moved Scott through the bank full of people. Men backed up and a clerk gave a sigh of fright, covering her mouth. Dawson stopped at the door and shoved Scott back against his own men.

"We've a problem here, gentlemen?" Sawyer held a revolver and Dawson gave a silent curse. He didn't need his brother coming to his rescue. He'd just handled what was needed.

Scott and his men held the porch. "I suggest you keep your brother in line, Sheriff."

"Lower your weapons," Sawyer shouted, cocking his revolver.

Scott stepped up in challenge, folding his arms, speaking to Dawson. "Make threats in my bank again, and there won't be any law that can save you or that pretty little redhead."

Dawson made a run for the man, but Sawyer grabbed him and forced him back.

Scott tipped his hat and disappeared back into the bank with his men following.

Dawson jerked from his brother's grasp with a curse. "Damn it, Sawyer."

"You know better than that." Sawyer headed him off at the bank stairs.

"I did what I had to do."

Sawyer shoved him back, stopping him in the street. "And you are lucky Scott didn't blast you a good one."

Dawson held Sawyer's gaze and turned for the mercantile. "Best he got the message."

"And how about you?" his brother asked, as he stopped at the jail. "Scott's not a man to play with."

Dawson narrowed his gaze hard. "Wasn't playing."

Sawyer only looked at him and stayed behind at the

jail. His sheriff brother had warned him enough, but he wouldn't let Haven be harmed by Scott again.

Haven needed to know nothing about how things had gone down, but now he had bigger worries in leaving her alone while he went off to the negotiations. This added to his week where earlier another mishap at the fort had almost landed him and Leaning Bear in jail, both accused of knowing more details about the Dog Soldiers than they had revealed. In the end, and with the telling of their sighting of the random band, the captain had released them both with warning, remaining suspicious because one of his superiors from back East was present. Well, he knew no more about the Dog Soldiers than he did about Scott and his men, but he did know that no matter what it took he would lay down his life to protect Haven.

His heart still hammered against his chest as Haven came down the mercantile steps, waiting. He walked to her, meeting her hazel-eyed gaze, and wrapped his arms around her, finding for that moment all the world was once again right.

Chapter Fourteen

Dawson flipped the hood of his buffalo robe back as he arrived in Cheyenne. He sucked in a cold breath, heading to the saloon where he'd no doubt find his brothers, it being early Saturday evening. He'd left Haven's a short time ago, needing to pick up medications that Tess had ordered for the reservations. Evan had also left a horse for him at the livery, an animal he'd chosen a few weeks back that he could gift to Levi for his hard work on the barn and as a surprise for Haven.

He'd put off the trip, not wanting to leave her, but it had come. The negotiations would take him away from her by morning, the thought unsettling the wolf inside him.

He stepped into the saloon, finding Wyatt belly up to the bar alongside Brett. The saloon was full of men playing cards at several tables, some flirting with the fancy ladies Jacob employed. Cavalry, miners, and men from the mountains were scattered across the tables at the game or drinking and chatting, one table of soldiers rowdy in the far corner.

"The prodigal son returns." Wyatt kicked out a stool as Dawson removed his buffalo robe, covering the stool and sitting atop it.

"Aren't you the prodigal?" Dawson nudged his brother and took Brett's outstretched hand.

Wyatt sipped his whiskey and growled with the burn. "Nope, it's Sawyer, though he says it's Evan."

"Thought you'd be out with the herd." Dawson nodded as he let Brett's grip go.

"Good to see ya, Dawson." Brett nursed a glass mug of dark brew, the suds riding his thick mustache. "I'll leave this cold to the younger men. Evan and Zane are out there. Told 'em to haul in before dark, check the cattle come morning."

Dawson understood well the cold and being out with the cattle. He'd done his years of that as one of the hands. Between both ranches, the McCade and Morgan lands, there were over three thousand head of cattle that were minded by two shifts of wrangling hands. Evan managed the hands for both ranches with Brett still recovering, so he'd guessed his brother knee deep in the elements about right now.

Jacob leaned on the other side of the bar in front of Brett, a towel over his shoulder. "What'll you have Dawson, sarsaparilla or coffee?"

The man knew him well. "Coffee."

"Coffee it is." Jacob set the mug of black brew before him and continued speaking to Brett. "And not a word about where he's striking when he comes in here."

Brett angled a hard glance at the man. "Folks think Thorn's a bit touched, but he's been onto one pocket or another for years now."

Wyatt shook his head with a chuckle. "Ahh, Thorn's crazy as hell when it comes down to it, but he stays out of trouble."

Dawson sipped his coffee. The Cheyenne thought the man a spirit seer and maybe they were right. The old man was smart about things, though he spoke in riddles most often, which confused people.

"Might warm up faster with a good shot of rotgut." Wyatt tossed back what was left of his shot, setting a package of envelopes before him. "Dried meds, heart powder, and something for fevers from Tess."

Dawson blew across the tin mug of steaming coffee and sipped again. He stuffed the envelopes inside his buckskin tunic. "Thank her for me."

Wyatt settled a sidelong glance at him. "So how's the little woman?"

Dawson glared in warning. "It's not like that."

"All right, then, but I happen to know you've not been to your cabin for a good week or more." Wyatt tapped his empty shot glass for a refill and Jacob topped it off.

Brett chuckled as he nursed his drink further, abreast of the situation as much any of the family.

"Come on, Dawson, she's a right beautiful... woman. Don't tell me you aren't hanging around for more than handy work. You're as good as hitched, brother." Wyatt leaned back against the saloon stool, folding his arms.

"Just minding the fences for now," Dawson answered. No sense denying things.

A giant smile spread across Wyatt's face. "As I suspected."

His brother's teasing was often unmerciful now that he'd been married to Tess for a time. And while he'd admit little now to his family, he was already anticipating his return from the negotiations to make Haven his wife.

Brett leaned around Wyatt, adding his two cents.

"She's got a good head on her shoulders, that one."

All he could do was nod.

"Dodge and Mei Ling are planning for a spring wedding as we speak," Wyatt bantered, adjusting the hat on his head as he eyed the mirror on the wall behind the bar.

Dawson glared at his brother. "A bit soon for that."

"Best you can do is hang on tight and figure it out as you go." Brett was always good with advice when it came down to it.

Wyatt elbowed Brett in the side. "About like you're doing with Dodge?"

Brett narrowed his gaze. "Your mother defines the word complicated, no sense thinking she'll ever settle down, but in the meantime I'm smart enough to do what she tells me."

Dawson sipped his coffee, not wishing to incriminate himself further. His mother and Brett had carried on for years, no secret to anyone in town, but Brett had never been able to convince Dodge to marry him. It wasn't for lack of trying, as he'd asked her several times over the years, but she'd held out on him for reasons no one, save her, understood.

"Ah, you'll get there, when you think you'll go crazy without her." Wyatt added, lighting a smoke, and watching the mirror again.

Dawson glanced up the same, giving him a view of the Cavalry playing cards at the corner table. He didn't recognize any of them, but without a doubt, they'd all had too much to drink.

"Where's Sawyer?" Dawson asked, dropping his gaze again to his brother.

"Making rounds, not much crime with the cold,

though." Wyatt turned. "He'll be back here in a bit."

Brett stood and tugged on his thick leather duster. "Calling it a night, boys. Gonna head to the ranch before this storm hits, send Zane back home. If I don't send the boy back by nightfall, I've gotta answer to Rose and Dodge. Rather take a beatin'."

Wyatt chuckled, sucking on his thin cigar, a rare treat he kept from Tess when he spent time in town overnight.

Brett grabbed his hat, slapped a golden eagle on the bar and turned to go. "Stay warm, boys, and you..." He gave Dawson a light punch to the shoulder. "Mind those fences and she'll be yours soon enough."

Dawson let a smile slip. He was young when his father had been killed, but long before then it had been Brett as foreman of the McCade ranch that had taught him what he knew about ranching and life.

He sipped his coffee, warming enough to think about heading back to Haven's until morning. At least so he might hold her in his arms once more before being on his way to the negotiations.

"Didn't know they let Indians drink here." The largest of the soldiers from the back table hissed as he walked closer, the other two on his heels.

Wyatt swung around on his stool and stood. "You soldiers be on your way. Careful out in the weather."

The soldier with the comment stopped. "Not too sure 'bout a saloon serving Indians or the like, especially one who killed a soldier."

Dawson stood, holding the man's gaze. Well, how come this was no damn surprise?

"Move along, gentlemen, night's too cold for trouble." Wyatt stepped ahead, putting himself in between them with purpose.

The other soldiers urged the tall one to follow, but he met gazes with Dawson once more. "I know you, Indian Agent, and I know what you did way back. Word has it you know those Dog Soldiers that've been traipsing around these parts. They cause any more trouble, it'll be a damn shame for the Cheyenne on the local reservations to pay that price."

Dawson held the man's gaze. It wasn't the soldier talking, it was Captain Simmons. "Those Dog Soldiers are not Cheyenne. Best you let the captain know he has his facts confused."

"You challenging me, Indian lover? Want to fight another soldier to the death? Time's as good as any." The man laughed along with his counterparts, who waited near the saloon door.

Dawson glared, the tomahawk at his belt heavy and the saloon at a dead quiet.

"Best you soldiers take it back to the fort before the weather hits." Jacob turned them all, a shotgun in his hands.

The tall soldier eyed them both and smirked in laughter. "Come on, boys, there's a stench here anyway."

Dawson jerked from Wyatt's grip, but his brother grabbed him again. "Let 'em go."

It wasn't the first time he'd been called out as an Indian lover, and it wasn't the first time the Cavalry had provoked him.

"Captain Simmons thinks Leaning Bear and I know those Dog Soldiers, but they weren't Cheyenne." He shook his head. "And Simmons is harping on the past every chance he gets."

His brother studied him for a moment. "Swallowing down death is about like sucking down the full moon, it never goes away. I've taken more lives than you, and not a one of them has been easy."

"But you wear a badge." Dawson shook his head, focusing on Wyatt.

His brother shrugged. "Badge or not, it's all the same when it comes down to it. Fate don't let you forget and neither do others. They've been in here for hours, drunk, nothing more. And you leave tomorrow for the negotiations. Don't need no trouble from them there either."

He turned back to his coffee, trying his best to vent his anger, the wolf inside him restless. He had killed a soldier long ago, and it had been ruled the self-defense it was.

"You did what you had to back then, but I won't remind you the stakes are higher now than they once were." Wyatt lowered his voice in the attempt to explain. "It's not safe anymore, brother, and my guess is you might need to be thinking more about that pretty redhead instead of running off to play with the tribes."

Dawson's pulse still raced but he angled a sidelong glance at his brother as he sat again. "I've been thinking of leaving my position after this. Leaning Bear's known for some time he may head north, even into Canada, nothing for him here but the reservation."

Wyatt shook his head in apparent disbelief. "Well, it's about damn time. You're fighting the battle, brother, but the war is already lost. You can't win, and in the middle of it all, you have the most to lose."

Somehow, his brother's words cut through him. "Never known you to give up the good fight." He grabbed his buffalo robe, stuffing his arms into the sleeves and walking past his brother into the frigid winds, the wolf uneasy.

Wyatt was right, though. He'd worked hard to see that the Cheyenne on reservations got the promised rations and needed medicines, and not one damn thing about it had ever been easy.

He cursed the biting wind as he headed out. The town was deserted save a lone horseman on the far edge. Shopkeepers had closed up early with the cold, and while he dreaded the ride back to Haven, a kiss from her would be his small reward for this day.

Gathering his head, his ideas and his frustrations, he moved ahead toward the livery for Viho and the horse for Levi.

Something smacked across his back, sending him flat to the ground on his belly. Pain scored through his middle, taking his breath as he tried to stand. Someone had hit him, and his first guess was the soldiers from the saloon. He sucked in a rasping breath, but was slammed again, his body hitting harder. He coughed as he pushed himself up and was hit yet again.

"Best you not be telling me what I will and will not do, McCade." Whit Scott's voice filled the night.

Dawson rolled away from the oncoming kick. He should've seen this coming. He fought to right himself, but the two men with Scott grabbed him. The pain made him struggle to gain his footing as Pete rammed a fist into his belly. He coughed and doubled over, though the other of Scott's men held him. He reached for his tomahawk, but it wasn't there, Scott holding it high in the air.

Another fist hit his midsection and he growled

through the pain, swinging his own and catching Pete's jaw. He jerked free and piled into Pete and Scott with all he had, but then all three were on him. He punched Pete's nose, blood spurting and the man swearing, but a knee slammed into his side. *Son of a bitch!*

He couldn't take his next breath, but everything stopped with a revolver echoing into the night.

"I'll arrest the next man that moves." Sawyer held his revolver toward them all.

Dawson crawled to his knees, fighting to stand and spitting blood to the ground. The wolf inside him had been restless all along. He should have been prepared for this.

"Just gaining your attention, McCade," Scott shouted. "You may be the sheriff, but I will not be threatened by this half-breed brother of yours. That is my bank and I will run it how I see fit."

"Well, you're doing a right shitty job of things." Wyatt held guns in both hands, stepping up behind the men. "Running people off and harassing others. Cheyenne wasn't built for the likes of you."

"You've done enough damage to the citizens of Cheyenne. Best you think about moving yourself somewhere else." Sawyer cocked the weapon.

Dawson's side ached and the pain in his low back still took his breath, but he wasn't broken, as near as he could tell.

Scott narrowed a gaze on him. "Show up on my side of town again, and you won't have to worry about where you find that little redheaded gold digger."

The mention of Haven under threat tore through Dawson, and he darted, tackling Scott to the ground. The bastard couldn't leave well enough alone, and he laid into the man fist after fist until Scott curled away holding his face. He punched until Wyatt pulled him off the man, shoving him back.

"He's had enough." Wyatt kept Dawson back as Scott's men got him up, and they all ambled away.

Sawyer grabbed him by the arm. "You hurt?"

"No." Dawson pulled from his brother's grasp and headed toward the livery, touching his chest, the package of medicines still there. His entire body shook, not from the fight with Scott but from the inward turmoil of the wolf. The time had come, and now he saw things clear. It was over. The tribes were on reservations and that would never change for any of them.

"What the hell happened to you?" Lang scampered out of the livery, tugging a saddled Viho toward him, Levi's mount tied to him.

"Scott and his men happened," Wyatt answered for him, his brothers having followed.

Dawson checked Viho's saddle, speaking without facing any of them. "Should've seen this one coming."

"We all should've." Sawyer handed him the reins, the moment holding between him and both his brothers.

"Get your negotiations done and get the hell back home." Wyatt gave him a pat to the shoulder, his blue eyes sincere.

Sawyer stood for a long moment, holding his gaze. "Look out for yourself, Dawson."

Dawson nodded and grabbed the saddle horn, mounting up before his brothers. The pain in his back and side ached, and his fists burned, but somehow the pain was appropriate.

With one more nod, he made off for the

homestead—to Haven, because she was his only reason anymore.

Chapter Fifteen

Dawson dismounted at the homestead, the bitter cold biting through the buffalo robe, his hands near frozen. The spirit of the wolf had remained restless inside him as pellets of sleet pounded across him on the ride to Haven's homestead. His back ached and his side pained but he wasn't broken, just angry, tired and for the most part, confused. He led Viho and Levi's horse inside the barn, knowing Sosha would bark his arrival soon enough.

Shuddering against the cold, he relieved Viho of the saddle and blanket. He gave both horses a quick rubdown with Josie's brush and stalled them on opposite ends of the small barn away from the mare. The old cow mooed her annoyance at the cold but went back to chewing her cud. Tucking the robe tighter around him, he stepped outside and glanced at the house, which gave a soft glow from the one lamp Haven left in the big room each night.

It was late and she would be sleeping by now, but somehow all he needed was her embrace. He made his way to the porch, blinking at the sleet falling from the cold, dark sky. Sosha's warning growl came, the dog sniffing at the door from inside as Haven's muffled whispers hushed the animal.

"Haven, it's me." He leaned closer to the door as it opened, and there she was, all he'd come to need in the world.

She wore a night robe over her sleep dress and his breath caught, stopping the words he had yet to figure. He'd seen glimpses of her before, but she'd been quick to escape to her room as he slept on the pallet by the hearth. He stepped inside and removed his gloves, shuddering with the warmth that engulfed his frozen body. Sosha greeted him, the dog's cold nose hitting the numbness of his frozen hands, startling him from his gaze of her.

"Dawson, you're near frozen." She tugged him further inside, closing the door behind them. "I thought perhaps with the weather you went to the ranch."

Ice dropped from his hair and eyebrows and she helped him remove his buffalo robe. His back carried the soreness of his attack, but somehow that mattered little being near her.

"I waited up, but I'm afraid I dozed." She fretted to hang his coat up and he stepped by the fire to warm himself, turning to memorize the view of her once more.

She clucked her tongue and called Sosha, letting the dog into Levi's room and shutting the door to keep the dog there. She trotted back to him, smiling though it faded as she touched his swollen lip. "You're hurt?"

"I'm fine, just..." he whispered, taking her hand in his. The fight was nothing and now the one thing standing between him and having her for a lifetime was the negotiations. He studied her for a long moment. He loved her, and right now that was all that held any certainty for him.

"Dawson, what is it?" Her voice was tender in the still night.

Overwhelmed at the beauty of her, he embraced her hard against his body. She shuddered at the cold but relaxed against him. After a moment he spoke. "I brought a horse for Levi, in the barn."

Haven narrowed her gaze. "Oh, Dawson, really? But you shouldn't have…"

"He worked hard on the barn, deserves a good ride." He smiled at her happiness. "You can tell him tomorrow."

She touched his lip with tentative fingers. "You've been in a fight?"

He sucked in a ragged breath, letting her go with reluctance and turning toward the hearth, searching for words he'd rehearsed a thousand different ways. "It's fine."

"No, you were in town. Mr. Scott did this, didn't he?" She waited on an answer he didn't give. "Because of me."

He turned back shaking his head. "Because of a lot of things. Not you. He's just spouting off as usual."

"But he retaliated because you spoke to him…about me." She wasn't asking. She'd figured it well, though he'd never mentioned the details of the encounter to her in full.

"It's not important, Haven. Men like him…never amount to much in the end." He glanced back into the fire. "I need you and your brothers to stay home while I head out to the negotiations, like I asked you this morning. Stay clear of the claim until I return. It's best for now."

He turned back to her. "Scott and his men jumped me, but Sawyer and Wyatt came along…the fight wasn't much, but Haven…there are so many things I want to tell you…before I go. I…"

"Come, I need to see to your injuries." She urged him to follow, but he resisted, holding her beautiful gaze as he took her hand again.

"I'm just bruised, but Scott's the least of worries. Everything's coming down like rain, Haven, the Cavalry pushing the rules on the reservation, the braves can't keep their families fed. Leaning Bear can hardly go to the fort without harassment, and he warns me about the soldiers and the captain, as do my brothers. Change is coming he says, and even my own brother, Wyatt, sees it clearer than I have."

He sucked in a deep breath and blew it out, looking at her again as the words poured from him. "I've worked so hard all these years…all the time away trying to make a difference for the tribes, thinking there has to be some way they can live in peace, but the damn government following through for once is never gonna happen. It's not the passes and the reservations. It's life…a life where a man can be free to feed his family, hunt like the brave he is. No matter what I do…I can't fix it. I can't stop what's happening, and all I've ever stood for is already gone."

"You can't give up your work…" She stepped closer to him. "When you came through the door, I could see it in your eyes, like you were lost."

"Haven, I wasn't lost until I found you…until I had a reason enough for all I do *to* matter." He touched her chin with his thumb and smiled. "So I'm going to the negotiations and I'm gonna do what I need to do once more, but then I want to come home…here to you, make you my wife."

He drew her closer, uncertain how she would

respond. "I want to tell you so many things. I know the Cheyenne ways are different from your own, but when I took my dance with the sun...the wolf brought you to me. I was never sure why, but things are changing like Leaning Bear says, and he's been talking of going to the Northern Tribes. So much of the world is gonna be different from now on. The land filling up with more and more people. The wolf knew long ago this day would come and so he brought me...you."

"Dawson..." Her voice broke as those sweet hazel eyes held him.

He kissed her, savoring her mouth and favoring his swollen lip. "Haven, you are my Heartsong. So I'm gonna do what I promised the Cheyenne, and then I'm never leaving you again." He waited for a breath of seconds, his heart pounding to the surface of his chest, and then it came, her sweet whispered response.

"Yes..." Her smile was tear filled.

Overwhelming warmth encircled him as he bent and took her lips. She was warm in his arms and against the fullness of his body.

She pulled from the kiss breathless. "I've had my brothers to raise, and I suppose I never thought to ask myself if I was entitled to my own dreams...with you."

"Only want to do right by you and your family. Make you happy. Take care of you and your brothers as my own." He took both her hands in his.

She turned, leading him toward the hallway, clinging to one of his hands so tightly he couldn't let go.

He hesitated, stopping her and shaking his head, not wanting to speak enough to alert Sosha or her brothers, because he couldn't...do what she was intending.

She placed a finger to his lips and tugged him along into the room with her bed and shut the door behind them. The lamp burned, a slight flame leaving a glow of orange across her sunset hair. His breath caught as she touched the buttons of her night robe, letting it slide to the floor, leaving no question as to her intentions.

"Haven...there's time for this...but your brothers and Sosha..." He well knew better than to let this happen.

"An uncertain month is a long time...to wait. They will sleep." She touched his tunic, and against his better judgment, he helped her lift it over his head, leaving his torso bare and his breath short. He'd thought of this so often, of touching her, of joining their bodies as one, but...

"Haven..." He spoke in a whisper that was cut short with her hands placed on his bare chest. It had been so damn long since a woman had touched him, and he shuddered the full length of his body as she explored further.

She glanced up at him. "Do you remember when you first kissed me at the meadow?"

He hadn't soon forgotten the moment that he'd held her in his heart.

She smoothed her hands over his chest, igniting his body further, and it occurred to him she had no idea how bad he wanted her...needed her this night.

"Not one day or night has gone by where I didn't wonder, of this...with you." Her words were strong, though her voice trembled as did her hands.

She traced the dotted scars of his upper chest.

"From your dance with the sun?" She questioned, his body shivering as she let her hands drop lower to his ribs. "You're bruised from the fight."

He nodded, damn well able to feel the soreness, but more intrigued at her exploration of his body and the ease at which she touched him. There was something so right about being with her, something that calmed the wolf and made him see clear for the first time in years.

"So many scars. And here?" She pushed her thumb across the long smooth scar on the right side of his belly. For a moment he wondered if she was stalling for time, the nerves in her voice evident though she deserved an answer as she studied him.

"A fight from a long time ago." It was part truth. He'd suffered the lash from the soldier he'd killed trying to defend himself, but he'd not get into that right now.

"And here…" She tilted him toward her and kissed the white scar along his brow that she'd never asked about.

"A warning, long past." One day he'd tell her about all his scars, but tonight, the one thing crushing him, the thought of leaving her behind come morning.

He bent and kissed her, dancing his tongue along hers. She moaned as he pulled her against him, allowing his hands to run down her sides to her hips, full and rounded. He wanted to groan at the beauty of her dark nipples underneath the fabric of the linen gown she wore.

There were things he should say to her, let her know this first time might not be so pleasant for her, but words didn't seem to be needed as he held her gaze and eased the gown from her shoulders. She kissed him, her hands tracing his sides, kneading him into a frenzy of want, but he wouldn't rush this, not say the words he was feeling, the words she deserved. "I love you, Haven…now and always."

"And I you…" She was breathless as he tugged her gown to let the garment clear her shoulders, keeping her breasts covered for the moment, a deep blush befalling her freckled skin. He placed his lips to her cheek and left kisses down to her neck and across her upper chest, using his palm to push the gown further, exposing her breasts. She was so beautiful, and he'd know every inch of her body this night but not before he'd shown her the first pleasures of her passion.

He stroked a thumb across the dark bud of one breast and took the other into his mouth, and the full of her body shivered, a soft sigh leaving her. His groin tightened further, and he backed her to the bed, urging her to sit as he freed himself of his moccasins, struggling with the laces and standing to remove his buckskins and long underwear, leaving him bare.

She was glancing the length of him when he lifted his gaze, the hint of scalded red across her cheeks. He urged her back as he covered her with his large frame, finding her tiny by comparison. He kissed her, teasing her lips open with his tongue and resting a hand on her flat belly, letting it slide ever lower.

Dawson lifted his gaze as he rested a hand across the tight auburn curls, groaning at that unexpected surprise. He bent to take a nipple in a soft tug, teasing as he rubbed a palm across her.

She trembled, letting her hands roam his shoulders and back, her eyes closed. And he continued for a time, easing his fingers to her and receiving a gasp as he touched the pearl of her pleasure, teasing until her hips lifted. He urged her legs apart and eased his fingers just inside her.

Haven trembled, her breath short, though after a time, she relaxed, holding his gaze. He dipped his fingers further, groaning as he found the barrier he'd expected.

He touched the tiny pearl again, and her hips rose to meet him, her eyes half glazed as she began to move with his efforts. He wanted to taste her, but his need was too urgent, and he upped his efforts as he drew hard on one nipple to the other. He pressed his fingers inside her again and she whimpered, writhing and twisting with the speed of his assault.

"Please...." Her urgent whisper came, her body reaching.

"Come to me..." He moved his fingers with purpose, and she clenched tight around them as he swallowed the sweetest cry that escaped her. Her hips moved, her chest heaving as she clung to him in her rapture. And he stayed with her and as she stilled, he seared his fingers past the barrier.

Haven tossed her head back in a small cry as he whispered, kissing her chin. "Shhh, I won't hurt you as much now..." He eased the motion of his fingers, showing her the pain was gone.

Haven gasped, biting her bottom lip as Dawson pressed himself to join them. This was nothing like the pleasure he'd brought to her moments ago, but somehow, she wanted this pain, the pressure of him as close as possible and she willed herself to take him.

His large body trembled as he held back, unmoving, a heavy moan leaving him. She supposed this was as her mother had told her, the pain that came with love. He rocked, groaning in his apparent pleasure of her, his blue eyes holding her as he moved within her again. And she let her legs fall further open, wanting him there, still trying to understand the pure bliss his fingers had caused inside her and the sheer pain he caused her now.

He didn't rush, moving slow and steady to fill her with the gentle motion of his hips and after a time, the pain eased. She explored him, rubbing his back and shoulders and running her hands into his hair, drawing him to her breasts. His mouth was warm as he licked and teased each of her nipples to hard peaks, and she closed her eyes as the draw upon them touched her where he filled her.

"Haven...move with me." He spoke the last part in Cheyenne and settled to his elbows, holding her breasts between them as his hips drove harder. And she lifted her pelvis to meet him, wrapping her legs around him. He thrust harder and harder, the hair hanging across his shoulders mingling with her own, the muscles of his body growing tense. He was beautiful, and he loved her and wanted to return to make her his wife.

"So perfect." He whispered again in Cheyenne closing his eyes as he rocked back and forth. Lord, but this *was* as perfect as she might have imagined, and she followed his prompt, meeting each impact of his body into hers and wanting the hints of pleasure that were reaching her deep inside.

Dawson traced a hand down her arm, to her hand, raising it above her head, his fingers gripping hers. Her body built as it had with his fingers touching her, and it was somehow too much, and she shuddered, trying to writhe away from the intensity. He pinned her then, moving faster and faster, his breath hard as she hovered on the edge…

Dawson's deep voice vibrated through her. "Come to me…" His Cheyenne words were her undoing and she shattered, tendrils of bliss rolling through her, the cries filling her ears, her own. And she held him to her, as he followed, calling her name and shuddering so hard it surprised her.

Haven took the weight of him as he collapsed, not wanting him to move from within her now or ever. His body shivered several more times and he rolled from her, embracing her from behind in his large arms. She played her fingers across the fur on his forearm, and as she reached his fingers, he gripped her hand, his breath heavy.

He kissed her shoulder and spoke in the Cheyenne she was beginning to understand. "And all the beauty I hold is you."

She turned to face him, tangling further into the sheets with his warmth and meeting his deep blue eyes, the flicker of the lamp tossing oranges and yellows across his bronze skin and long dark hair.

He touched her face, this time speaking to her in English. "I'm not sure once will ever be enough. I hurt you?"

She kissed his hand, wanting this night to never end. "I'm all right."

He ran a hand to her hips, pulling her against him. "Always the brave one."

"Maybe. I just…" Heat rushed her cheeks. It had hurt more than she had anticipated but the pleasure had hidden the pain with his tenderness of her.

"There's nothing we can't share." He waited until she looked at him again.

She played her palm across the muscles of his hard chest. "I just didn't know...how it would feel...I mean..." She dropped her gaze, embarrassed. "It was very overwhelming, the...pleasure. Leastwise we didn't wake Sosha."

He pushed her back, raising himself over her again. "You're special, Haven, and I knew that from the start. Want you to be mine, now and always."

"Always." She whispered.

He kissed her, tender and searing, leaving her breathless once more. "You are my Heartsong now and always...and when I come back, if you'll have me, I never want to part from you again."

She gulped the lump in her throat, offering him a smile. "Yes...I wish I could put off morning."

"It'll come anyway, and I'll go before your brothers wake, but I will take you with me here." He placed her hand to his chest, the strong beating of his heart beneath.

"Show me...again this night..." She pulled him to her, laying a leg over his hip, kissing him and speaking again. "Whisper the Cheyenne words to me when it comes." Heat scalded her, but she wasn't done loving him yet.

"Come to me..." He spoke it in English and then whispered it in Cheyenne as he joined her once more. "Come to me..."

Chapter Sixteen

Dawson sat across from Leaning Bear inside one of the large lodges on the reservation. Hours had passed with little progress, but the Cheyenne and a few Sioux leaders pushed the window of time by sharing the fire and peace pipe with the officials, who at best were not amused.

Leaning Bear handed off the pipe to Dancing Fox, who glared Dawson's way. They had exchanged no words outside of proceedings, but it would come. Strange he'd not seen the brave in years, but time had changed things little. The Cheyenne handed off the pipe, breaking his gaze, and Captain Simmons took the pipe and in disrespect passed it to the next man.

Dawson let his mind drift to Haven, who seemed to consume his thoughts no matter his doings. There were times, lying in his teepee at night, he could hear the soft sighs she'd made due to his touch. She'd been so beautiful lying with him, and her full acceptance of him had been a surprise, making him scold himself at times. He'd known better and for her sake he should've waited until they were wed. Well, he'd take care of that soon enough, though the recent passing of the old chief, Stalking Eagle, had delayed the negotiations by several days. His last conversation with the Cheyenne leader who had accepted him as a son entered his mind.

"It is…with you, Proud Wolf." Stalking Eagle had

greeted, his body trembling with lack of strength.

"I am well, Grandfather." He'd bowed his head to the man who was the last link in the tribes that would have known his father, John McCade, the thought overwhelming at times.

The old man coughed. "The great wars…are over…no more…will it be in the Cheyenne to…put in place resistance of the white man's ways."

Dancing Fox had leaned over his father. "Father…we will honor you with this continued fight against the ways that do not belong to our people."

Stalking Eagle's voice rose again. "The buffalo are gone…and our people are hungry. When the animals…are gone…so are the people. It is Proud Wolf who will lead us…into the ways of the white man…so the tribe lives."

"I will take the Cheyenne's burdens, Grandfather." Dawson had responded out of respect, still certain of no real gains for any of the tribes.

Dancing Fox had resisted. "My father, we must fight once again. We will not live as white men or within their confines of these borders we do not honor."

But the old Chief had held both of their hands and brought them together, he and Dancing Fox bound for that moment in a handshake of mutual respect if nothing else. It was then Stalking Eagle spoke his last words. "There is…peace, nothing more to seek, my sons."

Dancing Fox had jerked his hand away and lay across his father's chest screaming his cry of pain and chanting the prayers to send his father on his journey to the camp of the dead. "I will grieve my father alone."

It was as it should've been. A man had the right to

grieve in peace, and Dawson had nodded, holding the brave's angered gaze for a moment more before leaving him to his father. And now, he sat in the continued negotiations, smoking a peace pipe with soldiers who would, on order, slaughter every Cheyenne brave without a thought. And alongside them stood the Chief's son who would bring down their wrath on all the tribes, causing more harm than good to all the Indian nations, if he had his way.

Across from him, Captain Simmons had remained quiet after several warnings, but it appeared the man was about to burst with sitting still. The Army had sent three men from Washington, and it wasn't like any of the three thought much different than anyone else in the United States Government. The red man would find eventual extinction in the current growth of America or adapt to the push for attending white man schools, cutting tribal ties and supporting agricultural learning with little more in the way of preserving the tribes.

Dancing Fox took over the conversation, speaking first in Cheyenne and then in broken English. "We have followed the white man's policies, but our children are hungry while the bellies of the soldiers remain full. Tell me this time how is it anything will become different? Your word is no good. The Cheyenne and the Sioux and the Arapaho and the Pawnee have listened and waited for empty promises."

Dawson held the gaze of Dancing Fox, their differences from the past not encircling them yet. The brave—chief now, with his father gone—wasn't calling for war but was rightful in his words and what often lacked with promises from the government.

General Dodd spoke, using a hand to calm his men

who chattered at the perceived threat. "Endeavors of war, as such would be futile. I am of the personal belief that our government, while attempting to support the tribes on reservations, has done a very poor job of it. Instead of haggling for hours over all the past details, I need to let you know I have seen the conditions on the reservations and find them despicable. I will hold these soldiers to make things right with what the treaties will provide."

A smirk from Captain Simmons drew the group's attention. "Sir, with all due respect. The government cannot promise the provisions even my soldiers do without. And Dawson McCade and the medicine man push my men at every chance, harboring up passes and allowing the Indians freedoms that have been limited."

Dawson broke in. "We allow more passes so the men can feed their families. We allow more time to hunt for the same. Little promised has been sent, and the Cheyenne are a literal people, believing the treaties which fail them time and again. Most present would bid on the freedom to hunt and better rations when they are sent and not the last pickings after the soldiers are done."

The captain was quick to the defense. "My soldiers have taken nothing from these people, but to have the Indians out hunting at will would stir up this side of the country."

The general stopped Simmons from further remarks. "These are peaceful proceedings, Captain Simmons, and you will be the first to make it so. I will make the appropriate recommendations to Washington. In the meantime, the soldiers will maintain proper respect as will the tribes present. And tomorrow afternoon, we will meet to sign the formal treaties for the continued status of the tribes. But in the meantime, I do prefer to hear what Mr. McCade can share with us on the status of the reservations that he has shown to me."

Dawson took a deep breath to begin as the captain postured, bowing with anger. "Our discussions aren't about freedoms from the reservations, but they are about the betterment of living conditions. The braves are allowed a few passes at a time to hunt, which doesn't provide enough for all in camp or even a single family at best. They are not allowed in some of the towns, and when they have the chance to trade their goods and pelts, it is often at much less than fair. If they are to acclimate, then they need the same rights as white men to trade for full payment of their goods. You want them to live as white men, then give them their freedoms the same as white men and spell them out in these treaties."

Silence filled the lodge as he'd expected but he continued. "I've worked this job for more years than I was ever paid for and little has changed for these people. I'd like to think at some point in the future things will improve for the betterment of the tribes. But for now, along with the status reports I've attached my letter of resignation from the Department of Indian Affairs, effective with the close of these negotiations and with all due respect to those involved on either side."

Deafening quiet held for a long moment until the general nodded. "Your dedication to the office and tribes is well known all the way to Washington, Mr. McCade, but I urge you to retain your position. I assure you I will review this report in full and respond with what my superiors will approve for the tribes."

Dawson nodded to a few other officials who commented on his work ethic. There was no need for further words from him. His journey where the tribes were concerned had come to an end, and while he was sure of his decision, the feeling of defeat held him. Leaning Bear would go north by spring, and somehow things would never be the same, even if he agreed to continue the line of work he'd always known. He hadn't spoken to Leaning Bear of his decision, but it was understood when he held the medicine man's gaze.

"We will convene tomorrow at noon to finalize the official documents." With that, the general and his men left the lodge.

Dawson stood, waiting as the tribal elders followed still speaking with Leaning Bear, who translated further what the general had stated. Dawson lifted his gaze to meet Dancing Fox, who had remained behind, the moment holding almost as long as the years between them.

"And you think the white men will not fail us again, my brother." The brave spoke in Cheyenne, his words bitter.

Dawson picked up the remaining stacks of paper he needed to return to his teepee. The brave had not called him brother in respect. "I think there is a proper process to access what the tribes seek."

The Cheyenne laughed. "Always passive, even with Winona."

Well, it had been bound to come, even though he'd long let Winona go from his life. "She chose her own path, brother."

Dancing Fox tilted his head. "But not the one you would have chosen for her."

Dawson held the man's gaze and the Indian continued, "She died of the white man's disease of cough and blood." The brave explained, glancing anywhere but at Dawson, as he spoke his native tongue. "But on her last breath it was your name she called. Yours!"

There were no words to say, even though he hadn't known that.

Dancing Fox stepped closer. "And I will hold that, brother, for all of my life just like I will hold to war in my father's honor." With that, he stepped outside the lodge.

Dawson shook his head, his feelings for Winona were no longer important in his life. Time had moved and dwelling on things of the past never proved to change them.

He grabbed his buffalo robe and stepped from the lodge, not surprised at Dancing Fox's display. The negotiations had passed one day at a time and tomorrow would be the presentation of the treaties. A formality for show, though any follow-through by the American government would be months away if at all.

Dancing Fox had long spoken of building the various tribes to an army, but he wasn't able to see the years past and the full slaughter of men, women, and children that Stalking Eagle had lived.

He also couldn't see the extinction of the tribes if he did so much as cry war in these proceedings, but the old chief was holding them both to nothing more than peace for the sake of the tribe.

That was why he was here, to do what was needed

for the Cheyenne and all the tribes...at least this one last time.

Chapter Seventeen

The numbing wind blew snow across the divided group of men, adding to the tensions from the weeks before. The presentation of renewed treaties was a formality to complete the last day of negotiations. Dawson glanced at Leaning Bear, not speaking the words best left unspoken as General Dodd signed several of the documents, bending over a small table. Temperatures had held low for weeks, but since the night before, winds had become frigid and snow had begun as the telegrams from back East had hinted. It was strange that folks back East could predict what the weather thousands of miles away would do, but it appeared this time the continued wires of a blizzard were right.

He tugged his buffalo robe tighter around him, squeezing his numb hands inside the thick gloves that helped little. At least as it was, these proceedings would be over by the afternoon, and he'd find his way back to Haven for a lifetime. If he thought hard enough, he could still smell the lilac that rode her hair and taste the salt of her freckled skin.

The general continued to read aloud a summary of the government-issued treaties as he signed each one. Nearby, Captain Simmons and his men waited, armed and dressed in their best, but it was Dancing Fox who stepped up to speak when the general lifted his gaze on the final document.

"The Cheyenne have been on this land for more years than white man. We choose to live in peace but will have our freedom to live as our ancestors have lived before us. The white man says the white government owns the land. Who gives the white man this right? We will receive no treaty that feeds our families. Tell me when does this path of destruction end for the Cheyenne? Will the white man's government promise more death to my people? Will my children cry of hunger each night? My father is now in the camp of the dead, but the Cheyenne would choose no war, though the tribes will rise once more when it is time." Dancing Fox held his gaze to the men in the tribe.

With that, he lifted his bow to the air and gave a shrill cry, the hundred or more braves behind him doing the same and causing the soldiers to poise weapons without order. Leaning Bear stepped in between the soldiers and the tribes, holding his hands up to stop both sides, but the thunder of cries still filled the air.

"The government will process the contents of these treaties. You have my word on that," the general shouted, stepping beside Leaning Bear and waving off the soldiers to lower their weapons. "I've seen the conditions on the reservations and have permission to make sure that good rations and supplies break the lines of the soldiers, or anyone else who would try to stop this."

Dancing Fox gave a great belt of mocking laughter, folding his arms and glaring at the general as the men behind him continued with a new chant of war to come.

Dawson scanned the area around them. Something wasn't right and goose flesh rose on his skin though it wasn't from the cold. The tribes had been restless, but the intensity hadn't risen to this level until now.

Lieutenant Carl Bartley stepped in beside Dawson, glancing around them. "Tell me this is just for show."

Dawson gave the soldier a slight nod. "Not so sure."

"Think they know they can't win with this many soldiers?" Carl let his gaze travel across the chanting Indian nation, clearly outnumbered.

Leaning Bear stepped over to Dancing Fox, and their initial conversation quieted the tribes, settling the anxious soldiers for the time.

Dawson waited, perplexed as the cries for war faded.

"The Indian nations can rest assured that I will see the measures done." The general raised his voice along with his hands, trying to explain further, and glanced Dawson's way. "In support of all that is due to the tribes, I am asking Dawson McCade to assist in making sure that all the treaties are followed in full before resignation of his position."

Dawson held the general's gaze. He'd already turned in his notice, these negotiations ending his time in translation, but he gave a reluctant nod in an effort to calm the situation, knowing he'd have to follow through for a time.

Captain Simmons stomped closer, speaking to the general. "Sir, McCade has stepped from his post as an Indian Agent. His time here is done."

The general glared. "Captain, stick to running your fort and your soldiers."

"Sir, I highly suspect Dawson McCade of not using the government's money wisely. With all due respect, I believe I can handle your provision with much better skill."

Dawson stepped closer. "I've never cheated the government of anything, and most often, my minimal salary is returned in one form or another to the Cheyenne people for food and medicine."

The general spoke to Simmons again. "This is not the time or place, Captain. You will remove yourself, Sir, from these negotiations for the time being. Do I make myself clear, Sir?"

The captain stepped back with a salute, glaring hard.

General Dodd turned back to them all. "Now, it's freezing, gentlemen, and all the treaties have been signed by both sides. I bid you a good day and to stay warm…"

An arrow pierced the general's chest, sending him backwards to the ground with a hard thud, stopping him mid-sentence. Soldiers drew their weapons, firing toward the tree-covered incline before them, with Captain Simmons falling to his knees beside the general, urging his soldiers to the fight with a shout. .

Dawson pulled his revolver, meeting gazes with Leaning Bear, who grabbed his bow from his shoulder, lacing it with an arrow, his friend telling the story in Cheyenne. "Dog Soldiers."

The riders were Indians on horseback wearing dark paint and firing with bows and rifles as they invaded the camp. Dawson ducked behind a wagon, catching what breath he could and watching as the Cheyenne, including Dancing Fox, fought alongside the soldiers in defense. They should have all known with Dog Soldiers in the area this was inevitable. He caught the warrior's gaze. In the brevity of the moment, it was clear the brave knew nothing of this, same as he and Leaning Bear, all of them trying to stop the attack.

With a nod to the medicine man, Dawson ran toward the pounding hooves, merging with the Cavalrymen, the roar of gunfire filling the air along with the hiss of arrows and smoke. Leaning Bear ran alongside him, both of them waving off the Dog Soldiers, who never stopped the attack. Glancing behind him, soldiers fell with injury as before him war-painted Indians rode to their death, falling from their mounts in the white blinding snow.

He turned to Carl, who had followed. "You have to warn the reservation! Move the women and children to hiding! Go!" At this point, the village had no braves, and it was the elderly, women, and children who might be at risk from the Dog Soldiers and even retaliation from the Cavalry.

"I'll go, but the captain thinks this is you and Leaning Bear..." Carl glanced over his shoulder where the captain was pointing their way.

"Arrest the agent and the medicine man. Now!" The captain shouted to the soldiers, having left the general behind on the ground. "Apprehend them, now!"

"We must run," Leaning Bear yelled, lacing another arrow into his bow and sending a Dog Soldier to the frozen earth.

"Go." Carl shoved him ahead and disappeared in a haze of smoke and blinding snow.

An arrow whizzed past Dawson's head, skimming his ear and making him duck for cover. He grabbed his bloody ear and lifted his gaze to Leaning Bear for a brief second, both aware of their limited options. If they allowed themselves to be arrested, the captain would try hang them, but running sealed their fate as guilty men. The medicine man gave him a single nod, and they turned back for their horses, away from the Cavalry and Dog Soldiers alike.

Dawson covered ground to get to Viho and mounted the animal without worrying of anything he might be leaving behind, his revolver and tomahawk all he carried. It was vital they flee the area, with soldiers already mounting up behind them at the captain's orders. He whistled and Viho skirted away, Leaning Bear behind him on his own mount, both racing past the Dog Soldiers, toward the eastern slope of mountains.

Snow whipped across Dawson, stinging his face, as Viho made it to the far line of trees, the skirmish continuing and mounted soldiers following. Leaning Bear caught him and sped ahead a length, as Dawson urged Viho with a swift kick to the flanks. The horse picked up speed, the dangers of the icy ground ignored.

Pain pierced his side and Dawson froze, as before him an arrow embedded in the bark of a tree. It had sliced right through him. He blinked, shocked, waiting on the pain that followed, enough to double him over his horse. He lifted his body and held on, glancing ahead and grabbing the arrow that had ridden through his side, pulling it from the tree. Struggling for a deep breath, he broke off the feathered end. Dog Soldiers had hit him.

He continued ahead, the warm trickle of blood dripping from his side and bile filling his throat along with the nausea the pain brought.

Making it to the rise of mountains and dense wooding, Leaning Bear led the way, the trail they both knew well covered in at least a foot of snow. The horses struggled for footing across the frozen earth, the soldiers tracking them and falling further behind. When the gunfire ceased in the distance, they slowed their horses, Dawson's rapid breath turning white against the air before him.

Leaning Bear slowed his horse, turning. "You are injured?"

"It went through. Gotta keep moving." He held his friend's gaze, the burning pain slicing through him still.

Leaning Bear gave him a second skeptical glance, both men struggling to catch their wind. "You find white medicine woman?"

Dawson shook his head. "They'll look for me there." It was true, his name was known, and he'd meet with certain disaster if he rode for the ranch or if he sought care from Tess. "Storms picking up. I'll manage." Now that he wasn't moving, he could damn well feel the sting of the path the arrow had taken through him. Hell, he'd die from this if he wasn't careful.

"Your injury will lead them to you." Leaning Bear nodded at the bright red blood dripping to the snow off the side of Viho.

Dawson glanced down. "Storm'll cover my tracks."

"I must help village. Circle back, go north." The medicine man slung a leg over his horse, dismounting, and reached into the bag he always wore across his shoulders. He approached Dawson, urging him to open the buffalo robe and lift his leather tunic.

"You'll meet capture there." Dawson groaned at the sight of the slit on the left side of his belly, shivering.

"Yarrow leaf, stop bleeding." Leaning Bear placed a pouch of herbs against the wound to his side. He groaned, tossing his head back as the sting of the herbs took hold. The medicine man tugged his belt over the injury to hold the pack in place. "Must keep tight. Make journey to Woman with Frying Pan, closer."

Dawson held his friend's gaze. They each stood a better chance alone.

"Make a wise journey." Leaning Bear reached into his tunic and held his hand out to Dawson.

He eyed his friend and opened his palm where Leaning Bear laid a small knife. It was the same one he'd given to the young brave he'd first met as a boy, Leaning Bear almost eight years his senior. They'd traded at the river, the knife for the bear claw that Dawson still wore on a thin rope around his neck. They'd swapped many times over the years to the point there were times he forgot which one he possessed. He held the medicine man's gaze as he tugged the claw free and handed it back to his friend.

Leaning Bear mounted up. "When we meet again, my brother, I will want knife back and this claw will be yours once more."

Dawson held his side, the situation dire. "May our paths cross again, my brother."

****

The blinding whiteout of a blizzard limited visibility, confusing even his horse. Dawson shuddered and held his side, damp with oozing blood. Maybe he was the one that confused Viho, as he'd been pushing the exhausted animal for enough hours to feel the symptoms of lost blood blurring his vision. He was growing weak. He needed to find shelter as neither he nor the horse was doing each other much good.

He glanced at his tunic, hanging from under the buffalo robe, blood staining it and his leather pants all the way to his knee. At least the heavy snow was covering his trail of blood. The blizzard made travel weary but the best he could guess was Haven's homestead wasn't far. His damn hands were near frozen inside his thick gloves, and he figured by his lack of focus he'd already lost too much blood to survive anyway.

He'd seen the reluctance in Leaning Bear's eyes with their parting, but more than that, he'd seen the disappointment with the fact their paths might never cross again. He glanced at his belly, the searing pain calling his attention and a quick reminder he'd never belonged to either side anyway, and with his current role, he was now without a doubt labeled altogether something different—outlaw.

The Cavalry would report him and Leaning Bear as renegades soon enough, leaving them nothing but running to the road ahead of them. Hell, with his injury, it might be he didn't have such a far road to travel, and it would be nightfall soon.

He closed his eyes as Viho carried him further in the deep snowdrifts. He was beyond pain, the cold numbing his mind with the dropping temperatures. Somehow the thoughts of Haven warmed him, her sweet face etched into his mind. And in the haunting powerful drifts, with snow sticking to his brows and lashes, he could feel her body once more...

Viho stopped, sending him from the saddle right into a drift of deep snow. The powder flew around him, covering his face and making him cough as his lungs inhaled the frost. He lifted his head. He must've dreamt and fallen, causing the horse to stop.

He closed his eyes. Death never came easy to any man, though death came for all. Maybe he'd lost too much blood. Funny, it was now he who struggled with where he might end up in the afterlife—the Cheyenne camp of the dead or with the Christian God he'd known as a boy, neither of which would make claim of him. He opened his eyes, ignoring the heavy flakes of snow that gathered along his lashes, distorting his vision further. He had to get up or he'd die of exposure instead of his bleeding side.

Viho nudged him, and he grabbed the stirrup of the saddle to pull himself up, the effort taking what energy he could summons. Making it up, he leaned across the saddle, the still whiteness broken by the roof of a small barn in the distance.

So Viho had seen purpose in nudging him. Focusing on the rooftop of the barn, he glanced to where a small cabin stood, several hundred yards further. Smoke escaped the chimney, whirling in a stream across the darkening sky.

"Haven..." The whisper jolted him alert, but the trudge ahead would be the death of him in the heavy winds and snow.

He grabbed Viho's reins as the horse led him ahead, ice crunching under his moccasins, his heart pounding heavy inside his chest and pain scorching through his side. He leaned hard to push inside the barn once there, kicking snow from the wide swinging door. Making it inside, he urged a reluctant Viho in behind him, the horse startled with the wind and blowing drifts of white powder.

Inside, he dropped to his knees into the cold dirt, breathing hard and letting his eyes adjust to the darkness, his entire body shaking in fatigue. He sucked in a deep breath inhaling the smell of earth and animal. Willing himself to his feet, he moved unsteadily to Viho. If he didn't see to the horse now, he wouldn't be able to. Pulling hard he freed the dark leather saddlebags and the frozen canteen, letting them fall to the dirt floor. Knowing he couldn't lift the saddle off the horse, he rounded his hand along the animal's belly, struggling with the buckle and letting the saddle fall to the opposite side.

Nearby, Josie whinnied, and the cow lowed from the corner of the barn as he fought to stand again, his vision blurring. He gasped for breath, doubling over to clench his side and blinking hard trying to remain conscious. He had to make it to the house, but the barn spun around him and his focus faded. He fought to raise his head, to lift himself up to no avail. He had to get to Haven but he fell back, the darkness closing in around him with a force he couldn't fight.

Chapter Eighteen

"Haven, you have to come!" Levi barreled through the front door, wind and snow whirling through behind him with a roaring hiss.

He dropped saddle bags to the floor by the door and Haven's heart fell inside her chest. "Dawson?"

"He's in the barn, hurt." Her brother shivered, tugging her coat and hat from the hook on the wall and shoving them her way.

"Hurt?" Haven pushed her arms in the heavy coat, and put the hat on her head, wrapping the thick scarf around it to keep it on. The winds from the blizzard were harsh and as she pulled on her gloves a moment of panic took her. Dawson, injured…what on earth?

"He's bleeding, and I couldn't wake him." Her brother was breathless as he held the door waiting. "The blizzard's too much and I can't hold the rope with him, it's hard moving out there." The dangers of losing their way from the house to the barn with the heavy winds and snow were serious and a rope stayed tied to the porch that stretched to the barn door.

She turned to James who scampered up. "You stay here, James, at the door, and bang the spoon hard on the pot to let us know where the porch is, but you must not come off the porch at all, do you understand?" She pulled her heavy boots onto her sock-covered feet in a hurry, the flurry of her skirts whipping with the wind from the open door.

"Yes'm." James ran to close the door behind them with Sosha barking as he followed them out into the freezing storm.

Haven's heart pounded against her chest as the cold took her breath, her mind whirling around what might have happened. Good Lord, what if she hadn't sent her brother out for a brief check on the animals?

Levi grabbed the rope and wedged it into her hands, his voice muffled by the winds. "We have to hurry."

The darkness of the snow was blinding as she followed her brother, keeping both hands on the rope as he led the way. Strange she'd woken earlier this morning with a dream of Dawson calling to her and a large gray wolf howling in the distance. She wasn't sure how much of his Cheyenne ways had meaning, but the vivid dream must have been his totem wolf letting her know he was in some kind of danger.

She stepped behind her brother into snow as high as her hips, fighting her way through, the cold stinging her cheeks. She slipped as her boot snagged and she fell, but Levi was there, pulling her up.

"Not much further." Her brother yelled against the harsh whistling winds, his face scorched red to a burn from the freezing winds.

She got back to her feet, still clinging to the rope and stopping behind her brother as he wedged open the barn door. Entering, she shuddered hard against the cold, trying to focus her vision in the darkness of the barn.

"He's here." Levi bent before Dawson, who lay on the dirt floor. "Viho was loose but I put him in the stall and covered Dawson with the blanket."

Haven froze for a breath of seconds, touching Dawson's brow as she bent. His teeth chattered as he moaned, but he wasn't coherent. "Dawson?"

"He's bleeding from his belly." Levi lifted the blanket and the buffalo robe. "Guess it's a bullet."

Haven viewed the wound and patted Dawson's face, leaning closer. "Dawson, look at me...please, look at me." Tears rimmed her eyes. There was no way she could care for him in the barn, even if they had a better lantern.

After a moment his eyes opened, and he sucked in a deep breath. "Cold."

His voice was a whisper and she placed both her hands on his frozen cheeks. "We have to get you inside. I can't care for you here."

"Viho." He blinked several times, shuddering hard.

"Viho's fine." Levi's worried gaze met hers.

"Dawson, you have to stand up." Haven scolded as Dawson tried to close his eyes again.

She and Levi grabbed his arms, bringing him to sitting with great effort. He grabbed his side. "Haven..."

"I'm here, but we have to get you up." She answered as she and Levi fought to get him to his feet.

"That's it." Levi strained to hold him, Dawson's weight making it difficult as Haven wrapped an arm around his middle.

Dawson yelped, and Haven withdrew her gloved hand from his back, the garment saturated in blood. "The bullet must've gone through."

She grabbed him again. He'd lost so much blood, by the looks of his tunic and trousers. Even his buffalo robe was matted in the same dried blood that traced his moccasins.

Dawson's large body shivered hard. "Arrow…went through."

"An arrow?" Haven whispered.

Levi tugged harder to keep him on his feet as he swayed. "Gotta help us, Dawson."

Dawson staggered with her and Levi supporting him. Levi grabbed the door, pulling it open, and together they fought to find the rope in the droves of white snow and darkness.

"Take the rope." Her brother shoved it into her hand. "I've gotta have two hands to hold him up."

She could scarcely hear Levi's words above the whip of the wind, but she held to the rope and Dawson with all the might she had, while the echoing of James pounding on the metal with a spoon played in the distance.

Dawson's hand gripped tight to her coat and he moved with them as the cabin came into view.

The wind gusted hard, sending her against Dawson, who groaned and grabbed his side, falling to his knees. "Ahhhhhh…"

"Pull him up, Levi." Haven fought to keep her stance and pushed with her brother to get Dawson moving once more, struggling to keep the rope in her hand. Sosha barked, leading the way to the porch.

Dawson struggled ahead, hanging on to her and Levi, though he made moving ahead difficult as he didn't lift his moccasins to take the steps, but pushed through the snow drifts, moaning with each step.

"Don't let go of the rope," Levi yelled, his hat flying from his head and off into the weathered distance.

She hugged herself to Dawson. "Come on, take a step," she yelled, the wind hissing around them taking her breath.

Levi settled in behind Dawson, pushing him along, and as Haven took another step her boot hit the porch behind Sosha. "Step up."

Levi's dark hair was covered in snow as was Dawson's face and brows, his long hair whipping to cover the pain of his face.

"Dawson, step up." Haven let go of the rope and grabbed him with both her gloved hands, pulling him up as Levi pushed. And with great effort he made all the stairs one by one, his eyes closed.

James opened the front door, still banging the spoon to the pot, Sosha scampering inside. Haven pulled on Dawson, and all three of them fell through the doorway onto the floor as James slammed the door closed. Haven raised her head to look at Dawson and Levi climbed to his feet. Dawson was breathing hard, covered in snow and ice, as were they all.

"Viho?" he whispered, opening his eyes, shuddering.

"He's in the barn, safe." She touched his face. He was burning up in spite of the cold that chilled him. Fevered and confused. She got to her knees, tossing the hat and scarf from her head and removing her coat and gloves, letting them fall beside her. "Levi, let's get him to the pallet."

Together, with James helping, they managed to drag him to the hearth and onto the heavy blankets where she'd left his pallet all this time, expecting his return. "Help me get his coat off and his moccasins.

Leastwise, his gloves were still on or he'd have frost bite. He may still."

Her brothers went to work unlacing Dawson's moccasins and she tugged at his gloves, the heavy leather of them frozen in place. She took each hand in turn checking for frostbite, but while they were red and cold, it didn't appear so. With a quick glance of his feet, she covered him in the blankets as they were fine too.

"What happened to Mr. Dawson?" James stood over him. "He's a-bleedin'."

"Arrow," Dawson whispered, "went through."

Levi helped turn Dawson so Haven could free him of the heavy robe, but the effort made him cry out in pain. She tossed the fur aside and sucked in a deep breath as she lifted his blood-soaked tunic, struggling with the belt that held a pouch of yarrow leaves in place over the wound. "Levi, go get the dressing basket and my herbs from the wardrobe in my room. James, put two more logs on the fire and bring some drying cloths. Levi put more water on the fire to boil, hurry."

Sosha sniffed Dawson's buffalo robe and lay down against the rockwork of the hearth with a whimper.

Haven tugged Dawson's tunic up and over his head, fighting to free it from his muscular arms and shoulders, making him grimace. She leaned over the wound to his belly, which seeped bright red blood, and lifted her gaze to Levi, who bent to his knees on the opposite side of her.

She touched near the slit of a wound, wondering what damage the arrow had done inside. Belly injuries were the worst, from what she understood, but at least the arrow had gone through. If she could stop the bleeding maybe there was a chance, and her heart couldn't take anything less. She placed tentative fingers near the wound, which was an angry red.

Dawson groaned and touched her hand, wincing in pain.

"I've gotta stop the bleeding, Dawson. I'm afraid it may be painful." Her heart was in her throat and her mind was spinning around what best to do. But if she couldn't stop the bleeding… "We need a doctor, but…the weather. Let's look at his back."

Levi helped hold Dawson on his side, so she could view the wound to his back, which was smaller and clotted off with no bleeding. She cleaned around the wound and dug in the basket for ointment and a dressing and made haste in applying the bandage.

With effort. James walked around them to add two more logs to the fire with effort. "Is he gonna die like Papa?"

Fear pounded through her so profound she couldn't draw breath. "No, I won't let him die." She met Levi's gaze in warning, but he didn't say anything more, only shivered. "James, get a warm blanket for Levi."

Levi took the blanket when James returned with the one from his bed. His and Dawson's hair dropped chunks of ice to the bedding and floor.

Haven grabbed a pile of cut dressings and placed them to Dawson's wound and pressed, eliciting a heavy yelp from him. His eyes jerked open and he grabbed her wrists so hard she had to stifle a cry of her own. "Dawson, it's all right. I've got to stop the bleeding."

The pressure of his grip eased, but he didn't let her go as he blinked, his blue eyes holding a moment of confusion. "Haven…"

"Levi, hold this." She put her brother's hands to the

dressing. "Keep pressure here."

As Levi took over, she leaned closer to Dawson. "I don't know how to stop the bleeding. I've more yarrow, but what else should I do?"

He shuddered with the cold, not letting go of her wrist. "Just need…to rest."

Haven grabbed the small tin of leaves she had traded for at the fort. She eyed the poultice she'd removed from his belly and the leaves inside it were folded long ways and broken.

"What is it?" Levi studied the poultice she built the same as the one she'd found.

"Yarrow, but…I've got to clean around the wound first." She padded a cloth with the herbs and dampened the leaves with a bit of the hot water and set it aside. Dipping another into the water and wringing it, she held her brother's gaze. "Hold him."

Levi gave her an uncertain gaze but leaned over Dawson to hold both his arms at his sides. Haven pressed with tenderness on the knife-like wound, causing Dawson to shake hard, but he didn't resist her brother.

"Still bleeding." She held the yarrow leaves to the wound, glancing at Levi and back to Dawson.

Dawson gritted his teeth, speaking in a growl, shivering still. "Levi, get a bullet…from my… revolver."

Levi glanced at Haven, but it was James who dragged over Dawson's saddle bags that still lay by the front door.

"His gun's in here, ain't it?" James squatted as Levi took up the weapon and opened the barrel, using a fingernail to remove a single bullet, laying the open gun back inside the saddle bags.

"Got it." Levi waited with the bullet in hand.

Dawson swallowed hard. "Use the tool there…to open the bullet…get to the powder."

Levi lifted the gripping tool and struggled with great effort to remove the cap on the back of the bullet, setting the tool aside and holding the open-ended bullet.

In that brief second Haven understood and shook her head. She'd read that black powder could stop the bleeding from wounds

"Get a match." Dawson held her gaze, his breathing short and rapid.

Haven's mouth dropped opened and she shook her head. No, they couldn't…lighting the wound would cause him terrible pain and she couldn't do that, could she? "Dawson, we can't do this…"

"I'll…die…if not…" He smiled as if it was funny, then grimaced at the effort.

She looked into his deep blue eyes, swallowing back the fear that consumed her. "Dawson…"

"It'll…stop the bleeding, Haven." He placed a hand to her cheek. "Light it." It took effort for him to swallow, the Adam's apple at his throat bobbing. His face carried a few day's stubble and he was perspiring, though his shiver was constant.

"Levi, go get Papa's whiskey. James, take Sosha to your room and he can sleep with you. Go on to bed now." She nodded to her brothers, knowing she would need Levi's help but thinking James too young to witness such.

"Aw, I want to stay with Mr. Dawson," James protested, but Levi took him by the hand and led him away, clucking his tongue to urge Sosha to follow.

Dawson chuckled softly. "Might be…something he can tell…grandchildren about."

Haven brushed a hand across his brow.

"The negotiations…were near done, but…the weather turned and out of…nowhere, Dog Soldiers…attacked." He coughed, placing a hand over hers that covered his wound with pressure.

"Leaning Bear and me, we tried to…stop them, but they…kept going, fighting soldiers and Cheyenne." He shook his head. "And the captain…ordered his men to arrest us…but we knew nothing…of the attack…"

Tears dropped from Haven's eyes, spilling down her cheek. "They can't hold you responsible for this."

"Not so sure…" He closed his eyes for a moment. "Captain's had it in for us for a while."

Haven leaned toward him, placing her lips to his and kissing him as more tears came. "I will do this because I will not let you die, Dawson McCade."

He rubbed a hand on her cheek as Levi returned and bent before them, handing her a half full bottle of whiskey.

She glanced at her brother, who opened his hand, his thumb covering the opening of the bullet. Haven took it from him and forced herself to the task, pouring the powder in and around the wound.

"Got a feeling…dying might just be…easier…" Dawson said it with a hiss but took the bottle of alcohol and drank amply. He handed the bottle back to Levi and closed his eyes, bracing, his fists gripping the blankets beneath him. "Gonna rest now. You light it."

"Dawson…" she whispered, still uncertain.

He urged her ahead, through gritted teeth. "Go on…"

Haven lifted and struck the match with her fingernail and it sparked to life, glowing golden. "I can't." She fanned the match out, the smoke whirling in a thin stream before her face.

"We got…little choice here." Dawson shook his head, his face growing pale.

She nodded and extracted another match, striking it, determined this time, but Dawson halted her.

"Wait…" He held up a hand. "More whiskey."

Levi handed him the bottle and this time he gulped more than once and growled when he pulled the bottle away, giving her a nod. "Light it."

Haven bit her bottom lip and struck yet another match. With a quick glance at her brother, she let her hand fall closer to the wound, and with a last effort, let the flame touch the powder. It exploded in a singe of fire, and Dawson lifted from the mattress with a growling cry that startled them all. "Ahhhhhh…"

Haven's tears began as Dawson's body went limp against the blankets, the wound smoking. "I'm so sorry, breathe, please breathe…"

Levi touched her arm and then Dawson's chest. "He's passed out, Haven, but he's breathing."

She placed her hand on Dawson and wiped away more tears. The smell of powder and burnt flesh filled the air. Good Lord, how had he taken that kind of pain? The wound was charred but bled no more, and she inhaled a deep breath of relief.

"Levi, if you would check on James, take him some of the beans and ham and feed yourself, and you boys go on to bed. It's best I don't leave Dawson for now." She whispered, it being late and darkness long past them.

Levi nodded, and made haste at getting two plates for supper for him and James, who had stayed in his room as told.

Now alone with Dawson, Haven touched the hair on his brow and bent to kiss his hot forehead. With effort she placed ointment and the yarrow dressing along the wound and took her time rolling a bandage around him, made difficult due to his size. She ran a hand across his chest, remembering the night he lay with her in her bed, so tender in teaching her how a man loved a woman. But now…now he was injured, and she guessed a fugitive, and she couldn't think what would be best to do. Exhausted and hungry, she lay down beside him and tugged the blankets over them both, whispering a silent prayer that morning held the continued storm—for now.

Chapter Nineteen

Dawson fought the dreams plaguing him, the ones where he rode Viho against the storm, trying to outrun mounted soldiers. He'd be hanged if they caught him, but the unrelenting pain in his side would be the death of him. He was dreaming and knew so. He groaned and placed a hand to his side as he found delirious consciousness, the world spinning around him and the cold burning him up.

"Shhh. It's all right." A cool rag scorched his head, and he shivered so hard the wood beneath the pallet creaked.

Pulled from the dream, he focused as best he could on Haven, his sole reason for still drawing breath, uncertain why the fever or loss of blood hadn't taken him. "Haven…"

"I'm here." She placed a hand to his cheek and brushed her lips across his brow. He was safe for the time being.

"It's all right. Rest." She spoke again, the cold rag offering relief to the burning heat that made his teeth chatter.

"Cold." he managed. His vision blurred as did his thoughts. Come the Cavalry or not, there wasn't much he could do now anyway. Moving was futile and made the wound cut like a knife through his side once more.

"You've a fever." She lifted his head and a tin cup

touched his lips. He drank, not caring about the taste of the foul liquid but coughing at the burn to his dry throat. He pushed the cup away, the raw pain in his side making him grimace.

He grabbed Haven's hand. "How many…days…?"

She brought her face close to his, the smell of lilac surrounding him. "Three."

He fought to rise from the pallet on the floor by the hearth. That was too long. The soldiers would be hunting him without any doubt. "It's a danger…for me to stay…here."

He held his side, searing pain taking his breath.

"No, Dawson, you mustn't. Levi!" Haven shouted as she and her brother wrestled him back to the pallet.

"There's still a full blizzard. Ain't no soldiers gonna come here in this." Levi fought to push him back down.

"You could be in danger…is there any word?" Dawson groaned through his pain, but Levi held him still as Haven lifted the blankets, checking his wounds.

"You'll start bleeding again. Please, lie still. With the blizzard, we've seen no one." Her sweet voice was enough to calm all that fretted inside him.

His head pounded but the searing pain that scored his side took his breath still. "Whiskey…can't take this…pain…"

Levi relinquished his hold. "Want me to get Papa's whiskey?"

"Yes." Haven nodded at her brother as she sat beside Dawson. "The wound has stopped bleeding, but if you open it again, I'm not sure I can stop it."

"I'm sorry…you had to do that." He touched his side. Her face had held sheer terror at his request, and he didn't remember much except her unsteady hand as she had lowered the flame to ignite the gunpowder inside the wound.

"Oh, Dawson...I don't think the soldiers will come here now. They have to know you had nothing to do with knowing those Dog Soldiers, though." She tried, her voice tender but sure.

He closed his eyes to the nausea. "Viho?"

"The animals are fine." Levi watched as Haven poured a bit of the whiskey into the cup of willow bark tea, stirring the mixture.

Dawson took what she offered, struggling at the bitterness of the combined liquids. Hell, if that didn't kill him... He coughed and then yelped with his side, causing Sosha, who lay near the hearth to whimper.

"Drink slower, come on, all of it," she urged, and if he didn't love her so much— He drank and growled through the rest of the cup, the alcohol hitting his head rapidly enough to make him dizzy.

"Rest now." Haven smoothed a hand across his brow. He was scalded from fever. Infection from the wound would do him no good in trying to escape what was coming, if he was guessing right. But at this point he was at no liberty to move more than to let his body rest as the alcohol dulled his thoughts. With what strength he had left he traced his hand to hers and let the waiting darkness have him.

****

Haven lifted her head, disoriented for a brief second, but placed a hand on Dawson's chest as she sat up beside him. His chest rose and fell, yet he shivered and moaned in his sleep. She touched his brow expecting fever, but his forehead and cheeks were cool.

She shifted, lifting the blanket to inspect the dressing on his side, which was dry.

The house was still dark, with the hint of dawn peeking through the windows. The wind howled as she gathered herself up and glanced outside. It appeared the storm had yielded for the most part, droves of snow piled high against the house and barn. How had either of them slept with such a storm?

Turning, she went to her bedroom to wash her face and change her blouse and skirt, which were rumpled with her restless night next to Dawson. She still thought so often of the night before he'd left for the negotiations and the way he had taught her body what it meant to share her bed with a man. Heat flushed her face and she pushed thoughts of that from her mind. He was too injured for that, and now with the storm letting up everything seemed uncertain. Surely Dawson couldn't be accused of crimes he hadn't committed. He'd even rescued them both from the Dog Soldiers.

It was early and with the winds still blowing frigid, she'd need to boil snow and get to some of the washing of linens and Dawson's blood-soaked clothing. Her and Levi's clothing hadn't fared much better due to helping him, but stuck inside, the wash would keep her close to Dawson should he need anything.

Returning to the kitchen, Dawson remained unmoving by the hearth. He'd need willow bark tea for pain and a dressing change so she could check on his wounds. She went to the stove and struck a match and tossed it inside, where it smoldered against last night's partially burned wood, igniting.

The boys would be hungry when they woke, and she was famished herself. Johnnycakes would be hearty along with salt pork and the dried beans she'd soaked overnight. She bent and lifted the cast iron pot to the hearth into the ash. Reaching for two lengths of wood she glanced again at Dawson while she stoked the fire to life. Sosha ambled into the room and waited at the door. She turned to follow the dog, giving him a good rub and letting him outside. It was bitter cold, and the harsh winds continued blowing snow across the area between the house and barn, but at least the blizzard was over.

"No, Dawson you shouldn't get up. Haven!" Levi's voice found her with warning.

She ran back inside, where Dawson was staggering to his feet and swaying at the effort. That she'd managed to work his bloody buckskin clothing from him the evening before; he was wearing an old pair of her father's long underwear. "Dawson you must lie down. The bleeding may start again. Please."

He pushed against her with a groan, his eyes half open but he wasn't seeing her or her brother as they tried to stop him.

"Gotta...go." His voice was a whisper, leaving her to think he was confused as he headed for the small back door off the kitchen.

"Please, you cannot leave in such condition, and you're not even dressed for the cold." Haven tried again but he pulled free of both their grasps with a deep growl of pain. He struggled with the latch of the door, fighting against her to step outside. She couldn't imagine where he thought he was going, but he halted at the edge of the porch.

"Dawson, the bleeding will start. You must..." Haven stopped with Levi's chuckle behind her and

Dawson moaned in relief as he fumbled with the front of the long underwear and urinated from the porch.

She turned away to face her brother in humiliation, heat scalding her face as Dawson continued his sigh of relief. Good Lord. She supposed the fact he could get up was to his benefit and hers when it came to this, no matter they had been intimate.

Levi's continued smile flustered her even more, but she gave in to a grin at the situation.

"What day is it? How long?" Dawson's entire body shivered as he turned around and grabbed hold of her arm to steady himself, shivering, his naked chest holding gooseflesh.

"It's been four days. You were awake for a time yesterday evening." She held onto him as Levi shut the door behind them.

Dawson was making his way back to the pallet and she tugged at him. "No, we're gonna put you in my room so you have a real bed. I can sleep with James because we moved Levi into Papa's room a few weeks back."

"Don't wanna be no…trouble." He spoke as they made it into the room, and he took to the bed without further fuss. His breath was short as he held his side and scooted to a position of comfort, his body trembling in his efforts.

Haven moved his hand away from the dressed wound. "I'll have breakfast soon with willow bark tea for you and then I can redress the wounds."

Dawson nodded. "I'm just sore."

A fierce dread worked its way through her, and she sat on the edge of the bed. The impact he was now a wanted man didn't seem possible. "Dawson, I could send Levi for your brother, the sheriff. He will know what to do since maybe you're a fugitive."

Dawson shook his head. "Sawyer's no jurisdiction over the Cavalry or Federal Marshals, and they'll come too. I'll have to hide as soon as I can move better, leastwise until I can work out the details, find out the charges."

"But where will you go?" The reality of the situation hit her. He'd been coming back to make her his wife and now all she'd ever wanted lay open to unanswered questions. "There has to be a way. You saved me from the Dog Soldiers. Surely that has to be worth proving your innocence."

He groaned. "Not sure, depends on how things went after we left. I suspect Leaning Bear went further north, but there's the feathers of an arrow in my saddle bags that proves it was Dog Soldiers who got me…if nothing else."

"They've specific arrows?" Haven shook her head, not sure she understood.

He sucked in a deep breath. "The feathers are specific to tribes, and this one won't match the Cheyenne or Sioux from this area. Might be of some help."

"Oh, Dawson, I am sure you can explain this." She pleaded, unsure of any of the Cheyenne ways of things.

"Captain Simmons did this and he won't stop until…" He held her gaze, his deep blue eyes weary.

"There's the cave. No one would look there." She offered, "There are lanterns for warmth and the bedding where James sleeps while we work. It's a small stream for water inside."

James called from his room. "Haven?"

"Levi." She urged her brother to attend to James. He scampered out of the room with a roll of his eyes.

"That'll work for a time if I need a quick escape from here, but I can't make that right now." He let his hand rest on her thigh, his serious blue eyes studying her reaction.

"But you and I..." Her heart was broken at the options left to them.

He held his side, hugging her to his chest. "Nothing will change about that, once I've cleared me and Leaning Bear of this."

She jumped to her feet with a knock at the door, her first thought it could be soldiers as she scurried to the front of the house.

Levi waited at the door, shotgun in his hand, holding her gaze, but he set the weapon aside with a smile. "It's Mr. Wyatt."

Haven nodded, relief pouring through her. Surely, Wyatt had taken a chance on being seen by showing up, even in this storm, but maybe he would have ideas as to what was best for Dawson.

Levi eased the door open and Sosha flew ahead of her, yapping with effort as Dawson's brother stepped inside. Dusting himself of snow, Wyatt removed his hat, shuddering from the cold and tugging off his gloves.

"I hope I'm not imposing." His deep blue eyes, much like Dawson's, showed a hint of worry, though his voice held steady.

"Mr. Wyatt, did you bring candy?" James trotted closer, interrupting.

Wyatt's bearded face lit with a smile. "Sure did, but..." He reached into his coat and lifted a wrinkling of brown paper. "Only with your sister's permission."

Haven nodded, and James snatched the bag, making off with it.

"James, your manners." Haven scolded as she folded her arms, studying Dawson's brother, who chuckled at her youngest brother.

James' echoed thank you came from his room, Sosha disappearing with him.

Wyatt turned back to her and shucked his heavy coat and hung it on the hook by the door. "I'm hoping, since Viho's in your barn, I can find my brother here."

"He's been injured but he is doing much better. This way." Some part of her heart was relieved it was Wyatt McCade. Perhaps he would have news that might clear Dawson of any charges.

She led him down the hallway to her room, where Dawson was sitting up in bed, the blanket high across his chest and one hand underneath.

Wyatt leaned heavy against the door frame, neither man speaking at first. "Got yourself a nice likeness hanging on the wall outside the jail, making a mockery out of us men of law even in this hell of a blizzard."

Dawson muttered a curse and lowered the blanket, leaning his head back to catch his breath. He held his revolver; he must have gotten it from the top shelf of her wardrobe where it was placed out of James' reach.

Haven's heart sank at the idea of Dawson on Wanted posters. All in town would know him, and if this was true, what did it mean? Men were hanged for as much, and the thought scored pain right through her center, bile collecting in her throat.

Dawson's brows arched as he angled a sidelong glance at his brother. "What am I charged with?"

Wyatt stepped closer, folding his thick muscled arms. "For being behind the attack by Dog Soldiers. Seven counts on the Cavalry killed. Desertion—among other things they will think up."

Dawson shook his head with a sarcastic chuckle, holding his side, sweat forming along his brow. "Desertion? I'm no soldier…"

"Nope, but the Cavalry don't care much." Wyatt spat. "Sawyer's grasping at straws trying to find you a way out of this one but…it's not looking real good."

Dawson knocked his head against the headboard in frustration. "Didn't do this, didn't plan a cent of it."

"You hurt bad?" Wyatt angled a glance her way and faced Dawson again.

"Arrow went through. I'm mending."

"We got Cavalry all over town. Dodge and the women are worried." For the first time his brother sounded serious. "Gonna have to think hard on this one or you'll be paying hell, brother."

"You shouldn't have come. Anyone could have followed your trail." Dawson lifted his voice and groaned with his side.

"No one's out in this blizzard. Saloons are full of Cavalry, no one else much moving. It's all good, but we gotta figure what to do about you." Wyatt moved around to the other side of the bed to take the small chair. "Where's the Indian?"

"We parted before I made it here." Dawson shook his head. "He was gonna check the reservation first…I don't know, probably headed north."

"Well, can't stay long, but I brought you something." Wyatt reached into his trousers and tugged a pouch free, setting it on the bed, the coins inside jingling. "Might come in handy. Papers with an alias in case you need to disappear, which would be best when you can move."

Dawson held the pouch and set it back down. "I'll see what surfaces."

Wyatt lifted his brows. "You let the soldiers snag you and you'll end up swinging from a rope just your size."

A long moment held between Dawson and his brother before he spoke. "Take Viho with you to the ranch. Let Evan keep him mixed in with the other horses. He'll be a problem if discovered here. Sawyer know you're here?"

"Won't take him much to figure," Wyatt added, but then the brothers held quiet again. "I'll get Viho to the ranch, might make a run through the fort. See what the talk is, once this weather clears."

At first, Haven had thought turning himself in the best option but now she wasn't so sure. It didn't seem his brother was very sure of anything either, and he was a deputy.

She glanced at Dawson and back, interrupting. "Please, would you join us for breakfast."

"I'd be obliged for a small bundle to take along," Wyatt answered with a smile.

"I was just about to make our breakfast, I'll see to it." With a nod and a quick glance at Dawson, she turned from the room but halted outside as Wyatt spoke.

"Dawson, they're on a manhunt. Best you move from here when you can." His brother's rapid whispers held urgency.

Haven's breath caught in her throat and she had to

fight tears that blurred her vision and her thoughts.

"I need to find out about General Dodd. He took an arrow, but I know he could clear our charges," Dawson explained, his voice sure. "I've the feathers of the arrow that got me, proof enough it was Dog Soldiers."

"The general's alive, unconscious they say. Seven soldiers dead, a number of Cheyenne. And you and the Indian take off running." Wyatt's tone was sarcastic.

"We had little choice, Wyatt. Carl Bartley's the soldier who works the reservation. He's a good man, might be of some help." Dawson groaned in pain.

"I'll find him." Wyatt's voice sounded certain.

Haven scurried down the hallway to the stove, lost to think what she needed to pack for Wyatt. Dawson was accused of so many things, how would he ever be freed?

Moments later Wyatt returned to the kitchen, waiting as she bundled the food for him. "You, uh, need anything, send that brother of yours to the ranch. But if the Cavalry show here, it's best to say you've not seen Dawson at all."

She nodded, understanding, though dread plowed through her so profound the pain was real. "Please, if anything changes, can you send some kind of word?"

Wyatt's deep blue eyes held hers, and while he gave her a nod, she read the truth. Dawson was a fugitive and there wasn't going to be much that could be done. She followed his brother to the door and looked on as he rode his horse toward the McCade ranch with Viho in tow, leaving her a deep fear of what they all might be facing.

Chapter Twenty

The edge of darkness hung in the sky as Dawson moved with ease through the back streets of Cheyenne. Town was quiet, but no one would recognize him in the darkness if he managed to avoid Cavalry who lingered on corner streets. He stopped to catch his breath, having sent word by Levi that he'd meet his brothers in the one place no one would be looking—the jail.

It wasn't the wisest thing, and Haven had been upset to tears as he wasn't healed yet. It had taken some doing, but he'd convinced her he had to know more about what was going on.

His wound was mending, though it pained him and fatigue he hadn't expected took his wind. He'd rested too long, and even worse, put Haven and her brothers in more danger than he should have. So he'd meet with his brothers, weigh the best measure, and do what he needed to in order to hide, but it wouldn't be much longer he could remain at the homestead.

He scurried past the livery and across the street, having hidden Whistle, Levi's horse, outside of town. He adjusted the hat to his head, one he'd borrowed from Levi and tucked his hair underneath. That and the regular clothing wouldn't be fast to alarm anyone if he were spotted.

He lingered behind the jail, holding tight to the tomahawk he'd shoved into the back of his belt beneath

Haven's father's overcoat. The single lamp on the desk inside the jail office let him know his brothers were there. Otherwise the jail would've remained dark, something he and his brothers had used quite often over the years to say passage was safe.

He bent to the small window inside the storage closet of the jail, a room where little was kept save a broom, old files and broken chairs Sawyer refused to throw out. The window moved up, allowing him to struggle his large frame inside, making him hold his wound.

A click was the next sound he heard, that of Sawyer's revolver cocking across the room.

He gave a quick whistle, and Sawyer's whisper came as the closet door jerked open. "Federal Marshals rolled through here yesterday asking questions. Best you should've stayed hidden instead of planning this."

"Wanted to see if anything new had surfaced." Dawson glanced around as he stepped from the closet. The shutters to the two windows were closed and the lamp dim and low, but enough.

Sawyer shoved the revolver back into his holster and of all things gave him a pat to the shoulder. "You look almost normal dressed like that."

Dawson held his eldest brother's gaze. "Thought it might hide me a bit better."

His brother turned, moving to lean against his desk, his gray eyes dark. "We got soldiers a mile thick in town. You're not gonna prove much out there besides getting yourself captured if you don't lay low."

A tap at the door stopped them and Sawyer opened it, letting in Wyatt, Evan, and Brett.

"Got the damn Cavalry, drunk as hell most of

'em." Wyatt spat, dusting his shirt as he bolted the door behind the other two.

"The hell you say, Dawson?" Evan grabbed him in a bear hug. "You look sure enough like some cowpoke from Nebraska dressed like that, brother."

Dawson gave a groan at his belly, figuring Sawyer and Wyatt thinking it best not to tell their youngest brother all the details until now. "Good to see you too."

"Hey, take it easy, he's injured." Wyatt warned as he walked closer.

Dawson held his side, the searing pain always there.

"You healed?" It was Sawyer who studied him.

"Partly. But holding a fever at times." That was the partial truth. The fever he could handle but the outright searing pain made him double. The ride to town was something he'd pay for in a short time, by his figuring.

"This is not a day to be here in town. You be careful on your leaving." Brett folded his arms.

"You still look rather puny there, brother." Wyatt added, "But got a bit of color back in your face."

Dawson glanced at all of them. "Don't know much more than what I'm charged with but...not gonna be able to run, hurt like this. It was all I could do to make it here."

"Should've stayed your ass on that mountain." Wyatt shook his head and glanced at Sawyer.

"We're grasping at straws. Soldiers all over the place, the Federals lurking. Murder, adding up for the seven counts for soldiers killed. Eight if General Dodd dies." Sawyer shook his head. "I've telegrammed Rose's lawyer friend, Max Ferguson, in New York. He'll represent Leaning Bear as well, but he thinks surrender is best until the trial, to give you both a better chance."

"They won't believe him," Evan retorted, slamming himself down in one of the chairs.

"It's a gamble. Never met a soldier I trusted farther than I could toss him, but if the general survives, I believe you'll have a shot." Brett added his two bits. "You've a horse out there?"

Dawson nodded, having hidden Whistle well enough.

It was Wyatt who spoke then. "You need to get on that horse and ride. You seen the Indian?"

Dawson shook his head. "Nope, but I suspect he didn't go far." His brothers wouldn't understand it, the connection he had with the medicine man, but he'd been certain at times Leaning Bear was near and hadn't ridden north.

"What do you have in way of an alibi?" Sawyer leaned against the large desk, his brother's serious gray eyes hard.

Dawson ordered his thoughts. "If the general survives, he knows both Leaning Bear and me well enough to let them know we had no plans of the attack. Carl Bartley can put in a good word. Are the soldiers looking for Dancing Fox?"

Sawyer shook his head. "He's not on a Wanted poster, name's not mentioned."

Wyatt interrupted. "Dancing Fox is at the reservation, evidently not a concern, and that young soldier friend of yours, Bartley, ain't talking. Captain's made threats to his wife and little girl."

Dawson held his side tighter. That was no surprise as Simmons could be ruthless to his men. "The captain turned those soldiers on us. They all saw it and they all knew we didn't know anything. Roberts at the livery knows the captain has it in for us too. I've the arrow that went through me from the Dog Soldiers."

Sawyer ran a hand through his dark hair. "It'd be best you leave the homestead soon, Dawson. Things are heating up fast with the arrival of the Federals, though they moved on this afternoon. Leastwise, I've got word Hank Somersby may be tied to the case, and he's a fair man."

Dawson nodded, the Federal Marshal a close friend to his brother and someone they could trust.

Pain surged through his chest. "I'll be gone shortly." Though he had one more thing to take care of in town before he left.

Sawyer nodded. "It's best none of us know where you are for now."

"Either side of this fight, I lose." Dawson leaned back further in the chair. "You think that lawyer's right, surrender?"

The room held silent until Brett took off his hat, walking closer. "You hide for now. We need you to surface, we'll leave some signs around. You turn yourself in now, they'll hang ya."

"Surrender's a gamble but an option." Sawyer lifted his brows, shaking his head.

"This here isn't about the law anymore, brother. It's about survival. You ride the hell out of here and don't you look back." Wyatt poked a hard finger into Dawson's chest.

Sawyer bristled. "They find him with that alias and a pocket full of golden eagles, they'll toss the rope right there."

"He's gotta try something. Can't you lawmen do something more?" Evan stood and stomped across the room, shoving his hands in his trouser pockets.

Dawson studied them all. The sheriff brother who believed in the laws he served, the bounty hunter brother who'd break them all to keep him safe, and the horse-whispering brother who would fight anyone to prove his name clear. And then there was Brett, the one man who'd stood by the family and his mother since long before he could remember.

"Guess my path's set then." He said it with dread plowing through him. "But I'm asking you to all look out for Haven and her brothers until I can clear my name."

Sawyer shook his head. "You hide, and you damn well hide good. I'll get word to you if I need to, but don't show back in town or at the ranch."

Dawson gave Sawyer a nod and glanced at Wyatt, who walked closer.

"Go on with yourself. Don't need to hang around here much longer." Wyatt's strained voice filled the room.

Dawson stood and glanced at Brett and patted a hand across Evan's shoulder, his youngest brother not lifting his gaze. It was rare he'd seen any of his brothers fight tears, but the situation was grim at best. With another nod at them all, he turned and exited out the closet as he'd come in, but he wasn't heading out of town right away. There was a score to settle first.

The darkness of Cheyenne made it easy as he covered the back streets of town. It was risky, but he settled outside Whitney Scott's home, waiting and shivering in the bitter cold. The fancy little house at the end of town had cost more than the damn bank itself but was dark with the night. One of the men that protected Scott, the one called Pete, sat on the porch, guarding. Easing himself onto the porch, Dawson made a quick lunge and wrapped both his arms around Pete's neck, cutting off his air.

The man struggled and eased into unconsciousness and went limp. Dawson laid him on the porch and turned the knob, slipping inside. Listening to the quiet, he moved up the stairs to the top floor and stopped outside the room where Scott slept alone from what he could tell.

Easing into the room, he lifted the tomahawk from the belt in his trousers and held it high as he approached the sleeping man. Without hesitation, he slapped a hand over Scott's mouth, holding the tomahawk to his neck. Scott struggled, but then froze.

"Your life will be short if you ever lay hands on her or her brothers again." Dawson kept the man from talking by pressing harder on his mouth. "Understand?"

Scott gave a nervous series of nods, making no sound.

With that, Dawson slammed his tomahawk into the center of the fancy headboard and held the banker's gaze a moment more then escaped the room quickly. Leaving the weapon wasn't the wisest of things, but he had several more and he wanted Scott to have no doubts he'd do more should he ever bother Haven or her brothers again.

Pete still lay where he'd been, out cold on the porch. Dawson glanced up and down the way, the street clear. With one more glance behind him, he took off for the woods where he'd tied Levi's horse.

The animal gave a soft whinny as he lifted the reins. Mounting up, he turned the horse and headed in the direction of the homestead once more.

Risking things to meet his brothers was one thing, but threatening Scott had settled him little. No matter, now he wouldn't have to worry as much about Haven's dealings with the man in his absence, which would be soon. In fact, it was time he found a way to tell Haven goodbye for now, something he'd been putting off for as long as he could.

****

Haven closed the curtain, having looked on as both her brothers followed Thorn on his old mule up into the mountains. Levi and James both rode Whistle and would return home late afternoon the next day, this being common when the weather was good. They'd often gone with the old man to help him tan the hides he'd brought in off his lines. With the weather having turned a bit warmer, how could she resist their excitement to see the bearskin he'd claimed to take off a grizzly?

It might be that old Thorn had gotten a grizzly, but his tall tales were sometimes just that, stories. She giggled and let the curtain go, having sent Sosha along for protection.

She went to the hearth and added another log to the fire and put away the dishes from supper. Dawson had made his way outside for mending the barn door, which had been loosened by the heavy winds of the storm. The thought he was doing better gave her reason for momentary panic at times, and without a doubt he'd have to leave soon, though his recent trip to town had set him back. He'd slept for several days on his return, fatigued and sore. But her concern held with the fact he still carried a fever, something he played down when she asked.

With the boys away and Dawson busy working, she poured the hot water from the hearth to the small metal tub in her bedroom. She lifted her hair, twisting it together and pinning it atop her head.

She bent and dipped the rag into the steaming tub and stood again to squeeze the warmth of the water over her shoulders, moaning as the tendrils of heat dripped over her body. She always ran the boys outside when she wanted to bathe, but now she could enjoy her warm bath without interruption. She did the same again and washed her face and neck, the trickle of warm water lacing down her body.

Sensing movement, she continued, knowing Dawson was there.

He didn't say anything at first but pushed the door wider, stepping inside, his deep blue eyes holding her gaze. He was barefoot, wearing just his buckskin trousers as he did when he stayed inside at night, always polite enough to step out of his moccasins just inside the door and hang his shirt when he wasn't wearing it. "Should've knocked."

"I suppose that's not necessary between us." She reached for the towel and held it closer, though her body dripped the warm water, her center quivering at his extended view. It should've given her pause as he watched, but somehow it didn't. Neither did it when he took the cloth from her hand and stepped behind her to place its warmth across her back. She shuddered at his touch.

"I've been watching you all these days, so

beautiful..." His deep voice vibrated through her, warming her so far down inside herself, her body tightened. He moved the cloth with a slow, searing tenderness and leaned to place his lips against the dampness of her shoulder.

"You're not well." She whispered, and it took all her might to do so.

With that he stretched his arms about her and relieved her of the towel, laying it over the back of the chair and using the cloth to wash her upper chest and breasts, teasing her pert nipples.

She sucked in a deep breath, and he whispered in Cheyenne and she translated. "A flower in the storm."

He chuckled and corrected her in English. "A flower in winter."

He hadn't been well enough for this and she wasn't sure it was a good idea at this time, though her body heated to deceive her. His lips touched her shoulder and the rag slipped lower, covering her there, where she already felt him. Taking an even breath was impossible as he washed her intimately, the cloth dropping and his fingers finding her in a slow massage of pressure.

"Dawson..." She whispered. How could she do this here, standing in a pool of water and dripping wet?

"Shhh. Lean against me." His words touched her as well as his fingers, easing her into a relaxed state of bliss and her body moved of its own accord. Lord, but his touch turned her inside out, making her want what he would bring. She closed her eyes as the intensity grew and she flexed to encourage his touch, the first shudder reaching her and his Cheyenne words following. "Come to me...my Heartsong..."

His command, in words he was teaching her, fired

her center and heat spread through her as she rested against the warmth of his naked chest, sighing through the tender strokes of release. His whispers continued as he eased her to the bed, her feet leaving a trail of trickled water. She tried to protest as he nudged her back to the bedding, pushing her legs open and falling to his knees before her.

"Dawson..." Heat flushed through her body, open to him, nothing between them.

"I will have this..." He spoke to her in Cheyenne once more and his warm mouth seared her, his tongue rasping across the pert tenderness of her. She flung herself back gripping hard at the sheets, not understanding what was happening. Was this what a man desired of a woman, that she too would find the bliss of loving? It was all so confusing, but this was Dawson, and this was her heart. She let her legs fall further open, wanting to give him all of her, wanting to feel his touch in any way it came to her, right or wrong.

It had been more than a month since they had been together intimately, and her courses had come and gone, but he was here now, and her body betrayed her as he manipulated her tender flesh. She moaned, as it was all so foreign that a man would do this with his mouth. Her mother had explained the usual way a man loved a woman, but she hadn't spoken of this. Oh my, never this...she moaned...

Dawson eased one of her legs over his shoulder and she gasped and tangled her hands into his hair, twisting and fighting what was to come. Wanting it, but uncertain her body would break again as she drew tighter...

He pressed his fingers inside her and without

warning the blissful spasms took her. She cried out in Cheyenne, because they were his words, because they were him and because she was his...

She opened her eyes, Dawson standing before her naked. Unsure how he'd lost his buckskins so fast, she lifted her brows, having no more words as he drew her up to stand beside him.

"I didn't know of that..." It was all she could do to whisper and let the heat ride her cheeks.

"You liked it?" He took her hand and backed up to the chair and sat, pulling her astride his knees, his erection full and a warning she'd hurt again, but somehow, she didn't care.

"Yes." She answered his question. She had liked it, his mouth on her.

He smiled and drew her down, moaning as he filled her little by little. She bit her bottom lip, surprised the pain was there but not as bad as it had been the first time. It was awkward for a moment, finding how to sit along him and the fullness caused a deep shrill of pleasure to pulse through her.

"You aren't fully...well." She glanced at his wound, which remained charred and scabbed.

"Well enough..." He flexed his hips, searing her deeper.

She gasped at the stretch and he moved her on him again before she could decide it was comfort or pain. His hands trembled at her hips, making her wonder at the fragileness of a man when he took a woman, his eyes glazed and serious and his large body rigid.

"Takes some getting used to..." She held to his shoulders, almost grimacing with the continued motion.

"Let your body relax, I've got you..." He lifted her

with both hands and eased her down again closing his eyes with a groan of deep satisfaction.

It surprised her when he spoke, opening his eyes again. "Your courses came?"

Now her face heated, and she dropped her gaze as she whispered, "Yes."

"When I'm free of all this...I'd like it if they didn't come." He kissed her lips and pulled on the bottom one, making her smile.

"A child?" She kissed him back. "Always dreamt of my own children."

"A child, time with you, holding you each night in my arms, kissing...and this." He tugged her down again and urged her continued rocking motion against him. He closed his eyes, leaning further back in the old chair and flexed his hips in no seeming hurry. And the flow of them as one began to grow, slow and burning and consuming as any fire.

Haven arched in a small shudder and he watched her as she took the motion, certain angles tugging pleasure from inside her. He traced his hands up and released her hair, playing his fingers through it, resting his callused hands along her breasts. He bent and took his mouth to one and she watched as he drew hard on the nipple. She gasped at the clench of her own body to his thickness, the need for her release close.

He chanted in Cheyenne, words she knew well as his fingers made their way to the core of her, rubbing the pert flesh there several times. "Come to me...Come to me."

She hovered at the edge of bliss whispering his name as her entire body went tight, his moans mingling with her cries.

Haven collapsed across his chest unsure her breath would come and she held him as his large body shuddered into her so hard, she wasn't certain where she ended, and he began. He lifted her, separating their union, and laid her in the bed, still resting between her thighs. She traced her fingers through his long dark hair, massaged the heavy muscles of his shoulders and back until the softness of his breathing let her know he slept.

And she held him until the dimly lit lamp at her bedside had burned itself out, leaving her in the darkness with the weight of his body proof enough he was hers, if only for now.

Chapter Twenty-One

A thump at the door startled Dawson from deep slumber. He jolted upright, holding a finger to his lips to keep Haven quiet, both of them naked. He eased up and lifted his buckskin trousers and stepped into them without bothering with the laces.

Haven pulled her nightdress over her naked body, causing him a lift of his brows at the view of her. The sound had been a thump, something knocking at the porch, and he eased himself toward the revolver, lifting it and moving to the curtain at the front window. He waited a breath of seconds, cocked the revolver and held it before him as he lifted the bar and slung open the front door, leaving it wide. Nothing but the wind whirled across him as he stepped onto the porch and glanced around the homestead.

"Look." Haven stepped outside, pointing. "Someone left us meat, skinned and smoked."

On the left side of the porch, leaning against the cabin, was a side of elk hindquarter.

Dawson studied the forest to the right of the house where the wind whipped the shrubs and cottonwoods in a whisper of stillness he knew well.

"Who would have done this?" She turned to him.

"Leaning Bear." He had no doubts as he scanned around them for any sign, but the medicine man never showed until he was ready.

"But I thought Leaning Bear was going north." Haven touched him, startling him away from random thoughts of why the Indian would have remained so close.

"When we parted, he turned back to warn the tribe, but…he's here." He scanned the forest again, knowing he wouldn't find a trace of the Cheyenne, the man able to disappear with a whisper of wind. But more than that, it was a sign it was time for him to leave. He was better, though his wound still pained deep inside his belly as he suspected it always would.

He lifted the hindquarter and carried it inside, following Haven, who shivered from the chill. She closed the door behind him and looked on as he set the meat on the counter.

"Perhaps he stayed to make sure you were all right." Her words held a hint of sadness, though she didn't lift her gaze to look at him.

"When I go, I'll find him, but it'll still be a few days." He touched her blushing cheek with his palm. Damn, he loved her, and leaving her was cutting the heart right out of his chest.

"I know you must go…" Her words were a soft whisper.

He kissed her forehead, remembering the night before. Bathing her, tasting her and burying himself deep inside her had been worth the bit of setback he felt this morning. Her sweet cries of pleasure had ridden through him but lying with her naked for the night had given him a peace he'd never known.

As much as he didn't want to leave her, it was time, though he had to get Viho from the ranch. He'd send Levi for the animal when he returned and in the next few days make his departure. Leaning Bear providing the elk was his first call. He wouldn't have to find the Cheyenne; the medicine man would find him soon enough.

She spoke again, this time her voice cracking. "I've never been good at saying goodbye, so I won't, not ever…"

He drew her to him, holding her as tight as he dared. "I don't know what's gonna happen, Haven, but I will come back to you…no matter what."

Tears streaked her face though she brushed them away. "I will be waiting. Always."

He placed his hand on hers. "It will still be a few days more. If you're not opposed, I'd like to send Levi to return Viho. Not sure if the soldiers were concerned about Dancing Fox, but it seems he's still on the reservation, and Leaning Bear and I might find a few answers there."

She angled a glance at him as he sat in the chair and tugged the leather ties and feather from his hair, letting it fall around his shoulders.

"I need you to cut my hair, not too short." He said it with reservation, shaking his head. "And maybe with that and this beard, I can keep out of sight a bit more easily."

"But…" She shook her head.

"It's best." He touched the length of his hair, uncertain he could let her do it.

Haven opened the drawer of the counter, lifting scissors and laying them on the table. "I'll need to smooth it with my brush."

He looked on as she trotted to her room and returned carrying the silver-plated brush and lifting a segment of his hair. He'd not cut his hair since the death of his father so long ago.

Haven lifted the scissors. "I cut the boys' hair all the time, but…"

"Just do it." Hell, if she didn't start, he might think of something better than changing his appearance.

She drew up a segment and began talking to him as she clipped, letting his hair fall around the chair.

He needed to warn her about things since he wouldn't be close. "When you go to town to pay Scott, go by the mercantile and tell Dodge to send me a couple of trousers, suspenders, and button shirts such as Wyatt wears. Boots too, and a dark hat. And you give the payment for Scott to Sawyer to pay for you."

She shook her head, holding the clippers high. "I am paying on my own to face Mr. Scott. I shouldn't do anything out of the ordinary to alert anyone in town of anything different."

He knew her determination well enough. "Then you take Levi and Sosha with you, but my guess is you will have little trouble out of him."

"You had words with him again?" Her voice dropped off as she gave him a sidelong glance.

"Not so much words, but…a warning of sorts. Just pay him and get out of there," he explained and edged his fingers through his hair that now touched his neckline. If it hadn't been she was present, he might have cursed at the atrocity.

"It's not too short. Shorter than Sawyer's and not as neatly trimmed as Wyatt's." She clipped around his ears. "You look like your brothers."

Well, he didn't find that amusing and folded his arms across his chest with a grump of defeat. He rubbed the edge of the stubble covering his face. He'd never worn a beard for long, never liked the few days it took to come in full, itchy and hot in the summer, but perhaps now with the cold it was added protection.

Haven bent before him, snipping bangs into place and edging the clippers ever closer. Still in her night dress, her breasts rode against the fabric as she used the brush to smooth the strands she cut.

"There you have it." She made another quick snip above his right eye and laid down the scissors, and handing him the mirror she'd brought with the brush.

He shook his head, staring into the reflection of his father. "Been a long time."

"I think you are very handsome, though I will miss the length, too." She grabbed the brush and scissors. "I'll start breakfast."

Dawson stood and gathered her against him. "Your brothers will be a while yet. Why don't we skip the breakfast part?" As he talked, he led her by the hand to the hallway toward her room.

"You will be hungry later, Dawson McCade," she teased, though she gasped as he wrapped his arms around her, easing her gown off as they met her bed.

"I'm a wanted man, an outlaw, but only you could bring me to my knees." He whispered in a growl, burying his face in her neck.

She giggled as he fumbled with his trousers. "And all I have to do is say the word and Sosha would eat you."

"I think Sosha likes me." He chuckled as he pressed her back to the bed, falling in place between her thighs. She sighed with his deep entry and in no time cried out her pleasure against his shoulder, taking him with her, where the worries of freeing his name mattered little and the wolf inside him howled in triumph.

****

Dawson opened his eyes, blinking back his confusion as James shook him. "Soldiers. Dawson, soldiers are coming."

The boy scurried away, running into Haven's room in a flurry of fear.

Dawson jumped up and pulled his shirt over his long underwear and stepped into his trousers and moccasins, hurrying to half tie the laces. He lifted his newly made tomahawk and revolver and shoved them into his belt. Haven and Levi had left earlier for the trip into town, taking Sosha with them, and he must have dozed again after she kissed him. *Son of a bitch!*

He wasn't sure what James was doing, but he eased into the living area to lift the curtain. Cavalry were indeed riding up on the homestead in formation, around eight from his quick count. He turned back around as there was little time.

"James, what're you doing?" The boy was still scrambling around Haven's room in a flurry and stuttered all over his words when he came into the hallway.

"I gotta hide it all and you gotta run to the cave like Haven said." The little boy was near tears lugging a heavy velvet bag.

"Come on, we're gonna leave." He tugged the boy toward the back door, helping him into his coat and toboggan as he bobbled the heavy sack he carried. Turning for the back door, he opened it, startled by Thorn, who caused him to draw the tomahawk without thought.

"'Tis a wise thing ya go now." The old man cackled in a rhyme as James ran past them both, into the woods behind the house.

"James, wait. James!" Dawson gave a harsh whisper not understanding what the boy had even been talking about, though it dawned on him the bag must have held the gold Haven kept hidden.

"I'll go after the boy and stall the soldiers." Thorn shoved him ahead. "Now ya go. No time to chat 'bout it, man."

The old man was right, but what if the soldiers hurt him or James? Dawson nodded, the chill catching him off guard, though. There was no time for his buffalo robe at this point. It was too dangerous to run for one of the horses, so he took off on foot, making his way off trail toward the cave. If nothing else, he could disappear there for a time. He ran, quiet and brisk through the drifts of cold snow and winds, ignoring the pain in his side.

Time seemed to race faster than he could move, and he stopped, long from the homestead. He leaned against a large frozen cottonwood to catch his breath, holding his side. Glancing down, his tunic held a blood stain the size of his fist, where his escape had opened the wound.

It was well enough the soldiers had no dogs, or he wouldn't have found escape. He took off on a trot again and eased to a faster run, holding his side. If he could cross the river and make it to the cave, he could cover his tracks before he pushed himself inside.

Hesitating at the river, he had to reach hard inside himself to step into the freezing rush of water. He hissed, losing his breath as he waded deeper, and then the unforgiving water hit his side, making him shriek in pain.

He fought to keep his stance and with one last effort pulled himself out of the water and fell into the hard-packed snow on the other side. His breath was short, and he fought the numbing cold that threatened to take his mind. It wasn't far to the small mouth of the cave, but he had to circle around and mark up the snow with tracks back to the water. Forcing himself to do so, he stopped at the edge and scooted a pile of frozen snow into the river and did the same in several places.

They would track him, but ahead was where the mouth of the cave hid. He fell at the opening and dug with his hands at the hard-packed snow and pushed his way through the opening with a groan of effort. He fell, hitting the damp dirt of the cave below. The searing pain in his side plagued him with nausea, and he gagged as he rolled to his knees. He had to close the opening and light the small lantern for heat.

The cave was dark, and he could see little as he tried to gain his footing. All he had was his tomahawk and wet revolver should the soldiers find him. He fought to light the lantern with fingers so cold he couldn't feel them. So damn tired, and this would be his life, hiding and on the run, though he suspected he could remain here for a time.

Grabbing the lamp and crawling to one side of the cave, he lay down across the makeshift bed Haven kept for James. Rest. Just for a minute and he could get out of his wet clothes, check his wound and clean his gun. Just as soon as…nausea hit him again and he fell back, closing his eyes and shuddering in the cold. Starting a fire at this point would be dangerous, so he drew the lamp closer and studied the flame until the covers about him warmed him. He closed his eyes, just rest for…a short time…

****

Josie darted ahead of Levi's horse as Haven rode alongside her brother into Cheyenne, Sosha running ahead of them both. She'd warned her brother it would be best for them to go to the mercantile first for supplies as usual and for a chance to speak with Dawson's mother about the supplies he needed

"Lot of soldiers," Levi whispered as he stopped Whistle and dismounted outside the store.

She nodded. "Best you stay with the horses. Keep a mind to Sosha."

"All right." He grabbed Josie by the reins, as Haven climbed the stairs and stepped inside the mercantile, her heart racing. Ambling to the shelves of dry goods, she picked up small bags of sugar and flour and made her way to the front, each weighing her down as she set them on the counter for her purchase.

Behind the desk, Dodge spoke with a woman who pointed to a tea set inside a catalog. Dodge glanced up, catching Haven's gaze as she continued to talk to the woman and then leaned back to call to the storage area. "Mr. Lester can help you with this order, so I can take care of another customer. Burt?"

The older man turned the corner from the storage room and nodded when Dodge handed him the paper and pencil. Without any hesitation, Dodge had Haven by the elbow leading her into the back.

"How is he? The boys said he was doing well," his mother asked, the concern in her eyes pleading.

"He's mending. The wound has remained closed and the fevers are less." Haven glanced around them, cautious.

"Is there anything you need?" Dodge touched her hand.

"Only the flour and sugar. But Dawson wanted…regular clothing, boots and a hat," Haven explained.

"I've worried so about him." Dodge grabbed items from the shelves before them.

"Truly he is much better, Mrs. McCade." Haven held her gaze.

"Please, it's Dodge," she said as she lifted down denim trousers. "I suspected you might come in first of the month for your banking, but I must tell you…"

Haven waited as Dodge hesitated, her expression of heavy concern.

"I know Dawson was here in town to meet with his brothers days ago. But…his plight is now worse. Haven, Mr. Scott was found dead the next morning." Dodge whispered, glancing behind her and back.

Haven fought for breath. "Mr. Scott, but how…"

"Dawson's tomahawk was slammed into the headboard where Mr. Scott was found." Dodge shook her head. "They have added this to his charges."

"But…he wouldn't do such a thing, I know he wouldn't." A dread of pain rushed through Haven't chest and she swayed.

Dodge caught her by the arm. "It's one of his tomahawks and my guess is he warned the man, but you and I both know he didn't kill Mr. Scott. You must let him know and send him away until we can find a way out of all this. He's done none of what he's been charged. I won't say Mr. Scott didn't have it coming, but my son didn't do it."

"Oh, Dodge…" Haven's eyes rimmed with tears she couldn't control though she hurried to wipe them. "I'll get the payment on the homestead made, and Levi and I will see Dawson on his way."

Dodge nodded, handing her the bag of supplies. "There's a revolver and small case of bullets inside here should either of you need it."

"Yes, and he would like a dark hat." Haven's heart raced at the idea of the need for a weapon.

Dodge lifted a dark brown hat from the mix of hats on the shelf behind her. "He never has liked to wear a hat with that mop of long hair."

"Well," Haven juggled the hat and bag of items. "He had me cut his hair, and he's grown a beard."

Dodge angled her wide blue eyes toward Haven again. "Did he now? That would be a sight for me to see, but it's best he stays in hiding until we get all this figured. The Cavalry are thick as flies around here, and I have no doubts even the Federal Marshals are watching everything."

"I'm so frightened for him." Haven thought perhaps she had spoken too much, but as ashamed as she was to think it, paying on the homestead should be much easier with Mr. Scott…dead.

"Haven, should the need be, you're to keep you and your brothers safe, regardless what happens to Dawson. You must promise." Dodge's voice cracked as she spoke.

Haven swallowed the lump in her throat with a nod. "He was to come back after the negotiations, after he resigned his position and…"

"He resigned his position?" Dodge tilted her head in surprised.

Haven spoke the truth of it. "Yes. He asked me to become his wife."

To her surprise, a smile eased across Dodge's face. "Well, I knew he'd lost that heart to you when you were at the ranch. You hang on to that, and we'll get him freed of this, I promise you that."

Haven shook her head. "I suppose I'd rather see Mr. Scott a hundred times over than have Dawson face any of this."

The older woman closed her hand around Haven's. "Be on your way and be careful. If you need anything, you ask."

Making her way back to Levi, Haven had him strap the packages on Josie. Levi added the sacks of flour and sugar to his own horse, calling for Sosha, who came running from around the edge of the mercantile porch.

"Levi, you must listen to me. Mrs. McCade said Mr. Scott was found dead and…isn't sure but that they may blame it on Dawson." She took Josie by the reins as he led his horse alongside her.

Levi shook his head. "Dawson wouldn't do such a thing!"

Haven held her brother's gaze. "No, but his tomahawk was nearby. You and I both know he wouldn't do it, but I suppose others wouldn't see it the same. Leastwise, making homestead payments might be a bit easier."

"What's Dawson's family gonna do?" Her brother followed as she pulled her coat tighter. It was rare she kept anything from Levi, but his face frowned in worry she hadn't expected.

"I'm not sure." It was the truth she spoke as they passed the sheriff's office and her pulse all but stopped. Outside on the wall, posted for all was the image of Dawson and Leaning Bear.

She'd left Dawson sleeping this morning, kissing his forehead before she and Levi left. He'd stirred and held her a long moment, whispering in Cheyenne for her to be careful and to go and return on different paths, which she would do.

She stopped outside the bank and glanced at Levi. "Well, I suppose this won't take long now."

"Leastwise someone gave Mr. Scott what he deserved," Levi whispered.

"Levi." Haven scolded but couldn't blame her brother for his thoughts. "I'll be right back."

Inside, she loosened her coat and tugged free the pouch of gold dust that would make the current payment on the homestead.

"Yes, Miss Oakley, I believe your payment on the homestead is due." The clerk pushed his glasses back, took the pouch and took a moment to weigh the gold, swift and efficient.

"Thank you." Haven waited as he measured and figured her payment onto a tablet.

"Seems just right. Thank you, Ma'am." The clerk didn't look up as he jotted the payment weight and nodded for the next customer.

The simple satisfaction made Haven smile as she turned to leave the bank, though the worry of Dawson now hung like a boulder across her shoulders. She hadn't been sure how to react to the banker, given he had known how Mr. Scott had treated her. On the porch she glanced toward Levi, who was playing with Sosha, tossing a stick for the dog to return.

"Might I have a word, Miss Oakley?" Haven turned, finding a uniformed soldier on the porch steps.

She glanced again at her brother and back to the soldier. "Yes."

The soldier removed his hat, stepping closer. "I am sorry if I startled you, Ma'am, but I'm Lieutenant Bartley. I work with Dawson on the reservations..."

Panic took Haven, and she shook her head. She could speak to no one about Dawson. "I'm sorry, I know nothing of Mr. McCade."

"Wait, please. I...wanted to warn you in case...you'd seen him, Ma'am. Soldiers were heading out to search just a short time ago, toward your homestead." The young man's eyes were serious, as far as Haven could tell.

"I thank you, kindly, Sir, but I have no inkling of Mr. McCade's whereabouts." Haven turned, taking the stairs off the porch and mounting up on Josie. It took all the strength she had not to look again at the soldier. Her heart raced as she contemplated how long it would take her to get back home. What if Dawson had met with capture, and what if James was harmed? *Oh, dear God, please...*

She urged Josie ahead, her brother following on Whistle and rushing to keep up as Sosha trailed ahead.

"Haven, what's wrong?" Levi caught up to her outside of town, and she stopped Josie. "Levi, the Cavalry are headed to the homestead for Dawson. Listen to me. I'm taking Sosha, and I want you to ride as hard as you can to the McCade ranch and bring Viho. If the Cavalry haven't arrived yet, Dawson can make his escape. But you have to ride hard, Levi, and be careful."

He nodded his understanding and took off in the direction of the McCade ranch, Sosha whining as he disappeared over the rise.

"Come, Sosha." She called the dog and took Josie to a gallop, the chill knocking against her racing heart.

The ride was long, and the wind was brisk as she pushed Josie to race across terrain. It was certain the Cavalry would be ahead of her and her hopes were that Dawson and James had managed to hide.

Chapter Twenty-Two

Haven's heart panicked as she arrived at the homestead. Cavalry horses lined the fences outside the corral. Inside the barn, the old cow bellowed at her arrival as she took her gaze to Thorn, who sat against the porch, a soldier holding a gun on him and a streak of blood across his forehead.

Haven dismounted, dropping Josie's reins, and grabbed Sosha, who rumbled a growl. "Sosha. Come." The dog tossed his ears back but followed her, baring his teeth as she arrived at the porch where Captain Simmons stood, eyeing her with a knowing grin.

Haven's heart pounded inside her chest with worry of James, but she ignored the captain. "Thorn, where's James?" She climbed the steps and Captain Simmons stepped to block her way to the old man.

She jerked from the captain's grasp. "Thorn?"

"Oh, the boy is well, Haven, dear. He'll be under his bed, a might afraid of the soldiers." Thorn didn't struggle, though he wasn't focusing on her as he held his head.

Haven tried to walk by the captain, who caught her again. "Let me go. My brother's in there and you have no right."

He shoved her back toward Thorn. "Not your brother we're looking for, Missy." He turned to the soldier standing over Thorn. "If the dog moves, shoot it."

Haven narrowed her gaze, jerking free and grabbing Sosha by the collar to tie him on the far end of the porch past Thorn. She returned, intent on entering her home for James.

The captain stood to block the door, whispering in spite of the soldier who held Thorn at gunpoint. "If we find what we are looking for, you'll hang right alongside him for giving aid to a fugitive, missy, unless of course, you'd like to make a little deal ahead of time. I save you and you save me, so to speak."

She didn't skip a beat, though heat rose to her cheeks at what the man was insinuating. "I've no idea what you are speaking of, Sir, and your forwardness is out of line."

It occurred to her it was better that she down play who Dawson was to her and that she hadn't seen him. She could only hope he'd made his way to the cave or had hidden elsewhere, but he still wasn't well and that was more of a worry.

The soldiers inside the home were knocking over shelves, furniture and tossing items from drawers. Inside her room, hidden away, were the gold nuggets and dust she kept secret, but that was not as much a worry as getting to James, who gave a shrill scream.

"James, no!" She pushed against the captain who whipped her around to him, grasping at her breast, the soldiers on the porch laughing as she tried to free herself.

A tall skinny soldier made his way to the porch, carrying James around the middle, her brother fighting. "This be what you're a-huntin', Sir?"

Captain Simmons laughed as Haven struggled

away. "Ah, that's a bit smaller than the one I want."

James shrieked, screaming as Haven took him away from the soldier in spite of the captain trying to keep her back. "Leave him be!"

She held James as he wept and clung so tight to her she could scarcely breathe. "It's all right, James. Shhhhh."

She wasn't sure what James might have been through, but Thorn had become quiet where he sat wearing Dawson's buffalo robe, in an effort to throw the soldiers off from finding anything belonging to Dawson.

"Thorn?" She touched his brow and the old man stirred, smiling at her as he held his head. "Hang on, Thorn, and we'll get you to bed to rest."

Haven stood with James and faced the captain as two more soldiers exited the house, not having located Dawson, to her relief.

"All clear, Captain, even the barn." One of the soldiers reported, eyeing her closely.

"Now, Captain Simmons, if you and your men are done frightening children, beating an old man, and tearing our home apart, I'll bid you good day, sir." She waited, worried about Levi arriving with Viho.

"My men will be watching. Best, if you haven't seen McCade, you don't." The captain tipped his hat and left the porch to her surprise. She lingered as each mounted up and followed Captain Simmons in formation toward the fort.

She tugged Thorn to his feet, James still clinging to her, the old man shivering in spite of the thick coat that belonged to Dawson. "It's all right, Thorn, come on."

"James, the soldiers are gone. Did they hurt you?"

Haven looked at her brother's eyes, rubbing a hand across his dark locks.

"I...I ran and waked up Dawson and I got the gold and I hid it." Her brother stuttered. "And Thorn found me...and I hid under the bed."

The gold—she'd not thought again about the stash under the floorboards under her bed. "The gold, James, where did you hide it?"

He wiped his eyes and glanced at Thorn. "Papa's place where he can watch it. And I put my pretty rocks on it. I tried to be brave, Haven, but the soldiers are mean, and I couldn't help but cry. You won't tell Levi I'm a 'fraidy cat, will you?"

Haven breathed a sigh of relief and hugged him to her. "Oh, you're the bravest boy I know, and I won't tell Levi a thing."

"McCade made off in time, though I fear he'll be a might frozen." It was Thorn who spoke then, opening his eyes.

"He'll find his way, Thorn. Thank you for caring for James." Haven wiped the blood from Thorn's forehead. The gash wasn't deep but badly swollen. "James, I need to untie Sosha and get Josie stalled. Can you sit with Thorn? He needs you right now because you're so brave." She was surprised when James took Thorn's wrinkled hand in his own.

She turned, near tears and stepped to end of the porch, taking the rope from Sosha and praising the dog. "Good boy, Sosha." She scanned the horizon that held no more sign of the soldiers, though her heart hurt at the worry about Dawson. She guessed he'd gone to the cave, but now what should she do? She held the frozen horizon, uttering a whispered prayer that no matter what, Dawson was hidden, and Levi would return soon with Viho.

****

The frigid air filled the darkness as Dawson followed Thorn through the heavy woods outside the cave. Hiding had proven little yet allowed him time to dry his clothing and nurse his bleeding side. There was pain, but nothing he couldn't live with as he and the old trapper made their way toward Haven's homestead.

Dawson leaned against a tree to catch his breath and waited outside the house to make sure things were quiet.

"Best to ya, that you make a care of your wound and head north to escape the soldiers." Thorn held his gaze in the darkness. "The troops'll return to seek ya out should ya stay any time."

He nodded. "I've no intentions of bringing further danger to Haven or her brothers. I'll take my leave within a day or so." As he said it, he wasn't certain he had the ability to escape far, given the soldiers and the fact the reservations were being guarded. He glanced at the porch, the flame of a single lamp adding a slight glow inside the quiet of the cabin.

"I'll be on the trail, let ya know should soldiers amble near, aye." The old man stepped ahead and turned back. "'Tis safe to go on. Haven will see to your wound."

Dawson looked on as Thorn disappeared into the woods. With a deep breath, he made his way to the porch and whispered with a slight knock. "Haven?"

The bar lifted with a squeak and Haven stepped out into the cold and wrapped her arms about him. "Oh, Dawson...I was so worried."

He held her a moment and pushed them inside, closing the door. "Thorn let me know it was safe to return for a bit."

She helped him with his buffalo robe and frowned. "Your wound."

He glanced at his bloodstained tunic. "Doesn't pain much. Everyone's sleepin'?"

"Yes, for hours now." She gathered dressings from the cabinet and turned to him, waiting as he lifted the tunic over his head, laying it aside.

"I've more yarrow, but the wound must heal from the inside out. I sent Thorn when the soldiers didn't return." She pushed a chair out and he sat.

She touched the wound to clean it with warm water and he fought not to grimace.

"It's not bleeding further, but you must rest or..." She stopped as he touched her arm, holding her gaze. Damn, he loved her, and he hadn't wanted this, to live on the run.

"I'll rest for a time, but I need to head to town, see what Sawyer or Wyatt might have figured, though my guess is little." He tried. "I've gotta find a way..."

She shook her head. "No, you mustn't. Town's full of soldiers."

"If I stay, I put you and your brothers in more danger than myself." He rubbed her hand in his.

"Dawson, I was in town, it's how I knew the soldiers were coming to find you. Lieutenant Bartley stopped me to let me know, but I didn't act as if I knew of you. When I got here Thorn was injured and James frightened of the soldiers." Her voice cracked, and he took her into his arms and held her onto his lap.

"I had to run, but Thorn went after James, which

was best at the time." He shook his head. "Leastwise Levi got Viho here, and I'm obliged."

"Levi has kept him hidden in the barn for now," she added, though her voice broke.

"Shhhh...It's time, Haven. I've got to leave here, but I can't hide in the cave all the time...or run for the full of my life..." He smoothed her hair and inhaled the lilac as she clung to him.

"Wait..." She went to the cupboard again and returned to his lap. "Levi found this on the porch."

Dawson's pulse raced as he took the two hawk feathers, tied with beads. "When?"

She shrugged. "Yesterday morning, from the night before, I suppose. It's from Leaning Bear, isn't it?"

He nodded.

"But what's it mean?" She asked as her fingers smoothed across one of the feathers and she gripped the bright beads.

"He's here. Tomorrow we'll have to head out, probably the middle of the night, but I've gotta go to town first." His medicine man brother had indeed been watching things, but a jaunt to town would let him know more of what might be going on.

"But your wound, Dawson—you're still not strong enough and your body needs to heal." She held him and in spite of his discomfort his body reacted to her fingers tracing the scars of his dance with the sun. He kissed her, taking the full of her mouth.

Reluctantly, he let go. "I have to go, Haven, do what I can to clear myself of this, so I can come back here to you." He placed his hand to her cheek and kissed her pouting lips again with effort until she sighed and pulled back.

"I'm so afraid for you," she whispered.

He lifted her chin to make her look at him. "I'm gonna do all I can, Haven, to come back here to you, but you have to keep saying you haven't seen me. Your brothers too. Just go about things normal and should you need anything, you go to the ranch."

She nodded, the pool of tears gathering in her eyes ripping through his center.

"Hey, none of that…you and me…we're gonna get through this…" He took her face in his hands. "You're my Heartsong, Haven, and no one will take that from either of us. But I won't leave here without I see your beautiful smile."

And even with all the unknowns that held between them, she held his gaze and let her lips curl into the smile that warmed his heart. That alone gave him the courage he needed to plan the escape to free his name—though he had little idea of just how he might do that.

****

Dawson held Viho steady as the whistle drifting across the wind found him. That of Leaning Bear's night call as if a flurry of birds nesting had been disturbed. He waited, holding the horse as a brisk wind stirred the trees. The Indian appeared on his mount, settling his gaze on Dawson.

"Image of father with cut hair." The medicine man spoke in Cheyenne, making light of him. Sometimes he forgot that Leaning Bear had once known his father.

"Better than looking like myself right now." With that, he tightened the saddle on Viho, glancing at the porch where Haven waited. Her tears would be the death of him, but she was more than enough reason for the fight ahead of them both.

The medicine man drew closer and spoke in English. "You are healed?"

He nodded, though he was far from well when it came down to it. "You never went north."

The Indian smiled. "Eyes on you for keep out of trouble."

"You'll pay hell trying to do that." Dawson smirked and took the knife from his saddle bags to make the trade. "Never gonna get that damn knife back for good, am I?"

The medicine man shoved the small weapon into his belt and handed him the bear claw necklace. "Walk as free men, get to keep knife once more in this life."

Dawson smiled, dressed in his heavy buckskin tunic and trousers, moccasins, and the leather strap with beads and feathers that Haven had made for him. The chances they would walk free of charges seemed far off and both held it in their gaze.

The Cheyenne studied him. "You have said farewell to Woman with Frying Pan?"

He tugged Viho around. "And what would you know about it anyway?"

"Know where man finds comfort before long ride." The Indian chuckled.

"Never figured you a spy." Dawson scolded, though it was apparent the medicine man had been watching, and he'd spent the night before in Haven's bed. He'd made love to her slow and consuming, not ever wanting to let her go, but he'd held her long into the night just as he'd held her tears at his leaving. He drew his mind away. "My brothers have nothing much to help. Think the trail north is clear?"

Leaning Bear's dark hair whipped in the wind.

"Clear where we ride."

A certain dread filled him with a deep longing about leaving Haven behind, but he'd never find his way back to her if he didn't clear his name. There were no choices here for him or his Cheyenne brother, and he turned to Haven once more. Taking the steps two at a time, he took her in his arms.

"I'll pray every hour." She held him, though she was brave in not allowing tears.

He let his gaze roam over her. The light from the cabin dabbed tendrils of her hair a golden orange. His fingers strayed through it as he held her. "Never wanted to cause you this kind of pain."

She brushed her tears back, offering him a brave face. "You will return to me, Dawson McCade, or I will never forgive you."

He traced a finger across her chin. "I will be back as soon as I can."

"I know you will." And of all things she smiled.

Damn, how he loved her, so much so it hurt to know what he'd brought to her. "You go to the ranch if you have any trouble." He kissed her, pushing back the thoughts of how long he might be away from her. "I love you…Haven."

"And I you." Her whispered words held him, and he let her go, the force of it almost bringing him to his knees.

"You're surrounded! Stand where you are!" The voice arrived a second before mounted Cavalry with weapons encircled the porch.

Dawson froze, not turning but holding Haven's gaze. No doubt it was Captain Simmons. His pulse raced. He glanced behind him as soldiers placed rifles to him and Leaning Bear, there being no escape. He'd let his damn guard down and risked too much in returning, putting Haven and her family in danger.

Haven gripped his tunic with a whisper of fear. "Dawson?"

"No matter what happens, get yourself and your brothers to the ranch. You'll be safe there. Take your gold and the cow and stay there. I mean it." He whispered again, "You are my Heartsong now and always."

"I won't let them take you." She held to him, but the soldiers climbed the stairs and took him by the arms, one with a rifle aimed at his head, the other shoving Haven aside.

"Leave her be." Dawson shoved ahead to Haven's defense, but the butt end of the rifle hit him hard across the forehead, knocking him senseless, blood dripping across his cheek.

Haven screamed as he fought to keep the soldiers from her, the rifle crashing across his back as the men fought to subdue him, dragging him from the porch. He fell to his knees and one of the men kicked him across his belly. He doubled over holding his wound, unable to take his next breath with the searing pain.

"No, please! He's injured." Haven screamed, though they held her back. "Dawson, don't fight. Please, he's hurt." Behind her, from inside the house, Sosha barked, and Haven shouted. "Stay inside, Levi! Don't come out."

Dawson fought to keep from passing out as Captain Simmons walked closer.

"It's a funny thing a man's want of a woman. Knew right where to find you, McCade. It was only a matter of time." The captain chuckled.

Dawson struggled to take in air, glancing up at the man who'd caused this entire thing.

"Tie and mount 'em up." The captain hissed. "My, my, but you have been rather elusive, McCade. Guess you got all cleaned up to hang. You almost look civilized."

The soldiers drew Dawson's hands together and tied them before him as he held the captain's evil gaze.

"Well, you'll get what's coming to ya. You and the Indian both." The captain spat. "Bringing in Dog Soldiers, injuring and killing some of my men, including the general, who may not survive."

"He didn't do any of this, and you know that!" Haven fought against the soldiers holding her and made it to the bottom of the porch steps in spite of them. "You cannot hang innocent men. I was rescued from Dog Soldiers by Dawson McCade, and he nearly lost his life in doing so."

The captain stepped closer to her and put a tentative hand on her cheek. "Be careful, little Missy. Harboring an outlaw might wind up with you hanging right beside him."

Dawson crashed against the soldiers holding him, making for the captain in a rage, but a rifle cracked down across his shoulders again, sending him to his knees once more.

"Kill the Indian!" The captain shouted, and Dawson stopped the fight.

Across the way, the soldier holding Leaning Bear placed a pistol to his temple. "Just give me the word, Sir."

The captain jerked Dawson up by his tunic. "You

don't behave on this little jaunt and I'll have a bullet sent through his head quicker than you can say 'dead.' Mount him up." The blow to his belly from the captain's fist took what breath Dawson had held, and he coughed and sputtered. He was shoved to Viho, his hands tied to the saddle horn. It was done. They were both dead men.

"Dawson…" Haven shrieked from where a soldier held her back.

He shook his head, trying to stay on the horse with the pain coursing through his middle, but he spoke to Haven in the Cheyenne he'd been teaching her. "Go to the ranch. Don't come back here."

The medicine man spoke to him in his native tongue as they were driven toward the fort. "Be still for now. We will find a way."

He gave a nod, though the soldier leading Leaning Bear smacked the butt of his rifle against the Indian's thigh, and he said no more. Ahead of them were the miles to the fort, and the death of cold as they awaited their fate. Fighting the pain in his side, he focused on the darkened horizon, thinking of Haven and knowing he would do whatever it took to get back to her.

Chapter Twenty-Three

Haven urged Josie up the rise, the McCade ranch spread below them for miles. She'd watched as the soldiers had ridden away with Dawson and Leaning Bear, crushing the very breath from her. After, she'd wiped her tears, gathered their belongings and taken her brothers from the homestead, stopping for the hidden gold at her father's grave. The remainder of the gold from their father would stay buried nearby where no one would ever suspect.

Levi had been distraught over leaving the claim, though he rode Whistle, tugging along the cow, Buttercup, behind him. And packed on the old cow was a crate holding the three chickens, which Levi had covered to keep the wind from them. James snuggled across her lap and slept for most of the ride bundled in a blanket. The weather was frigid, and with the McCade home in her sights, and worried about Dawson, tears blurred Haven's vision in relief.

It was shy of dawn, but the large house held a bit of light, as two men exited the barn to meet them.

The first nodded. "Morning, ma'am. A might early."

She remembered Billy as he smiled, the hand that kept the horses saddled for the family as needed. He'd been very kind to her when James was ill, letting her know he'd take care of Josie.

"Please, I need to see Dodge." She let James down, and he wobbled to keep his footing as she dismounted behind him.

"I'll let Evan know." Billy nodded, glancing toward the house. She hoped there would be no more questions. She wasn't sure what the family had spoken of Dawson to the hands that worked the ranch, and she needed Dodge or Dawson's brothers.

"I'll get your animals brushed down and fed." The other gentleman began taking their belongings to the porch with Levi's help.

James moseyed over to the steps and leaned against the railing, his eyes closed as his tiny body swayed and shivered in the cold.

Haven turned from her younger brother as Sawyer bolted through the door with Dodge behind him, and Evan bringing up the rear, struggling into his boots.

"What happened?" Sawyer buttoned his shirt as Dodge ran to her.

Haven began to explain, not expecting her emotions as she tried. "He was with Leaning Bear and the soldiers came. They beat them both and that captain threatened to hang me along with them. Dawson told me to come here. He could hardly ride, and his side was bleeding again. Oh, Dodge."

"I'll head out to town and warn Wyatt." Evan was off to the barn, running past her as her eyes blurred in tears. Her heart raced, and her body shivered in the frigid cold she'd ignored.

It was then the warmth of Dodge's arms spread around her and offered her what hadn't been available to her since her mother's death. With that she let go of her tears, her heart racing and her mind easing away from her body as if she were watching the whole thing from afar. She was going to faint, the fear and the darkness swallowing her whole.

****

Haven startled awake, not remembering where she was until Doc Tess spoke to her, a gentle hand on her arm.

"It's all right. You're at the ranch. You passed out, I'm afraid." Dodge sat down on the bed beside her, the mattress giving little.

She eased up, rubbing her aching temple, dizzy and trying to remember what on earth had happened. "My brothers…"

She coughed, and Tess lifted a tin cup to her lips. She took the cup, remembering the quick travel to the ranch and then passing out near the porch. She sipped the warm tea.

"You gave us quite a scare. Your brothers are downstairs having breakfast." Dodge glanced at the door as Mei Ling ambled into the room. The petite Chinese woman placed a plate of scrambled eggs, bacon and a biscuit on the table by the bed.

"And Dawson?" Haven's heart all but stopped at remembering the night before. Lord, but the soldiers had taken him, and his side had been bleeding as they beat him. All because he'd tried to protect her.

Dodge let out a deep breath. "Sawyer wired for assistance, a good attorney friend of Rose's in New York may be of help, and Wyatt took off for the fort to see what's going to happen."

"Must eat, gather strength back." Mei Ling lingered a moment offering a smile and turning for the door again.

"I'm sorry. I didn't mean to be so much trouble. I'm not sure what happened, perhaps my worry for Dawson." Haven tried to explain in her uncertainty.

Tess and Dodge exchanged glances and Dawson's mother laid a hand across hers, holding her gaze with a kind smile.

"Haven," Tess began, the physician hesitant at first. "You passed out because you hadn't eaten, and because you're...with child."

Haven dropped her gaze in already knowing the truth of it. Her courses had come the once, and it hadn't seemed the full course. And her lack of appetite she'd begun to think was from morning sickness, though she'd tried her best to ignore all the truths of it. It was a long moment before she glanced between them. "I had suspected as much."

Tess touched her shoulder again. "All is well, though, I believe, and you need to eat and make sure to drink a lot of water and milk during the day."

Haven glanced at the plate of food which had been enticing until now. What must they all think of her with this news? "I suppose you all find disappointment in my circumstances, but I hold no regrets in carrying Dawson's child no matter what anyone thinks of me. But my brothers...mustn't know for now."

Dodge shook her head, giving her hand a squeeze. "Nonsense. You'll find no such judgment here, though at this point, I think this is best kept with us women."

Haven fought tears given the kindness. "We're to be married, but...now."

Dodge rubbed a hand along her arm. "And you will still be married, once we figure all this out."

Haven whispered. "I do love him, Dodge...no

matter what anyone would think."

Dodge used the napkin from the tray to dab at her cheeks, drying the tears that continued. "Never seen him care for someone so much as you, so don't fret over any of this until we know more."

Down the hallway a baby began to cry, and Tess grabbed her breasts, each with a hand. "I believe Zachariah is hungry. Rest and eat, and if you feel well you are fine to do as you please."

Haven forced a whisper. "Thank you, Doctor."

Dodge lifted the plate of food and set it before her. "A child before marriage is very frightening, Haven, but I once found myself in the same situation, not that a woman ever has to tell. It's best Dawson sent you to us."

"I worry little of myself, only for my brothers and Dawson. But they hurt him, and he isn't healed fully. He fought harder because the soldiers shoved me." She sighed, taking a deep breath.

Dodge lifted the fork and stabbed at the eggs. "This is far from over. They're not going to hang my son, and they're not going to hang you. You are going to eat and spend the afternoon helping in the kitchen. It'll keep your mind from things. Zane is spending time with your brothers." Dodge lifted the fork to her, and she took it and ate, holding the edge of the plate.

"Now," Dodge said. "Is there anything more that needs to be checked at your homestead? I could send Evan."

"No, that isn't necessary. We brought everything of importance." She glanced around and across the room. Even the bag full of gold was there. "It might only be Thorn who worries of us, but I left him a note where he'd know to look."

Dodge chuckled. "How on earth is Thorn doing these days? He hasn't been to town in a while."

"The soldiers that first looked for Dawson hit him, but he is better, off to his traps from what he said." Haven stirred the food around her plate. "He's been very kind to look after us since Papa died."

"Thorn's been around these parts since I was a young woman, it seems. But, Haven, I know about the claim your father had and that it is still yielding. I suspect all is hidden well." Dodge lifted her light brows.

Haven looked at her for a long moment. "Yes, things remain hidden."

"Come down to the kitchen and we'll make all these boys some cookies in a bit." Dodge stood and turned back to her at the doorway.

"I'd like that." Haven tried for a smile as Dodge slipped from the room.

Haven began on her breakfast again, still shocked at the truth she was carrying a child. Dawson's child. A child she'd dreamt she would one day have.

But the dread of worry found her over Dawson. Would he be tried? And if his family couldn't find a way to help him, would he hang? No, she would not sit here and think the worst. She brushed away more tears with her hands.

But of her condition. She'd known it could happen and she'd suspected it had, but now she knew for sure. Her parents would have been hurt by this, and should the word get out, she'd be shunned in town, to say the least. But she'd made her own choices with no regrets where it came to her love for Dawson. He'd made her a woman, his woman, and she would do all she could to help with clearing his name.

She glanced at the window, where in spite of the bitter cold the morning sun was peeking through. And somewhere out there was Dawson, and all she could wonder was if he was warm and fed. She touched her low belly, muttering a prayer in his Cheyenne words and gathering her determination, got out of bed and headed to the kitchen.

****

Dawson jolted against the irons, shackled to one of the wagons in the elements. He must have dozed, even in spite of the cold and pain. Sleep was dangerous for a man when it was frigid, and worse when losing blood. He glanced around him, his left eye so swollen it didn't open, but there was nothing much to see, save the inside walls of the fort which bustled with activity as usual.

Leaning Bear, tied to the wagon wheel opposite him, whispered in Cheyenne. "Be still, you are weak."

He growled as he adjusted his position, sticky blood lacing the front of his tunic. It would do him no good his wound had opened again. It was no doubt infected, giving him to shiver, perspiration settling across his brow.

"What're they sayin'?" He groaned, the soreness in his back and shoulders unrelenting. Leaning Bear had suffered the same beatings, even though he hadn't resisted. What a hell of a predicament.

"No words. Soldiers quiet." His friend spoke in a whisper not looking at him again.

Dawson gave a nod. Shackled, there was little chance of escape, that was for sure, and his wrists already carried torn and blistered skin. The one chance either of them had left was if his sheriff brother might have a little something up his sleeve, but even that was doubtful.

Leaning Bear glanced behind them. "Think not much trial but hang for sure."

Dawson doubled with the pain in his belly he couldn't relieve with touch. "Ahhhhh, I think they'll want to make it more elaborate, showy." So much for a chance to clear their names of charges. They were dead men with no doubt.

He thought of Haven. He'd promised her a future, and now it wasn't that he would have the chance to follow through. The terror on her face as the soldiers had beaten him was enough to haunt him still, but he had to think she had gone to the ranch for safety.

"Not talk, best." Leaning Bear gave a grunt of satisfaction.

"They won't be asking much." Dawson tried to move to a more comfortable position, but the shackles didn't allow it.

The soldier guarding them turned. "You two aren't supposed to be talking, now keep it quiet."

The medicine man angled a glance at the soldier. "Soldiers think all Cheyenne liars? You think this too? Cheyenne think this of most soldiers."

"I said to keep it quiet." The soldier saluted as the captain and a group of soldiers approached from the Cavalry office.

The Indian kept speaking. "I think all soldiers fear Captain Simmons, do captain's work, only think like captain think. Not think for self."

The soldier glared and then stood at attention once more.

The wind made Dawson shiver, though he lifted his gaze to the captain as Leaning Bear chuckled with his questions to the soldier.

"Not all fun and games now is it, Indian Agent?" Captain Simmons nodded to one of the soldiers. "Let them have a bit of water, no food. Got word from Washington. Your trial and hanging will take place in Cheyenne only because this fort hasn't a room big enough."

Dawson grimaced but said nothing as the captain bent closer. "That bounty hunter brother of yours is here. I'll send him out to chat with you, but any funny business and I'll have all three of you shot on command. He's no jurisdiction here. Best you warn him. Got yourself some real trouble now with bringing on that attack and leaving soldiers dead." The captain stood again, and Dawson saw it coming. The captain's boot found his middle and knocked the breath from him, leaving him groaning.

"Mighty cold out here. Think I'll go warm up a bit by the fire." Simmons stepped away, speaking to the guard. "I'll send his brother. Keep your weapon poised, and you will shoot him on the spot if he tries anything."

"Yes, Sir." The soldier took up his rifle.

Dawson struggled for breath and righted himself as the captain walked away and a group of three soldiers followed Wyatt out to them. That his brother was here meant Haven had made it to the safety of the ranch, if he were guessing. Wyatt had no gun belt, and it was surprising the captain had allowed the visit at all.

The lead soldier spoke to Wyatt. "You've ten minutes. Any funny business and we've orders to shoot."

Wyatt narrowed his gaze on the man. "I find nothing about this business funny." He leaned closer and all of a sudden yelled. "Boo!"

The soldier jumped back in fright, all the others with him, making Wyatt chuckle as he bent before Dawson. "Looks like they done a number on you both. They cut your hair for ya?"

Dawson looked on as his brother opened a small pack with him. "Haven?"

"At the house, scared out of her mind. Brought her brothers, the dog, the horses and the cow too, for good measure." Wyatt lifted his tunic to view the wound to his belly. "And three chickens near half frozen."

He winced, the wound bloody, sticky and red all around. "It's best she doesn't go back there to her homestead for now."

Wyatt nodded. "This looks angry, brother."

"Took a good beating, opened it again." He leaned his head back in a growl as Wyatt cleaned and dressed the wound and then added ointment to his eye and cheek with his smallest finger. Hell, it had been a long time since his older brother had cared for him as such. Memories from long ago flooded his thoughts. A time when he'd been beaten up by some older boys, and Wyatt had cleaned him up and then taught him how to fight back.

"Well, I'll leave this." Wyatt tucked the tin of ointment into Dawson's tunic pocket. "Maybe the medicine man here can help you. You hurt?" He turned to Leaning Bear as he tugged Dawson's tunic back in place.

"No hurt." Leaning Bear nodded, unable to move with his shackles.

Wyatt glanced behind him at the soldiers lurking close. "They've cleaned me out, so I've nothing to offer. They've been mandated you be brought to Cheyenne for trial, most likely due to Scott being found dead. They'll pin that one on you too. Too bad you can't thank the bastard for that, but there's question of a military trial."

Dawson groaned at the pain in his side. "I'm civilian employed, both of us."

His brother shook his head. "They know that too, but Sawyer's wiring Washington."

The moment held between them. No one needed to say much more on a full military trial, those were most often for the guilty to prove their innocence if it came down to it.

"Say the word, brother, and I'll gather a posse of outlaws to break down this whole fort..." His brother glared hard, his deep blue eyes holding a fear he'd never seen before.

"Live a life on the run? Been hiding long enough." He spoke it, thinking with the pain in his side he'd never make the trip back to Cheyenne.

"Sawyer's got that attorney Max Ferguson on the way here to represent you both. Keep your heads about you. I'll be seein' ya back to Cheyenne." Wyatt stood and studied him. "You look like Father with that short hair, brother. Damn."

"Wyatt. Thanks." He watched as the soldiers led his brother away.

The medicine man leaned his head back against the wagon wheel. "Trial in Cheyenne, change nothing. White man's trial, white man's town."

Dawson held his gaze, blinking with his bad eye.

"White or not, nothing much good's gonna come our way. But living on the run wasn't gonna lead us nowhere but back to this."

The medicine man gave a small grunt in agreement and closed his eyes. "Die by rope, die by hunger or gun, die by damned cold, of little choice. I vote gun, quicker, cold not so quick. Rope too long, hunger…belly has not always known food."

Dawson smiled. Leaning Bear and his humor was at least worth that. He closed his eyes, fighting a bout of nausea that he wasn't sure was from his wound or hunger. He let his mind drift back to Haven. At least with his family, he wouldn't have to worry about her and the safety of her brothers. And right now, that was all that mattered as he began his morning chant.

Chapter Twenty-Four

The frigid wind blew hard across the prairie, digging into his flesh. Dawson shivered the full length of his body, his teeth chattering with force. He fought to keep himself on Viho as he and Leaning Bear were escorted toward Cheyenne. They'd been woken before dawn and beaten by a group of soldiers for the bruises that would impress the townsfolk as they arrived in Cheyenne. He'd rolled into a ball, not letting them have his belly, though his back now held a constant ache. Leaning Bear had suffered, though, and now rode his horse hunched over the saddle horn with broken ribs.

Another couple of notches on Captain Simmons' gun, he supposed. Wyatt rode ahead of the formation, having been warned as well. Earlier he'd spotted Lieutenant Carl Bartley among the men escorting the procession to Cheyenne, though the soldier hadn't been allowed to speak to him either.

Dawson glanced at his belly, the wound still seeping blood and leaving him weak. He needed food and so did the medicine man, whose horse fell behind. The sun settled behind gray skies, threatening weather, and the winds were frigid and harsh. Well, that would be the death of him should rain or snow begin. He was so damn cold now he could scarcely feel his fingers and shuddered hard in the shackles, recognizing the landscape and the outskirts of Cheyenne.

Captain Simmons cantered his horse closer, a smirk crossing his face as he yelled for the entourage to halt, his large black horse snorting its disapproval. "Take 'em down, Sergeant. They can walk the next few miles to town."

"Aye, Sir." With that, two soldiers pulled them from their mounts with force. Dawson fought to keep his stance, but Leaning Bear collapsed to his knees, spitting blood with a hard cough. The soldiers remounted and took up the same pace, he and Leaning Bear parallel to each other, tethered to ropes tied to their shackled hands. He held tight to his rope to keep up as did the medicine man, whose struggle was far worse, his breath rasping with the exertion, the scowl of pain across his face.

The road moved by them little by little until Leaning Bear fell, hanging tight, to be dragged along, the soldiers ordered by the captain not to stop. Dawson wavered that direction and tugged hard on the rope to slow the horse dragging his friend, his shackled wrists on fire. With effort, the medicine man made it to his feet, bobbling along once more.

The streets of Cheyenne were damp with recent rains as they arrived, and Dawson lost track of Wyatt in the commotion. Mud caked their moccasins as they struggled to keep steady with the horses, people lining the edge of the streets in Cheyenne to watch the spectacle.

Leaning Bear spoke in Cheyenne, the medicine man's voice weak. "Hold eyes to no shame before your people."

He glanced around him at the faces, most of whom he could name. His family was here, or at least, his brothers would be, along with Brett. He met the gazes of those watching—they weren't his people any more than the Dog Soldiers who had put an arrow through him, or the Cheyenne he'd been sworn to protect. Cheated by all sides, he belonged to no one save himself, and the man who walked beside him whom he called brother.

Arriving outside the jail, there on the wall were the Wanted posters of him and Leaning Bear, Sawyer having no choice but to place them there.

"Good likeness." The medicine man spoke in Cheyenne and held a chuckle under wraps. Always the humor. But Leaning Bear's pain was evident, and he coughed, spitting blood to the ground once more.

The rumble from the townsfolk carried enough for him to hear the remarks of those who would just as soon they both hang. Not many in the settled towns could appreciate that a Cheyenne just wanted to live in peace, hunt and feed his family. Not any of them would understand a white man who worked hard to make that happen.

He lifted his gaze, catching a glimpse of Sawyer standing at the jail, keys in his hand, Wyatt and Brett alongside him. He didn't see Evan, but beside the others was Hank Somersby, Federal Marshal, a man Sawyer had called friend for years. He held the man's gaze wondering at his presence but gave a slight nod.

He stayed steady on his feet, though Leaning Bear swayed as he coughed again. There was little he could do to help his friend, but the Indian remained standing when men on the sidelines spat at him.

"Damn Indian, let 'em hang." A shout rose above the noise.

Another echoed from behind the crowd. "The only good Indian is a dead one. String 'em up now!"

Then the comments he'd expected erupted from various places around them. "Indian lover. Killed the banker too."

He was so numb from the cold he'd long since forgotten the pain in his belly that caused sharp aches through his back. Never mind he'd hang. If not, he'd die of this wound that took what energy he had left. He closed his eyes for a long moment, fatigue and hunger plaguing him and leaving him with a lingering of nausea.

He opened his eyes once more, and there she was. Haven. All that was good left in his world. He held her gaze, but the crowd shifted, and he lost her, his heart shattering into ten thousand tiny pieces at the tears streaking her face.

The soldier jerked harder on his rope, and he followed Leaning Bear ahead of him as they passed his brothers and Brett, entering the jail office. Once inside, he was shoved into one of the cells in the back, though he was surprised his shackled hands were released. Pain crept up his arms as the shackles were lifted, his hands numb and his wrists raw with remaining bloodied blisters.

It was the same for Leaning Bear who rubbed his wrists, shivering as both their cell doors were slammed in unison. The warmth of the jail enveloped him, making him shudder hard at the heat. He'd have to thank his brother later for the old stove in the corner burning strong.

He tucked his hands under the arms of his tunic as the soldiers, all but one, filed out. And then for the next few moments, he struggled to listen to what was being said in the office, though he could hear little.

He turned as Leaning Bear collapsed on the cot, easing himself back and closing his eyes as he held his chest. He'd taken much worse from the soldiers because he was Cheyenne, and would take even more as the days progressed, he suspected.

Dawson turned a circle, knowing the jail offered no escape, not that he'd take to it anyway. His brother had built this one himself, and there was no way out. Somewhere inside him the wolf howled in discontent, caged and beaten.

Then the captain's voice rose above all. "You men are his brothers and have no jurisdiction where the Cavalry are commanded. We will keep men on this jail to avoid the prisoners escaping."

"Captain, I will remind you these men are not military, and right now, I am in charge here, so we will be playing by my rules." The Federal Marshal, Hank Somersby's familiar voice echoed. "Sawyer McCade is sheriff, a man of great integrity, and I am allowing him the charge of his jail as usual. You may put your soldiers on guard outside the building as you see fit, Captain, but my job here is to make sure these men are treated properly while being detained."

"I'll be messaging Washington over this matter." The captain's tone jumped a notch.

"I *am* Washington, Sir," Somersby shouted. "It's absurd how these men have already been mistreated, and from this point, they will be treated with respect. Do I make myself clear?"

The captain said nothing, his heavy boots clomping outside, leaving silence.

"Thanks, Hank, leastwise they'll be harassed less." Sawyer spoke, his frustration evident as he and the Marshal entered the cell area, followed by Wyatt.

"You men need medical attention. We'll send for the doctor." Hank spoke further to him. "It's good to see you, Dawson, although not under such circumstance."

What was he to say to that? Hank would be here for the purpose of keeping order to things, and to see that rules were followed, but he really had no jurisdiction over the Cavalry. "I can appreciate what you have to do, Hank."

The Federal Marshal turned to Wyatt. "You get that wife of yours in here to see them."

"She's already on the way." Wyatt turned back to him and Leaning Bear, his face bruised. "Tried to stop the soldiers this morning."

"Wasn't much you could do." Dawson glanced at Leaning Bear, who lay with his eyes closed.

Sawyer lifted the hat from his head, fiddling with it in his fingers. "The weather's kept Max Ferguson and they aren't likely to delay a trial at this point."

"I figured." Dawson took a deep breath, holding his side.

"How's your wound?" Wyatt asked, leaning against the wall, glancing at his bloody tunic.

He shook his head. The wound was worse, but he wouldn't alarm his family. He supposed he was tired, hungry, and sore from the beatings more than anything. "I'm making it."

"Son of a bitch! Not so sure how things are gonna go here, brother." Sawyer whispered a growl through his teeth. "I suppose the captain took those fake credentials off you as well?"

He nodded. "And the money."

"Shit." Wyatt narrowed his gaze. "We can still fight that, Sawyer."

"With what? Getting you arrested too?" Sawyer folded his arms and cursed. "He and Leaning Bear ran, seven counts of murdered soldiers at the attack, a tomahawk found by Scott's corpse. Treason and murder are not taken lightly, or have you both forgotten? And…" Sawyer stopped, forcing a deep breath and exhaling.

Dawson grabbed the bars, nausea hitting him again. "And?"

Sawyer walked a complete circle and turned. "You got nothing, brother, save General Dodd making it and the talk in the saloons is circulating the story about the soldier…from before."

"That was self-defense, Sawyer, and all know it," Dawson roared, the wolf inside him restless. "I wasn't held responsible for that."

"Not gonna matter much right now. They'll pull it all back up." Sawyer held his gaze. "Damn, if you don't look like Father with your hair short."

Wyatt shook his head. "That's double jeopardy. He can't be tried for the same crime twice."

"No one forgets those things." Sawyer shook his head. "You get to the crowd, and I've wires to send to Washington."

Tess whirled in, carrying her bag. "The streets are filled with people. Wyatt, you be careful out there."

His brother kissed her cheek. "Just gonna get the streets cleared."

Tess glanced at Dawson, her mouth dropping open.

"You look so different with your hair short."

"See to him first, got busted ribs." He nodded toward Leaning Bear as Wyatt opened both cells. Tess made her way to the medicine man, who sat up for her with a groan of great effort.

Dodge trotted in, surprise crossing her face. She placed a palm to Dawson's bearded cheek and whispered, "I might as well have John standing here before me once more."

He supposed his haircut was shocking to her and his brothers. "Keep wondering what he would do."

"He'd tell you to fight to clear your name." His mother spoke sure. "This is preposterous, and I will not stand here and let anything happen to either of you."

Dawson's gaze drifted as Haven entered, easing closer, a hesitant smile crossing her lips. His breath held at her beauty, as always.

"Dodge, I'll need a little help to get his ribs wrapped, several are broken." Tess called from where she had the medicine man sitting up. "Leaning Bear, the dressing will need to be a bit tight, but you have to prop up when you sleep and let this heal. Is there any blood?"

The Indian nodded. "It is as you say."

"Then you may not move at all once I get you wrapped." She explained, "Your lung has been punctured. It may heal with little movement and allowing the bleeding to stop."

Dawson turned his gaze back to Haven, reaching his tentative fingers to touch her hair. "Are you all right?"

She smiled, though tears rimmed her eyes. "I'm well and the boys, too. Your wound?"

"I'm fine." He lied, but touching her once more, his heart pained at all he couldn't do to make this right for her.

She placed a palm on his brow. "You've fever in spite of the cold."

He took her hand and kissed her palm. "You deserve none of this."

Leaning Bear groaned as Tess and Dodge eased him back, stuffing a pillow behind him. "Thank you, Medicine Woman and kind mother."

"You're welcome, Leaning Bear. I've willow bark tea as well." Tess spoke to him, touching his cheek.

The Indian closed his eyes.

"I'll start the tea for both of them." Dodge made her exit as Wyatt closed Leaning Bear's cell door, the echo a reminder of their confinement.

Tess entered Dawson's cell and touched his tunic, lifting it. "Let's get your shirt off and have a look."

He tugged the damp tunic over his head, not taking his gaze from Haven. He wanted to hold her, take her in his arms and make everything right. He wanted to lose himself in the hint of lilac that held him now, and he wanted to fall into her for all of his days, forgetting all he was facing.

"Dawson, this is very angry." Tess pressed along his side until he groaned, his breath short. The pain coursed through his middle and settled in his back, making him take a step back from them both.

"It'll need a good cleaning. Lie down." Doc Tess dug in her bag as he settled on the cot and leaned back. The wound was festered. He'd known that from the fever, but there'd been little he could do.

Tess pressed the wound near his back, and he

yelped. "Dawson, this will need surgery, but I suppose for the time being I can at least clean it up and make you more comfortable. This cannot wait for long, Wyatt."

"They aren't going to let him have a surgery right now, Doc." Wyatt stepped closer, his face distorting at the sight of the wound which was still charred but held a ring of angry red, leaking pus and dark blood.

"Dawson, I'll give you Laudanum. This must surely pain you constantly," Tess offered.

"No." Dawson shook his head. "Gotta keep my head clear for all this. I'm good."

"I'll be back shortly." With that his bounty hunter brother headed out to the streets of Cheyenne.

"Willow bark will help, and I'll rest." Dawson shook his head. He hadn't been aware he'd need surgery but given the pain he wasn't surprised.

"Well, if nothing else, the salve will help with moving and not let the scab dry, so it can drain. Leastwise, we might get you more comfortable." The doctor, his sister-in-law, was the best there was at her work, but it wasn't like he could go through a surgery and still stand up in court.

He fought against the groans he wanted to give with her manipulation of the wound.

"It's all right." Haven brushed his bangs back and whispered. "Levi has enjoyed working alongside Zane, and James has spent time playing with Nicholas and Ella. Your family has been very kind to us, but I was so worried about you."

He bit his bottom lip trying to focus on her words, her voice and the lilac smell of her hair. And as she continued to tell him things, he let his mind wander to the first time he'd touched her, kissing her in the meadow. It had been the sweetest kiss of his life with because innocence. That and making love with her, tenderly, as she'd cried out her first pleasures clinging to him. He'd never seen anything more beautiful than that.

Her tender fingers continued to brush along his hair, calming the wolf inside and taking away the hurt that would be the death of him. In no time, it was over, and he sat up to take the tea from Dodge, thinking maybe he'd even dozed for a moment or two. He sipped the warm dark liquid in gulps to get it down.

Dodge sat on the cot beside him. "We're fighting, son, to get the trial delayed in order to get Max Ferguson here."

He nodded. "Never meant to bring the family this much trouble."

Dodge gave his arm a squeeze and stood again after a few minutes. "I'm going by the diner, and I'll bring you both a meal, to get your strength back."

Dawson shook his head. "Not sure either of us remember when we last ate something."

His mother touched his brow. "So like John..." And then she was gone, but not before he'd seen the tears welling in her eyes.

He stood and turned back to Haven and placed a finger to her lips as she tried to speak. Even with Leaning Bear so close, he brought her against him and kissed her.

He swayed, holding her, and she eased him back to the cot, encouraging him to lie down again and sitting beside him. He closed his eyes, not wanting to lose his sight of her, but exhaustion winning the battle within him. She placed her hand to his bearded cheek, rubbing and lulling him with her whispers. "Rest. I'll stay as long as they let me."

Chapter Twenty-Five

Dawson tilted his head back, nausea plaguing him to the point he thought he'd be sick. He supposed surgery was in order, but there would be no time for it, and if he wasn't sentenced to death, he was now certain this damn wound would no doubt kill him. He'd slept some, with Haven's coaxing, and he and Leaning Bear had both eaten their first meal in days, but the food had made him ill.

A cool rag touched his brow, making him shiver. They would need a good clean-up for the small hearing tomorrow morning about the trial. It was a shame the weather had held Max Ferguson's arrival. Without good counsel they'd be paying hell for sure.

"Leaning Bear seems to be resting better since the meal and tea, and you've dozed for a bit." Haven's sweet voice echoed the walls of their entrapment.

"They beat him far worse, but the meal was needed." He glanced through the bars where the medicine man lay on his side, his body much larger than the cot he lay on.

Haven touched him again with the cool rag. "Tess says the ribs have broken through his lungs, but he can still survive this with rest and his body fighting hard, though I fear you are just as ill."

"Not sure, Haven, if either one of us are getting out of this one alive." He said what they were both tiptoeing around.

She inhaled a startled breath. "You must fight, Dawson, and rest when you can."

Her tone had changed, and she carried no tears as he suspected she might with his words. He grabbed the bars to his side and pulled himself to sitting beside her. "The fight's in the courts where we have little alibi, especially if we get held to a military trial."

It was a moment more before she spoke, mingling her fingers within his. "When I first met you, your work was a part of you, that the Cheyenne would know more freedoms and purpose. And without you, they wouldn't know some of the things they do have. I know the government has to know the good you've done."

Leaning Bear adjusted his position, it being clear he listened to her as well.

"There is still a chance the general will recover, and Lieutenant Bartley, maybe he can speak to this." Haven tried, squeezing his hand.

Dawson shook his head. "Carl's not gonna talk with his family at risk, and the general may be weeks, if at all, recovering."

"You saw him, the Lieutenant?" she asked, lifting her brows.

He nodded. "It hasn't been safe for him to talk to us, but I did see him in formation when we were brought here."

"He's here in Cheyenne now?" she questioned, glancing away and back to him.

"Probably making camp with the other soldiers outside of town." He narrowed his gaze. "Haven, he's not talking, with threats to his family."

Her shoulders dropped, as did her gaze.

Dawson lifted her chin meeting her gaze. "He's held as captive as we are by the captain."

She shook her head, though he couldn't read her thoughts.

"I need to clean up and get some rest. You go on home with Dodge tonight. I'll see you in the morning." He tried, as she looked exhausted.

"I would rather stay with you..." Her voice cracked.

He hugged her close. "I know, but I need you to go to the ranch. In my room, in the bottom drawer, there's a pair of buckskin trousers and a fancier shirt made the same. I want you to get them and the other set there. Bring them to me."

"But Dodge thought you dressing in the regular clothing, and even the suit coat, for the trial would be best." She glanced where the pile of fancy clothing for him and Leaning Bear waited, his mother's doing.

"Haven, I am not the man you or anyone knows, dressed like my brothers." He shook his head in trying to understand it all himself. He would have little time to prepare for court, but as it stood, he'd go to court as himself, in buckskins.

She touched the bangs that hung longer in his face than when she'd first cut them, and of all things, she smiled. "I'll bring them."

"It's about time for Dodge and you to head back. Go on..." He kissed her on top of the head as they stood. "Tell Sawyer I need pencil and paper. I've need to order my thoughts on the trial."

She turned at the door of his cell and ran back to hug him once more. He took her, hanging onto her tight and inhaling the sweet lilac as he gave her a tender shove. He shut the cell door and turned to face Leaning Bear once she was gone.

Leaning Bear held his side and sat up with effort. "Sky-colored buckskins are for one day marriage to Woman with Frying Pan, not trial."

Dawson shook his head. The fancier blue tinted buckskins were made for him to wear one day when he chose a wife. "Not much of a marriage going to happen if this doesn't go well."

The medicine man nodded. "We dress fine for trial. But Cheyenne Indian best dead Indian, to court."

He stepped to the small window holding his side, not commenting. The pain was worse; he didn't expect relief any time soon. Town still bustled with people and soldiers, though the crowds had dispersed. He glanced at the sky, looking for answers that wouldn't come any better from *Heammawihio* or the Christian God of his childhood. A constant battle inside him had raged on and off since he'd taken up the ways of the Cheyenne. He bent, then, still wearing no shirt and gave his whispered Cheyenne chants to whoever would have them, praying for what was right for Haven and nothing more.

****

Haven made her way across town to the outskirts where soldiers had made a temporary barracks of lined tents. She had a little time before she and Dodge would head to the ranch, and if she found Lieutenant Bartley, it might be she could convince him to help Dawson's case.

The walk wasn't far, and as she stopped at a group of soldiers around a fire, she was well aware that all of the men in camp had followed her with their gazes.

She spoke sure, though her heart raced. "Excuse me. Might I inquire as to where Lieutenant Carl Bartley can be found."

"Last tent there." One of the men pointed and sipped his coffee, though she could smell the alcohol that laced his drink.

"Thank you." She hurried ahead.

"You don't find him, ya come back this way, Ma'am, keep me warm." The soldier cackled along with his friends, though Haven never acknowledged his words as she made it to Lieutenant Bartley's tent.

She gathered her nerves as she stopped at the tent opening, a small lamp flame inside. "Lieutenant Bartley, might I speak with you?"

It was a moment before the soldier pushed the tent flap back, the same man she remembered from town.

"Miss Oakley." He glanced around them and back, seemingly surprised at her arrival.

Haven pulled her heavy coat a bit tighter about her. "Lieutenant…I will apologize for not speaking to you at the bank, but at the time, I wasn't at liberty to do so."

He nodded. "I understand the circumstance, Ma'am."

Haven continued. "I was hoping you might testify on Dawson and Leaning Bear's behalf."

He nodded to the cut logs standing upright by the fire and waited, sitting after she did.

"It's not safe for either of us…for you to be here, Miss Oakley, and my wife and daughter have been threatened if I try to help." He spoke through a forced whisper, turning to glance behind them.

"I thought if you could speak for Dawson and Leaning Bear, maybe how hard they work for the tribes and that they weren't behind that attack, it would help their case. I know Dawson thinks well of you." She held the soldier's gaze, but the fear on his face was evident. "You are his and Leaning Bear's one chance at having a witness regarding how the captain treated them and about the attack."

He shook his head. "Captain has made it clear, if I don't lay low, he will..." He stopped. "I can't help you, Miss Oakley, as much as I so wish it."

Haven wasn't going to let him off so easy. "I fear for my family too, Lieutenant. My future with Dawson...a future we may never see. But let me ask you something. How will you face your wife and daughter if you ride away from here and Dawson and Leaning Bear are hanged for crimes they didn't commit? If you can't help us, is there any chance of General Dodd doing so?"

The soldier studied the fire and in a change of tone whispered through gritted teeth, "I can appreciate your position, Miss Oakley, but I'm afraid the general's condition is still very poor. He lingers but hasn't regained consciousness. I can't help."

"I don't understand. You know the good Dawson has done, giving to the tribes even of his own money to make sure even the last child eats and is warm." She whispered stern and sure, fighting tears.

The soldier stood, pacing away and glancing around them.

Haven lifted herself up from the log, shivering against the elements, but before she could speak again, Bartley turned. "The captain has threatened to...cut my daughter's hands off." Tears rimmed his lids. "She's a baby, just about to walk, Miss Oakley, and I cannot let that happen, not to mention how he would plan to harm my wife…you cannot possibly understand what I stand to lose here. He's evil, the Captain."

Haven held his gaze, interrupting. "No, Lieutenant Bartley, I cannot possibly understand, even as I carry Dawson McCade's child within me. I suppose that cannot be the same as your own struggles in doing what is right." With that she turned, her emotions gathering enough to bring about tears she wiped away in her new-found anger.

"Wait," Bartley called to her. "I've something."

She stepped closer as he rummaged in his tent and returned with a small bundle, handing it to her after a moment of hesitation.

"What's this?" She lifted the flap to find several feathers from arrows, not understanding.

"This one, the general took. These three match it, but this is from the Cheyenne on the reservations." He explained, touching each.

"I don't understand." Haven shook her head.

He glanced around them. "General Dodd was hit by the Dog Soldiers, as was Dawson. The Cheyenne have different arrows than those Dog Soldiers. Might help some, but you mustn't tell how you got these." He bound the pack again. "Just let Dawson know you have it. Be safe until you return to town, Ma'am. I'll watch to make sure." With that he said no more.

Haven turned back for town not sure she understood the arrows, except that in Dawson's saddle bags she'd brought with her to the ranch, the arrow he'd taken was there. Maybe she'd said too much in telling Mr. Bartley of her condition. She hadn't even told Dawson of the child within her. They should be celebrating instead of facing a trial that might take him from them both. She touched her low belly and bit her bottom lip as she turned for the main road to meet Dodge with a new hope that what she held might be of some help.

Chapter Twenty-Six

Dawn had come early, lighting the jail with a hint of cold gray sky. Dawson woke with a chill. He sucked in a deep breath, surprised he'd managed sleep at all with restless dreams of the wolf pacing in dark confinement.

He lifted himself as Leaning Bear, standing at the window of his cell, spoke in Cheyenne. "Your rest was uneasy?"

Dawson ran a hand through his hair, and with effort and holding his belly, stood to take in the view from his cell. "About as good as your own."

"Not good then." The medicine man wore no shirt and what skin was exposed outside his wraps held the terrible bruises of his beating, though his cough and the blood had eased.

Dawson narrowed his gaze to the hillside sprinkled with soldiers' tents. "Anything going on out there?"

The medicine man answered without looking at him. "Same."

Sawyer and Wyatt entered the jail office, their voices carrying, turning them both. He held Leaning Bear's gaze, no words needed to figure this day would decide a lot of things.

Wyatt pushed open the door, bobbling two plates of food and setting them at the opening in the irons. "Got you boys some breakfast, best the diner had."

Dawson took his plate and grabbed the fork, jabbing eggs and stuffing his mouth, and though his stomach turned, he knew he had to eat.

"Sleep any?" Wyatt angled a gaze his way.

"Had better." He continued to eat, fighting the nausea.

"It looks like Max Ferguson should make it here after all." Wyatt leaned against the cell wall.

"The weather let up, then?" Dawson asked.

"Trains are moving. He's bringing the family to visit Rose." Wyatt glanced at the doorway as Sawyer stepped inside, his eldest brother holding a serious gaze.

"Train's due soon. I got Zane waiting with the wagon to get Max's family to the ranch. Seems he's three daughters, so Rose is excited about the visit, even though Max has his work cut out for him." Sawyer shoved his hands in the pockets of his trousers.

Dawson gulped the rest of his eggs and lifted the biscuit. "I jotted down all we could think to list to our advantage and explained the things where there's controversy." He glanced at Leaning Bear, who coughed hard and held his side, though he had lifted the plate to eat.

"You both look like hell." Wyatt shook his head. "Bastards. Tess is fit to be tied as you both shouldn't even be moving around much."

Dawson studied Sawyer, reading what his brother wasn't saying. "Enlighten us, Sawyer."

"Hank seems to think they are going to push for a military trial as we suspected." His sheriff brother lifted his dark brows.

"We aren't military," Dawson blurted. "They all know that, even Hank."

Sawyer nodded. "Hank's jurisdiction here is to see you tried fair and held without more abuse, but Washington hasn't assigned him here. He came at my request."

"They can't try them as soldiers," Wyatt retorted, shoving his hat back.

Leaning Bear spoke without a glance at any of them. "Soldier trial. White man trial. No matter for Cheyenne."

It was true, no matter what kind of trial they were afforded, it wasn't like there would be any freedoms for Leaning Bear, who at best would be forced back to the reservation.

"I suppose we'll need to talk through all these points with Max, see his take on how to present them. He'll still represent in a military trial, and as for Scott's murder, it would most likely be a civil trial, following the military…if ya both don't hang." Sawyer leaned away from the wall, shaking his head.

Dawson looked on as his brother opened a pouch of arrows carrying feathers he recognized.

"Seems Haven visited Bartley last night to beg him to testify, but all he came up with were these." Sawyer held the feathered arrows for view.

"Damn it, I told you both to watch her. She has no business out there," Dawson scolded, eyeing the weapons.

"She's all right. Think these will do us any good?" Wyatt touched a couple of the arrows, comparing them.

"Those there are Dog Soldiers', and these here are Cheyenne," Dawson explained as he reached through the bars to point.

"Seems Bartley confiscated the arrow that hit the

general. Haven's bringing the one that hit you, said it was in your saddle bags," Sawyer explained. "We'll ask Max about it."

Dawson studied his brothers. "I'm asking you both again to keep an eye on her."

Wyatt nodded. "Got her in my sights, brother."

Dodge whirled in with Haven and Tess following, stopping their conversation. "Can't even drive a buggy through town this morning the streets are so full. Apparently, your charges have attracted people from surrounding towns."

"Guess I best see to moving folks off the streets." With that Wyatt kissed Tess and exited to his duties.

"My, you two clean up well," Tess teased, though the edge of stress in her voice and actions hinted at what they all held inside them. She had the baby with her, asleep in a basket she set aside. "Leaning Bear, you look much better after a night's rest. Has there has been no more blood with the cough?"

"No blood." The Indian nodded in respect as Sawyer let Tess inside the cell to see to his care.

Dawson met gazes with Haven, the worry having not left her eyes, but at least she offered him a smile as Sawyer opened his cell next.

She handed him a bag with a nod, making sure to whisper, "The clothing you asked about, though I had to let the guards outside search it."

He hugged her to him and drew her back. "You shouldn't have gone out there with the soldiers on your own."

Her face glowed pink. "I know, but the arrows may help."

Sawyer spoke. "I sent Brett to check on Carl's

family with Wyatt's suggestion he bring Bartley's wife and daughter to the ranch. They'll be safe there."

He hadn't known that, but it was best. "He let Carl know?"

Sawyer nodded. "He was agreeable, needs some way to protect them regardless. Seems he was roughed up last night in warning."

"It's my fault." Haven placed a hand to her mouth, upset at the idea.

"He's alright," Sawyer added.

Dawson lifted his gaze from Haven as Tess came to him, placing a hand to his brow. "How's your wound today? You still carry a fever."

"I'll get you both more willow bark tea." Haven squeezed his hand and went to the task as Tess urged him to lie back on the cot to change the dressing.

He grimaced, closing his eyes, as she began cleaning the wound. He could move around, and he had cleaned up just as had the medicine man, but the wound was little better. He was so incredibly sore, he groaned at his sister-in-law's efforts.

"I'm sorry, I know it hurts." She glanced at him. "This will need a surgery to clean the depth of the wound, I'm afraid. Sawyer, he can't go on much longer like this. The infection is much worse. This is a high and consistent fever."

Sawyer inspected the wound. "I'll see what I can do. Max might be able to delay things."

Haven returned with two cups of the willow bark tea that Dawson was beginning to dislike with a passion. He sat up and took the cup and met gazes with Dodge. The worry in his mother's eyes never ceased, but somehow words weren't needed.

"Tess, how long do we have?" Dodge asked as she laid a hand across his damp brow. The fever had plagued him most of the night, and his skin held a constant dampness.

"Maybe a day or two, but no more." Tess looked at him. "You need to drink as much of the tea as possible every few hours. And you need to take Laudanum, Dawson. Surely the pain is unbearable."

Dawson nodded, there not being any point each day where he didn't thirst, it seemed. He emptied the tea, grimacing. "I can't afford the confusion of the medicine right now, Doc."

"What's the recovery time if you do the surgery?" Sawyer folded the feathers back into the pack, setting them aside.

Tess shook her head. "Surgery for a day. Rest for at least a week, but several months to be back at his best. If he did well, he might sit for a trial in three or four days."

"We can try, get Max to push for the week. It's about time for the train." Sawyer held his gaze a moment longer and turned to go. His brother's lack of words said plenty. Neither Simmons nor the judge would ever give him a week, and in no way a month.

"I can give you Laudanum for the pain, Dawson." Tess rummaged a hand into her medical bag.

"No." Dawson shook his head again. "I need a clear head for all this."

"I've clients coming to the clinic and will be there most of the day if I'm needed." Tess lifted her bag and then the basket with her newborn son.

Dodge nodded. "And I've need of helping Burt at the mercantile. Town is full up it seems. Haven, I could use your help once you spend some time here."

"Of course." Haven turned back to him as Leaning Bear sat facing away from them to finish his food.

Dawson touched her hair and drew her mouth to his. She resisted at first, but after a brief glance at his friend, joined the deep kiss for a long moment. Lands but he loved her, the sweet flavor and the warmth of her. "Been waitin' on that."

She frowned, placing a tentative palm to his bearded cheek. "I can feel the fever inside you. Oh Dawson, they must allow this surgery."

"They aren't gonna go for any delay, Haven," he whispered and changed the subject. "How are Levi and James?"

The smile returned. "Levi now wants to become one of the hands. Evan's paid him the hours earned. James is ever leading Nicholas to all kinds of things little boys do, and he carries Ella with them, tending her for Tess. It's very sweet as he's had no little ones to play with much."

He smiled, the guilt that laced his thoughts over them leaving their home prevalent. Somehow in falling in love with her, he'd turned her world upside down, yet here she was making the most of it that she could.

"Do you think this lawyer from New York can help?" Her worried gaze held him.

"Perhaps." He ran a hand through the length of her hair, glad she'd pulled it back with a ribbon instead of piling it atop her head.

"I won't think of anything more than your freedom." She shook her head. "I would never survive it if you were…"

He touched his index finger to her lips, memorizing

her features, the light freckles across her nose and the deep hazel eyes that held him close. She looked different today. He couldn't put his finger to that or the reason she seemed to hold back her usual chatter, other than the situation and Leaning Bear so near to them.

"Why don't you go on, help Dodge? Keep your mind from things." He whispered, tasting her lips with a tender kiss. "We've work to do here, figuring things and talking with the lawyer."

She kissed his cheek as he waited for her to exit the cell. No doubt Dodge had summoned her help to keep her busy, which was best. He lingered there after she was gone, the reality of the whole situation hitting him hard. Should he be hanged, well, she didn't deserve that. And it was his job that those sweet hazel eyes should never know another day of pain.

****

Dawson held onto the bars as Wyatt opened his and Leaning Bear's cells. After an entire day of talking with his brothers, Brett, and Max Ferguson, the fancy-dressed lawyer from New York, they had managed to pull together a hearing with the judge. The mid-day hearing would take place moments from now in the large ballroom of the new hotel at the end of town.

"No need for the damn shackles. They aren't going anywhere." Wyatt snarled as he placed the cuffs on Leaning Bear, the two exchanging quick annoyed glances at each other.

There had never been much to Wyatt caring for Leaning Bear, but when Wyatt had been ambushed and left for dead a while back, it had been Leaning Bear who'd found him. It seemed since then his brother had been more cordial to the Indian when it came down to it.

"Damn, brother, you look like hell with that fever." Wyatt added the irons shackles to his wrists one at a time. "Maybe you should sit this one out."

Sawyer stepped in for a closer look at him. "There's plenty of reason for the Cavalry to think they'll run. Leastwise you both look damn respectable dressed as you are. Can you make it?"

"Yeah," he answered, though the fever had left him, even with the willow bark tea every few hours. He and Leaning Bear had worn the clothing brought to them by Dodge, but while he'd dress like his brothers today, he'd already decided he wouldn't do so for any trial.

"Father always said a man's appearance told the story." Wyatt brushed the sleeves of his new white shirt, leaving Dawson to roll his eyes and glance at the medicine man, who looked rather odd dressed as a white man.

Max Ferguson nodded to them all, the New York lawyer capturing each with his gaze. "There's no worries today of anything but haggling through what processes the trial will take. I've made a good case for all you've asked, and it's positive we've been allowed a hearing. Only…"

"Only what?" Dawson asked, as Leaning Bear stepped in place behind him.

"I've telegrammed for information on this judge. His name is Colonel Milton Garrett, and he's known to be about the rules, but opinions vary." Max nodded. "I've written up the reports for his review and made them available along with our requests, for a delay for a quick surgery and time for Leaning Bear's ribs to pain him less. I believe, however, we'll have a quick decision for a military trial."

"Think that's such a good idea?" It was Wyatt who asked. "Giving away some of the ammunition before the trial."

Max nodded, sure of himself. "Only the big things. My guess is if we play fair, offer what we can without the asking, things will go better."

"I suppose I don't need to warn either of you about your behavior." Sawyer eyed Leaning Bear but narrowed a gaze on Dawson. "Town's roaring with soldiers, just..."

"I got it, Sawyer." Dawson shook his head though the act made him dizzy, bringing on the nausea that had become his own personal hell.

Sawyer added a warning for Wyatt. "And no outbursts. You got it, Wyatt?"

Wyatt gave a reluctant nod along with a lift of his dark brows.

"Let me do the talking. If you've something to add, either of you..." Max held Leaning Bear's gaze for a moment. "I was going to ask that you write it down, but..."

"I write white man's words." The medicine man answered with a tinge of pride, his jaw held high.

Dawson gave Max a nod. It was true, Leaning Bear could write better than he could speak English if it came down to it, something that had come in handy for his friend over the years.

Moments later, and led by his brothers and soldiers, both cuffed with iron shackles, he and Leaning Bear ignored the jests and jeers from men on the streets of Cheyenne.

Soldiers stopped, and women at their shopping crossed the street to avoid them, but the quick jaunt to the hotel proved to be of little fanfare.

Inside, he glanced around as did Leaning Bear, the new hotel offering the fanciest building Cheyenne had ever seen. Large green curtains of velvet adorned windows. Carpets to match lined all the hallways and even the staircase. The dining room held fancy chandeliers of glass, and inside the meeting room, a table as long as the room itself would hold forty men by his quick count.

Sitting at the table was Captain Simmons, flanked by the judge and several soldiers, all dressed in their finest. Well, he'd expected a military trial, and there didn't seem to be much doubt about it now.

Dawson rested a gaze on Hank Somersby, who nodded. The Federal Marshal would be here for making sure order was kept, if nothing else.

"Gentlemen." The judge stood, wearing his black robe. "I'm Judge Milton Garrett. Alongside me are counselors Colonel Bennett Larson, Lieutenant Wallis Willams, and Captain Phillip Nalley, all United States assigned with current terms of office at present. I would also introduce you to Colonel Josiah McEntyre, who will be representing counsel for this case."

Each man nodded in turn as Max stepped up with a slight bow and a handshake to each. "I do hope, Sirs, that you've had time to read the information provided to the court."

Dawson fought a moment of nausea and tucked his shackled hands to his side, catching a glare from Captain Simmons. He kept the man's gaze until Simmons looked away.

The judge scooted his chair closer to the table, lifting a pencil and holding it above the tablet of paper before him. "Yes, I have reviewed the information from both sides of the charges. I have also considered the Cavalry's need for a speedy trial, as well as the requested time for surgery in the case of Mr. McCade and the time to recover for the Cheyenne, Leaning Bear. These considerations have been reviewed by all present."

Wyatt postured stiff in his chair, his brother's fists tight, but Sawyer didn't move and neither did Leaning Bear. The judge waited a long moment and looked at each of them in turn. "I will give my decision and I will hear from each side's counsel, but I will remind you that the decision will be final."

Nods came from both sides as the judge continued. "It is my recommendation that we proceed with a full military trial based on the evidence at hand, the untimely death of seven soldiers and the close working relationship both of the accused have held with the military and the Office of Indian Affairs. As for the local banker and the accusation that Dawson McCade be behind his murder, a civil trial will follow these proceedings in the event the accused in this case is found not guilty."

So it was as they all thought it would be. If he was granted his freedom on one trial, then he'd step right into the next.

"Our proceedings of the trial are set to begin tomorrow morning at eight in the room next to this, which has been set up in an effort to best serve as court. I will hear any rebuttal from each side, beginning with Colonel McEntyre." The judge leaned back in the deep leather-covered chair.

McEntyre, a large man, broad of shoulder and the tallest present, nodded. "Thank you, Judge. At this time, we do continue to support a rapid trial, given the number of soldiers displaced to town. We would also ask that the accused remain in restraints with the jail manned by the United States military. It is thought with Sheriff Sawyer McCade and Deputy Wyatt McCade being brothers of the accused, there is a heavy possibility of escape for both men."

The judge glanced at Hank. "Given the record of both men, we will allow Sheriff Sawyer McCade to continue to man the jail, but while outside their cells, we do feel confining the accused men for proceedings is best. Soldiers may remain outside the jail office as mandated by Captain Simmons."

The captain cleared his voice in annoyance but said nothing.

The judge glanced over his notes again. "And Mr. Ferguson."

"Your Honor, Dawson McCade and Leaning Bear, who is a highly respected medicine man, have been paid as civilian employees by the Office of Indian Affairs for several years now. With all due respect, we still request a civil trial be granted to both. As we sit here, Dawson McCade suffers a high fever from the wound that needs immediate surgery. We do not feel that it is asking too much to afford him to be the best he can for this trial, given his life may be at stake. Furthermore, Leaning Bear can hardly stay seated in comfort given the beating he has taken from soldiers under Captain Simmons' command, and he could clearly use a few more days to heal in order to help in defending his life as well."

The judge considered them both, taking a long look at Dawson who held his gaze and Leaning Bear who did the same. "Desertion is defined by any person employed by the military, as such, even civilian employees who leave service without the intention of returning. Given the costs to the government for the manhunt of both men, we find the term 'desertion' to in fact play a strong part of what charges are presented, and the risk of flight is high. This is also where we have come to the conclusion that a military trial is in order for both parties as The Office of Indian Affairs falls under military parameters. We will begin tomorrow with a speedy trial in the favor of both sides."

Max gave a nod, leaving Dawson perplexed as to how the New York fancy-clad lawyer would proceed with this trial. "Thank you, Sir."

The quiet held them all captive as the judge and panel left the room. Just as fast, Max stood and led the way for them all from the hotel, not offering the captain or his counsel even a glance.

Wyatt nodded for him and Leaning Bear to head out, playing his part as deputy, which he wasn't enforcing other than for show. Out on the streets, townsfolk had waited for a view of them once more. The numbing cold offered a relief of the heat scorching Dawson's face, though he shivered and moved toward the jail.

Sawyer plopped down at his desk as they all filed into the jail office. "Remove their shackles. You won't wear 'em while I man this jail."

Wyatt removed Leaning Bear's shackles and the man rubbed his wrists, waiting as Dawson's were unlocked.

Dawson ignored the sting to his wrists. "What the hell kind of hearing was that, incriminating before we get there?"

Max turned. "Don't be fooled by the simplicity of what just happened. It's best, gentlemen, to play nice. Now, Dawson and Leaning Bear, I'd like to hear it all again from the first, of you meeting Captain Simmons and all the way through the attack and after."

Dawson sucked in a deep breath, his mind heavy with fever. "He's been at the fort three years. Keeps his soldiers in a state of fear of retaliation against their families. Johnson, who runs the livery, has been about the only man we could trust at the fort, him and Lieutenant Carl Bartley, the soldier who helps at the reservations, though he's not talking with threats to his family."

Max nodded. "We can subpoena him, and he'd have to testify."

Dawson shook his head. "I'd rather not have his family under threat, though Wyatt had his wife and daughter moved to the ranch for protection."

"We may need him. The hard work for us, proving the times and whereabouts of you, the reasons you both were not behind this attack, motives, and in truth what played out that day from all views." The lawyer sat on the edge of Sawyer's desk making notes on a small tablet. "Our fight is ahead of us, but I think we have a good handle on how to undermine their accusations." The counsel looked at each of them.

"And if not?" Dawson narrowed a hard gaze on the man.

Max figured for a moment and smiled. "Then that,

gentlemen, is when we get ready to pay the very Devil himself."

Chapter Twenty-Seven

It was dusk as Haven lifted her gaze from where she sat across from Dawson in the sheriff's office. He was busy with his brothers and the lawyer and so distracted by it all, she'd stayed in the corner. Nearby, Dodge walked back and forth too nervous to sit, she supposed.

Haven had yet to tell Dawson of her condition, of the child she carried, as it seemed like bad timing. Sometimes, she wasn't sure if her morning nausea were the child or what Dawson faced along with Leaning Bear. Worse was looking on as Dawson suffered from his wound. He hadn't eaten well and the fever that burned through him day and night was high.

He kept a hand to his side, his shirt loose from his trousers as he listened. His pain was evident, and the willow bark tea wasn't holding the fever any longer. Lord, but she loved him, and as she sat, her prayers continued to be for his release from this burden. The talk now was full of tension and what would happen if he did receive a death sentence along with Leaning Bear. How on earth would he face that, and how would she ever survive it?

The medicine man was in pain too, his breathing short, but he was a man of few words. He was handsome for an Indian, with his bronze skin, and as tall or taller than Dawson with the same hard-packed body of muscles, making her wonder at his not being married within the tribe.

Fatigue had long taken her as it had them all, though Dodge had managed to keep her munching on small meals throughout the day.

Max Ferguson stretched his back, then settled his sights on her. "Forgive me for asking, Miss Oakley, if I may be so bold as to fully understand your relationship with Dawson?"

Haven's mouth dropped open, but she could scarce utter a word, Dodge and Tess aware of the truths she'd never confess to anyone save Dawson.

"No, she's not part of this…" Dawson's voice was as stern as she'd ever heard, startling her.

The lawyer continued, "Respectfully, Miss Oakley, of course." But he turned back to Dawson. "They *will* call her to the stand. It's unavoidable, with Captain Simmons' report stating that you've been residing there while remaining elusive from authorities. I need to understand fully what may surface in truth."

Dawson held up a hand and hushed them all as he gazed her direction. "She's to be my wife should I be freed of this. She should've been my wife long before now. I did stay with her and her brothers to help put a roof on the barn for winter and to keep her safe from Mr. Scott. She cared for my wounds right after the attack for several days, only because I gave her no choice." He grabbed his side, grimacing.

The lawyer jotted down a few sentences. "And you've stayed at her residence overnight on a number of occasions prior to being injured?"

"Yes, on a pallet by the fire, alone," Dawson shouted.

Heat rose in Haven's cheeks, though she never dropped her gaze. The quiet in the room told her what they all thought of the situation. It wasn't as if they knew she and Dawson had been intimate, but no one would see it proper that a young woman allowed a man into her home unescorted. Dodge touched her shoulder, and she held her thoughts, wondering if she would have to confess such a thing in court.

Max studied her for a moment. "Miss Oakley, this is well enough that Dawson was in protection of you and your family, but the court may ask even more difficult questions as to the relationship between the two of you. I don't want either of you unprepared for what might come."

"I'm certain, Sir, that I will be prepared for answering what is asked." She said it sure confidently, though her heart pounded hard. The strong urge to touch her belly drew her, though she simply held the lawyer's gaze. She didn't care what they thought so long as Dawson would have his life and freedom.

"And about Mr. Scott." The lawyer sat back down. "Tell me again of his harassment of you and your brothers. I'm aware you've reason to believe he killed your father, but I must understand why you think this. It might even be that the prosecution questions your play in Scott's demise."

A bolt of sheer terror rode through her, but she gathered her voice. "My father found gold on our claim and was killed shortly after. Because of my being a woman and my younger brother Levi not of age, Mr. Scott requested more than our homestead payment each month, threatening my brothers if it was not paid. Mr. Scott and his men returned my father to me after he was drowned, but my father could swim well, and the waters weren't frozen at the time. That's when the threats started, and I never went to the authorities as I was afraid he'd hurt my brothers."

The lawyer nodded. "I see, and Dawson, the attack on this man…regardless it will be a civil trial to follow, you have been accused due to the tomahawk located in the headboard of Mr. Scott's bed."

Dawson met her gaze and turned back to the lawyer. "Haven had been threatened by Scott, and even at one point bruised. So I rendered the man guarding him unconscious and went inside his home the night before he was found dead, but I didn't kill him. I made my way to him. Held a hand over his mouth and let him know he'd best leave Haven and her brothers alone. I slammed the tomahawk into the headboard as a reminder, nothing more. He was alive when I left. My best guess is someone else had the same intentions but carried it through. Strange the two men who worked for him have all but disappeared with his death. Anyone looking at how fast those two made out of town?"

"But they attacked Dawson one night long before, doesn't that count for something?" Haven blurted.

"I've notes on that one." The lawyer continued. "And this Captain Simmons, Dawson has let me know that he has harassed you when you went to the fort."

She nodded.

"Has the captain made any forward advances toward you?" Max waited.

Haven held his gaze. "Yes."

Dawson postured, sitting more erect as he held his side.

"On the night Dawson was captured. He told

me…" She stopped, heat flaming her face. "He suggested my favors to him might protect me from being detained for rendering aid to Dawson, and at the time he…touched me…inappropriately."

Dawson cursed, jumping up and pacing.

"Did Mr. Scott ever insinuate the same?" Max noted the details.

"Yes, though I stood up to him as well." Haven fought her nerves. Talking with Max had to be easier than talking to the others who would question her. "Will I be detained for this?"

Max Ferguson studied her a long moment. "I don't think so. If the captain didn't already press for that, it's good ammunition for our side. Why didn't he? Because he was interested in you? Because he has a vendetta against Dawson? And a bit of the same where Scott comes in, good ammunition for rebuttal if needed."

"No, I won't allow that." Dawson's voice rose above them all as he turned.

The lawyer nodded. "It's gonna take all we have, and this is just part of it."

"Please, Dawson, you have to allow it." Haven pleaded for his approval, though, deep down she wondered if she might have to answer the question of their intimacy and that of carrying his child. She had wanted to tell him, but he was so ill and that he was being detained only added to the situation. She hadn't wanted him to worry further about her well-being.

His blue-eyed gaze held her, and he shook his head. "Never wanted this for you."

It surprised Haven he would speak as such with all that were present.

Max shrugged. "Right now, we grasp all that might

help. But I think it's late and a good night's sleep for us all is in order. We'll pick up early tomorrow before the trial, and I'll be at some ideas tonight."

Haven stood, as did the men. It was now her heart raced, but she smiled when Dawson touched her hand before filing away behind Leaning Bear to the cells where his brother Wyatt locked them away from the world, from his freedom and from her, because there was no other choice.

****

Haven sat beside Dawson inside his cell, the night surrounding them and the jail quiet. He'd slept little and somehow, even though, she was tired, sleep would not come to her. Dodge had encouraged her to stay because it was time she told Dawson about the child, and with his mother's encouragement, she'd been sitting for a few hours trying to gather her nerves.

He'd said little and she'd asked nothing, but it was clear he thought a military trial the worst for him and Leaning Bear. It seemed he'd given up, his face stoic and lost, much like when he'd come to her that night on the homestead. But as she held to his hand, he was alive, his pulse rapid from the fever, and she struggled with the words. How could she tell him that there was more reason than her for this fight?

She scooted closer, the heat of his fever against her and his large arm around her a comfort she only found with him. "Dawson, you need rest, but you must fight in court tomorrow. I know you're upset at the possibility of me on the stand, but I'm not afraid of them. There's always a chance, and you have to believe that you will be free of this."

He didn't move but glanced across to the other cell,

where Leaning Bear lay on his cot, his back turned. She suspected the Cheyenne didn't sleep but wanted to give them time together. It saddened her that Leaning Bear basically faced this all alone except for Dawson.

"A military trial won't be a fair one, not unless Max has a few tricks to pull, but even he's not sure of that." He let his fingers play in between hers, tracing them but not looking at her. The lawyer, Max, had stated he was aware of military trial process and that they would still present a case worthy of the possibility Dawson and Leaning Bear would be exonerated of charges.

The quiet was overwhelming, but it was time she let him know the reason he had to give his best. The tiny life inside her was the one thing that mattered. "Dawson, you must fight, and I will ask this of you, for more than myself."

He held her gaze as she brought his hand to her low belly, unable to find the words to let him know of her condition. It was too early for either of them to feel anything, but it was time he knew he would be a father. She might have expected his protest or questions, but he left his hand there, resting, as tears spilled down his cheeks. And of all things, he leaned closer and wrapped both his arms around her.

She whispered, clinging to him with hope. "I've known for a short time…"

He still didn't speak but let his hand rub along her belly, holding her against him and speaking in Cheyenne. "All that has ever been beautiful in my life is you."

"Oh, Dawson, you must fight." She let her tears fall at his sweet words.

His forehead touched hers. "No matter what happens Haven, you can't say anything in the courtroom about this. Who knows?"

"Only Dodge, Mei Ling, and Rose. They and Doc Tess agreed to say nothing until I could tell you. Your brothers are not aware either." She studied his deep blue eyes, the darkness of the jail shading half his tearstained face.

"I love you, Haven." He lifted her chin and kissed her. "I promise I'll fight for you both, but you have to promise me, if this doesn't go well, you'll let my family help you, always."

"I will, but you will be there too. I know you will." She tried, her voice cracking.

He shook his head. "Haven, you have to know…at this trial, things will be said like Max tried to tell us. They will ask both of us…about us, Haven, and how we…or if we have…"

"I am prepared to answer any of the questions they ask, even to the point of you and me…of us being together. I do not fear what the townsfolk or the soldiers think of me as long as I have you." She could find no more words, not wanting to ever let him go, though Tess appeared at the door.

He spoke in Cheyenne. "My love is yours."

"I know. Now you fight, Dawson, but for tonight, please rest." She touched his heated face and he shivered.

"Haven, we've only a few more minutes." Doc Tess turned again, giving them a moment more.

Haven glanced back at Dawson. "The ladies are staying at the clinic, to be close to you. Max's wife's keeping the little ones for now, along with James." She hugged him to her again. "Please, drink the rest of the tea."

He held her for a moment more and nodded, urging her to follow Tess. While she wanted to let the tears flow, she held them at bay until she was outside the clinic following the doctor. And there she wanted to scream at the top of her lungs at the injustice of it all, though she let her hand ride along her low belly, reminding herself of all the reasons why she would be brave when the sun returned come morning.

Chapter Twenty-Eight

Dawn came early. Dawson rose from his knees, where he'd chanted his morning prayers, all of which belonged to Haven and the child she carried. His child. It had come as a shock, gutting him to his center that he might leave her to raise the child alone, but now he knew the reason for the glow about her. He pulled his fancy blue-stained buckskin tunic over his head and adjusted its fit, the shiny beads rattling and shimmering in the little light from outside.

Today, he wouldn't wear the clothes like his brothers. Today, he would reclaim himself and fight for the truth. Haven and Doc Tess hadn't shown, denied by the soldiers, he expected, so he'd changed his own dressing, the burn in his belly aching through to his back. It seemed now he fought nausea every few hours, and the fever had held him still. He had rested little and neither had the medicine man, who hadn't spoken since they'd awoken.

"You men ready the prisoners, keep them shackled." Captain Simmons leaned against the doorway, speaking to the two soldiers who entered before him, Sawyer and Wyatt standing nearby.

Dawson held the captain's gaze, though he glanced at Wyatt in warning. His brother looked ready to implode, but he shook his head and Wyatt let go of his bristle. Sawyer sent Wyatt to the porch with a nod. On his last conversation with his brothers the night before, he'd let them both know that getting themselves into any trouble wasn't worth their efforts. They both had families to think about—as did he, though that was a secret he still held.

"Aye, sir." One of the soldiers responded as he opened both cells.

The captain moseyed closer, smelling of stale tobacco. "My, my...the mornings do come early."

Dawson narrowed a gaze on the man that had caused every bit of this. "This how you wanted things, Captain, all wrapped up in a nice red bow?"

Captain Simmons snarled. "Don't worry, I'll have my best sharpshooter make it a clean shot. Then I'll see about that little missy you're so fond of, standing for her own trial in aiding fugitives."

Dawson's blood went cold as he stepped closer to the captain. He didn't fight Sawyer, who held him, but spoke through his clenched teeth. "If this doesn't go as you're planning, I expect myself and the Cheyenne will see you burn, one hot coal at a time." With that he pushed past the man, knocking him aside and following the soldier who led Leaning Bear outside to the streets.

His body shook hard at the prospect the captain would have cause to bring harm to Haven, and while he'd never liked the idea of killing, if the man laid a hand on Haven, the hot coals would be the least of his worries.

It was early, and small crowds had gathered to watch the parade to court. Shopkeepers hung in doorways and the saloon was quiet as he and Leaning Bear were paraded down the main street to the hotel. The rising sun shone on the faces of those he'd known all his life and ones he'd never before seen.

"You fight this, Dawson!" Lang, from the livery, cast his voice among the crowd with several cheers erupting, and Jacob from the saloon echoed in response. "Give them bastards hell, Son!"

He didn't respond to those that would support him, though they'd been men who had known his father. It had been his father who had spoken to him in his restless dreams. He'd been young when he lost his father, and it had been a number of years since the man's words had reached him, but the deep voice much like his own had found him.

'No matter the cause, be on the right side of the law and stand up for your beliefs. Find the good in all men and never lose the good in yourself.'

He wasn't sure why he remembered these words after all the years, but somehow it was as if his father had shown up once more in some kind of protection.

Soldiers stopped them inside the hotel, searching them and their clothing, and neither he nor Leaning Bear spoke a word. Dawson's head pounded, and he shivered with fever after having been out in the cold dampness of morning. The ache in his back caught his breath short as they were ushered into the courtroom, which was already full of people. His family, and Haven, waited toward the front of the court. The room went silent, and everyone turned to face them.

He caught a second of Haven's gaze before being moved ahead. She was radiant, in a dress she must have borrowed, a shiny sheen of pink held to her cheeks from the cold. She was beautiful, and inside her was their child. Well, come the wrath of hell he'd be there and rear his child beside her.

The hard chair next to Max Ferguson took him, jarring his back, and he closed his eyes for the moment focusing on breathing. Overwhelmed, he faced the court, gripping his fists so the shackles grew tight. Pain made things feel real and woke him to the thoughts he would need to keep current in his fevered mind.

Wyatt sat on the row behind the defense, with Sawyer beside him. His deputy brother leaned closer with a whisper. "Best dressed for the occasion, brother?"

He angled a quick glance, having expected wearing his Cheyenne best to rile his family, though it spoke the truth for him. "Not pretending to be someone I'm not."

With that his brother leaned back, annoyed. If the soldiers, namely Captain Simmons, could wear their soldier blues, then he would offer the same in his own fashion, clothes worn by an honest hardworking man, though there were those that would see the hate in his garments. Those who were hopeful to see all the tribes annihilated, one at a time.

Leaning Bear spoke in Cheyenne. "Fever takes more of you."

He shook his head. "I'll make it."

Max Ferguson turned to him and the medicine man. "How're you both holding up?"

"So far, so good." Dawson lied along with the medicine man's single nod.

"The doctor and your family are worried for your well-being, as am I." Max leaned closer. "When you need a break, we can ask it. This is going to be a long day, but I am hopeful to turn things around."

Dawson nodded, though it was hard to know if things would indeed be found in their favor.

The counsel leaned in closer, his dark hair hanging across his brow and his green eyes holding a sparkle. "But, uh, if you really want to halt things, you could pass out cold. Might get the surgery that way...it's a gamble but might just work."

At first Dawson thought the lawyer was kidding but then realized he was suggesting what he might do. "No need to delay things further."

"All rise!"

Judge Garrett entered with the other men on his court following. Dawson stood, studying the judge for what the day would encompass, though the man's eyes gave little away.

"Thank you, be seated." Judge Garrett nodded to the men beside him, who took their places behind the table, a rumble through the courtroom hushed as the crowd found seating once more.

The judge grabbed the gavel, smacked it down on the block of wood before him and began addressing the courtroom. "I am Judge Milton Garrett, and alongside me is Cavalry Colonel Bennett Larson, Lieutenant Wallis Williams, and Captain Phillip Nalley, all United States Army and with current terms of office at present. These men are called to act in the best interest of serving our U.S. Military and the Office of Indian Affairs for this trial.

Dawson adjusted in his chair, taking a glance at each man, none of whom had made eye contact with him or Leaning Bear.

The judge continued. "This trial is the Cavalry vs. one Dawson William McCade and the Cheyenne medicine man, Leaning Bear, both accused of being the force behind the recent attack on a group of soldiers as the military function of negotiations took place."

The quiet in the courtroom was deafening as Judge Garrett paused, scanning the crowd and landing his gaze on Dawson. It was clear the man was making a point for all in the courtroom to see. Without a doubt he and the medicine man were guilty until proven innocent.

"I will remind everyone in this courtroom that any outburst and negative comments will be dealt with promptly. Now, it is also my duty to remind the counsel and those who will be placed on this stand that these two men accused are just that, innocent until proven guilty by this court of military law." Judge Garrett nodded to the court.

Captain Simmons whispered to Josiah McEntyre, and the counselor nodded, giving him and Leaning Bear both a sidelong glance.

"Counsel, if you'd take to your statement first." The judge nodded toward McEntyre, who stood and made his way around the small table.

"Judge, counsel, and soldiers, I address you today to explain the details of sabotage and abuse to our Cavalry of the United States of America, in fact, murder, treason, and full out deceit of resources. As well, you all know a pack of murderers, Indian soldiers on horseback known as Dog Soldiers made a malicious attack on Cavalry, killing seven men, injuring many more, and leaving General Dodd near death at this very moment." The man turned, lifting his voice further.

"It is known, and we shall prove, that with their backgrounds, lack of work ethic, and disrespect of authority within the military that Mr. Dawson McCade and the Cheyenne Leaning Bear are accused of aiding this attack from early on."

A flurry of whispers flowed through the crowd and hushed.

The Counselman went on with an abrupt turn back to the room. "While these men were paid as civil employees, we are holding them to the military trial reserved for those who are accused of such crimes against God and Country, purposeful murder of soldiers. That is all, Judge."

"Thank you, Counsel. Defense, you may take the session." The judge nodded to Max Ferguson, who rose, turning to the counselor and then the soldiers with a smile.

"Your Honor, I would like to respectfully ask that while on trial, my clients be freed of their shackles and to remind the court that neither of these men are in much condition to finagle an escape from court." Max held his sights on the judge.

"I will grant this, Counsel, but only during court session." The judge nodded and one of the soldiers came to Leaning Bear first and began removing the medicine man's irons. "And further, as your shackles are removed, any attempts at fleeing the courtroom will be met with quick action."

Max bowed. "Thank you, Your Honor."

"Proceed, counselor." The judge pushed ahead.

Dawson held out his hands for the shackles to be removed, his wrists as raw and as bloody as his friend's.

It was a moment before the lawyer spoke again, scanning the room for a moment and settling to the remainder of his opening statement. "I'm sorry for my slight delay in speech, but as I look out across this courtroom, it's apparent the citizens of Cheyenne and the surrounding area have filled this room to capacity." Max held his gaze on those in the courtroom.

"That tells me a few things," he went on, stepping closer to the seats that held those who had come for the spectacle of it all. "One, that the people of Cheyenne have cause for support of the accused men because they are well known. It also lets me know that because of the type of work Dawson McCade and Leaning Bear do, there are certain prejudices, just as there are for the military and the government when it comes down to it." Max ambled to the other side of the court.

Dawson placed a hand to his side and tried to focus on what the counsel spoke, though his mind rambled through details faster than he could sort them.

Max went on. "Any trial is said to protect the innocent until proven guilty, and I aim to prove to you that these men accused of treason, desertion and murder have not been responsible for the crimes at hand. But, as I look before me at this crowd along with the military and counsel involved, biases must be put aside to do the just job of serving these men that they not be wrongly convicted. Both men are civilian hired employees who were unaware of the plans schemed to bring the Dog Soldiers' attack on the Cavalry."

Max walked across the room and picked up his Bible, making a show of holding the large black book. He opened it, lifted a piece of paper and began to read. "The term treason is defined as *'the crime of betraying one's country, especially by attempt in killing the sovereign or overthrowing the government.'* The term of desertion is reserved for *"those who leave military service or duty without the intention of returning."*"

Max studied the courtroom once more. "The plans to overthrow a government, when attacked yourself, is as difficult a feat as returning to any form of service where not welcome and accused..." The counsel chuckled and glanced at the paper he'd pulled from his Bible. "These two men are civilians and have never been held as soldiers to a post or battalion or assigned in any way by the military. I'll go on to define murder for you. *'The unlawful killing of another human being with malice and aforethought.'* Malice and aforethought."

Max faced the judges, then McEntyre and the captain. "In fairness to the men accused, and because as soldiers assigned to this military court-martial style trial you as the jury are held accountable to arrive at a decision that either frees or condemns the men at hand to death. Treason, desertion, and murder..."

Dawson's gut clenched. Neither he nor Leaning Bear had done those things, and no man on either side of this trial would ever know all they had done for the good of the tribes. He gritted his teeth to avoid shaking his head or giving the other side anything more to balance on.

Max turned back to face Dawson and Leaning Bear. "If you cannot look at these two men and fully know, without even the smallest doubt they did what they are accused, then it is your military duty to find them not guilty, so...help...you...God! May he have mercy on those of you who cannot or will not do what is truth in justice. May your judgment be as harsh." Max swung around with a smile and a nod to the judge. "Thank you, Your Honor."

Dawson lifted the mug of water before him and

drank, surprised at having cool liquid, and filled the cup again. He drank and emptied the cup, the cool temperature of the water making him shiver the full length of his body.

"Wyatt, he's very ill." The doctor's urgent whisper found him, but there was little anyone could do at this point.

He was worse, and it had become obvious to those around him. He'd fought the fever for more days than he cared to count, and the soreness had been as constant as the nausea. The urge to turn around for a glimpse of Haven tugged at him, though it was best he face ahead and gave no inkling of his thoughts about her or their child. Thoughts that cut him mid-belly at the possibility of not being there for either of them.

Chapter Twenty-Nine

Dawson shivered to the chill that rushed through him, proceedings in the courtroom progressing slowly and taking what energy his fevered body still held. It had been a short time since court had begun, but it seemed to him a full day had worn him down and it wasn't even noon.

Judge Garrett cleared his voice. "Prosecution, please call your witness."

"I call to the stand Captain Truett Simmons of the Seventh Cavalry." Josiah McEntyre took his chair as the captain stood and placed his hand on the Bible.

Dawson wiped the sweat from his brow and pulled a piece of paper and the inkwell closer.

McEntyre rose to his feet. "Captain, we will simply bypass the niceties of your duties. I'd like for you to start with how you know the accused, Dawson McCade and the Cheyenne, Leaning Bear."

The captain cleared his throat. "I've been assigned to the fort for nearing three years. I've close to three hundred men under my command at this time. Soldiers are posted at Fort Laramie and in and around the local towns and reservations. McCade and the Indian report every month as Indian Agents."

Max interrupted. "Objection, my clients do not act in the Indian Agent role. They are civilians hired for translation and to oversee conditions. Also, Leaning

Bear has a name and should be referred to as such."

The judge glared at Max, who sat back in his chair, a leg over his knee and a tablet across his lap. "Counsel, please refer to Leaning Bear by his name and let it be documented that the accused men are not employed as Indian Agents."

"What are your experiences working with each of these men, if you can be brief, Sir." McEntyre faced the captain again.

Captain Simmons angled a glance their way. "I've had nothing but trouble out of them both. Never where they need to be, offer more passes than allotted to the Indians. Let the Cheyenne leave the reservations without passes to hunt passed the border set to them. Breaking the rules set up by the government when it serves their purpose. Often creating rifts between my soldiers, themselves, and the Cheyenne. It's something all the time with the both of 'em."

The lawyer nodded. "Making it difficult to do your job?"

Max lifted his brows. "Objection, Your Honor."

"Sustained."

"Can you lead us up to the days of the negotiations?" McEntyre changed the question, folding his arms.

The captain gave a heavy shrug. "General Dodd and his party arrived, as did many of the Cheyenne, and Sioux and some other tribes. The first weeks were in preparation, the Indians gathering on the reservations and soldiers and military collecting at the fort. We were training the soldiers on the negotiations and preparing them for any uprising, how to handle the Indians. Any time you deal with the tribes gathering there is usually a lot of posturing and Indian chatter on rising up once more."

"And with that preparation, did McCade and Leaning Bear take part?" McEntyre waited, lifting his dark brows.

"No, as usual, Dawson McCade didn't show up for his assigned duty until a few days before the negotiations. And Leaning Bear just seems to pop in when it's to his convenience." The captain narrowed his gaze. "Not sure as to why the government would pay good money for his involvement."

"Objection." Max glanced up from his tablet. "Describing my clients in a bad light."

"I'll allow it."

"What in your opinion were the work ethic of these men?" The counselor switched up the question.

Dawson took a deep breath and let it out. This wasn't the least bit painful, and he jotted notes for Max, though his vision blurred. He had to blink several times, the ache through his middle cutting deeper as he wrote a rebuttal to a few facts.

Captain Simmons adjusted in his seat. "Poor at best, Sir."

"And lead us into the events, Captain." McEntyre turned back to the table, lifted his tablet, and faced the captain again.

"The negotiation for treaties by the Office of Indian Affairs went on for about three days with General Dodd leading. The events, for the most part, went smoothly. McCade and the Indian participated, leading in the tribal leaders and often chatting with them out of turn." Captain Simmons glared their way and back to the counsel.

"Out of turn?" McEntyre stepped back to allow the captain to be seen.

"Well, interrupting to explain in the other languages, Cheyenne, Sioux, making sure I suppose the Indians understood things and all, though I know for a fact some of those Indians speak English—"

"Speak English not mean full understand," Leaning Bear interrupted with a shake of his head.

The judge grabbed his gavel and hit the block. "No outburst in court, Sir. You will wait your turn to talk."

The medicine man held the man's gaze, acknowledging nothing.

"Objection. My clients are hired for interpretation," Max added.

"Overruled."

McEntyre forged ahead. "So when was it you were aware of this attack by Dog Soldiers?"

"We knew about Dog Soldiers being seen, but we had no idea of the attack. The Indians stayed a bit restless at these negotiations, as I've said. But until the last day while the treaties were actually being signed nothing hinted at an attack." Captain Simmons tugged at his collar and shook his head.

"But the son of the chief, Dancing Fox, stirred things up a little with some chanting and words of still not trusting a white government when the final papers were being signed." The man swallowed hard and wiped a handkerchief across his sweating brow.

"I have to say it made me and my men a bit nervous. Any time you got Indians, you gotta keep your guard up. They cannot be trusted. And McCade and Leaning Bear were always off in meetings with the Indians, I believe preparing for this attack. Soldiers kept hearing talk of war from the tribes."

"Objection, derogatory statement on my clients." Max raised his voice.

"Overruled, Counselor."

"I thought at first it had been Dancing Fox who had called on the attack, but he fought alongside my men in protection of his Cheyenne, as hard as any soldier." The captain's voice went up an octave and he gripped his hands to his knees. "The first arrow hit General Dodd in the chest, and Dog Soldiers seemed to come out of nowhere. Maybe a hundred or more." He glanced at his counsel and the jurors. "All at once the scene turned, and with the mix of Dog Soldiers and the current tribes fighting, it was hard to tell who was fighting whom, but I held my men together."

"During this attack, what were Mr. McCade and Leaning Bear doing?" McEntyre glanced their direction.

"They were running toward their horses, urging the Dog Soldiers onward as Cavalry fell to their deaths." The captain shook his head.

Dawson grabbed the pen and dipped it into the ink and began to scribble notes. He pushed the paper to Max, who gave him a wink and glanced back up to the court. Dawson sat back further in his chair, having already explained where their horses were and how the whole setup appeared. He'd drawn out the whole scene for the lawyer the night before.

Captain Simmons went on. "Never seen anything like it. They just shouted and encoured the attack. Such a blatant hate of soldiers I've never seen. But it seems one of the Cheyenne hit McCade."

"So McCade was indeed injured as he fled?"

"Took an arrow to his belly in running toward those Dog Soldiers to urge them onward toward all of us." The captain eyed him hard.

"So what happened then?" McEntyre asked, his questions, obviously rehearsed.

"I turned my soldiers to their arrest, but those two were on their horses and gone, though. I failed to mention the blizzard had begun that morning and my men lost their trail shortly after, in pursuit," The captain explained, folding his fists tight. "It took some time to bring these men in."

McEntyre went back to sit at the table. "Can you lead us through how you found them and brought them under arrest?"

Simmons nodded. "McCade and the Ind—Leaning Bear know the land, every nook and cranny along the mountains and rivers. Easy enough for them to hide in weather like that. They remained elusive until a tip came my way."

"A tip?" Counsel asked, his brows riding high.

The captain hesitated, but then lifted his chin. "Some in town have said McCade is rather fond of Miss Oakley, so I suspected to find him there at her home eventually."

Whispers scattered across the courtroom but hushed.

The captain glanced at Haven and back. "Kept watch, and sure enough, several weeks later when he and the Cheyenne showed up, we made their capture. Even found fake credentials on McCade, as if he was planning his escape, a name change and all."

"Submitting those credentials, Your Honor, for evidence." McEntyre handed the judge the pouch of folded papers.

"Miss Oakley, is she present?" McEntyre folded his arms.

Simmons hesitated, holding Dawson's gaze but after a blink moved his sights to Haven and pointed. "She's right there, Sir."

A rush of whispers filled the room, causing the judge to hit the block several times. "Quiet, please."

The weight of Wyatt's hand settled on Dawson's shoulder, keeping him seated. He didn't turn to look at Haven, though it was all he could do to sit still. While Max had been certain Haven would be named and that the questions for both might be difficult, he'd rather have lost this entire trial than have her face any of it.

"Was there any resistance met in collecting these men when found?" McEntyre asked further.

"Only a little from McCade over the woman, trying to warn her, speaking to her in that Cheyenne tongue she must understand. Rumor has it he spent time with one of those squaws on the reservation years back, too." He chuckled along with a few in the room.

"And these men stir up trouble, as you say, with the soldiers?"

"Well, McCade's like that, fighting the soldiers any time things agree little with him. Had a few scuffles with him myself, even heard he killed a soldier some time back." Captain Simmons glared Dawson's way.

So there it was, the resurfacing of the soldier from his past. Dawson sat still. The dread of what had happened had never left him, something that lived inside, stirring the wolf now and then as it did now. He wiped the sweat from his brow and adjusted in his chair, keeping a hand across his aching side. He glanced again at the clock on the far wall, which seemed to move little. And the mention of Winona was painful, but he'd told Haven of that, and their parting had been mutual. There was nothing to hide there either.

Max never missed a beat. "Objection, Your Honor. Double Jeopardy. My client was tried and found not guilty in the case of the soldier that died weeks after he attacked my client. For the measure of the court, it was ruled as self-defense."

"Sustained, and strike that from the record as Double Jeopardy for the past event." Judge Garrett made notes on the tablet before him. "Carry on, counselor."

"And all the time you have worked with these men, what weapons have you known them to carry?" McEntyre led the men right where he wanted them.

Captain Simmons nodded. "Leaning Bear has a bow and arrows, knives. McCade carries a revolver and one of those tomahawks like the Indians use. Heard that's what killed the banker here in town."

"Objection!" Max shouted. "My client, Dawson McCade, is not being tried at this time for the death of the banker."

"The unfortunate demise of Whitney Scott is at this time not being tried and will be dismissed," Judge Garrett explained.

McEntyre nodded toward the captain. "Let's get back to the attack, and so assuming that McCade and Leaning Bear are behind the attack, tell us more about how you are certain."

"Seems McCade had some dealings with Dog Soldiers over a mare he had at the fort. He met up with a few of those savages to gain the animal, which belongs to Miss Oakley. Seen her on it a number of times when she came to the fort," the captain explained. "I figured from all I've been hearing, he rescued the woman from these same men and later went back maybe to trade for her horse, not sure I know directly, but there seems to be a connection with him and those Dog Soldiers."

Max stuck the pencil behind his ear and folded his arms, leaning back in his chair to listen.

Leaning Bear leaned across the table and tugged the tablet to his side. Dipping one of the feathered pens into the inkwell. And with little sound and his left hand he began to draw a mountain scene across the paper.

Dawson closed his eyes to a stab of pain and a shudder of fever as the captain went on with all the reasons they had brought on the attack.

"You all right, brother?" Sawyer tugged at the back of Dawson's tunic.

Dawson opened his eyes and gave a nod.

"Captain, in the negotiations, how did these two men behave when things got heated in discussions?" Counsel questioned.

"We had some talk in the lodges around the small fires where the Indians wanted to share their pipes. McCade and Leaning Bear were a part of most of it, speaking back and forth with that Indian language." The captain folded his arms. "My guess is they translated falsely, and I believe that is why the Indians with Dancing Fox began their chanting right before the attack."

"So the accused have both provoked you as well?" McEntyre questioned.

Captain Simmons nodded. "McCade barged into my office several weeks back, threatened me. Turned over my desk. Rarely controls his temper in anything."

"What provoked him this time?"

"Oh, we got a couple of men good at boxing, and now and then we lay wages on a good match. Had Leaning Bear there in the ring, though he wouldn't fight, just stood there. I think that riled McCade. I tried to explain we were just funning the Indian for sport, no one harmed." The captain shrugged. "My men need to let off steam a bit that way."

"What further can you tell us in knowing these men were behind the attack?"

The captain tilted his head. "They kept their horses away from all the others, on the far end of the tree line where those Dog Soldiers rode in from. I watched them run toward those men, urging them on to the victory, not with the other Indians they've been sworn to protect. And I looked on as my soldiers, good men, fell and died by arrows and rifles. Indians with rifles I believe McCade and Leaning Bear supplied to them, maybe what they traded for that horse. Those two have no allegiance to anyone, much less soldiers and the United States Government."

"Your witness." McEntyre glanced at Max and took his seat once more.

Chapter Thirty

Haven sat still, watching Dawson as Max Ferguson stood with a nod to the people crowded into the hotel courtroom. The morning had progressed, and the proceedings seemed long already, though Max had warned them the trial would last, at best, one day.

She'd never been inside a courtroom and imagined not many would be this fancy. But that her name had already been mentioned, her heart raced, though her worries were for Dawson who wasn't well.

At the time the captain had spoken of her, Dodge had reached over to lay a hand on hers in support. But it seemed his mother also suffered in watching what Dawson had to go through.

Max stepped ahead, studying the captain who now couldn't help but fidget in his chair. "Having three hundred men under your command is very impressive I'd have to say, Captain Simmons."

The man hesitated but nodded as Max continued. "I am sure manning the fort, a few of the local towns and two reservations takes a great deal of skill and, would you say, organization and discipline?"

Again, the captain was slow to answer but nodded. "Indeed, I'm a busy man most all the time."

Max narrowed a gaze with the lift of his dark brows. "So…how many times a month do you make it to the reservations to check on conditions there?"

Captain Simmons narrowed his gaze. "I've men placed there that report in on a weekly basis."

"That's not what I asked, Sir. How often do *you* check on conditions at either of the reservations?" Max stepped back so the captain could be seen by all.

"A couple of times a year." The captain gave his reluctant answer, which was no doubt to any of them a lie.

Max continued. "The conditions at the reservations are poor, from what I am told. I should think if you are assigned to govern the reservations you would be there more often. What say you?"

"I'm not on trial here, but I place men to report in, as I cannot be in all places at once." Captain Simmons defended, his voice lurching higher.

"And…" Max reached for a piece of paper from the table and handed it to the judge. "I'd like to submit this list, which contains provisions for the tribes, never delivered to the current reservations, and still remaining in the guarded warehouse on site at the fort."

"We ration them out as we can. You have to understand if we give it fully to the Indians, it will be squandered and sold in the towns and to my own soldiers, those Indians looking for any way they can to make more money." The captain blurted the interruption, shaking his head.

But Max went on, walking closer to the captain and glancing at a notepad in his hand. "Seems these items were slated for the reservations some weeks back, enough so that spoils have been burned. Quite a façade going on there at the fort, along with harassment of the Indians that come there to trade, often at poor profit. Cheated there, made to box for the entertainment of your soldiers, and from what I understand, in the last few years under your command the fort has been rather, shall we say, out of order."

"Objection." McEntyre shook his head. "My client is not the one on trial."

"Overruled. Continue." Judge Garrett nodded.

Max went on. "Do you think you have control of the men under your command, Sir?"

"Yes, I do, Counselor!" The captain sat high in his chair, proud.

"Yet as we sit here in court, you have..." Max glanced across the courtroom behind him.

From the back came the count from Jacob Sanders, saloon owner. "Nine and six."

Max nodded with a slight curl to his lips. "Nine soldiers sitting across the way in the saloon, drinking and at a good game of poker. Six more, let's say occupied upstairs, most likely out of uniform, Sir."

Laughter broke out across the courtroom and the judge slammed his hammer once more. "Pipe down, folks. Mr. Ferguson, I am not sure what you are up to here, but this is a courtroom and not a circus. Please keep to the testimonies at hand, and no outbursts from the audience any further."

Haven glanced at Dawson. He'd moved little, and his hand still rested on his side. Her heart cringed to think he'd need a surgery once he was freed from all this. He'd glanced at her the once when he'd entered the court, but it was best he brought no more attention to their relationship until it was mentioned in court.

"What have been your expectations of Dawson McCade and Leaning Bear in their job duties?" Max waited, consulting his tablet again.

The captain spoke in a stern tone. "Acting as agents to watch the reservations—"

"Neither of these men have ever been contracted as agents, Captain." The lawyer interrupted as a reminder.

"I've expected they report on time, which they have not, regardless their titles," Captain Simmons snarled.

Max lifted another piece of paper. "This I submit is like copies of the contracts that Dawson McCade and Leaning Bear have signed and followed for a number of years. These have been sent by courier from The Office of Indian Affairs as current. I'd like you to read the areas I've marked, Captain."

The captain held the man's gaze and went ahead. "Acting in and according to the outlines of interpretation of the languages. To be paid as civilian contractors and in no way are to be considered military employees. To answer for duties as assigned by The Office of Indian Affairs."

"Objection, my client is not the one on trial." McEntyre stood this time.

"Sustained."

Much of the courtroom began to whisper. Max Ferguson was animated if nothing else. He was dressed in fancy clothing, Haven thought, very expensive, and he smiled and postured as if acting in a play. It was easy to see why he'd been successful as a lawyer in a place like New York City.

"Just establishing a few knowns for the judges." Max shoved a hand into his trouser pocket. "Captain Simmons, you say these men have squandered passes and broken rules."

The captain narrowed his gaze and his angry voice

came. "Yes."

"Are you aware that both of these men often do without their salary from the United States Department of Indian Affairs? That they instead use it for goods and medicines needed by the tribes." Max waited, his dark brows lifting in question.

"So they say." The captain smirked.

"And the rifts you describe, would they come from the fact you antagonize Leaning Bear, as well as Dawson McCade, any time they are at the fort because you assume they report to you?" Max waited, tapping his foot.

Captain Simmons glared. "I am in charge at the fort, regardless of who they report to."

"Answer the question, Captain. Do Leaning Bear and Dawson McCade in any way report to you?" Max spoke over the man.

The captain angled his jaw high. "No."

Haven glanced at Dawson again, wishing she were seated closer to him, but his brothers had insisted on the chairs behind him. She'd seen Wyatt hold Dawson steady at the captain's first mention of her. As terrified as she was, she would testify, no matter the thoughts some might carry. She glanced down at the pink gown she wore; Tess had insisted she wear it to look her best in court.

"I'd like to address again that my clients have deserted nothing, as they have never been soldiers." Max glanced at the judge and then went on with the captain, "So, let's move to the negotiations. You mention the Chief's son, Dancing Fox led some kind of chanting prior to the attack. Why then would he not have been detained as well?"

"I've said he stayed and fought hard right alongside my men, trying to stave off the attack." The captain rebutted, his tone stern.

"Well, sir, I'm not sure how you knew this, given your mission seemed to be taking down both my clients during the attack." Max set his notebook on the table and turned back to face the man.

"I had glanced the direction of the Dog Soldiers coming toward us and saw that those two were heading off to encourage the attackers, and I called my men to it." The Captain's tone rose, and he squirmed in his seat.

"Yet these men ran toward a group of attacking Dog Soldiers, their horses on the far side, away from the Cavalry's animals but nowhere near where they began to run. If I may..." Max grabbed a short rod and pointed to the chalk drawing he turned around at the front, the board on an easel.

"So according to your account, Captain, the attackers rode in from here." Max placed the end of the chalk stick at the area of trees drawn opposite the negotiations.

The captain nodded.

"And so these men, Dawson and Leaning Bear, were running this direction. Correct?" Max waited for the captain's second nod. "So, if you will, then can you please point to the area where the horses for the Cavalry were kept and then where the horses for the accused were placed."

The captain cleared his voice and stood to reach the board with the wand. It touched behind where the Cavalry were holding the negotiations, from what Haven could tell. She leaned over for a better view.

"All right, sir, and the place where Dawson McCade and Leaning Bear's mounts were waiting." Max folded his arms as the captain hesitated.

"Captain?"

Haven glanced at Dodge, who smiled as the captain laid the end of the poker to the board, showing that Dawson and Leaning Bear's horses were nowhere near where the Dog Soldiers had attacked, and in fact were further than the Cavalry's own horses.

"Here." Max took the rod back. "You pointed out my clients were running this direction toward their horses…but this is not where the animals were. My clients were running toward the oncoming fight to stop it. I'm not sure they were trying to escape with their horses behind them as they ran directly into the attack."

The captain said nothing and neither did his counsel.

"And you've spoken of the Indians beginning to chant. Why wasn't Dancing Fox hunted down and arrested along with my clients if this 'restlessness' as you described it was observed to bring on the attack?" Max waited with a cocked head.

"Because he didn't run and stayed to fight with us," the captain shouted.

"I understand that right before this display you'd been called down by the general for your actions." Max turned back to the table and sat by Dawson, folding his arms in wait of the explanation.

Captain Simmons eyed his counsel, who gave him a nod. "General Dodd and I had words over the fact he'd further assigned Dawson McCade to duties with the tribes, though McCade had submitted his resignation from the current position so he could pull this off, from what I believe."

"My understanding is you were asked to step away from the proceedings, having annoyed the general. So would that not make you care little about the fight but more about apprehending my clients for your own purpose?" Max leaned back in his chair, folding his hands behind his head.

"Objection."

"Overruled."

"I was asked to back down, leave the negotiations, right as an arrow took the general's chest, forcing me to assume command." The captain's gaze narrowed, and he talked through clenched teeth.

"My client did submit a letter of resignation from duties, but not so that he could desert what he never belonged to or betray the government and officials like you, and certainly not to bring on a Dog Soldier attack on men he chose to work alongside. While we are at it, the credentials, or alias as you referred to them, that Dawson McCade was carrying when captured, those would simply be another choice he decided not to take, though the three hundred dollars that was in the same bag has gone missing. What would you have to say about that, Captain?" Max never gave the man a rest, the flurry of details and questions seeming to fluster the man.

Simmons said nothing, his eyes wide with surprise as he eyed his counsel.

"Captain, surely you and your men confiscated that money at the same time. Where would that be located now, Sir?" Max lifted his brows.

"He said he had that money, but we found no golden eagles on him." The captain's tone was charged with anger and the man clenched his fists.

Max shook his head. "I never said my client claimed the three hundred dollars as golden eagles, Sir."

The captain sat speechless.

"Objection, Your Honor. Counsel continues to put my client on trial in an accusatory fashion." McEntyre smacked his hands on the table before him.

"Sustained."

Max stood again. "Captain, you mentioned you saw Dawson McCade take an arrow from the Cheyenne. I'd like to know how close you were to know that this arrow came from the Cheyenne." Max glanced at Dawson, who scooted his chair back, holding his side.

"Well, I didn't see exactly, but we all know he has a gut wound causing him fever." The captain fidgeted in his chair.

"And so, as a medical and weaponry expert, you can speak to Dawson McCade's injuries?" Max taunted, to another objection from the captain's counsel.

"Sustained."

Max stepped ahead, meeting the judge's gaze. "If I may, Your Honor, I call before us Doctor Tess Sullivan McCade and Dawson McCade."

Haven's mouth dropped open for a second as Tess rose from her chair and went to the front, standing beside Dawson before the court. Dawson stood, his face devoid of emotion.

Haven's pulse raced at catching his gaze, no words needed for her to offer him a smile he couldn't return. Sweat beaded his brow, his skin flushed with the heat of illness. Lands, this was harder than she'd ever imagined. Watching him suffer brought tears to her eyes that she blinked away.

Tess placed her hand on the Bible, spoke the oath and turned back to the courts.

Max spoke as she waited. "Doctor McCade is a graduate of The Philadelphia College for Women and, indeed, a trained professional surgeon within the finer hospitals of Boston, Massachusetts. She will be explaining to us the impact of the arrow's trajectory through Dawson's body and how it entered his back and not his belly as mentioned earlier. Go ahead, Doctor." Max was held up by opposite counsel.

"Objection, you cannot possibly show these wounds in court," McEntyre pressed, whispers filling the courtroom.

"I'll allow it, Counselor." Judge Garrett turned back to the physician.

Tess touched Dawson's arm and set her bag on the table as he lifted his tunic over his head, standing shirtless before the court.

Haven trembled as Tess began cutting away the old dressing, not believing that this would have to be done in front of all in court. Dawson held his gaze steady ahead of him, but he was shaking with fever, and didn't he hate this, being on display? Now the tears that Haven had held back scrolled down her face, though she remained silent.

"The entry is here." Tess turned Dawson, showing his back to the judges and counsel and then the courtroom.

"We know this was an arrow, as the wound along Dawson's back, just here under his ribs made a slice such as any blade would leave." Tess eased Dawson around again and held him steady. "The entry wound is often much smaller in diameter than the exit wound on most impaling injuries because the damage is done inside the body as it pushes through rapidly." Tess frowned, as she touched Dawson's skin and reached for a dressing cloth to pad the slight ooze of blood and pus from his side.

"And Doctor, please explain the path and angle of the hit and how—if Dawson was here, on a horse—how it would have happened." Max used the stick on the display board again to point where Dawson and Leaning Bear would have gotten to their horses.

Tess pointed to Dawson's back. "Arrows are incredibly sharp, often more so than the knives you men may carry. Sent from a bow, the impact is swift."

The physician then reached for one of the arrows and held it beside Dawson's body. "The trajectory is often straight, providing the arrow doesn't hit anything solid like bone."

She measured the angle by placing the weapon against Dawson. "In this case, it went on through the soft tissue of Dawson's body. So the injury is a straight path, but because arrows harbor a lot of dirt and are often not clean, Dawson has continued to suffer infection."

She let go of Dawson and turned to the judge. "All of you men, judges or not, should be ashamed. He is scorching with fever and has needed a surgery long before now."

"Objection," McEntyre shouted as he jumped to his feet.

Tess never floundered. "I have no care what the courts say here, and I am also not under military jurisdiction but caring for any prisoner, injured or not, as you have is inexcusable. Beating them until they cannot even stand is far worse."

"Dismissed, Doctor!" The judge spouted with a growl.

Doc Tess said no more as Max excused her back to her seat. Dawson tugged the tunic over his head, taking his own chair with some effort.

Dodge placed a folded napkin in Haven's hands. She opened the wrapped bread with a small piece of jerky and glanced at Dawson's mother.

"You must eat," Dodge whispered.

Haven took a deep breath, and even with her belly full of nerves, began to nibble as Max lifted the arrow that Dawson had managed to save.

"I am holding the tip of the arrow that went through Dawson McCade as explained by the physician. Max held up the piece still stained with Dawson's blood. "As we compare this to one from the local Cheyenne, you'll see this one hardly made the same and with dark feathers not found in this area. And here," Max picked up more tips from the large bag behind him. "These three were collected from the negotiations and kept by the Cavalry as proof of what the Dog Soldiers were sending. I also have here a fourth, the exact arrow that hit General Dodd." Max laid all the weapons before the judges, allowing them a moment, and then put them across the table before the jurors. "This proves Dawson McCade was hit in the back not by a bullet from soldiers, not by an arrow from the Cheyenne or Sioux, but by an arrow from the Dog Soldiers. He escaped in this direction because he had no other choice."

"Objection, Your Honor. How is it we have proof of any of these arrows." McEntyre stood, his face and ears turning bright.

"Sustained."

"Let's move forward, shall we? Captain, I'd like to know more about your capture of my clients." Max sat as he asked this time. "You say you received a tip that Dawson McCade could be found in or around Miss Oakley's homestead?"

"That's right." The captain shuffled in his seat as if annoyed in repeating himself.

Max held silent for a long moment. "Did you know that after Dawson McCade rescued Miss Oakley from the hands of Dog Soldiers, he later found her horse at the livery within the fort? He paid to gain the animal back and returned her to Miss Oakley, at which time he did stay on at the homestead to assist her younger brother with roofing the barn."

Dawson adjusted in his seat, holding his side. Haven never took her sights off him, worried he was worse all the while.

From behind him it was easy to see he trembled with fever, but the judge had paid little attention to Dr. Tess.

"As the months passed, so that nothing is kept from this courtroom, Dawson McCade had indeed begun to court Miss Oakley, something of which they have kept no secret, and should this trial be in my client's favor, the two will soon be married." Max nodded to the courtroom and turned back to the judge. "To further answer a few questions you have brought forth, Dawson McCade did have a relationship with a half Cheyenne woman named Winona, when he was a much younger man. The affair was brief, not that any of this is concern for the records of the courts. If, however, you knew Miss Oakley to be harboring either of my clients, why then would you not have detained her as well?"

A hush of whispers covered the crowd. Heat rose to Haven's face, but she held her gaze on Max. Why would he even mention that? What if they decided to put her on trial and hang her or jail her for life... Oh, God, what would happen to her brothers, and her child? Dodge took her hand once more and held tight.

The captain glanced at his counsel. "I was figuring Miss Oakley...might not have known these two were on the run and thought it best to not press those charges."

Max turned the subject once more, Simmons still stuttering. "We might as well address again the death of the soldier in Dawson McCade's past, as a reminder he was acquitted of all counts as self-defense. He was attacked and defended himself in a knife fight in which he took a bad cut to his belly." Max folded his arms and rocked on his heels. "And since you mentioned it, what do you know about the death of Mr. Whitney Scott?"

A scorch of dread flowed through Haven, and she closed the napkin of food.

"Well, I heard he was found dead by a tomahawk." Captain Simmons glanced around as a few whispers filled the courtroom.

Max handed yet another paper to the judge. "There was a tomahawk slammed into the headboard, but that was not apparently how Mr. Scott died. Doctor Tess examined the banker's body and her statement is here, where she draws up the cause of death to be asphyxiation, not even so much as a mark on the man's body related to the tomahawk."

"I'd also add these…" Max held up a stack of papers. "Official papers submitted by numerous citizens in and around Cheyenne, all filing complaints on being cheated by Mr. Scott related to payments on homesteads and claims, falsified deeds of ownership. And while this trial is not about the untimely death of the banker, I submit this to the courts to make a statement that a lot of people might have had reason to want Mr. Scott dead."

Judge Garrett hit the hammer hard, glaring at the attorney. "Mr. Ferguson, this is not the trial for the death of Mr. Scott, and you will leave it as such."

Max gave just a lift of his brows and a nod and then walked a full circle, waving his hands as he spoke. "So as to pull this all together, I find it rather interesting, Captain, that you fail to fight alongside your men as they are attacked. Why? Because you were too busy trying to apprehend my clients. You failed to name Dancing Fox as a possible connection to the Dog Soldiers who attacked as he chanted with all the other Cheyenne in some sort of uprising. You fail to prove your version of the direction my clients took to escape the soldiers. And you fail to arrest Miss Oakley, whom you say rendered aid to my clients." The attorney turned on a dime and held the captain's gaze. "You seem to fall very short in the control of your soldiers in town, leading one to wonder if it is the same at the fort."

McEntyre jumped to his feet. "Objection, Your Honor, this cannot continue." His voice echoed across the room.

Max smiled and bowed to the court, taking his seat. "That's all for now, Sir."

Chapter Thirty-One

The early afternoon came as court continued. Dawson and Leaning Bear had been held by soldiers in a side room outside the court. Dawson had forced himself to eat more than one of the slices of meat and bread. Nausea had scored through him, but once the food settled, he'd been better for it.

Returning to the courtroom behind his friend, both their shackles were once again removed, and they were seated under guard. He met brief gazes with Haven, his heart pounding at the idea Max had explained—he'd call her next. Dawson turned to face the court, uncertain he could take it without an outburst if anyone was unkind to her.

Max glanced at him. "She's ready. I spoke to her prior to coming back inside. The good thing is we are calling her first, as they are afraid of her testimony."

Dawson couldn't utter a word but gave a nod. He gripped his fists tight. He was supposed to be her protector, yet now, there was little he could do as Max stood.

"The defense calls Miss Haven Oakley to the stand, Your Honor." Max waited as Haven made her way to the front.

"Sit still." Sawyer's deep voice found the depths of Dawson as if somehow his father's voice reached him through his brother. He shrugged his brother's hand away and leaned to hold his side. They had all known Haven would be called to the stand, but he hadn't been prepared for the shredding pain that plowed through him.

He'd have surrendered to death if there had been a way to keep her off the stand. Following her gaze, he glanced behind him to where Levi and Zane had slipped into the back of the room despite being turned away by soldiers earlier.

He turned back, his vision blurring, causing him to blink several times, nausea coursing through him to the point he could have gagged out loud. He rubbed a hand across his face and forced his gaze back to Haven. "Miss Oakley, to begin with, please let us know where you reside." Max offered a nod of reassurance.

Haven's cheeks glowed pink, but she nodded. "My brothers and I live at the old Harper homestead, as most know. We've been there for several years now."

"Very well. I'd like to go back a little bit to identify when you first met Dawson McCade and Leaning Bear." Max slowed his words, inviting her calm response.

Haven cleared her voice. "Several months ago, I was collecting herbs when I realized Indians were racing toward me, so I took to my horse and tried to escape them. I soon realized that wasn't going to happen, and as I reached a place of cover, I jumped. I was injured and couldn't run well, and that's when Mr. McCade found me."

Dawson studied her words. *Mr. McCade...*Max had coached her to use proper etiquette instead of using his given name.

"And then?" Max asked, still at ease with his tone.

"Well, he led me to his horse, and we fled to escape, though the Indians followed for a time, until we hid in a crevice underneath the falls." She glanced at Dawson but returned her gaze to the counsel.

"So you both were in grave danger at the pursuit of these Dog Soldiers, and even my client, Dawson McCade, felt the need to escape them?" Max questioned, walking to lean against the table where Dawson and Leaning Bear sat.

"Objection. Leading," McEntyre shouted.

"Sustained." The judge gave a prompt response.

Max reworded his question. "Miss Oakley, did you suspect Mr. McCade of knowing those Dog Soldiers?"

Haven shook her head. "He was adamant to get us both from the area. He told me they were very dangerous for us both."

"Lead us into what followed with your injuries, your return home, and the recovering of your horse." Max stepped closer, waiting beside Haven but allowing the courtroom to see her.

Haven gave a slight nod, her hazel eyes serious. "Mr. McCade got us back to his cabin, where he cared for my injuries. The snow was heavy and there was no way to get me to a doctor. I rested for a few days and then he took me back home to my brothers."

Max nodded for her to continue.

"Several weeks later, I was out searching for herbs closer to home this time, when Mr. McCade found me, and he had Josie, my horse, with him." Her voice cracked with a bit of emotion. "I never thought I'd see her again."

"And did he tell you how he acquired the animal?"

She continued, though her fingers traced a seam of

lace along the skirt of her dress. "He said from the livery owner at the fort, Mr. Roberts. He's a very kind man and said he got her from Indians. I don't know much more than that, I'm afraid."

"Very well, and after this you saw Mr. McCade again when your youngest brother fell ill?" The lawyer gave her a nod, shoving his hand into his pockets.

"Yes, James had such a high fever I had to take him to the McCade ranch to see Doctor Tess. Thankfully he did well, and Mr. McCade escorted us home safely afterwards." She lifted her gaze to the judge and back to Max.

"Now, Miss Oakley, can you explain for the courts the reasons Mr. McCade was frequently seen at your homestead, even overnight?" Max held her gaze despite the hushed whispers that traveled across the room.

Dawson's pulse raced but he held himself steady, trying to focus. Behind him Sawyer cleared his voice in warning.

"Mr. McCade stayed to help my brother put a new roof on the barn, to teach Levi how. I believe he was also aware of the issues we've had with our visits to town to pay on our homestead..." She hesitated for a moment.

"Issues?" Max urged.

She nodded. "Most of the time Mr. Scott...well, he would require more than was due on our homestead's account, threatening me and my brothers should we not pay as he desired."

The whispers from the crowd increased until the judge hit the block. "Quiet in the courtroom."

"Is it fair to say that you and your brothers were harassed by the man, then?" Max asked.

"Yes." Haven's voice held strong.

"Can you explain if at any time Mr. Scott caused you physical harm?" Max waited with a lift of his dark brows.

"Well, I told him I was not paying extra on the homestead anymore and he...grabbed my wrist and made threats and inappropriate advances..." Haven stopped, the glow to her cheeks bright.

"And how did Dawson McCade react to this treatment, the bruising of your wrist?"

Haven glanced from Dawson back to Max. "He was very upset and went to the bank to confront Mr. Scott, in warning only."

Max nodded. "And do you think because of this harassment there would be cause for Mr. McCade to harm Whitney Scott?"

"Mr. Ferguson, I believe there are a lot of people in Cheyenne who were threatened by Mr. Scott. Many being forced to pay more than was due, like us. Mr. McCade could hardly be the only person who had words with him. No, I do not believe he would have imposed any harm, only warnings." Haven's voice was stern, and she straightened her back in the chair, holding full eye contact with the judges before her.

"Why do you think Mr. Scott had so many threats to you and your family as well as the advances you say he made toward you?" Max stepped closer to the table again and glanced at his tablet and back to Haven.

"He had reason to want the homestead..." She lifted her gaze. "Because...we discovered a bit of gold, and Mr. Scott kept upping the amount we needed to pay each month, telling me it would keep my brothers safe."

"So, while you've made no formal claim, you and

your brother, Levi, believe it was Mr. Scott who was behind the death of your father. Could you explain?" Max glanced behind him as the chatter and whispers in the courtroom caused the judge to smack his gavel again.

"My father...was brought back to us after drowning by Mr. Scott, only my father was an excellent swimmer, Mr. Ferguson. He had no accidents on the water, but because of threats from Mr. Scott my brother and I never went to the authorities. After he died, I believe Mr. Scott thought he would have our claim easily from us, and that is the reason for the excess payments and threats." Haven narrowed her brows, tears rimming her eyes.

"You believe Mr. Scott killed your father? How do you have further proof of this?" Max nodded for her to continue.

Haven swallowed hard but never dropped her gaze. "Yes. I know most of this town would believe little what Old Man Thorn would have to say, but he saw this happen, where Mr. Scott's men held my father under the water, but there was little he could do. And while he cannot speak, our dog Sosha would go crazy any time Mr. Scott came around. He was there as well."

Laughter erupted across the crowd as she mentioned Thorn.

Haven scanned the room and spoke again, her tone quieting the court. "I hear all the whispers about Thorn, but he is a very good man. Kinder than most of you in this town who make light of him. Thorn has been the only person to check on us when we lost our father and not one of you in this town cared, save Mrs. McCade, who allowed me to continue father's line of credit at the mercantile. Thorn spoke of seeing Mr. Scott and his men drown my father, and I know his word is true. He may talk in riddles, but he doesn't lie."

Max considered her with a smile of approval at her display. "Some might ask if you or your brothers had anything to do with Mr. Scott's untimely demise?"

Dawson shook his head. Ferguson wasn't leaving a thing untouched.

Haven went ahead with her response, holding her chin high. "Did we kill him? No, Mr. Ferguson, we did not, and for that matter, neither did Mr. McCade."

Dawson held her gaze. Telling all she had was giving every miner this side of the Powder River permission to traipse across her land. He'd threatened Scott twice, but he hadn't killed the man, though there would be those that would think otherwise.

Max changed the topic then. "How did you come to know my client Leaning Bear?"

"Well, to be honest..." She glanced at Dawson and then landed her sights on the Medicine Man. "He startled me, and I hit him with a frying pan."

Laughter halted proceedings until the judge pounded the hammer. "Quiet in the courtroom, please!"

Max folded his arms in question. "Really?"

"Yes, I'm afraid it's true. When I was recovering at Mr. McCade's cabin, Leaning Bear came inside and out of my fright over those Dog Soldiers, I nearly knocked him out." She held Leaning Bear's gaze and smiled. "Though I have apologized several times now."

Leaning Bear rubbed the back of his head, getting another round of laughter out of the patrons of Cheyenne. Dawson let go with a slight smile in spite of the pain, Haven meeting his gaze.

"And Miss Oakley, with it being said that Mr. McCade and Leaning Bear were frequently around your homestead, can you explain the relationship and reasons they would be there in better detail?" Max slowed his words, speaking in a relaxed tone, leaning against the table once more.

Haven nodded, a hint of pink crossing her cheeks. "At first it was to protect me and my brothers from Mr. Scott and to help Levi with the barn roof. But after Dawson was injured by the arrow, I found him in my barn, very near death. I did the best I could for him with the blizzard and no way to a doctor. He was so ill he couldn't have ridden far anyway."

Max remained quiet for a long moment. Dawson held his breath and then the counsel went on. "Miss Oakley, there are a lot of people in this courtroom and around town who would think it inappropriate for a young woman such as yourself to keep company with a gentleman like my client in secret for as long as you did. How would you explain this to those here today, for the sake of the courts and in respect of your own reputation?"

Dawson held back a curse, gripping his fists tight. Max had not gone over the details of this question and now he was giving the other side ammunition. *Son of a bitch!*

"Easy, brother." Wyatt's whisper reached him, though he settled little.

"Mr. McCade was the perfect gentleman when I recovered at his cabin. He allowed me his bed and he slept on the floor by the hearth in a different room, just as he did at my home when he was injured and as he worked on the roof. As we know, it was too cold to have him sleep in a barn that needed repairs. I provided his meals in exchange for the work. I cannot help what people will think, most will gossip about our relationship and his staying on at the homestead, but he was a perfect gentleman. In question of my virtue, I believe I owe no one any explanation beyond what I have stated."

The silence in the courtroom was deafening for a long moment, until Max smiled and spoke. "Indeed, Miss Oakley. Your witness, Counselor."

****

The courtroom remained quiet as Haven waited on the opposite counsel to question her. She glanced at Dawson, whose lips gave her the hint of an encouraging smile, but as it was, he'd closed his eyes. He wasn't well and what they were doing to him wasn't right. How could this happen as it had? She also caught Levi's gaze and her brother, looking so much like a man, nodded to her. It worried her that the questions to come would reveal even more than her brother understood. At this point there was little to be done about it, save answering as honestly as she could.

"Miss Oakley, you have stated you cared for Mr. McCade with his injuries. Were you, at that time, aware you were harboring a fugitive?" McEntyre stood and walked to stand in front of Haven, arriving close to her in what she thought was meant to be intimidating her.

"I suspected before he regained consciousness, that he was running from what had happened at the negotiations. He later told me he had been wrongly accused." She held her chin higher toward the man.

"So you willingly kept a known fugitive in your home?" The lawyer glanced at his handful of notes and eyed her again.

"I rendered what medical care I could to Mr. McCade in the middle of a blizzard. He was in no condition to seek help elsewhere. I have been honest with this court in explaining that." Haven held her voice strong and kept a stern gaze on the man.

McEntyre glanced at her again. "And if we step back to the incident of your rescue by Dawson McCade from the Dog Soldiers. You believe he had no relationship with those Indians?"

Haven nodded. "I've explained I do not believe he knew them at all."

"But you can't know this. Have you ever been on the reservations?" The counsel challenged.

"No, I have not been on the reservations, but as we escaped the Dog Soldiers, I was worried they had taken my horse. When Dawson came to my rescue, I had no idea if he knew those Indians or not. I was insistent about getting Josie back, but he gave me no choice and we fled out of necessity," she explained.

"I see, and did you know anything of Mr. Dawson McCade carrying alias credentials or the three hundred dollars, for this impending escape he and Leaning Bear were planning on the night of their capture?" McEntyre changed the question.

Haven shook her head. "I never viewed any papers or money."

"And even as you've told the courts, betrothed to Mr. McCade, did he not confide in you his involvement in the negotiations, and as such, the imminent attack by the Dog Soldiers?"

"Mr. McCade talked to me a number of times about the meetings and what would take place at the negotiations, but never once did he mention any uprising or attack." Haven shook her head but held the man's gaze.

McEntyre moved from the table, circling the room in thought. "And you say Dawson McCade angered easily over Scott's harassment of you?"

"Yes." Haven gave a tentative answer. It occurred to her that he was mixing topics rather fast.

McEntyre held her gaze for a long moment. "But you don't believe that Mr. McCade had anything to do with the untimely death of Whitney Scott?"

Haven held the man's gaze. "With all due respect, Sir, I have answered that question already."

"But you would have no way of knowing for sure. As most in the room know, a man's heart captured by a woman might lead him to take a life to keep her safe, would you not agree? I mean, all of this points very easily to Dawson McCade and his tomahawk on the scene the very night Whitney Scott breathed his last…"

"Objection!" Max stood. "We have covered ground on this topic already, and it isn't relevant to this case."

McEntyre stood alongside Max. "I am using McCade's reactions and known angry behavior as a way of stressing the man cannot control his temper or impulses, thus the reason he has the history he does."

"Dawson McCade is not on trial for the murder of Whitney Scott at this time!" Max stepped closer to the judges.

"And it has been easy enough for the prosecution to prove this point. Added to that is the fact that on the night of Mr. Scott's death, a tomahawk was found in the headboard of the dead man's room, and it is the same night that the Cavalry arrested both these men.

This picture is very clear to the courts, as Dawson McCade has no alibi for either issue."

"I'm afraid you're wrong, Mr. McEntyre." Haven's voice lifted above the arguments of the men before her. "Mr. McCade does have an alibi."

In that brief second, Dawson's heart skipped a beat inside his chest, and it was all he could do to force his words. "Haven. No!" She couldn't say what she was about to, but he'd caught her gaze.

"How is it you know, Miss Oakley?" Judge Garrett held a hand up to quiet both lawyers.

The courtroom fell dead silent.

"Because…he was alone…with me at my home that night." Haven glanced Dawson's way and back to the judge. "And as for the proof you will ask for next…I now carry his child." Haven held her gaze steady on the counsel as hushed whispers shrouded the courtroom. The judge slammed his hammer multiple times as the outburst continued to grow.

Dawson shrugged from his brother's grip, Wyatt fighting to keep him in his seat. Why would Haven think she had to tell this?

"Order, order." The judge hammered in rapid succession. "I demand order. Keep your seat, Mr. McCade, or you will be escorted to your cell for the remainder of the trial." Soldiers now held weapons toward him, and he jerked away from Wyatt once more.

A heavy hand settled across Dawson's shoulder and Max's voice found him. "Sit, now! It's all right!"

Dawson couldn't take his gaze from Haven as she sat looking toward the judges, waiting in silence. She'd done that to protect him and nothing more. His pulse raced at the ridicule she'd now face from all in town.

McEntyre spoke above the crowd. "No more questions, Your Honor."

Chapter Thirty-Two

The afternoon sun filtered through the fancy glass windows of the hotel courtroom. Dawson blinked into the sun, waiting for the warmth that never touched him. Haven had taken her seat once more and now a soldier was posted at the front of the room behind the judge's table due to his near outburst.

Whispers filled the courtroom as Leaning Bear was called to testify. The medicine man stood and made his way across the front of the room to stop before the soldier holding a Bible across a palm.

"Place your hand on the Bible and repeat after me." The soldier's monotone filled the room.

Dawson blinked hard, trying to clear his head. Haven's admission had stirred the courts and him. While it was the bravest of things he'd ever seen, she'd risked much in telling what she had. People in town gossiped and would be less than forgiving to an unmarried pregnant woman. If he did face death from this, then leaving her alone would be all the worse for her.

In the last few hours, the fever that gripped him was worse because now he no longer sweated but stayed frozen to the point his teeth chattered.

"Leaning Bear, you are mandated to take the oath of truth on the Holy Bible." Judge Garrett lifted his voice.

Leaning Bear didn't move but spoke. "A man speaking truth cannot be proven by hand on book. In book, this Jesus speak many truths of government being corrupt."

The soldier lifted his brows toward the judge. "Sir?"

"Mark it for the record the oath was refused and not understood." Judge Garrett gave up.

Leaning Bear turned to Dawson and back. "Understand fine. Believe book hold many truths. Believe white government hold little truths."

Laughter filtered across the room as the Judge stood and leaned across the table. "Your beliefs, Sir, may be your own, but you are on trial here for murder of numerous counts, and you will abide by my rules in this courtroom. You must tell the truth. Do I make myself clear?"

Leaning Bear held the man's gaze. "If speak truth all that is needed, then why this court to decide?"

The judge glared. "Have a seat, Mr. Leaning Bear, or I will have you detained elsewhere, and your trial will go on without you."

Dawson gave a sidelong glance to Max, who sat smiling, amused with the display.

Dawson cleared his voice and made a slight guttural sound from his throat to urge his friend's cooperation. The judge didn't know he was dealing with a Cheyenne medicine man who feared little but was very well educated when it came down to it. His friend had settled to the fact they were walking dead men. He glanced at the paper where Leaning Bear had drawn the likeness of all in court, a blend of faces merging with detailed accuracy.

Leaning Bear settled his gaze on the Cavalry counsel, who stood waiting as he sat.

"Leaning Bear..." McEntyre began but hesitated, looking at the tablet he held.

A wave of nausea rode through Dawson, making him grip the table and hope he didn't gag out loud or pass out. Hunger plagued him, though thirst beckoned, and he reached for the tin cup before him, shaking as he brought it to his lips.

Behind him, Tess whispered, "Wyatt, he can't go on like this..."

He was far worse, and he damn well knew it, as did Doc Tess. He was having a hard time and had to focus on each word as the lawyer continued with Leaning Bear.

"Can you please explain for the courts your relationship to Dawson McCade, as well as your place among the Cheyenne tribes?" McEntyre folded his arms.

Leaning Bear began. "I am medicine man but not belong to tribes. Belong to all Cheyenne nation. Dawson McCade is my brother."

A hush of whispers flowed through the room.

"Brother?" Counsel questioned.

The medicine man nodded. "Blood is not only thing to make men brothers."

Leaning Bear's comment made Dawson open his eyes. They did indeed have the kinship as close as he and his own brothers. He wondered now where the small knife and bear claw had wound up, given all their possessions had been taken, but it was evident neither mattered now. Most likely Sawyer held what personal items had been confiscated, all but the money the captain had made off with.

Leaning Bear went on. "Work for tribe with Dawson, food and medicine for tribes. Translation of many tribes Sioux, Arapahoe. Teach Dawson Cheyenne language long ago, to talk to white government for my people."

"And during this work, would you say you illegally gave extra passes to the Cheyenne?" McEntyre pushed further, taking a step back and folding his arm.

Leaning Bear nodded. "It is as you say."

The lawyer glanced at the judge. "Sir, do you and Dawson give unauthorized accesses to the men of your tribe, regardless of the rules?"

Leaning Bear never hesitated. "Piece of paper tell a man you may now hunt in small area to feed family. Paper worthless when family has hunger."

The lawyer postured, his muscles going rigid. "Yes or no. Do you give more passes than allowed, sir?"

"It is as you say." The medicine man held the counsel's gaze.

Dawson thought for a moment to chuckle. Leaning Bear was amusing himself, though it wasn't working for the judge or counsel.

"Fine. Were you aware of Dog Soldiers being in the area, and do you or have you ever known these Indians?" McEntyre backed down, scrubbing a hand over his face.

Leaning Bear held his chin high, following the counsel with his gaze. "It many years since Dog Soldiers part of tribe. Yes, I know these men back then when the white man slaughter tribes."

"Just answer the question." McEntyre glanced at Judge Garrett.

The judge nodded in agreement, motioning the medicine man to continue with the wave of his hand.

"Long ago I know Dog Soldiers. Now I know none." Leaning Bear answered once more the same.

"Can you tell me in your opinion how the negotiations proceeded?" McEntyre asked but took a step back and leaned against the table beside the captain.

Leaning Bear pushed his shoulders back, adding a nod. "Negotiations for white man with papers. Much promised is broken. Treaties worthless papers. Tribes upset at death of chief, chanting for peace only."

"And you think Dancing Fox began this chanting because the chief passed on?" The lawyer pursed his lips, tapping a foot along the wooden floor.

Leaning Bear thrust his chest out and gave a nod. "Dancing Fox talks no war, except to respect death of father. Cheyenne and all nations speak war, but all know that fight means more death. You believe Dancing Fox lead this, why Dancing Fox not brought to court? That is question for you to find the answer."

Dawson had to smile, though it was a struggle. Leaning Bear would play them the entire time if they continued. His belly burned deep inside and nausea made his head spin. He closed his eyes for a moment.

The counsel turned back to the court. "During the time of Mr. McCade's healing, you and he remained in touch somehow to plan escape from all this, did you not?"

"We part after negotiations. He rode toward Woman with Frying Pan, only way for help in blizzard with the wound he carried." Leaning Bear place both palms to his knees.

"Yet the night of your capture, and the night Mr. Scott was killed, you met up with Dawson McCade with a set plan to escape. You must've conversed at some point, and perhaps you even know if Mr. McCade had anything to do with killing Mr. Scott?" McEntyre rocked back and forth on his heels.

The Indian lifted a single brow at the question and then spoke. "When timing right, spirits speak to each."

The lawyer cocked his head. "Sir, do you know the details of Mr. Scott's death at the hands of Dawson McCade?"

"Not killed by hands of Dawson McCade. You say killed by tomahawk or suffocate." Leaning Bear held a serious chocolate-eyed gaze at the man.

Laughter erupted and ceased just as fast with the judge's glare.

"Did Dawson McCade kill Mr. Scott?" McEntyre raised his voice an octave.

The Indian angled his gaze at the man and shrugged. "Don't know. Not there. This not my question."

Laughter filled the room, and Judge Garrett slammed his hammer again. "Leaning Bear, I take my court seriously and you will do the same. Please answer the question."

"It is as you say. Tomahawk kill banker. Pillow kill banker. Cannot speak to who hold tomahawk or pillow." The medicine man held a stoic face.

Max poured more water for Dawson and handed him the tin cup. Dawson hadn't been aware he'd closed his eyes, but he angled a glance at the lawyer, who spoke. "You need a break?"

He shook his head. If they let him lie down, he

wouldn't get back up. "I'm good."

"Now, in your line of work, it's been pointed out that you and Mr. McCade's work ethics are rather sporadic. If you will. Let me phrase that more elementarily, that you show up when it's convenient for yourself. How would you explain this?" McEntyre changed the subject as he settled back to his chair.

"Not need simple words. My people need medicine man often, show up where needed most." The Indian's brows narrowed.

"Yet the government pays you for acting to assist the soldiers with the tribe. Taking pay for a job not done is considered fraudulent." McEntyre folded his arms with an accusatory brow.

"Pay for Dawson is half more than pay for medicine man. White government ethic of more question in honesty than my show at captain's request." Leaning Bear stood, though the posted soldiers placed rifles toward him.

"Take your seat, Leaning Bear." Judge Garret slammed his gavel on the block.

Dawson studied his friend, the number of years between them uncounted but understood. It was true that Leaning Bear made less wages, though he'd little ever complained of it.

"The United States Government is not on trial here, Sir." McEntyre rolled his eyes, setting the tablet aside.

"Maybe should be." The medicine man added with a smirk as he sat again. "And who says this of not good character? Good character not the United States Payroll Department."

Laughter rumbled again, once more quieted by the beat of the hammer across the block.

Dawson found himself amused. He lifted the glass and drank more of the cool water, a shiver rushing through him.

"Your Honor." The counsel turned to the judge, pleading.

"Leaning Bear, please just answer the question instead of offering another." Judge Garrett rolled his eyes and laid the hammer down.

McEntyre rushed to start again. "To go on, you have an established relationship to the Cheyenne on the two reservations in this area. It is said you have no relationship with the Dog Soldiers, though those Indians were seen on both reservations by soldiers on numerous occasions. How would you not have known these men if this is the case?"

Leaning Bear took a long moment before his answer. "The white soldiers not good at identify each Indian. See all Cheyenne the same. Cheyenne have Dog Soldiers with tribe, but not the same as the men that attacked at negotiations."

"So you are saying men of trouble are on the reservation, but they are not the ones who led the attack. And how is it you have proof of this?" The counsel shook his head with a shrug.

"How I have proof *you* not know Dog Soldiers?" Leaning Bear's dark brows lifted, his chocolate eyes serious.

The lawyer drew in a deep breath and let it go. "Did you or did you not know the Dog Soldiers that attacked the negotiations?"

"No. Did not know these men now, but long ago." Leaning Bear shrugged. "I repeat this again for white law man for making simple."

Cackles from the courtroom brought on the judge's hammer again, quieting the crowd, though Leaning Bear gave a lift of his dark brows.

McEntyre went on. "You say you tried to stop the attack, yet you and Mr. McCade were quick to ride off from the fight when the captain ordered you to stop. How is that?"

"Captain order arrest. Not fond of death by soldiers." Leaning Bear lifted his dark brows.

The crowd erupted in whispers and giggles.

"All right, folks. Quiet down." Judge Garrett smacked the anvil several times.

Dawson jumped, his head pounding right along with the clack of hard wood. He rubbed a hand across his face, finding his palm covered in dampness.

McEntyre continued to waltz around the front of the court, gesturing with his hand. "And so, this act of cowardice was out of fear of facing the consequences for assuming the responsibility of urging the attack at hand."

"Objection." Max lifted a swift hand.

The judge waved him off with a brush of the hand.

"This act of coward for rope or bullet, not captain." Leaning Bear went on. "Captain not fight with soldiers because of wanting arrest for Dawson and medicine man. No choice but flee."

The counsel turned to face Leaning Bear once more. "It's been said you hid right along with the Dog Soldiers. If this is not the case, how is it we have proof?"

"Why white man need proof of all things? I find Cheyenne Dog Soldiers, I wake up dead. You find Dog Soldiers, you wake up dead." This time the medicine man offered a smile.

Dawson chuckled at his friend's humor though it was short lived when McEntyre continued. "So, as it stands, in summary, you rarely show up for your assigned work, take the government's pay, and you have no proof as to not knowing the Dog Soldiers who attacked and killed seven Cavalrymen. But you ran and hid, planning things with Dawson McCade to escape as cowards, and then met him as you'd schemed only to be caught." McEntyre repeated it all using his fingers to count each item he mentioned.

"Run not proof of coward. Run proof of wrongly accused. White men find all Indians liars and cheat. All Indians guilty long before trial." Leaning Bear leaned back in his chair, chin held high.

The judge slammed his hammer to the bursts of chatter in the court. "Quiet in the courtroom."

"When the Dog Soldiers attacked, what were you and Dawson McCade doing?" Counsel went on, pacing the room once more.

"Try to stop attack. Then captain turn soldiers to follow as Dawson and medicine man flee." Leaning Bear sat stoic, his eyes fixed on the man.

"It seems odd the Cheyenne stayed to fight, and you fled, even while your new chief stayed to defend the tribe." The counsel shrugged with a lift of his dark brows.

"Odd to you, but guns facing me. Ride fast." Leaning Bear held a serious gaze on the counsel, though laughter echoed the room.

From behind him, Haven's giggle found Dawson and he turned for a brief second. Somehow, he held her in the brevity of their gaze. Her laughter so easily found even with all she had endured and all that was to come. He turned back to face the court. She'd been determined to afford her brothers a good life and she would do the same for their child, whether or not he was present. Damn…he had no patience for all this, his body boiling itself to death one slow minute at a time. He reached for the water again, shaking hard as he drank, spilling drips of the cool liquid from his chin.

"I will ask this one last question. Leaning Bear, did you and or Dawson McCade plan for the attack on the Cavalry that took the lives of seven men and leaves the general near death at this hour?" McEntyre's voice covered the courtroom as he stamped a foot to the wooden floor.

Leaning Bear waited a long moment. "No, this I did not do. This Dawson McCade did not do."

Chapter Thirty-Three

Max stood, a hand pressed to Dawson's shoulder for a brief moment before he took the front of the room. The court had paused for a thirty-minute break and it had done him little good. Tess has insisted on his drinking more willow bark tea, though he reckoned it wouldn't help much. The worry in the physician's eyes had told him the story he already knew. He was near death and except for Haven and the child might even welcome it.

He took a deep breath and willed away the fog of fever that held him captive. The lawyer from New York had been supportive but stern in saying they were up against a wall that he'd do his best to tear down. The counsel had questioned Leaning Bear with thoroughness and while part of that had been comical, it was now his turn to take the oath.

"I call to the stand Dawson McCade." Max nodded, a hush falling over the confines of the courtroom.

Dawson stood, holding the table to steady himself before he moved to the front. The soldier held out the black leather Bible. "Place your right hand on the Bible and repeat." Dawson eyed the Bible before him, something he'd cherished his entire life in spite of his Cheyenne beliefs, which merged with what he knew the big book carried. Without hesitation he laid his hand on the Bible, his prayers for Haven and the baby alone.

"Do you promise to tell the truth, the whole truth, and nothing but the truth, so help you God?"

"I do." Dawson sat and adjusted to comfort with the length of his forearm pressed to his side. The pain there never ceased, and a hard shiver ran the length of his body even with his will to keep himself still.

He glanced around the room, viewing the gaze of his family and many from town who knew him well. Some in support and some interested in the spectacle alone. He didn't linger with the quick glimpse of Dodge who had worn her best and was sitting with her usual proud posture, offering him a smile. She'd made it clear he would not lose, and while McCade money could be stretched far, it was his best guess that these proceedings weren't about who had the biggest purse.

He took his gaze to Haven, who sat between his mother and Doc Tess, and in spite of the fear holding her sweet hazel eyes, she let the edge of her lips curl.

Max studied his page of notes while standing. The lawyer had said he would lead things slowly and systematically. The man had coached none of them but had prepared them for the difficult issues at hand.

"Dawson, let's start at the beginning with your background, where you assumed your role as a civilian contracted by the government." Max pulled his shoulders back and shoved his hands into his trouser pockets, non-assuming.

Dawson cleared his voice and searched his thoughts. "For some years I've helped the Cheyenne with understanding the treaties. It's going on ten years since Leaning Bear and I were asked to take the assignment in the best interest of the tribes, mostly for translation."

Max nodded with a tilt of his head. "And with this translation, what other duties are you assigned?"

Dawson shrugged, focusing on a deep breath. "The work evolved from translating into both of us becoming go-betweens for the Cheyenne and the Cavalry, a way to keep better order for the tribes and less harassment in the long run."

"Objection," McEntyre shouted, raising a hand and letting it fall again.

"Overruled."

"And that would involve the passes that are in question?" Max nodded for Dawson to continue.

Dawson wiped the sweat from his brow with the sleeve of his tunic, nausea cutting his thoughts "Each reservation receives government signed passes good for two men at a time to hunt or trade off the reservations."

"It's been stated that you and Leaning Bear hand out more of these passes than are necessary, for lack of a better word, and you would agree to this before the court?" Max glanced behind him at the courtroom full of patrons and back.

"I give men passes to feed their families as needed and yes, in excess. Most simply want to hunt for small game or to trade their pelts somewhere besides the fort where they can gain a better price. Few cause trouble," he added, gripping his hands to his knees.

"I see, and do some at times abuse this privilege?"

"Sure, but not for long, most returning when their hunt's successful. Game isn't always plentiful close to the reservations." He clutched his side, closing his eyes in a hard blink to the nausea again.

"Is there any reprimand for those that return late?"

"At times, further harassment from the soldiers. These men know they risk their families and a good beating if they return late." He eyed the captain, who sat stoic.

"And the rifts the captain refers to, and the bickering with him and the soldiers, come for what reasons?" Max asked, giving him the freedom to speak.

"The women on the reservations are often teased unmercifully and the men made a spectacle. It never seems to end." He answered as best he could, blinking hard in fatigue.

"And it's true that provisions slated for the reservations often do not make it there."

He nodded. "I can imagine if you go to the fort now, the two storage houses are full of spoiled goods."

"To change things up. Return of Miss Oakley's horse had nothing to do with you knowing the Dog Soldiers that gave pursuit to you both?" Max leaned on the table. "You believed your own life in danger?"

Dawson worked to focus on him. "I came upon them and saw her running in the distance. They would have killed us both had we not hidden."

"Explain your time spent with Miss Oakley was to add the roof to the barn and to keep her and her family safe from the harassment by Mr. Whitney Scott. Did you know of the yielding claim that Miss Oakley and her brothers worked?"

Dawson angled a glance at Max, wondering at the question. "I helped with the barn's roof, taught Levi how, and yes, I worried about the harassment by Scott. But I have no interest in the claim."

Whispers filled the courtroom, halting them for the moment.

"So, to speak of Mr. Scott, explain the words you had with him at the bank after he harmed Miss Oakley." Max nodded.

Dawson shook his head. "She'd taken enough abuse verbally, but that day, she came to the mercantile, clearly upset and her wrist injured."

"And you went to the bank to confront the man. Can you explain in clear detail what happened?"

"I walked across town, into the bank, and into his office. I pulled my tomahawk and held it to his neck and let him know harassing Haven and her family would no longer be tolerated." Dawson's pulse raced. He'd not lie about any of it, and while he had threatened the man, he hadn't taken the banker's life.

"Seems rather stern…" Max lifted his dark brows.

"A man like Mr. Scott wasn't easily convinced and surrounding himself with guards should be clear evidence enough of his abuse of those owing the bank," he explained and added. "Since his death I understand his armed guards have all but disappeared. Is anyone looking at the idea of their quick departure?"

"Seems the course. And then, the night Mr. Scott died, you were there again?" Max went on with a nod for him to continue.

This was a loaded question. He'd come to town that night to meet his brothers but admitting that wouldn't be the best thing to do unless asked. "I had mended enough to make it to town, and as I knew I'd be leaving Haven and her brothers to Scott's mercy I planned to warn him. I got past the man guarding the front of his home, found Scott asleep, held my hand to his mouth and let him know he'd best leave her and her brothers alone. With that I slammed the tomahawk right into the headboard and escaped back outside. I was warning him by the fact I got past his guard."

"So, Dawson, did you kill Mr. Whitney Scott that night?"

"No. He was alive when I left." A hard shudder slammed through his body and his teeth chattered audibly.

Max glanced at the judge. "Your Honor, this man is clearly too ill to be sitting here. We request a break of these proceedings."

"Denied. Continue on after he has more water." The judge glanced toward the table at the water pitcher.

Max glared but reached for the tin mug Leaning Bear pushed toward the edge of the table.

Dawson took the cup and drank, forcing himself to have steady hands then handing the cup back.

Max pushed on, setting the cup on the table behind him. "In town just after your first warning to Whitney Scott, he and his men jumped you and a fight took place where the Sheriff had to intervene. Is that right?"

"It was short lived, but unexpected." He nodded. "He and his men sparred with me and my brothers, but no harm came from it."

"We've already settled on the facts of the negotiations and how things occurred. Would you have anything more to add at the time of the attack and at the time you and Leaning Bear were forced to flee the scene?" Max spoke slowly, walking a small circle before the court.

"I was shocked when the attack happened. The chanting with Dancing Fox started right before, and so I didn't see the Dog Soldiers until the general took that arrow." He held his arm tighter to his aching side. "I turned and realized what was happening, and even though Leaning Bear and I tried to stop them, they kept coming. The captain called us out to his soldiers and bullets started hitting the ground around us." He stopped, his breath short. "I got to Viho…and we rode off and the arrow went through me about that time."

"Even so, in trying to escape, you thought to grab that arrow that rested in a tree after hitting you?"

"I didn't know at first the arrow had gone through me. The pain came seconds later, and I saw the arrow ahead of me. At the time, I only thought to grab it, thinking I'd find the man who sent it one day." He fought to take several breaths.

"You made your way in the blizzard to Miss Oakley's for help?" Max lifted his dark brows.

"I remember little about getting there, but I woke, and she and her brother got me inside their home, helped me to stop the bleeding. I was so weak it was a while before I could leave." He was freezing one minute and burning the next.

"And the alias you carried?"

"I planned to use it if I needed, to clear my name, is all." He held a steady gaze on the counsel, not wanting it mentioned he'd gotten those papers from Wyatt.

"And the three hundred golden eagles were taken from you when apprehended?"

"Yes, by the captain, the papers and money in my saddle bag." He glanced at the man who wouldn't meet his gaze.

"Objection."

"Sustained."

"Can you tell us your reason for resignation from

your position prior?" Max moved with the intention of allowing him a quick gaze of Haven.

He held her there for a long moment. He'd never been certain he would become a father, but should his fate set him free, he would be there to raise his child as it should be. He'd watched children tame his older brothers. Given the chance, he had no doubts at all he would find himself content taking care of Haven, her brothers and their own children. He forced his gaze back to Max.

"I've done this job for a long time and seen little improvement for the tribes over the years. Conditions become worse and I'm afraid if I cannot make a difference then it's hard for me to find satisfaction in my work. I was planning to leave for that and…the fact I will soon have a family."

Max smiled. "That's all for the defense, Your Honor."

****

Dawson's heart raced as he remained on the stand awaiting McEntyre's questioning. He held a gaze to the man, the ache through his middle unrelenting as well as the fever that spread sweat across his brow. He was scalding, so hot it felt as if he were freezing. Damn, if he was released from these crimes, he'd still have a hell of a surgery to face.

McEntyre rested a gaze. "Mr. McCade, I see no point in repeating much of what has been said, except to question you further on some of the issues at hand."

Dawson held unblinking, though his vision continued to blur.

"It's been said you've picked fights with the Cavalry, even attacking Captain Simmons at one point.

There is also the fact where you've stated you held your tomahawk to Mr. Scott's throat in warning and slammed the same into the man's headboard after your intrusion into his home. As you were taken into custody, your apparent injuries remain as you resisted time and again. And while you have seemingly explained these actions away, would you not agree you are a very aggressive man by nature?"

"Objection, Your Honor," Max broke in.

"Please refrain from judgment, Counsel." Judge Garrett leaned forward across the table.

Dawson angled a gaze at McEntyre. "Each action I've explained was met with far worse for those I was attempting to help. I believe my aggressive behavior was warranted for the harassment of the tribes and Leaning Bear as well as Miss Oakley and her brothers."

"And how do you feel about seven dead soldiers and the general, who lies near death, Sir!" McEntyre didn't give him time to speak but went on. "Oh, that's right, seven dead now and one in your past, which explains much."

"Objection, Your Honor. Double jeopardy." Max stood and then sat again.

"Overruled, Counselor." Judge Garrett nodded for him to continue.

"I've men from the Cavalry reporting a bit of a scuffle the same night you fought with Scott and his men. Can you speak to this?" McEntyre waited with lifted brows.

No matter how he answered any of these questions, it seemed the tone of questioning was accusatory. He blinked hard to clear his vision. "This was before the negotiations. I'd gone to the saloon to meet my brother,

Wyatt, in order to pick up medication Doc Tess had ordered for me to take to the reservations."

He stopped, his head swimming in search of the details, the order of things. "I...was only in the saloon a short time, but it was the soldiers who became aggressive."

"I see, and afterwards, it was Scott and his men who attacked you?" McEntyre consulted his notes.

Dawson nodded, his mouth so dry the words were harder to find. "That's right."

"Well, it must come in handy that your brothers run the law here in Cheyenne, making it easy for you to, let's say, not be held accountable for your actions over the years, much like your father Colonel McCade in taking advantages where needed." McEntyre held a close gaze, a clear effort to rile and challenge him.

"Objection!" Max stood. "Colonel McCade has been long deceased prior to these events and with all respect, his character has no play here in court today."

Dawson shook his head and spoke over his own counsel. "No, I'll answer this. My father was well respected as Colonel, serving the country that I still try to protect. He taught me to stand up for what I believe is right and even encouraged me in my protection of the Cheyenne and other tribes who he thought of as his own equal..." He sucked in a much-needed breath, forcing himself to continue as he held his side. "My father would've taken one look at the fort and not tolerated the disorder and disrespect of citizens there."

McEntyre went on. "Mr. McCade, you turned in your resignation and have explained your time with the tribes as done because things have not 'changed' as you had wanted them to. That leads the counsel to believe perhaps you were planning an attack, one last fight of the Dog Soldiers against the Cavalry before you left it all behind...isn't that right, Sir?"

"No!" Dawson fought nausea, his head pounding. "I didn't know anything about the attack or that many Dog Soldiers being in the area. When I found Miss Oakley, there were only the four of them on horseback." The force of his words hurt once more, his body shaking as he clutched the pain in his side.

"And of Miss Oakley, let us suggest, with her family having a yielding claim, your alias on hand for a quick escape and your resignation signed, perhaps, you were going to escape with what you could of her gold, using your affections for her to make such a feat easy, is that not right, Mr. McCade?"

Dawson grabbed the edge of the judges' table, jumping up. "No, that's not the case..." He pushed harder trying to keep his stance as soldiers moved in to grab him. His vision blurred, and his head pounded but he would never have done such a thing to Haven.

Judge Garrett slammed his hammer several times. "Have a seat, Mr. McCade."

Dawson glanced around the courtroom, to his mother and brothers and then to Haven, though he didn't sit, even with two soldiers shoving him toward the chair. "No, I would never do such a thing...I love her, as I have loved no other, and I will not allow you the right to take that from me, even if you do take my life with this trial." He jerked free of the soldiers and grabbed the table, his vision blurring as blood dripped to the floor.

He held Haven's sweet face, his mind fading and the strength leaving his legs. He was losing consciousness and he couldn't take in enough breath. He was gonna be sick, or maybe…the roar of the room made him close his eyes as he grabbed for the table and fell into the darkness.

Chapter Thirty-Four

"Dawson!" Haven jumped to her feet as did most of those in court when he fell to the floor, overturning the judge's table and spilling water.

Doctor Tess pushed through the crowd trying to get to Dawson, and Haven clung to the physician to make it as well. His brothers were already there, from what she could tell as she got closer, Dawson unmoving. *Oh, please Lord...*

"Order!" Judge Garrett shouted as the other men righted the table. "Let the doctor through."

"Dawson?" Tess laid a hand across his damp forehead. "His fever's too high. We need ice right away."

Haven bent to her knees, wanting to touch Dawson, hold him to her, but letting the doctor work.

Suddenly, Dawson startled, blinking his eyes, fighting until Wyatt held him, Sawyer shouting to clear the courtroom for a brief halt.

"Lie still." Wyatt pinned him with little effort.

It was clear he was confused as he glanced around, lying still as his brother had told him, his cheeks scalding red beneath the beard that covered his face.

Tess glanced at her. "Grab the pitcher of water, and I need a cloth."

Haven scrambled up, grabbing the tin of cool water from the table behind her. She stepped through to hand it to Doctor Tess. Haven had no cloth but ripped a section of her petticoat away and handed it to Tess, who dampened it and ran the cool liquid over Dawson's face and neck. He shuddered a violent chill.

"Dawson, lie still." Doc Tess spoke, holding the cloth to his brow.

"I'm…fine." His words were less than a whisper as Haven bent beside him once more. She could still hear in her mind how hard he'd hit the wooden floor. And she touched his cheek and smoothed his hair as he glanced at her.

Doc Tess used her stethoscope and listened to his chest and grabbed his wrist, speaking to the judge. "Sir, you must call a recess. His fever's extremely high and he can't sit for this. We can get it down with ice and cool water, but he can no longer sit on the stand."

The judge nodded. "Very well. Recess for one hour, ladies and gentlemen. Clear the courts."

Haven glanced around as the courtroom began to empty, Sawyer ushering people from the large hotel room. She turned as Dodge bent with a bucket of ice.

"Oh my God, Dawson…" His mother poured the ice across him, and she and Tess made short work of rubbing the cool large chips across his chest and under his tunic.

He fought them until Wyatt stopped him again and then he settled his gaze on Haven, his blue eyes weak but seeking.

"Always so brave." He shivered hard as he focused on her.

"For you. For us." She whispered. He closed his eyes, his entire body shuddering with fever.

"Dodge, we need willow bark tea and more water."

Tess continued to rub ice along Dawson's chest as Dodge scampered from the courtroom.

"Let me...up." Dawson's teeth chattered as he tried to rise, even with Wyatt holding him.

"Rest for a minute while you can," Wyatt coaxed.

Haven took her shawl from her shoulders and rolled it, placing it under his head for comfort as Tess raised Dawson's tunic to look at his wound.

"Oh, my..." Tess grabbed her bag and took scissors to cut away the bloody dressing to his middle.

Dawson groaned in pain, but Haven bent to him. "It's all right. Doc Tess is gonna fix you right up." She ran a hand into his damp hair. "Close your eyes and rest a bit."

He winced at the doctor's touch, but closed his eyes, one hand hanging onto hers and squeezing as Tess struggled to clean the festered bloodied wound. How on earth could he keep going?

He opened his deep blue eyes again. "When I get back home...to you. Gonna make sure you...always wear beautiful things like this." He touched the dress at her shoulder, his teeth chattering.

It was then that Max, standing above them, spoke to the counsel. "I assure you, judge and the courts, that if this man dies at your hands for not allowing him the time he needs and the surgery required...The McCade family will sue the entire Cavalry, Office of Indian Affairs, and the United States Government for his treatment, or lack thereof."

And with that the judge's response came. "Court will reconvene as stated. The accused may stay seated with the doctor alongside him if needed."

Dawson held Haven's gaze again. "I'll be all

right."

"Of course you will." Tears streaked her face as he closed his eyes once more.

****

Dawson stood alongside Leaning Bear as Judge Garrett and the other judges entered the courtroom, all the citizens rising in respect behind him. He'd been allowed the hour of rest and a bit of time for his fever to come down, though it still raged inside him. His brothers and Brett had been allowed to see him for a time, but none of them had any more answer than did he. Max had stayed positive, but he'd read in the lawyer's eyes the worry.

None of the officers looked at either of them or at each other in taking their seats, the courtroom silent for the impending judgment, the day of court complete to this point. And now he stood alongside Leaning Bear awaiting their fate.

His body trembled in fever and focusing was difficult. He'd been allowed a rest for a time because he'd passed out cold. Doc Tess had redressed his wound yet again, but even with a bit of the willow bark tea, his fever was scorching from the inside out. His head pounded, and his pulse raced to the point even sitting had been difficult. But now to stand, his legs shook as did his hands in trying to balance.

He'd sat beside Leaning Bear as both lawyers gave their final statements. McEntyre had painted a perfect picture that pulled it all together in a neat little package where the two of them had committed all the crimes they were accused. Max Ferguson had answered each of those with all the reasons they hadn't committed any of the charges against them. The lawyer from New

York, with a wealth of experience behind him, had done a good job of it all, but this was a military trial.

Beside him, Max held a smile, though it was apparent he too expected the worst. He'd even explained to the family that should a guilty verdict come, he already had telegrams waiting to be sent to Washington to push for an appeal on the basis it should have been a civil trial and to claim it all a mistrial. He'd mentioned also, if acquitted, the family would do well to turn around and file a suit against the military for the delay in Dawson's medical care and for the wrongful accusations.

The fever still raged as he stood beside the medicine man and waited, not allowing himself to turn to his family or Haven. He'd woken on the floor with her sweet voice coaxing him to survive when he'd passed out. She was so brave, and she carried his child, and though he'd never regret holding her in his arms, he had reason to think he should have waited. If this didn't go well, she'd have to raise their child alone and she didn't deserve the heartache that would follow.

Judge Garrett began. "As with any militant trial, the panel of judges present have cast their vote as to the counts charged against Dawson William McCade and the Cheyenne medicine man, Leaning Bear. And so the votes have been tallied and the accused will remain standing as the verdict is read. The three judges beside me, along with myself, have come to a unanimous decision."

Strange that while Dawson's life was on the line with the next few moments, he already knew, the wolf inside him howling in defeat.

The judge glanced at him and Leaning Bear. "As I

read the verdict, the courtroom will remain quiet. Any outburst will not be tolerated. If the court finds these men guilty, then they will be detained and removed from the court by soldiers and will face a firing squad at dawn tomorrow. Should these men be found innocent of the said charges, then they may walk free from this court without harassment on the streets of Cheyenne."

It took a moment, but the room quieted, and the judge began to read. "For the count of aiding and encouraging an attack on Cavalry by Dog Soldiers and continued neglect of duties and responsibilities and for being behind the death of seven soldiers, the Cheyenne Leaning Bear and Dawson William McCade are both hereby found…guilty as charged."

Dawson's knees wanted to buckle, but he forced himself to remain standing. Behind him, Wyatt cursed as soldiers came before him and Leaning Bear. Sawyer removed his hat, swearing as Dawson glanced behind him, the court filled with the noise of cheers and those voicing against the verdict. Beside him Max Ferguson didn't move as the judge continued, "To the charge of one Dawson William McCade in relation to the death of Mr. Whitney Scott, there will be no civil trial of justice given the current verdict."

Dawson closed his eyes and opened them once more. So there it was. A fate neither of them owned.

Max laid down papers before the judge. "We appeal, Your Honor, and call for a mistrial given a civil trial was denied to men who are not soldiers. This appeal has already arrived in Washington and you are mandated to allow for a response."

The judge spoke around him. "Take the men into custody. As spelled out by the law, the convicted fugitives will now remain in the armed guard of the U.S. Cavalry and will face a firing squad at dawn. Mr. Ferguson, your requests are further denied."

A soldier grabbed Dawson's wrists and shackled him as another did the same with the medicine man, leading them toward the back doors of the hotel courtroom.

He searched for Haven in all the commotion, but she and even most of his family were lost to him. His ears rang, and his heart pounded inside his chest as he was shoved ahead. Grabbing his side, he fought the nausea, stumbling as Leaning Bear held him to his feet in spite of the soldiers jerking them along. Then he lifted his gaze, catching Haven's sweet hazel eyes and in that moment, his entire world stopped to the sound of her tears.

****

Dawson glanced from where he lay on the cot, fever ravaging his body, and a shiver forcing through him. Guilty. Both he and the man he'd long called brother would die. Outside the jail, to his surprise, drums echoed where the Cheyenne had gathered out of respect for Leaning Bear, he supposed, the presence of Indians upsetting the town of Cheyenne further. But the city had quieted at the mid of night with Jacob closing down his saloon, something that had never before happened, the man refusing to sell his liquor to soldiers.

He stared at the ceiling as his brothers and Max, in the next room, haggled over avenues that might be found to halt the early morning firing squad. He'd never feared death. He'd face it head on in its coming but telling Haven goodbye was something he could never do.

He'd been told family could visit, but he didn't know when, and no matter, he had to find the words of comfort Haven needed, words that eluded him now. He closed his eyes to the fatigue and the fever wracking his body. Maybe death wouldn't be so bad, and relief would come for the endless pain, though his heart ached for what might have been with Haven and the fact she carried his unborn child.

****

Haven's pulse raced and a pain as fierce as any she'd ever known held in her chest, cutting her breath short, but she waited outside the jail because she wanted to be with Dawson if the soldiers would allow it. There were no more tears her body could make as terror rode through her time and again. How could they do this and kill innocent men? How would she ever take a breath again with Dawson put to death? She wanted to scream the injustice, but his family was already scrambling to find a way, though Washington had not replied.

It had been several hours now since the courtroom had exploded with the roars of chaos at the verdict Dawson and Leaning Bear had been found guilty of all charges. She'd jumped up alongside his family unable to speak amid the protests as his mother shouted, trying to get to him herself. But people stood, blocking aisles, and before even his brothers could react, Dawson and Leaning Bear had been escorted from the courtroom, with his brothers and Brett Morgan held at gunpoint by soldiers.

When they couldn't get to Dawson, Dodge had held her as she wept until her own ears rang. All the women had cried, his mother, Mei Ling, Doc Tess and

Rose, all hanging onto one another in this disaster of wrongdoing. But it was his brothers who had been detained for a time, as soldiers took over the manning of the jail from Sawyer and Wyatt.

Cavalry lined the jail now, the streets quieter than she might have expected. Cheyenne, the town where Dawson had grown up, offering him nothing more than his place to be put to death. Bile rose in her throat, nausea creeping close enough to make her cover her mouth and force herself to swallow.

Someone took her hand, and she glanced down at the familiar strength. "Levi." She whispered as she let go of Dodge and fell into her younger brother's embrace, and the tears began all over again as her brother held her.

"The soldiers wouldn't let me or Zane inside, but we got in once things started." His words were soft, and he trembled as she clung to him.

"I know. James?" she asked, worried for both of them.

Levi brushed a sleeve across his damp cheeks. "He don't know nothin'. I left Sosha with him at the ranch, and Rose's friend, Muriel, is there with all the children. Haven, they can't do this…but…" He pulled her aside and hesitated.

"Levi?"

His tears were real as he spoke in a hoarse whisper. "I didn't say it, but Thorn…Haven, I should have told you, but I didn't know it would be like this, I didn't really…"

"What about Thorn, Levi, what?"

Levi shook his head. "Thorn talks so crazy sometimes, but he said something about the banker, meaning Mr. Scott, would no longer be a problem…what if he did it…I should've told you."

"I'll ask when I get to see Dawson, but you don't say anything more. Dawson was not tried for his death, so it won't matter." Haven could hardly believe what her brother had told her. What if Thorn had killed Mr. Scott? Would it change things now? She had no words for him or for herself and she squeezed his hand tighter.

"Pa, you have to do something." Zane spoke in anger, his face red with tears that matched her brother's. "You have to stop it."

Sawyer stepped closer to his son, letting go of Rose. "Zane, son…"

"No, you have to stop it. You know people. They can't do it. I won't let them. Do you hear me, all of you? I won't let them do it." Zane pounded his fists as Sawyer subdued him in his embrace, holding him until his body went limp, defeated.

Sawyer's own eyes rimmed with tears that fell in streaks as he held his son, Rose putting her arms around them both as Zane cried hard into his father's chest.

Wyatt stood stoic with Tess dabbing away her silent tears alongside Dodge who hadn't wept since the verdict. Mei Ling stood beside her, using a silk cloth to dry her tears.

Just past them all was Evan, who stayed to himself, though Haven had seen his tears as well. He'd spoken angry words to Sawyer and Wyatt, but it was Brett who had turned him away, talking to him in the distance.

McEntyre stepped outside the jail, his darkened gaze scanning across them all. "You're permitted to visit for a time. I've made sure the soldiers will give you privacy by stepping into the office."

Wyatt nodded, as did Sawyer, and all entered the jail, with many of the citizens of Cheyenne looking on. Haven stepped inside, her brother still hanging onto her hand and Dodge walking just ahead of her as they all faced Dawson.

She had thought Dawson would be angered, even distressed, but he moved little, due to his condition. Sweat streaked his cheeks and neck and the wound was seeping through to stain his fancy buckskin tunic.

Dawson glanced at them all one by one as he began. "There's no need...for a lot of words here. Not gonna try to say something profound, but I need to know all of you will go on...with your lives no matter this is happening." He focused on his brothers.

Haven dabbed at her tears with a handkerchief Rose had stuffed into her hands at some point upon entering the jail.

"All of you did what you could. No letting any of this eat you up inside once it's done. None of you." Dawson lifted his tone. "And...I gave Sawyer a list of things to take care of once this is done. Things to make sure of...for me." He caught Haven's gaze and her heart jumped inside her chest and more tears threatened.

"Gonna ask you all to go. Let me do this as best I can. Don't want you looking on tomorrow either. Sawyer, take the ladies home tonight." His voice softened, and he held his side, shuddering in fever.

Rose burst into tears, hiding her face in Sawyer's chest, but it was Dodge who stepped to him with a smile. "We are all going to respect your wishes, son. You've always made me proud, even now, Dawson." With that she drew him closer and placed her lips on his cheek and turned, wiped her eyes and spoke again. "We ladies will be at the clinic throughout the night, but we will not leave you. Wyatt, if you will allow Haven a bit of time and see her to us when she's ready."

Haven held Dodge's gaze, in awe at her show of strength, which she was sure she didn't hold herself. Wyatt nodded as Tess touched his hand and followed Dodge, her arm around Rose, who tugged Zane to follow in spite of his efforts to resist.

Mei Ling had remained quiet but now stepped to Dawson, her voice but a whisper. "Had ever I a son, he would be as you."

Dawson touched her cheek through the bars, and she turned to follow Dodge, weeping audibly.

Haven gave Levi a nudge. "Please, go with Zane. I'll be all right."

"I'll wait outside for you, no matter how long." Her brother turned to follow the others, his head down. She wasn't sure when Levi had become a man, but today was surely that day.

Brett held a hand through the bars and Dawson gripped it for a long moment, it seeming no words needed between them though the older man spoke near tears. "You say the word, and I'll blow this whole town with black powder and take down that fort with all I can give it."

Dawson smiled. "Best you stay out of trouble."

Brett stepped back, brushing a hand across his face.

"Got a couple of things." Dawson's blue eyes held serious and hard. "The captain...watch him, he's not done yet."

"We got the captain." Wyatt raised his voice in a stern tone.

Evan stood nearby, his face streaked with tears and he stepped before Dawson, who smiled. "Keep yourself out of trouble and the ranch in order."

Evan nodded, but gave no words.

Dawson held Haven's gaze for a moment and turned to his eldest brother. "Sawyer, you've my list. Make sure of it all. Allow Zane the mare and give Nicholas the colt. And I want you to give Viho, to Levi and when James is older, my knife to him."

Haven turned, wiping her eyes and forcing herself not to allow any further tears. She had to be strong for Dawson, and if his mother could do so, then she would push herself to do the same.

Sawyer shrugged. "Still no response from Washington, but I'll keep at it. Max is sending more telegrams to call for a mistrial or an appeal, whatever we can get. Hank's trying to get word he can bring you back to Washington for sentencing at a later time."

Dawson shook his head. "I'd never make the trip." Hell, he could hardly stand up now. "This here's not your fault, Sawyer, and Max did all he could. None of you are at any fault. It just happened. Don't need you out on some revenge as you did for Father. Nothing good will come of it, and you've families." Dawson walked away and turned back to them. "Now leave me to it. I'd like to talk to Haven…"

One by one his brothers filed out, Evan lingering until Sawyer urged him away, his youngest brother bursting into tears. Dawson watched them and turned back to her and of all things gave the hint of a smile.

With the weight of all that shadowed them, Haven stepped toward him, increasing her speed until she met the bars, falling into what embrace he could offer through them. He clung to her, his fingers mingling in her hair and his tears matching hers. "Never wished any of this for you."

She lifted her gaze. "I'll never be sorry for one second spent with you, but I will not tell you goodbye, ever. But Dawson, Levi…he didn't know it would matter, but it seems Thorn may have been the one who killed Mr. Scott, as he said as much in his roundabout way. Would that help? I could go to Max or even the judge."

Dawson shook his head and held her. "It would only be those charges not the others. No one would believe Thorn anyway, Haven."

"But we have to try everything."

He wiped her tears. "No. Haven, I want…you to know…I never knew love until you. The song of my heart. But promise when the time comes…one day you will love again. You deserve to be loved for your lifetime, by a good man."

She shook her head. How could he ask such a thing? Yet she agreed for him, so he could be brave in the final things he wanted. "I promise."

"Haven, this is done. No more tears…happy times are coming." He touched her belly through the bars. "The wolf came to me. He showed me a little girl with flaming hair like her Mama. Name her Asha when she comes."

Haven smiled, though tears scrolled down her cheeks. "Hope."

He nodded as Wyatt whispered at the door. "We've been ordered to go until morning."

Dawson held her tighter and touched her lips with his thumb. "Haven, look at me. She'll be beautiful like you, and I'll be there too, watching as she grows. Always remember the sun will rise come morning so you can smile, not hurt. Give her the stone I gave to you, when she's of age, so she will remember my love. I'm going to ask you not to come tomorrow, Haven...I can't do this with you there...I can't see you and go to it..." His voice cracked, and he drew up her chin, taking the last kiss she would know from him. She stole one more before Wyatt tugged her gently from him, escorting her outside the jail where she fell once more into her brother's arms.

Chapter Thirty-Five

Dodge sat alone on a bench inside the small church at the end of town, the double doors open, a single lamp lit at the altar as a frigid wind whipped across her and gooseflesh rose on her arms. She refused the shiver her body demanded, preferring the sting of the cold, the stale night filling her with more dread than she had ever carried at one time.

She fought for a deep breath, her thoughts staggering over the last few days and the final word from the judge this afternoon. Dawson and Leaning Bear would die come morning. Her son would be put to death for crimes he had not committed against man and country. And his longtime friend would die just the same, for doing nothing more than what had been asked. Yet sitting in the dark, it was her own heart struck by the impending bullet in her ability to do nothing more to save them both.

She wasn't sure what had compelled her to make her way inside the church and the needful call to pray away her own sins of the past. Well, she'd leave those how they were, tactful in praying in even bursts of Sunday morning confessions. She glanced at the lamp on the altar, yet didn't speak her prayers aloud, letting her heart rest there at the front for her son.

With the judge's final words, she'd fought hard to get to Dawson as he and the medicine man were shackled and pulled from the room. But she had watched her son lift his head high and walk from the room in dignity, as proud as he had always been.

And now he waited, as did she through this hopeless hell of a night. Nothing could save her from the vicious sucking pain that scored through her center, settling in her heart.

The clinking of Brett's spurs met her long before his shadow fell across the floor. His six-foot frame slid in beside her, the bench creaking at his added weight. He was here to comfort her. Her constant friend since long before she'd ever needed him and years before she'd admitted her love for him. It was a breath of seconds before he placed his hand on hers, always a man of few words. She glanced down as she joined their fingers, accepting what he offered.

"Do you remember when Dawson was born?" She continued with his nod, though he didn't look at her. "John was off in Nebraska or some hell's half acre, and Mei Ling had gone for a visit to the Orient with Da Ming. It was just us, you and I."

She let the quiet surround them. "You held him first, even before I did, I was so weak." She'd been alone trying to care for Sawyer and Wyatt, though it had been the wee hours of an early morning when Brett had helped her deliver her third son.

His lip curled into a tentative smile under his thick gray mustache and his green-eyed gaze found her own, the glistening there catching her by surprise. It occurred to her then she'd never seen him cry, not once, and she caught herself staring at the small pool of tears as he spoke.

"I used to watch you from where I was working.

Spitting nails at John for never doing right by you. But no matter his neglect…you flowered so beautifully without any need of either of us." He studied their hands and continued, "He didn't deserve you or these boys, and I would trade places with Dawson if there was some Godforsaken way…"

The quiet settled between them again. He was right, but deserving or not, it was John McCade who had set up all their futures. The land, the cattle and the money, though none of that could save her son now. Her beautiful son who had always loved all life, who'd given of himself for the cause of oppression to others.

"Oh, Brett. Tell me how to do this. Tell me how to watch my son die…" She collapsed against him and he held her tight. She wept for her son, for herself and for the man she clung to, who had always deserved more than he'd ever asked to have.

He added nothing more save rocking as she beat her fists against his chest in an anguish so deep, she was sure she would never take another solitary breath. "They can't do this to him. I won't let them…I will not watch him die with sunrise…Tell me what to do, how to do it, tell me…tell me…"

He brought her no words, but he didn't let her go, not until her tears would come no more and her body fell limp against him in defeat. Then he lifted her and carried her out into the cold unforgiving streets of Cheyenne, all the way to the clinic to be with the other women. Inside he took her to one of the small beds, covering her with a blanket as he lay down beside her and held her shuddering body against the cold as they both waited for the dreaded light of dawn.

****

Dawson held himself as erect as he could facing the streets of Cheyenne ahead of the soldiers, a step behind Leaning Bear. His heart thumped so hard inside his chest he heard it, but it wasn't from fear as much as the fever he bore. He had already resigned himself to a good and proud death. All men had their day of death, and this would be his, as good a day as any. Too bad the Cavalry hadn't left him to the fate of the wound that was killing him one slow minute at a time.

Outside in the Cheyenne winter, the elements might consume him and his medicine man friend long before the firing squad they were traipsing to face. He shuddered again with fever so intense his thoughts had blurred from his family, leaving him to Haven. Somehow, it mattered little to him, the bullets coming his way, when compared to the weight of her tears.

Wyatt had promised to take her away, not let her watch as the soldiers did what they must. The town was full of people lining the streets, making him wonder at those who would make a spectacle out of watching. He closed his eyes as he marched behind a better man than himself, the medicine man truly his brother. And while his morning chant had calmed the wolf a little, he'd let them go from the spirit of the wolf inside him to the spirit of the child Haven carried.

He stumbled, catching himself to continue in formation to the wall on the far side of Cheyenne. Hell, maybe the infection inside him would win yet, as it seemed he could no longer make a clear picture of the world around him. But as they turned the last corner, as far as he could see the Cheyenne lined the streets, and among them Dancing Fox chanted in prayer.

Soldiers held formation and townsfolk filled in the

streets, some in tears, even the men. Then there were his brothers. All three of them along with Brett, holding their spot so as not to leave him alone to his fate. So they'd managed to keep the women away, and he'd guess that Sawyer would have had to lock Dodge and Mei Ling in the jail to make sure. A part of him should laugh at that but nausea caught him, and he grabbed his side which had bled a steady stream of blood most of the night. Dizziness pushed him to fight to keep his stance, and it was Leaning Bear who kept him on his feet as he blinked hard, stumbling forward.

Before them both, seven soldiers in a line held their rifles at their sides. The judges and captain stood inside one of the large army wagons that held no canvas, the captain's arms folded and a smile of delight across his face. Well, here was their show, a chance to prove themselves the men they were. With any grace, they'd be about it before he couldn't stand up and die like a man, the damn fever scorching him.

They were separating them, he and Leaning Bear, several feet from each other, and both were offered blindfolds they refused. If these men were going to pull the triggers, then they could damn well look him in the eye and take their own brand of punishment.

"I have been proud to call you brother." Leaning Bear spoke in Cheyenne.

Dawson nodded the words he couldn't speak, wondering if he could even stand any longer. "I will meet you again, my brother."

The judge read the words aloud, the crowd hushing. "For the planning of an attack on the United States Cavalry and the death of seven soldiers, Dawson William McCade and the Cheyenne, Leaning Bear, you are to be put to death by firing squad at this time. Have you any last words?"

Dawson met gazes with the judge and then the captain. What good would words be at this time? But Leaning Bear began singing his death song in Cheyenne. The medicine man's voice filled the streets of Cheyenne as others from the tribe joined him in a hollow echo.

"Arms," Captain Simmons shouted from his perch and the soldiers before them shouldered their rifles.

Dawson gazed at his brothers, each in turn. Sawyer, who gave him a nod, a nudge that he'd done it all well. Wyatt, whose anger bore down on him defeating him to fight the tears that fell anyway, and Evan, whose face streamed tears he didn't bother to wipe away.

"Make ready." The men took their stance in unison, lifting their weapons to aim, the seconds ticking in slow motion.

Dawson pulled his gaze to each of the soldiers. His heart pounded, but the fear was gone. His death would be instant, and bullets couldn't make him hurt any worse than he already did. He focused his mind to Haven, thinking of her warm embrace and of the child she carried, all he'd ever wanted in this life.

"Take aim." The captain's voice rose above the silence of the crowd as if an echo.

"Wait!" A shout filtered to them all. "Stop the squad. By order of Washington!"

The men held their stance, weapons poised for command, as the crowd parted and a lone soldier on foot led a horse carrying a large man in civilian clothing with a dark hat closer.

Dawson stumbled but kept his footing with confusion as the roar of the crowd increased, making his burning head pound. Who had called for a halt? He shuddered at the cold, hard enough to shake the shackles on his wrists and ankles. But then he heard her voice and glanced past the line of soldiers.

Haven, alongside Carl Bartley, stopped before the judges with the man on horseback.

"You must stop this, now!" Her sweet cry reached him as did her gaze.

"Wyatt!" Dawson yelled at his brother who had promised to keep Haven from this. Dawson swayed, and Leaning Bear grabbed him, growling in his own pain at the effort in keeping him on his feet.

Dawson forced his eyes open. Carl Bartley was shouting to the judges. What was happening? His damn brother knew to keep Haven from here.

The soldiers held their stance, rifles poised as the captain shook his head. But Dawson let his gaze stray, searching for Haven, whom he lost in the crowd, his vision blurred, and his head pounded with the fever.

The man dismounted and began to speak, holding up a piece of paper. "I'm General Dodd, and I have come to this of my own accord, in dress not fit for a general but still in possession of such a title. I order this court martial null and void as I hold in my hands a full pardon for both of these men, Dawson McCade and the Cheyenne Leaning Bear, from President James A. Garfield of the United States of America. You will lower your arms and unshackle these men at once."

The soldiers lowered the rifles, as confused as them all. The noise of the crowd grew with protests and cheers that made Dawson close his eyes, his mind confused as Haven found him, wrapping her arms about him, the smell of lilac finding him as he began to fade.

"You've been pardoned," she shouted, as she clung to him.

He couldn't focus, and even though she was touching him, he couldn't hear her above the roar as Leaning Bear stepped in front of them both, shoving them back. It was then Dawson caught a glimpse of the reason, with Captain Simmons drawing his revolver and taking aim. Seconds passed, his mind whirling as he focused on the situation and fought to keep Haven behind him, the bullet sounding and scattering the crowd.

Dawson ducked, crashing into Leaning Bear, lifting his gaze as the captain fell from the wagon into the dirt.

Haven had screamed but now held tighter to him as he lifted his gaze to Carl Bartley, who had made the shot, killing Captain Simmons.

"What..." Dawson tried to speak but no more words would come. His fevered mind confused him further and he was sure he wasn't going to be able to stand much longer. He clung to Haven, uncertain she was at last in his arms, as he stumbled to stay erect.

General Dodd handed off the paperwork to the judges. "These men are free. Unshackle them both at once. This pardon should've never been needed, Judge Garrett, and I am damned ashamed of the treatment they received on account of the soldiers here today. It's inexcusable."

Judge Garrett lowered his head, glancing at the papers. "We followed proper procedure, Sir."

"These men are of the highest character I've ever

had the privilege of working alongside. All you men working under Captain Simmons take a good look at your leader. Judge Garrett, I am decommissioning you from your post. Soldiers of the Seventh Cavalry, you now answer to Lieutenant Carl Bartley."

Carl touched Dawson's shoulder. "I'm sorry it took so long, if you can forgive me. The general still isn't well, but I would have never gotten him here without Miss Oakley's help."

Dawson's vision blurred as he listened to the roar of the crowd, his breath short. Pardoned? Haven held him, but the pain edged too close, making him stagger. All the voices surrounded him with the wolf howling in triumph, taking him as if in a vision. The chant of the drums pulled him ever deeper as he fought to keep his sights on Haven, but it was too late. Too damn late.

Chapter Thirty-Six

The dim flame of a single lamp lit the clinic surgery to a deep golden orange, casting shadows across Dawson's face. Haven placed a cool rag to his forehead. The fever inside him still raged even though Doc Tess had done her best to clean up his wound with two surgeries. He'd yet to regain consciousness, and it hadn't gone past her, the worry that rode the doctor's face.

She let her fingers trail through Dawson's hair, tangling in locks. His family had encouraged her to rest, but how could she? He was free now, pardoned of the crimes that had never belonged to him, and yet she wasn't sure he'd understood that before he passed out.

Haven had prayed nonstop for him, asking God for one more chance to hold him in her arms and that he would be with her as their baby came into the world. She touched her low belly where the first days of quickening had started, as Tess had explained to her, a shuddering feeling that seemed to have no explanation save the tiny life there.

She traced Dawson's top lip with her finger as she leaned closer and placed her lips to his. How could he die not being able to relish the freedoms he'd gained once more? It hadn't taken long for the Cavalry to clear out of town under Bartley's command. He'd been by to see Dawson and let her know that his family was well.

And he'd left the general resting in one of the rooms down the hall under Doc Tess's care.

Leaning Bear, with his own injuries still healing, had left town with the last of the Cheyenne, letting her know he would return when he could.

Tess wandered in, taking a look at Dawson by lifting the lid of one of his eyes. She took his wrist, counting the beats of his heart.

"His fever's still there?" She spoke to the doctor in question.

Tess nodded. "It's a bit less of a fever, but he still lingers in the stupor of no response. Dodge says he's stubborn that way, but I think the body responds when it can. Fever like that can be as bad as a shotgun blast, when it comes down to it. We have to give him more time."

"And that's exactly what we are going to do." Dodge entered with a bouquet of flowers. She added water to one of the medical pitchers on the counter and placed them inside. "These are for you, Haven, from your brothers."

Haven's mouth dropped open. "My brothers… really?"

"James and Levi were out early. Gave them to me before I headed to town." Dodge brought the vase closer and let Haven smell the sweet pink flowers.

"They're lovely." She turned back to Dawson as Dodge set them back on the counter.

Dodge touched his brow. "I'm still not used to him without that long hair. He's so much like John, a better likeness than the man himself."

Sawyer eased into the room, one of Dawson's brothers always near. "I guess with his hair and buckskins, we lost sight of who he was all these years and what good he was doing."

"I don't think we lost him, I think we just stepped aside for him to do what he had to do." Dodge angled a gaze his way.

Sawyer lifted the pocket watch from his vest. "Gotta meet Wyatt to wire some items to Washington. We'll be back in a while."

"Let Burt know I'll follow shortly," Dodge added, rubbing Dawson's forearm.

"I'll wait outside." Sawyer turned to leave the clinic.

Haven brushed Dawson's hair back and he gave a slight cough. "Dawson?"

He didn't move further as Tess and Dodge stepped closer.

"Open your eyes." Tess rubbed his chest hard with her knuckles trying to rouse him. "Dawson?"

"Doctor?" Haven asked, confused. He'd coughed, and didn't that mean he was waking, at least a little?

"Dawson, wake up..." Tess tried again. "Sometimes the effects of Chloroform can linger but...Come on..."

"Wake up, son," Dodge added, rubbing his arm again.

"Haven, you try your voice. Be stern with him, remind him about the baby." Tess offered, giving her a nudge.

Haven touched his brow. "Dawson, please open your eyes."

Tess nodded. "Scolding."

She'd do anything if he'd wake. Even yell at him. She took a deep breath. "Dawson, you wake up this minute. If you think I am going to raise this baby alone, you are mistaken. Now, you open your eyes right this minute."

"Don't want you...to be...alone. My head..." He opened his eyes and squinted at the light, his voice a whisper.

"I knew you'd come back to me." She kissed his cheek, tears streaming in relief.

"Dawson, where are you?" Tess asked.

Dodge wiped her tears. "You gave us such a fright, son."

It took a moment, but he answered. "At...the clinic. How...many days...the soldiers..." Haven had been right that he hadn't even grasped he'd been pardoned. "You received a Presidential Pardon because of General Dodd. You and Leaning Bear are free." She sat on the edge of the bed to get closer to him. "You've had surgery twice now and your wound is healing. You're free...Dawson, pardoned."

He studied her face for a long moment, reaching for his side. "I hurt...so damn...bad. The baby, you..."

"We are fine." She whispered. "Rest, I know you hurt."

Dodge kissed him. "The President himself sent the pardon."

Tess wiped tears away as well. "I can give you a bit of Laudanum for the pain, but Dawson, you must rest in order to heal."

He nodded and never moved as Tess injected his hip and checked his dressing and followed Dodge outside the room.

Haven touched Dawson's brow. "I was so worried when you fell, and I knew you didn't know you'd been pardoned. Oh, Dawson, the general rode in and called the firing squad off, and Mr. Bartley had to shoot the captain."

"Don't remember much..." He took her hand, shaking in his weakness.

"You passed out and the Cheyenne with Dancing Fox came and lifted you, carrying you to the clinic, and a hush fell over the crowd in respect." Haven whispered, wiping a tear that strayed down his cheek. "And the men in town on the streets lowered their hats in respect..."

"Dancing Fox?" He narrowed his gaze.

"Yes, he and several braves, with the rest of the men from the tribe following behind. Dawson, you slept so long after the surgeries, it's been days." She touched his cheek.

"Not feelin' much, like I'm...gonna live now." He closed his drowsy eyes and opened them again. "Didn't want to...leave you...and all I...could think...was you'd be alone with the child..." He groaned, gritting his teeth. "I...didn't want to die and leave you...never want to leave you. Hurts...so much."

Haven stopped his hand from touching his side across the blankets. "Doc Tess had to open the wound twice...the medicine will work soon. Rest Dawson, and I'll be right here." She held him as he wept and finally closed his eyes to the medication.

****

The spring sun wove its way through new leaves of spring hanging from the trees by the stream, a reminder that winter was behind them all. Dawson folded his hands before him as he stood alongside Leaning Bear and the Reverend Prather. It was strange that his pulse raced as he waited for Haven's arrival. After today, a lifetime for him to love her would never be enough, but he'd take that for all the remainder of his days.

The winter had been a hard one with several blizzards, and he'd spent months recovering from the multiple surgeries to clear his body of the infection. Sometimes, the long days had been a blur of a confusion that lingered at night with the nightmares that still haunted him from time to time, But Haven had been there through it all. Now months later, he was well enough to take his place before their friends and family so all around them would know she was his wife.

With the spring upon them, it was his turn to bring her the happiness she deserved after all they'd been through. He glanced around where Dodge, Mei Ling and his sisters-in-law had decorated various chairs and benches with drapes of white flowers and pots of planted roses. Even the trees were adorned with white ribbons and sashes as if they were part of the coming ceremony.

Mei Ling met his gaze nodding her approval, sitting on a bench near Tess who held her infant son Zachariah across her knees, the baby fretting with Ella sitting quietly beside her. He locked a gaze on Sawyer who assisted Rose to her seat, their daughter, Stella, sleeping in her arms. His brother held a toddling Uriah's hand and sat, taking the boy into his lap and urging Nicholas to his seat beside James, the two inseparable pals these days.

Standing behind the chairs along with Evan, were a number of hands from the ranch, a few men from town, and Brett.

Dawson hadn't needed all this fanfare if it came

down to it but agreed as it seemed Haven deserved the wedding of her dreams, even if she was a bit reluctant, with the roundness of her belly. All had reassured her at the occasion of the wedding there was no need to worry, but she had fretted over every stitch and bow, from what he understood, sewing the dress she would wear herself.

"Frying Pan Woman good choice." Leaning Bear's tone was low. "I tell you this long time ago."

Dawson held the medicine man's dark-eyed gaze. "Well, if she'd knocked any sense into you with that frying pan. It's time you found yourself a wife as well."

Leaning Bear lifted his chin with pride. "Wife can be much problem."

"You've been pardoned...best you find a good woman to keep you warm nights and out of trouble," Dawson added, giving the Reverend Prather reason to adjust his collar at the conversation.

The buggy at the main house began a slow descent to them, capturing Dawson's attention. He sucked in a deep breath and dusted his fancy blue tunic and trousers in anticipation.

He held the carriage in his sights as Wyatt slipped in behind Tess to take Zachariah, who hushed in his father's arms.

It occurred to Dawson he'd be next holding a little one. It was hard to imagine being a father, but he'd wear it as well as his brothers. Off by the trees Zane began to play his violin, the tones of the strings mixing with the light wind.

Reverend Prather opened his Bible, sifting through the pages, as Leaning Bear held to the feathers and herbs that would be a part of his portion of the ceremony. Dawson continued to watch the carriage, led by Levi, who was dressed in a fine suit, ready to give his sister to be wed.

The carriage stopped, and Brett ambled over and assisted Dodge down and they both waited as Levi helped Haven step to the ground.

All the breath Dawson held left him, the world standing still. Haven was the most beautiful thing he'd ever beheld. Her hair was down and full of tiny white flowers. Her gown was full to the ground, swaying in the wind and glimmering in the sunlight. She wore white slippers that Dodge had insisted on ordering from Chicago, and she carried a bundle of white flowers.

Brett escorted Dodge to her seat and his mother lifted her brows. He wanted to chuckle at the fact she'd known all along, but he glanced back at Haven as Zane's music began a slower tune for her walk to him.

"She's all beautiful." James gasped and everyone around him laughed.

Well, he was right. Dawson held Haven's gaze as she gripped Levi's arm.

The Reverend Prather began. "We are gathered here today in the sight of God and an abundance of friends and family to see to the marriage of Dawson McCade and Haven Oakley. Who gives this woman to be wed?"

Levi stepped up. "My brother and I give our blessings." And with that he handed Haven's hand to Dawson.

"Marriage is a holy promise to each other before God, to love one another, honor one another and obey one another according to God's laws. When a man leaves his father's home to take his wife, he promises to provide for her and care for her all the days of their lives. It is the same that the woman who leaves her father's home and promises to love, honor and obey her husband according to the laws of our God in heaven."

"Do you, Dawson McCade, take this woman, Haven Oakley to be your lawfully wedded wife?"

Dawson held Haven's gaze and was surprised that she hadn't come to tears, but the smile she carried was the sweetest he'd ever seen. "I do."

"Haven Oakley, do you take this man, Dawson McCade, to be your lawfully wedded husband?" Reverend Prather waited.

"I do." Haven's sweet voice filled his ears and then it came, the single tear he might have expected. He was quick to use his thumb to wipe it from her cheek as Leaning Bear moved in front of them. Zane began playing as Leaning Bear spoke in Cheyenne.

"Now you will feel no rain, for each of you will be shelter for the other. Now you will feel no cold, for each of you will be warmth to the other. Now there will be no loneliness, for each of you will be companion to the other. Now you are two persons, but there is only one life before you. May the beauty surround you both in the journey ahead and through the years, may happiness be your companion and your days together be good and long upon the earth."

Dawson held Haven's gaze and whispered, as Leaning Bear continued, "I love you."

"This day is all the happiness my life will ever need." She whispered, squeezing his hand tighter.

Leaning Bear went on with the Cheyenne language that no one save he, Dawson, and Haven understood. "Treat yourselves and each other with respect and remind yourselves often of what brought you together. Give the highest priority to the tenderness, gentleness and kindness that your connection deserves. When frustration, difficulties and fear assail your relationship, as they threaten all relationships at one time or another, remember to focus on what is right between you, not only the part which seems wrong. In this way, you can ride out the storms when clouds hide the face of the sun in your lives, remembering that even if you lose sight of it for a moment, the sun is still there. If each of you take responsibility for the quality of your life together, it will be marked by abundance and delight."

Dawson took the feather from his hair and tied it into Haven's, smiling as the task was done, and then he took her hand again and placed on her finger a golden band.

Haven glanced down. "It's beautiful."

He smiled and touched the blue stone she wore around her neck as the Reverend stepped back in place. "Ladies and gentlemen, I am proud to present to you Mr. and Mrs. Dawson McCade. May happiness always surround you both."

The crowd of family and friends cheered and clapped as he placed his palms on each of Haven's cheeks and kissed her lips for longer than necessary. The coughs and teasing of his brothers and the other men drew him away. He kept his face close to her. "I love you, Haven."

"And I you." She fell into his embrace and he wrapped both arms around her as the family joined them. Handshakes from his brothers and the other men drew him from her as the women made over her dress and the ceremony. He stepped back and took a mug of sarsaparilla Wyatt offered to him and watched Haven enjoy her time.

The beauty of her dress had hidden her belly for the most part, but he didn't care who knew. She carried his child and of that he would never hold any shame nor would she. Today, this was her day as it should be, and the rest of the afternoon would be filled with food and dancing right along the stream that was his favorite place to spend time. Haven smiled and hugged everyone, including her brothers, glancing back to him from time to time and giving his heart all the reason it needed to smile for the rest of his days.

Epilogue

Fall 1882, Cheyenne, Wyoming Territory

The fall sun plagued the afternoon with a steady wave of Wyoming heat. Dawson leaned against a fallen cottonwood at the edge of the meadow. He glanced at his bent knees where Asha flailed her tiny arms, as content as he to be outside the house. He placed a palm to her small head, touching the strawberry wisps the very color of her mother's.

"You like the sun, little one." He spoke in Cheyenne to his daughter as she cooed back to him. He smiled as he traced his large hand down her tiny body and caught her feet in his palms.

Living with Haven as his wife had been all he'd ever needed, but holding his daughter was more joy than he'd never known before. His recovery from his injuries had been long coming, and he still wasn't back to his full self, pain gripping his belly at times. The multiple surgeries to his wound had taken much from him last winter, as had putting all the events of his arrest behind him, but life was good now. Even the nightmares had faded, the ones that had woken him in a cold sweat for months after his pardon.

He'd spent a hard winter fighting to heal one day at a time and coming to grips with all he'd been through. He'd found himself again, little by little over the last half year, in finding his life with Haven, her brothers, and now his daughter.

He'd paced right along with the wolf a month ago as Haven had struggled to deliver Asha on a cool fall evening. And of all the things he'd ever seen in his lifetime, Doc Tess placing his daughter into his arms had brought him to his knees with tears of joy. She was the most beautiful thing he'd ever held, save her mother.

He glanced across the meadow as Haven bent to pick wild mushrooms, dropping them in her bucket and trotting toward them. She'd recovered well from the birth and had already mentioned she'd want another child in the near future.

Haven plopped down beside him, setting the small bucket aside, Sosha following to lie in the comfort of the shade. "What are you two talking about?"

He took the baby's tiny fingers each in a hand and she clung tight and gave a fuss. "We've secrets, Mama, but I think someone's hungry."

Haven placed a hand to the baby's belly. "She enjoys being outside. Did you read the letter?"

He gave her a nod. "It's General Dodd's request that once I'm fully recovered my employment will be waiting."

He wasn't sure how he felt about returning to the reservations which would be moved further north in the coming year. The job would take him from home, and glancing at his daughter and his wife, his decision was an easy one. "I've no business that far north. Besides, I've got a little something that's gonna keep me busy here."

"I know when you are being sneaky." She giggled.

"You're not to be trusted."

He handed her a piece of paper from his tunic, something he'd been saving for her birthday.

"What's this?" She unfolded the sealed paper.

"Happy birthday." He kissed her, lingering for a moment. "Go ahead."

She opened it, studying it for a long moment. "Dawson...this is a deed..."

He pointed to the document she held. "It's for the post office in town. Well, it's no longer the post office, with the new one by the rail station, but it's yours, the building."

She looked at the paper again. "The post office?"

He nodded. "It needs some work. Gonna gut it, redo a bit of it. An apothecary needs quite a bit of shelving and cabinets. There're a few boards to the flooring that need replaced, but I would imagine by next spring you could be up and running. Wyatt's gonna help me get a start on it next week."

Haven's jaw dropped open. "My own apothecary?" She wrapped her arms around him, kissing the side of his face and running her hands into the length of his hair.

Her joy in anything was the heart of him. "I figured with Levi hiring on with Evan, if you went into town daily, James could start at the new school."

"James would love that, but you're not fully well yet." She scolded, her hair blowing free across her shoulders, enticing him to run his hands through it and tug her closer.

"I'm getting there. Wyatt can do the heavier lifting. Won't be much rush for now," he added, though he was well aware of the limits to his exertion.

She nodded. "You're so good to me. Oh, and Dodge wants us to sup on Sunday, as usual, but she has a party for Zane planned. He leaves next Thursday for Denver again."

"He's ready, been aching to get back to his courses." He added, proud of his nephew.

"I'm afraid Levi will miss him." She glanced at the deed and then folded it once more.

"Denver's not so far."

"Rose was in town, too, had Stella with her, she's crawling, about to walk any day." The light in her hazel eyes captivated him and he studied her because he could.

"I suppose it doesn't take long, they grow fast." He glanced at Asha, who fussed again.

"What are your thoughts on the reservation?" She asked what he'd yet to answer. "I've no interest in work that takes me from you and Asha. I'll keep busy, help at the ranch, work with Levi inside the claim, though I think the yield's about done. Remodeling the post office will keep me busy for a time, that and rebuilding my cabin."

"But I think once you're well you will miss your work. The Cheyenne need you." She nudged him after a moment.

"Maybe one day, but later on." It might be that he'd return, but for now he was content. He closed his eyes to the sun and the beauty of just being with his wife and child.

"Dawson?"

"Huh?"

"Levi said he saw Thorn a few days ago. I still worry that he'll be discovered." She shook her head. "I know we never said, but...what if anyone else found out?"

He shook his head. "Doubt that will happen. No one would believe him, Haven, most think he's touched and all. He did the town a big favor, right or wrong. It's best left as it is."

"I suppose." She tickled the baby, who fussed, chewing her fingers. "Do you think Leaning Bear might join you if you go back? I know you miss him."

It was ironic she'd mentioned the medicine man. He pulled a small knife in its leather pouch from his tunic, the weight of it a reminder of the friend he called brother.

"He's here?" She glanced around them, across the meadow.

"Found it this morning tied to Viho's saddle with two dove feathers." His gaze joined her scan of the land before them.

She touched the knife. "So he'll come two days from now?"

"Probably. He'll want the bear claw back. It's a good thing you had Carl get the knife and claw for us." He'd missed the medicine man, as he'd not come around since the wedding, though he'd figured it would be a short time before his friend found his way back.

"It's been so long to put it all past us." She leaned into him, her journey just as difficult as his own.

"I know I've had a long recovery, and things weren't easy for you then or with having the baby. But the sun feels good and the nightmares come less. Just having you is all I need."

"I would do it all a thousand times over to be with you like this," she whispered as her hazel gaze found his and he kissed her.

He spoke to her in Cheyenne and touched the necklace she wore, which held the blue stone from his medicine bag. "As would I, my Heartsong."

She snuggled into his shoulder as he handed the baby to her. He tangled his fingers in Haven's hair and watched as she nursed Asha. In the distance a wolf howled from the mountains, a reminder that it had been the spirit of the great predator that had brought him through it all, leaving him with the wife and daughter promised from long ago. He tugged Haven closer to kiss her forehead and held the moment with her beside him as he would for all of his days.

Kim Turner

Author's Note

Throughout this story I have done my best to respect the Cheyenne and all American Indian nations while depicting a story as close to historically accurate as possible.

I have chosen to use the Apache Prayer even though the character Leaning Bear is a Cheyenne medicine man. The references to the Dog Soldiers are truly fiction, as by the date of my story, most tribes were, unfortunately, placed on reservations. Any mistakes regarding Native American history are completely my own but made with a heart intent on giving the utmost respect.

Additionally, I have written a shortened version of a military trial in the interest of moving the story forward. Any mistakes or omissions related to the process of such a trial belong to me as well.

A word about the author...

Kim Turner writes western historical romance. She first discovered her passion for writing at the age of eight by writing poems, short stories, and journals.

Kim graduated from Clayton State University with a Bachelor's of Science in Nursing and holds a master's degree in Adult Education from Central Michigan University. Working as a registered nurse educator for over twenty-six years, she enjoys studying the medical treatments of the Old West as well as keeping up with the latest western movies and television series. While she loves reading anything from highlanders to pirates, she claims to have an unquenchable thirst for the American cowboy when choosing her reads.

Kim lives south of Atlanta with her husband and calls her greatest accomplishment the birth of one daughter and the adoption of another from China—neither of which came easy.

Kim is a member of Romance Writers of America and Georgia Romance Writers and says her beta readers are the best thing that ever happened to her writing. Kim's motto: It's All About a Cowboy and the Woman He Loves.

Visit her at:
kimturnerwrites.com

Thank you for purchasing
this publication of The Wild Rose Press, Inc.

For questions or more information
contact us at
info@thewildrosepress.com.

The Wild Rose Press, Inc.
www.thewildrosepress.com

To visit with authors of
The Wild Rose Press, Inc.
join our yahoo loop at
http://groups.yahoo.com/group/thewildrosepress/

CPSIA information can be obtained
at www.ICGtesting.com
Printed in the USA
BVHW061105060120
568694BV00025B/1584/P

9 781509 228492